The Flaming Sword

The Tethered World Chronicles

Book one—The Tethered World
Book two—The Flaming Sword
Book three—The Genesis Tree

The Flaming Sword

Book Two of
The Tethered World Chronicles

Heather L.L. FitzGerald

The Flaming Sword
Published by Mountain Brook Ink
White Salmon, WA U.S.A.

The website addresses recommended throughout this book are offered as a resource. These websites are not intended in any way to be or imply an endorsement on the part of Mountain Brook Ink, nor do we vouch for their content.

This story is a work of fiction. All characters and events are the product of the author's imagination. Any resemblance to any person, living or dead, is coincidental.

Scripture quotations are taken from the King James Version of the Bible. Public domain.

ISBN 9781943959037

The Team: Miralee Ferrell, Lissa Halls Johnson, Nikki Wright, Susan Marlow, Cindy Jackson

Cover Design: Indie Cover Design, Lynnette Bonner, Designer

Mountain Brook Ink is an inspirational publisher offering fiction you can believe in.

Map illustration by William Love@sevenoversix.com

Printed in the U.S.A. 2016

Dedication

This one is for you, Mom. Your strength of spirit and character, and your loving support and resilience are legendary (like some of the creatures in this book!) Above all, I appreciate the legacy of faith you've passed on to me. Your life has been an example of unwavering belief in God's goodness and power. I love you.

*"Then I heard every creature in heaven and on earth and **under the earth**…saying: To him who sits on the throne and to the Lamb be praise and honor and glory and power, for ever and ever!"* Revelation 5: 13

*This book is a work of fiction from a Christian worldview. The ideas are strictly from the author's imagination, portraying what might be possible in places that Scripture is silent.

** A cast of characters' list with descriptions is located at the back of the book for your convenience.

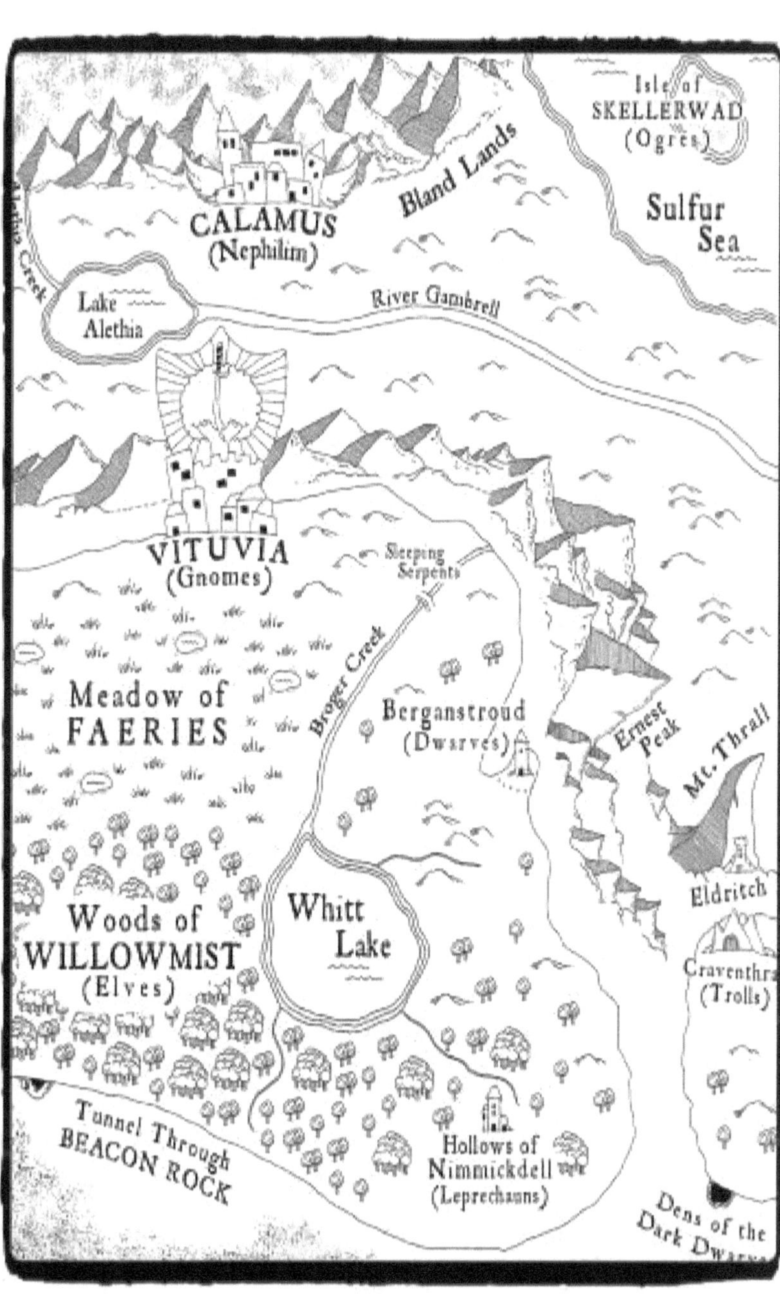

Isle of
SKELLERWAD
(Ogres)
Sulfur
Sea
Bland Lands
CALAMUS
(Nephilim)
Harlins Creek
Lake
Alethia
River Gambrell
VITUVIA
(Gnomes)
Sleeping
Serpents
Broger Creek
Meadow of
FAERIES
Berganstroud
(Dwarves)
Ernest
Peak
Mt. Thrall
Eldritch
Woods of
WILLOWMIST
(Elves)
Whitt
Lake
Craventhra
(Trolls)
Tunnel Through
BEACON ROCK
Hollows of
Nimmickdell
(Leprechauns)
Dens of the
Dark Dwarves

CHAPTER ONE

"Is she dead?" Shock shimmied up my spine at the sight of Great-Aunt Jules crumpled in my mother's arms. I couldn't tear my gaze from her conspicuous black eye, the size and color of a plum.

"Sadie!" Mom shot me a scornful look and shifted from under the weight of our Irish aunt. Not hard to do since she was smaller than my eleven-year-old sister Sophie. "Why do you always imagine the worst? Run and get a wet washcloth for her face."

My breath came in shallow spurts. I dashed to the guest bath and scrounged a cloth from the cupboard, turning the tap full blast. Maybe it would drown my growing alarm. It takes a certain strain of vicious behavior to attack an elderly woman. And I've got my reasons for imagining 'the worst.' With vindictive force I wrung out the washcloth and darted back to Mom.

"Sophie and Brady," Mom shouted. "Downstairs. *Now.*"

Mom snatched the washcloth and pressed it against Aunt Jules's forehead. With her other hand she stroked the crimson curls around our great-aunt's face, speaking in hushed tones. If not for the unnatural angle of Aunt Jules's body, she might have been sleeping peacefully.

I knelt beside my mom. "What's this?" I reached for a piece of paper that Auntie clutched against her chest.

"Don't touch it." Mom's tone made my fingers recoil. "Someone ransacked her house. They left a note."

My mind reeled. Her tidy beach bungalow was in a safe, gated neighborhood where everyone looked out for each other. Uneasiness continued to swell.

Footsteps bounded down the stairs. Brady and Sophie

stumbled into each other at the sight of our aunt.

"Oh, no!" Sophie's hands flew to her face. "Is she dead?"

"For Pete's sake." Mom shook her head. "What's with you kids? No. Aunt Jules fainted."

"When did she get here?" Brady crossed to the couch. His lanky, fifteen-years-and-growing body towered over Mom and the patient. "Is she sick?" He crouched beside me. "Wow. Now that's a shiner."

Mom ignored his comment. "Carry her upstairs to Brock's bed. She's hurt...and who knows what else. Prop her feet on a pillow."

Aunt Jules moaned when Brady scooped her up.

"Sophie, get an ice pack and a glass of water." Mom pointed toward the kitchen. "And Sadie"—she gave me a serious look— "call your dad. Tell him, 'code word *curator*.' It's a word we picked to alert one another in case of danger or a family emergency."

"Code word? We have *code words* now? I thought all our bizarre family secrets were finally out in the open." I was treading on thin ice for sure. But the last six weeks had uncovered a host of skeletons from our family's creepy closet. Living specters that had rocked my world.

"Not...now." Mom looked ready to snap.

With a huff, I turned to find the phone. I used speed dial to call my dad at the Camas School of Cosmetology, the cosmetology college he owned. His occupation was only one of the numerous quirky things about my family. It helped that I was homeschooled—yeah, that qualifies as quirky too—so I didn't constantly have to explain things like this to a multitude of people.

"Camas School of Cosmetology. This is Dinah. How may I direct your call?"

"Dinah? Hey, it's Sadie. I need to talk to my dad."

"Sorry, Sadie. Your dad hasn't come in yet. Did you try his cell?"

"What? Are you sure?" I leaned against the wall. "He left like two hours ago."

"Hmm. Lemme double check. I'm usually the first person to see him, but maybe he snuck past. Hold on."

I wandered into the kitchen, dodging Sophie and her ice pack and water.

"Oh, my goodness." I froze.

My two-year-old brother, Nate, sat in his booster seat, covered in oatmeal. In all the uproar, the poor kid had been left to mind himself while strapped to his chair. Supporting the phone with my shoulder, I grabbed a bunch of paper towels and mopped the gummy stuff from his face.

"Sadie? No sign of your dad. Sorry."

"Okay, thanks for checking. I'll try his cell." The oatmeal had migrated to my fingers. I leaned over the table and let the phone plop from the crook of my neck.

Nate clapped his sticky hands together, making slimy, suction noises between his fingers. "Mushy, mushy." He smiled at the goo. The pale-colored oatmeal contrasted with his chocolaty Ethiopian skin. I envied my adopted brother's year-round tan.

"Yep. It's mushy, little man." I crossed to the sink for more wet towels and caught sight of my youngest sister, Nicole, outside on the tire swing. "Hey, Nicole," I called through the open kitchen window. "I need your help. Come 'ere."

A moment later, she opened the patio door and peeked inside. A pink, plastic tiara nestled lopsided in her honey hair.

"Would you finish cleaning Nate? I have to do something for Mom."

"Sure." Nicole took the paper towels and zeroed in on the moving mound of muck. At only seven years old, she tackled most of Nate's needs with the skill of a seasoned babysitter.

I picked up the phone and headed to the privacy of the living room. Something about using code words made me feel like I'd better keep the convo under the radar. While Dad's cell rang, I wandered to the front window and thought about the random word my parents had chosen. Curator? Isn't that an old person in charge of a museum or something?

"You've reached the voicemail of Liam Larcen..."

I caught sight of my haphazard reflection in the window. I didn't want to dwell on the pimple on my chin, the cowlick in my brown locks, or the smudged mascara I forgot to wash off the night before. Instead, I focused my attention past the mess that was me and peered outside while I waited for the voicemail beep.

Is it okay to leave code words in a voicemail?

Aunt Jules's old VW Beetle was parked crooked in our driveway and blocked both of our family vehicles. She obviously parked it in a hurry.

Wait.

"Oh, my." I smacked the phone onto the windowsill and booked it upstairs. "Mom, Mom!" Nausea swirled in my gut. I whipped around the corner and skidded to a stop in my brothers' bedroom. Everyone—who was conscious—jerked their heads in my direction.

I took a deep breath, then another, dreading what I had to say.

Mom paused in the middle of placing a blanket over Aunt Jules. "Sadie, please. Spare us the dramatics."

I slowly exhaled. "Dad's car is still in the driveway."

The blanket slipped from Mom's hands. "What?"

"His car. It's there." I thumbed in the general direction. "Parked." The words impregnated the room with sinister implications. My mind flashed back to earlier this summer when both my parents went missing.

Mom shook her head. "No. He kissed me goodbye. I watched him walk out the door."

Sophie shoved the icepack at Brady and brushed past me.

"Sophie!" Mom's eyes flashed. "No, ma'am. Get back here."

Sophie shuffled back in the room, arms crossed and chin set.

Mom raised a warning finger. "*No one* goes outside."

"Amy?" Aunt Jules's eyes were still closed. "What's going on?"

Mom clasped her hand over Aunt Jules's clenched fist. Unconscious or not, Auntie kept a stranglehold on her scrap of paper. "Someone broke into your house, remember?"

Aunt Jules's mouth pressed into a frown, an uncommon sight for the cheerful woman. She blinked. The swollen bruise twitched. Her gaze settled on Mom. "I know what happened t' *me.* Did somethin' happen to Liam?"

Mom bit her lip. She appeared to weigh the wisdom of sharing bad news on top of bad news. "Uh, not sure. He left for work a couple of hours ago, but his car's still here."

"Ya think it's related to what happened to me?" Aunt Jules tried to roll onto her side. Her emerald eyes winced with the effort.

Mom gently pushed her shoulder back onto the pillow. "That remains to be seen. I still don't know what happened to you. You barely made it into the house, mumbling about a break-in, when you passed out." She handed Aunt Jules the ice pack. "Here, use this on your eye. When you're feeling better, we'll talk."

Aunt Jules shoved the pack away. "Won't be needin' that. Nothin's wrong with me that a steamin' cup o' tea won't fix. It's painfully clear we've got loads of talkin' to do."

"Um..." Sophie looked at us like we'd been struck with amnesia. "Dad's *missing*. Shouldn't we call the police?"

"It's true, your father's not here." Mom swallowed. "But...that doesn't mean he's missing. I mean, not in *that* way. It's doubtful." Her voice grew quiet. "Not after what happened before."

"Family meetin'. Soon as the kettle whistles." Aunt Jules worked her legs out of the blankets.

"Nonsense." Mom barred her way. "You've had a terrible scare. You're hurt. Now lie down and ice your eye...please. We'll bring you the tea."

"Amy Ann Larcen! If I say I'm fine, then I'm *fine*." The spunky little redhead swung her legs off the bed and stood. "I won't be lyin' here when earth-shatterin' events are takin' place right under our noses. You've no idea how serious this is."

Sophie, Brady, and I exchanged troubled glances.

Mom looked resigned to Aunt Jules's insistence while she grabbed the ice pack. "Fine. But you're going to keep this on your eye. You've got a terrible *periorbital hematoma*, and it needs attention."

"Poppycock!" Aunt Jules straightened her twisted velour sweat suit. "Don't throw that highfalutin' medical talk at me, *nurse* Amy. Nobody dies from a black eye. If ya don't mind, I'd like to speak to ya about *this*"—she waved the scrunched paper at us—"or somebody else is likely to go missin' while I'm lyin' here like a helpless lump o' sugar."

"Yes, let's talk about that." Mom looked like she was teetering on her last available nerve. "Before we do anything else, would you mind explaining what kind of burglar beats up their victim and leaves a note?"

"It wasn't a burglary." Aunt Jules shook her flaming curls. "Nothin' valuable is missin'. These intruders weren't thieves. Leastways, they weren't today because they didn't find what they came for. Which is why they left this for me." She indicated the note and sat back down on the edge of the bed.

Mom looked puzzled. "Okay…"

"Ya think me brain is addled, don't ya?" She leveled her gaze at Mom. "Listen, there's somethin' stirrin'. And it has to do with me late husband—and so much more."

Mom shifted her weight and looked impatient. "I'm not following you. What could the intruders possibly want in regards to Uncle Daniel? He's been dead for over thirty years."

I scooted closer to my brother and sister, their expressions a mixture of confusion and skepticism—exactly like my brain.

One lone tear slipped down Aunt Jules's cheek. "Thirty-eight years, actually." She stroked the crinkled letter repeatedly across her lap. Her head shook slowly. "This note. I wouldn't believe a word of it, but…" Another tear dripped.

"But *what*?" I burst out.

"But I'd know this handwritin' anywhere. I know who penned these here words like I know the wrinkles on me own face."

Mom lowered herself onto the bed and placed a gentle hand on top of our aunt's nervous fingers. "*Whose* handwriting?"

Aunt Jules let out a ragged sigh. "The date, see?" She pointed. "This note was written last week. But I'd swear by the dragon's lair that the handwritin' belongs to me dear husband, Daniel."

CHAPTER TWO

BRADY OFFERED TO CARRY AUNT JULES downstairs, but she stubbornly refused. He settled for helping her totter to the kitchen and then returned to his empty bedroom. He hadn't slept well for the past six weeks—ever since he had been separated from his autistic twin brother, Brock.

Brady paced in tight circles, trying to calm a sickening sensation that *something* must be happening where Brock lived since life in the Larcen household was, once again, in a state of chaos. Brady had protected Brock all of their lives. Protected him from bullies who didn't understand the blond little boy who refused to play tag on the playground and rocked back and forth to music only he could hear. Protected him from unkind customers at the mall who didn't like having to step around someone who stopped the flow of shoppers. Brady had endured a few black eyes for his brother's sake. Gladly. But now...now he could no longer run interference, and it left him feeling lost. And empty.

Brady plopped onto the beanbag between his brother's bed and his own. Brock's blanket lay skewed from where Aunt Jules recovered a few minutes earlier. Brady grinned to think how Brock would react to seeing his bed in such a disorderly mess.

On Brock's nightstand sat seventeen Matchbox cars—his favorite number. They were always placed in precisely the same way—front bumpers aligned in a semicircle. Did Brock miss his cars?

Does Brock miss me? Brady bit his lip and stared at a picture of the two of them—identical on the outside, but for the smudge of a birthmark on Brock's collarbone—but so different beneath the surface.

As twins, the two hadn't been apart for more than the occasional night or two. But earlier this summer, things changed in major ways. It began with their parents being kidnapped and taken to a world that none of the kids knew existed. A world where Brock now lived as an apprenticed future king—away from the watchful eye and quick fist of Brady.

Though the whole family, Brady included, loved the fact that Brock's autism made him the perfect fit for kingship—Brady struggled to find himself outside of his position as protector and interpreter for his quiet brother.

Clearly he was having an identity crisis. One that left him restless, worrying about Brock. Wondering what part, if any, he himself would have in this strange, new place that had invaded their lives.

The thought of what might be happening to his dad—and by default, to Brock—left him with a mix of fear and exhilaration. Fear for the safety of those he loved. Exhilaration that he might be going back to this world to do something about it.

I silently volunteered to put the kettle on for tea and made a beeline for the kitchen. How was it that missing people and family meetings had become an integral part of our lives?

In the kitchen, I filled the teapot and looked out on the perfect summer day with sadness. The treehouse and tire swing called to my childhood. Gone were the blissful, carefree days of pretending there were Dwarves and Dragons lurking about. I now knew how very real they were and missed the ones I could control with my innocent imagination.

Nicole carried Nate piggyback across the yard to the shade of a tree. Our little Corgis, Ollie and Mindy-loo, romped about nearby. Mom's warning suddenly blared in my brain. *No one goes outside.* I ran to the door and yanked it open.

"Nicole! Nicole, let's come back in the house." I trotted across the cool concrete patio and into the dewy grass.

"Is it time for school already?" Nicole slid Nate from her back.

"No. I don't think we're having school today." Nate reached his chubby arms my direction, and I lifted him to my hip. "Aunt Jules is here."

"What? Oh, awesome." Nicole zoomed into the house.

"Awesommme," Nate crooned.

I kissed his curly head. Glad someone could find a reason to smile.

Back inside, Brady helped Aunt Jules into a chair at the breakfast table. She still clutched the crumpled note.

"Guess this means I'm not getting my driver's permit today." Brady glanced at Mom. "Which also means I cut my hair short for *nothing*."

Mom sighed. "No. Sorry. Not today." She brought a box of Darjeeling tea to the table. "But thank the Lord for small favors. Your hair needed to be mowed worse than grass in springtime."

"Why can't Brady get his permit?" Nicole asked. "And how did Aunt Jules get that black eye?"

"I'll explain, later. You and Nate may go watch one of your shows."

Nicole glanced at me. She seemed to sense something in the air. I shrugged and gave her a wink, then watched her disappear into the living room with Nate.

"Lucky," Brady whispered to me. "Our lives hadn't turned into a freaky fairytale when you were getting your driver's permit."

I gave my brother a sympathetic grin. "Wish I could help ya out."

He plopped into a chair.

"Hang on." Mom held up a hand. "I know it's probably pointless, but I want the two of you to accompany me outside to look for clues to your father's disappearance. There's safety in numbers." She turned to Aunt Jules. "Auntie, we'll be right back. Let that tea work its magic, and then we'll talk. Sophie will stay and keep you company."

"But, I wanna—"

"You're *staying*, Sophie. Don't argue."

Sophie clammed up but looked on the brink of tears. She

had more guts than me, hands down. When our parents disappeared, she handled it with grace and courage—something I couldn't claim. Death-defying circumstances seemed to bring out the best in her...with a side of annoying, overeager behavior.

Mom led the way to the front door and stopped. "Look for any sign of struggle. Stay close."

"Gee, that won't look suspicious." I glanced at Brady.

"I'm not really concerned about appearances at this point, Sadie." Mom tugged the door open.

We slowed every few feet, inspecting the hedges, the walkway, the brick, and so on. Once in the driveway, we walked around both vehicles looking for anything out of the ordinary. Our minivan still sported three claw swipes from earlier in the summer when my parents were abducted by Bigfoot.

This seems like a good place to point out another quirk about my family...my mother's occupation. She's an expert on Bigfoot, as well as Leprechauns, Elves, and other mythical creatures. This bizarre hobby has always been a source of embarrassment for me—wackier than my dad's flair for hair.

That is, until their kidnapping set off a chain of events that led my siblings and me to travel to a world inhabited by the very creatures she studies. This world, we learned, exists within our own planet. Seriously. It's called the Tethered World. And Bigfoot is one of the villains living there. Whatever you want to call him—Sasquatch, Yeti, Abominable—those are mere cultural names for something else you've probably heard of: the infamous, villainous *Troll*.

Beyond that interesting factoid, my brother Brock was now spending the summer in the Tethered World as High King in training with some of the good guys. While he stayed behind to learn how to run a powerful realm of—get this—*Gnomes*, the rest of us have been missing him terribly, counting the days until he returns from his first round of training.

As I combed the yard for signs of my father's disappearance, I wondered what implications this real-life plot twist had for Brock. Was he in danger? Did something happen to him today, as well?

"There's nothing here," Brady said.

We had made concentric circles around the driveway and

yard, but it looked undisturbed.

Mom puffed out her cheeks and expelled a breath. "Well..." She placed her hands on her hips.

"What about Mr. Marshall?" I pointed to our neighbor's house across the street. The man stayed rooted to his front porch, or behind the front window, watching the world go by. There was rarely a time when he wasn't sitting there in a fog of cigar smoke or silhouetted behind the glass. He had blinds installed a couple years ago, but when the light slanted in at the proper angle, I could still glimpse his stout body positioned in its regular spot.

"Good thinking." Mom turned toward our nosy neighbor's house. "If anyone happened to see something, it would be him."

We traipsed across the road, and I noticed the blinds snap shut at our approach. Mom raised her fist to knock, then turned and looked at my brother and me. She whispered, "Let me do the talking. I need to ask him a few things without telling him anything."

Good luck with that.

CHAPTER THREE

MR. MARSHALL PULLED THE DOOR OPEN before my mother could knock.

"Well, well, looks like we've got company." The balding man wore a newsboy's cap and stood in a swirling cloud of smoke. His cigar dangled from beneath his mustache so precariously, I expected it to fall at any moment.

"Hello, Joseph." Mom nodded. "How are—"

"Who's at the door, Joe?" a shrill voice called from behind the man.

Mr. Marshall hollered over his shoulder. "Just the Larcens paying us a visit, Abigail."

"Oh. How nice." Mrs. Marshall peeked over her husband's shoulder, but he didn't seem inclined to move and share the doorway. "Why don't you invite them in?"

"No, no." Mom held up a hand. "We can't stay. We, uh, wondered if you saw unusual...activity...in front of our house. This morning."

Mr. Marshall closed the door farther, so that it framed his plump, crinkled face. "See anything like what?" His voice was low.

"Out of the ordinary." Mom sounded impatient. "C'mon, you look out your front window 24/7. You probably know what *unusual* looks like better than we do."

His eyes narrowed. I don't think he appreciated my mom pointing out the obvious. "Sorry, but I don't know what you mean. Abigail feels under the weather and has required my care most of the morning. I haven't been paying attention to much of anything besides my dear wife."

Mom nodded. "Okay, okay. Sorry to have bothered you."

"No bother, Amy." Mr. Marshall grinned, biting his cigar

between his teeth. The smell was getting to me. "You mind telling me what I *should* be looking for?"

Mom shook her head. "Nope. Nothing that we won't be able to take care of. Soon as Liam gets home, I'll discuss it with him. If he thinks there's reason to be alarmed, then I'm sure he'll talk to you and the other neighbors."

A strange look flashed across Mr. Marshall's face. So swift, I thought I imagined it. "Very well." He took a drag from his cigar and blew the smoke out of his nose.

"See you, Joseph."

Our own front door opened before we left Mr. Marshall's driveway. Sophie stared a hole through us as we approached. "Well?" she asked, when we were within earshot.

"Nothing." Mom shrugged.

We stepped inside and Mom locked all three deadbolts, slid the chain in place, and locked the doorknob—precautions we hadn't bothered with since sleepwalking Brock stayed behind in the Tethered World.

I linked arms with Brady, needing to siphon some of his bravado to face the long, disturbing conversation I knew awaited us. Sophie danced ahead into the kitchen. I didn't know if she felt giddy with excitement or needed the restroom. Either way, I found her obnoxious.

My disposition was slipping back into resentful, fearful territory and I felt powerless to stop it. Having to face these family demons again, so soon after our big "showdown" earlier this summer, seemed like cruel and unusual punishment. I only wanted my senior year to get started. At this rate we wouldn't begin the new school year anytime soon.

Aunt Jules sat staring at her empty teacup. I grabbed the kettle. "You want seconds?"

"Yes, guppy, I surely would."

A measure of calm washed over me. It registered that guppy was the first pet name Auntie had used since she arrived. Pet names and Aunt Jules were synonymous. I felt better already.

Crossing to the stove, I fingered the necklace my father gave me "just because" after our adventures this summer. A tiny silver charm shaped like a book. He told me to wear it as a reminder of things to come. A promise that I wouldn't have to lose the things I love in the midst of this new part of my life in the Tethered World. I often found myself messing with it to calm my nerves.

"Lovey, tell me what ya found." Aunt Jules held her used teabag under the stream of water as I poured.

Mom shook her head. "Nothing. Nada. We even went across the street to Mr. Marshall's house—you know, our oddball neighbor who *always* seems to be watching us—but he claimed to be taking care of his sick wife all morning."

"She didn't sound sick to me," Brady said.

"Yeah, I noticed." Mom brought an empty mug to the table. "My guess is that Mr. Marshall is so disagreeable, his wife puts on a happy face to make up for it. Even when she's ill."

"So, *now* can we call the police?" Sophie jutted her hip sideways and crossed her arms.

"You don't get it, do you?" I snapped. "Dad isn't here. Not topside, anyway."

"How do *you* know?"

"Because, I do! What happened to Dad and Aunt Jules is obviously connected." I plunked into a chair.

"It's not obvious to me. I don't see how Aunt Jules fainting has anything to do with Dad disappearing."

"Sophie, open your ears and close your mouth for once. You don't—"

"Sadie!" Mom interrupted. "You need to take your own advice." She arched an eyebrow and pointed her finger at me.

I pressed my lips tight. Before today, things had finally begun to feel normal—and I wasn't ready to revisit the bizarre side this soon. Though I came around to accepting my family's connection to the world below, it hadn't taken long to slip back into my old attitudes.

Aunt Jules reached a hand to Sophie and gave her shoulder a pat. "Have a seat, peanut. This is complicated."

I drew my legs up and hugged my knees. The last big pow-wow we had with Aunt Jules around this table had left me shaken, scared, and angry. When our parents disappeared, Auntie came to stay and spilled the beans about our ancestral connection to the Tethered World and the main hub within it called the Land of Legend. She had been the one to pull the curtain back on a history that included our family and the world at large. Things you'd never read in a history book, guaranteed.

One thing she shared was that her twin sister, Judith, was

the current queen of a special realm within the Tethered World called Vituvia. All our lives we'd heard that this sister lived "abroad." This is why we had never met her. Made sense. Turns out "abroad" was a very *broad* term that included the world below. The very place where Brock now apprenticed *with* Queen Judith, learning how to rule Vituvia when the time came for her to retire.

Hearing that our discussion would be "complicated" didn't inspire confidence about the subject matter. This time, instead of dealing with waves of alarm that grew with each revelation unveiled by Aunt Jules, panic wrapped its tendrils around me nice and tight, right from the start.

CHAPTER FOUR

"May I see the note?" Mom pointed at the paper that our aunt still clutched.

Aunt Jules slid the paper across the laminate. Her fingers shook. Mom gave her hand a squeeze and took the note. She tried to smooth it flat on top of the placemat while her eyes scanned it.

"Well?" Sophie drummed her fingers on the table. "I'm dying to know what it says. Are you going to—"

"Sophie. Sit tight." Mom had that edge to her voice that meant everyone better chill. She continued to read.

Brady gave me a cross-eyed look. He probably noticed my anxiety and wanted to help, but my sense of humor had vacated. I turned away.

"May I read this aloud?" Mom glanced at Auntie.

Aunt Jules's tiny frame looked smaller than ever hunched in her seat, staring into her teacup. In my mind, she always seemed cast from pure optimism. But now, her gaunt, bruised face and trembling fingers made me fight back nervous tears.

"Aunt Jules...did you hear me?" Mom touched her arm.

Auntie jerked her head up and blinked. "Sorry?"

"The note." Mom held it up. "May I read it to the kids?"

She gave a hint of a nod. "Certainly, dove. The more information we have, the better. Even if it's a wee bit painful."

'Wee bit.' That's the understatement of the year.

Mom looked around the table, cleared her throat, and read:

"'Darling,
In exchange for family secrets, my captors have permitted

me to contact you. This is both a hello and goodbye, I'm afraid. Due to illness, my days are numbered. Before I pass from this life to the next, however, I begged for an opportunity to tell you of my enduring fidelity and love. Daily thoughts of your beautiful smile have helped to chisel away the pain over these many years.

I'm sorry that you must hear from me in this manner. Though I hated to divulge any information to my captors, it was the only way to break through the barrier that has divided us for so long. I hope you can forgive me and understand why I cooperated.

Now, please give them what they want. Resisting is useless, as I've learned in the most difficult of ways. What you have is a means to their razor-sharp end—an end with a hilt that they intend to seize one way or another.

Do not try to find me. It would be impossible, and I'm not long for this world anyway. Remember me as I once was, my love. Let that young and vibrant man remain like an image, carved in your mind. As it is, you would not recognize the man I have become. Pain and hardship has chipped away my identity.

To hear such things may convince you that my heart is hard as granite—but trust that I think of you daily and pray for you. What is most important, my darling, is for you to do what I ask. Alerting you to my wishes is the only way for me to protect you. There is mortal danger flaming in this illness of mine, and I fear it shall consume me. Since we've not been granted much time together in this life, I'll look forward to an eternity with you instead. Please understand what it is I need from you.

Engrave my love upon your soul,
Daniel.'"

Mom lowered the paper and sighed. "Goodness. Are you certain Uncle Daniel wrote this? It seems so unlikely."

"Whoa." Sophie sat back, blinking her wide brown eyes. "Just when you think it can't get any weirder around here."

Mom gave a lopsided grin. "Agreed." She reached out and stroked Aunt Jules's arm. "I must say, if Daniel wrote this, he sure has an unusual way of expressing things."

Auntie didn't look up.

"You okay?" Mom leaned in to her.

Aunt Jules continued to stare at her tea like the answers

to all our questions might be swirling in its depths. "Im-*pass-ible*."

"What?" Mom scrunched her face.

"You read the note wrong. It doesn't say that findin' him would be *impossible*. It says it would be *impassible*. I remember.'"

Mom looked bewildered. She scrutinized the note. "Yes, I, uh, thought it was a mistake. *Impassible* doesn't make sense. That's just a misspelling."

We stared expectantly at our redheaded aunt. I tumbled around the words my mother read but couldn't make them fit into a sensible spot. It was easier to do something rational, so I hopped up. "Anyone want a bottle of water?"

Brady nodded. I grabbed a couple and returned to the table. Sliding onto my seat, I had a sense that time was suspended. No one seemed to have budged.

"It's a code." Aunt Jules broke her silent contemplation. She looked around at all of us. Fire sparked in her green eyes. Her face split into a smile. "It's a code."

Oh, great. Another code.

Mom gave an uncertain chuckle. "Okay. How's that?"

Aunt Jules sat up straight and whacked the table with her palm. Her curls bounced in response. "It's a *code*. Read it again, tulip. It's important we don't overlook a thing."

Mom read with slow deliberateness. Aunt Jules nodded here and there, bit her lip, and grinned to herself.

"Ya see!" She gave the table another victory smack.

"No..." we said in unison.

"Beyond the ominous undertones about his captor's conspiracy, what themes did ya notice, doodlebugs? What sort of images does this letter conjure up?"

We contemplated, exchanging curious looks.

"Rocks." Sophie punched her fist into the air. "He keeps talking about stone and rock-type things—like carvings."

"Yes, m'dear." Aunt Jules offered Sophie a high-five. "Precisely. And *that's* why he wrote that findin' him would be 'impassible.' Stone is impassible. He's tryin' to give us clues about his captors, and, more importantly, what they're up to." She applauded. "Oh, Daniel you're a brilliant man."

"What? Wait." Brady shook his head. "Seems pretty clear he *doesn't* want you to come rescue him."

"Yer right. He doesn't. What he's sayin' between the lines,

however"—she narrowed her eyes—"is of utmost importance. His choice of words insinuates that the safety of all, both above ground and below, is in imminent danger. And he's lettin' me know who's stirrin' it up. The implications are subtle but clear."

Mom grimaced. "Those are very serious conclusions to draw."

"Who *is* stirring up all this trouble?" Sophie leaned on the tabletop and curled her legs beneath her. "And what do you have that he wants you to give to…to whoever left the note?"

"Hang on, pet." Aunt Jules held a finger up toward Sophie but looked at Mom. "Like I said, dear: he's writin' with code. Whoever allowed this note to be written would've had to approve of its wordin'. Daniel is tryin' to appease his captors and alert *me* to what's most important. And that's *who* his captors are, and *what* they're intendin' to do. He had one shot to make his point."

"Couldn't the note be forged? I mean, thirty-five years is a long time without contact." Mom held the paper toward the bright window like she might find proof that it was counterfeit. "Plus, I thought he died in Vietnam."

"Missin' in action was the official declaration. After this many years, it's natural fer most to presume that he'd passed. Remember, it's been thirty-eight years, pumpkin. Not thirty-five."

"Okay, thirty-*eight*. Three more reasons this seems so unlikely."

Aunt Jules reached for the note. "This…this is me Daniel's handwritin'." She tapped the paper with her index finger. "We wrote so many letters durin' the war that I could pick his manner of writin' out with a glance. Look at the little loop on the letter 'y' and how he makes the lowercase 'e' as if it's a capital, only shorter. It's *Daniel*. I always felt in me heart he was alive. That's why I still wear me weddin' ring. I've never lost hope. Not completely."

I watched Aunt Jules twist her intricate, gold band. That kind of love seemed inconceivable. As unique as the ring she wore. How had she continued to hope—and wait—for so long?

Mom looked tearful. "So, now what? What do we do? Your husband is—is somewhere with creatures plotting world domination. My husband isn't here." She pressed her lips together and tears trickled down her cheeks. "D-do you think that Liam has been taken to where Daniel is? Why do you think *he* disappeared at the same time that this note showed up?"

My eyes blurred. Queasiness fluttered deep down. Images of Ogres torturing my parents played in my mind. The Trolls handed Mom and Dad over to those big, sweaty thugs after kidnapping them. I recalled the smell of the nasty oafs, sitting on bleachers above me in a primitive sort of coliseum. The din of their chanting, *"Hu-man games!"* The utter helplessness while I watched, from my hiding place, the spectacle of my parents dying a slow, sickening death. A last-minute rescue saved them. But now…was my dad once again in their clutches? Or in the dungeon of the Trolls or another nightmarish place?

Why, God? Why? I'm pretty sure we've met our quota for hard times for, like, the rest of our lives.

I rubbed the miniature book charm between my fingers, reminding myself that Dad had hopes for me that I was meant to fulfill. And I needed him here, with me, to help it happen.

Aunt Jules cleared her throat. "I can't answer that, Amy. I'm not sure of the connection between the two events beyond the clear indication that things must be quite unstable below ground. And the safety of that realm has everything to do with the safety of those we care about. In order to bring our loved ones home, we're gonna need to learn what sort of hullabaloo is happenin' down below."

"The only way to do that is to go back, isn't it?" I dreaded, and knew, the answer to my own question.

Aunt Jules nodded.

Sophie whispered a victorious sounding "Yesss." My expression dared her to show excitement.

"What?" She gave me an innocent stare.

"You know *what*." I shook my head. This wasn't the time for a spat so I looked away. My little sister would move to the Tethered World in a heartbeat. Something I couldn't fathom.

"Sadie." Mom leveled her gaze on me. "It's okay that Sophie likes being in the Tethered World. We will all have to travel there many times in our lives. With Brock becoming King of Vituvia, there are numerous trips to look forward to."

"Look forward to?" I chuckled at her choice of words. "The

best I can do is *try*, Mom. Try to face it. Try not to fear it. I confess, I've missed being there. I totally miss Brock. And several other friends that live there. Maybe if trips down below didn't involve dangerous rescues, near-death experiences, and, you know, monsters from nightmares, I could embrace the idea better."

"Fair enough." Mom shrugged one shoulder and glanced at Aunt Jules. "Do you know what the code means, Auntie? What's with the stone and rock symbolism?"

Something washed across Aunt Jules's face. A foreign flicker of fear crept into her voice. "That's the worst part of all, lovies. There's only one creature that has the characteristics that Daniel hinted about. And they make Trolls seem like lovable, overgrown teddy bears."

Oh no! This conversation was heading further south in a hurry, but I forced myself to face whatever came next. A bead of sweat meandered down my temple.

Aunt Jules leaned in and whispered, "What's made of stone and stands guard over cathedrals and castles and other important, ancient buildings? Something that looks demonic."

"Gargoyles?" Brady guessed.

No way.

"Bingo."

No way!

"How's that possible?" He stiffened and sat back.

"The images that are carved in stone—that can be seen with yer eyes—aren't the real Gargoyles. They're replicas of the ones that live below. They're imps that were banished from the Land of Legend. But they still roam the far recesses of the Tethered World."

"Are they made of stone too?" Sophie's eyes were round as Ping-Pong balls.

"From what I understand, they can make themselves appear to be stone. Even topside. But that's not their real form. The stone masons who carved these images—actually known as *gargoyles* and *grotesques*, dependin' on their use—practiced dark magic and interacted with these bein's. They designed their statues to look like the evil apparitions that were conjured up in their twisted, pagan ceremonies."

My mind reeled through a mental file marked "creepy creatures" and came up empty. "How come the Gnomes and

Dwarves never mentioned these Gargoyles?"

"I don't know, chipmunk. From what I understand, these goonies were banished to the boonies long ago—far from the Land of Legend. Only the good Lord knows how far that part of the world extends beyond the main territory and who or what might live there."

Mom shook her head. "In my research over the years, I've come across rumors of this sort. But I dismissed them as exactly that. Why haven't you shared this information before?"

"That's what *I've* been wondering all summer," I grumbled.

"Sadie..." Mom glowered at me.

"I've never known for certain meself." Aunt Jules grimaced. "It's been a few generations since anything has been mentioned concernin' them. And the notes in the family journal are vague at best."

"Family journal? What family journal?" I pushed my chair back and stood. "Can we just put all the deep, dark secrets on the table? I think we have a right to know the entirety of what we're involved with—*involuntarily*, I might add."

"There are plenty of things *I* don't know, Sadie." Mom's eyes sparked. "Like the Gargoyles, for instance. We're talking about centuries of history. Many generations of our family have had little to no dealings with things in the Tethered World. Details are shared on a 'need to know' basis."

"Well, *I* need to know, Mom." I sat back down. Tears drizzled my face, and I could barely speak.

She reached over and stroked my hair. "I understand your reluctance, dear. All I can tell you is to pray. A lot. Your involvement is not coincidence. It's a calling from your Creator. And He made you for the calling. I think you found that out when you were there the first time."

I watched a few tears plop onto the table. Though what she said rang true, I didn't want it to be true. The things that happened in the world below took me from sheer terror to sheer joy in barely over a week.

There were people and creatures there that I would give my life for, and I knew they would do the same for me. But I'd managed to convince myself that any future contact would be on happy terms, like my brother Brock's coronation. Further life-threatening activity hadn't been on my radar. I thought we had done a decent job of putting the finishing touches on a horrible situation, righting all the wrongs, and walking away with our sanity. It wasn't supposed to unravel so soon.

My life has become a roller coaster with no chance of getting off.

And I hate roller coasters.

"So, Uncle Daniel is being held by these Gargoyles. What about Dad?" Sophie twisted a napkin like it might be the neck of said Gargoyle.

Mom shrugged. "I'd say it's a realistic possibility. But we have a lot of enemies in the Tethered World. They could be working together."

We had enemies? I'd never thought of it in such stark terminology.

"What's the game plan?" Brady looked ready for action. When we were in the heat of battle, rescuing our parents, my little brother had become a young man. The struggles we faced seemed to bring out his best. I didn't think he would say the same about me.

"We have to go back." Mom slid the note over to Aunt Jules. "Something's going on down there. Which brings us to the next point. What are they after, Aunt Jules? The note said to 'give them what they want.' Well, what do they want?"

CHAPTER FIVE

AUNT JULES SWALLOWED. SHE APPEARED TO weigh her words. I gripped the table, bracing myself for some new piece of information that would be my undoing.

Before she could reply, Nicole and Nate wandered into the kitchen.

"The cartoon is over." Nicole sidled up to Mom.

Mom stretched in her chair. "You can watch another one."

Nicole looked at Mom like she spoke gibberish. "We can? You never let us watch this much TV."

Mom laughed. "I know. Desperate times call for desperate measures." She reached an arm around Nicole for a hug. Nate squirmed between them.

"What's that mean?" Nicole tried to push Nate out of the way.

"It means it's probably going to be a long day. Grab some fruit snacks and a blanket and get comfy. Pick a long movie." Mom kissed Nicole's forehead and poked Nate in his bellybutton.

"Sounds like a *fun* day to me." She turned to Aunt Jules and pointed. "Where'd ya get that big bump?"

Auntie grinned and touched her goose-egg. "Oh, just gettin' old and clumsy I suppose. Came home from walkin' the beach this mornin' and stumbled over a big mess on me floor. Smacked me face on the table good and hard."

Nicole looked Aunt Jules up and down. "You need to put your toys away next time. Or get a maid. Mom always tells me we can't get a maid so I *have* to pick my toys up."

"Good advice!" Aunt Jules winked. "I'll think about it."

"C'mon, Nate." Nicole skipped away.

Nate toddled in a circle while pulling up his shirt with one hand and probing his navel with the other.

Mom poked his belly again. "You better go find your sister, little man."

He ambled after Nicole, and the mood shifted back to pensive.

Mom gazed expectantly at Aunt Jules and didn't mince words. "So, what do you have that these creatures want? If they're willing to expose the fact that they have Uncle Daniel, you must possess something of great value."

"Indeed I do. What I have is intrinsic to the whole of what they desire." Aunt Jules squared her shoulders and lifted her chin. "They were turnin' me house inside out for a certain, significant key. Without this key, they cannot unlock the power they strive to possess."

"A key?" Mom narrowed her eyes.

"Yes. There're only two such keys in existence. They've been around since God moved some of the inhabitants of Eden below ground. Given to members of Noah's family before the flood. Passed along through his descendants. Our family, sweet'ums, is part of this long line of key keepers. The second key has been kept with another family somewhere else in the world. But—but I've heard a rumor that it may have been lost."

Mom gave me a look of amazement. "See. I told you there were things I didn't know."

Aunt Jules patted Mom's forearm. "It was a conversation we were goin' to have soon, candy cane. It's time to pass the job to someone else."

Oh joy. "And, uh, what exactly is this key for?" I took a sip of water and hoped to appear nonchalant.

Aunt Jules anxiously tapped her wedding ring on the table. She leaned in and lowered her voice. "It's a key to the seat of power. Like I said, it's part of the bigger scheme of things. A key that, if it fell into the wrong hands, has the potential to tip the odds in favor of darkness—precisely what Daniel was alludin' to in his note. No one has ever used the key, and no one ever should."

Right when I think I've heard the worst. "You have possession of a key that could start an underground Armageddon?"

Auntie grimaced. "Yes. And no. It's not as simple as that."

"Of course not." I rolled my eyes. "We don't do 'simple' in

this family."

"Are you gonna give it to 'em, like Uncle Daniel said?" Sophie bit her fingernail.

"Never mind what he said, kitten. He said what he *had* t'say in order to write that note and make contact with me. Trust me. What Daniel most definitely *doesn't* want is fer me to give them the key." She pointed her finger at no one in particular. "There'll be a time in the future when the Maker requires both of them to be handed over—and lost or found, He knows right where they be. Still, as long as the Larcens are alive and kickin', no one shall get their hands, or paws, on ours. Except..."

Aunt Jules sat motionless, finger in the air.

"Except?" Mom leaned toward Auntie.

"Except the rest of that rumor gives me the jitters." She lowered her arm. "Two years ago, a couple o' Gnomes paid me a visit. They wanted to impress upon me the importance of vigilantly guardin' the key. Ya see, they'd recently learned that the other key may have been recovered—or perhaps *discovered* is a better word. And not by the good guys. But all efforts to learn more came to naught."

"Who do the Gnomes suspect?" Brady asked.

"Why, none other than our cuddly pal, Chief Nekronok. But such a boast could easily be fabricated by the big ape to intimidate his enemies."

"Then it's probably still lost, right?" Sophie twirled the salt shaker on her placemat, leaving a smattering of crystals in its wake.

"That would be an optimistic but naive assumption, sugar. It's safer to err on the side of caution." She lowered her voice. "Ya see, if these two keys fall into the wrong hands they have astronomical potential. Together they have the power to release the Flamin' Sword of Cherubythe."

Duh...the sword. How could I lose track of the real trophy in the Tethered World? Kidnapping and torture were but a means to an end, for the Trolls anyway.

Brady let out a low whistle.

"Yer familiar with the story of Excalibur, the legendary sword of King Arthur?"

We nodded.

"How do ya think such a legend came to be? Some that knew of the Sword of Cherubythe—the sword that the angel used to protect the Garden of Eden once Adam and Eve were exiled—had their own retellin' of such history. Over time, such a fantastic tale took on a life of its own. Much like the rumors of Leprechauns and Dwarves and the like over the years. Each of ya know they're quite real, but most tales about 'em are fanciful folklore."

"I don't understand why there's a key at all." I threw my hands up. "If God placed the sword where it needs to stay until He's ready for it, why would He hand out keys that could release it and start a war? It's not like *He* needs keys to do what He wants to do, anyway."

Aunt Jules gave me a searching stare. "Why would He place the tree of knowledge in the Garden and forbid Adam and Eve to eat from it, darlin'?"

Good point. I sighed. And shrugged. "Obedience...a test...or both?"

"Fer some reason, the great God of the universe chooses to carry out His plans through the likes of weak and imperfect people like us. Rather than question it, we ought to be flabbergasted and excited to have such a privilege granted to us, don't ya think?"

"Definitely!" Sophie gave me a satisfied smirk.

"Sophie..." *She never lets up.* "Don't you realize that being a part of this means our lives are *always* in danger? Yetis kidnapped Mom and Dad. Ogres tortured them. Dad's been taken again. This ought to cause a bit of fear and trepidation—not celebration."

My sister straightened and looked me in the eye. "You know how scared I was when we were there. I'm not saying I'm not afraid. Or that I like it when something bad happens. But we're all here for a reason. If our reason is more dangerous than someone else's, that doesn't mean God isn't with us, right?"

I nodded. Barely. What could I say to that?

Aunt Jules patted Sophie's arm. "That's the spirit, youngun'. That's the attitude that'll carry ya through these trials." She looked around the table. "We all must come to grips with this in our own way. Though in the past our family has had little to do with the goin's on below, that's no longer the case. And if we continue to sit here and wrestle with it, we continue to waste precious time. Yer father needs us. Daniel needs us. But more importantly, the sword must remain securely with the Gnomes."

"And that's *our* problem?" I snapped back.

Mom shot me a look, but Aunt Jules ignored my rudeness. "Actually, yes, it is, pumpkin. The safety of the sword has always been—and always will be—somewhat in the hands of our family." She cocked her head. "I don't know the details of that because we haven't been needed for many generations. But somethin' in this note," she said tapping it with her fingernail, "is hinting that we are needed now for somethin' bigger than either yer father or Daniel. The decision has been made fer us. The Maker is not askin' how we feel about it. We must go back."

"But what about the key?" Brady drummed the edge of the table with his two index fingers. "Is it in a safe place?"

"Of course, dear."

"Where?" *Note to self: stay far away from the location of this key.*

Aunt Jules silenced me with a serious look. "That's one of those things on a need-to-know basis, pet. And right now, ya don't need to know."

CHAPTER SIX

MOM ASKED ME TO PACK A week's worth of clothing for Nate and Nicole. She would call her brother, Brent, to see if they could stay with his family. Where did Uncle Brent fit into the scheme of things? Surely he knew about our strange family lineage—he was raised in the same household as Mom—yet I hadn't heard his name mentioned in connection to the Tethered World.

The day's activities revolved around preparing to leave and all the implications such a trip held for those both going and staying. Our jaunt earlier this summer had left Aunt Jules at our house babysitting Nicole and Nate. This time she would embark on the journey with us.

I was shocked to learn that although her sister had been the ruling monarch in Vituvia for the past forty-one years, Aunt Jules had never traveled below for a visit.

"It's never been an option fer me," she said. "Me sister Judith would occasionally come up fer a visit from Vituvia—just show up on me doorstep with a couple of Gnomes in the middle of the night. Other times, I'd take me dragon, Odyssey, to one of the lairs that connect to the tunnels. Judith would meet me inside, and we'd have a picnic and camp out fer a night or two. But I've never felt that goin' was permissible. It's hard to explain. But today, wild mongooses couldn't keep me from chasin' after me Daniel, let alone doin' what I can to ensure the sword's safety."

Aunt Jules doesn't actually keep a pet dragon, in the way people keep a dog or cat. She uses the dragon for what she considers "official business." My siblings and I rode on this flying reptile when we set out on our first trip. With my aversion to roller coasters, you can imagine how delighted I felt about hopping on the back of this legendary creature, minus a seatbelt or crash bar, and taking to the sky. Admittedly, I had fun seeing the world from this vantage point—once I woke from blacking out with fear.

Odyssey brought us to one of his lairs: a large cave hidden inside a monolith that connects to the Tethered World. The closest one to where we live, here in Orchards, Washington, is Beacon Rock. It sits along the Columbia River gorge, towering over the divide between Washington and Oregon, about thirty minutes from the side east of Portland—by car, anyway.

Aunt Jules lives within view of a different monolith crowning the Oregon coast. Haystack Rock is Odyssey's regular hangout—which apparently makes it easy for my aunt to communicate with the big beast.

How she goes about such an odd feat, I haven't a clue. Though she would deny it, I've always felt there was something unique about Aunt Jules—maybe even a bit magical. I've accused her of being related to the Lucky Charms Leprechaun, but she assures me it's only my imagination.

Then again, if you were to look at one of these monoliths, you'd be hard pressed to imagine where a dragon's lair might be lurking. There are no visible caves or crevices that one could use to get inside. But I visited one myself.

And I definitely didn't imagination it.

"Mr. Marshall is downstairs." Brady stood in the doorway of Nate's room, where I rummaged through stacks of size 3T clothing.

"Really? Why?" I followed Brady to the top of the stairs. We stood in the shadows and listened.

"I'm sure when Liam gets home, he'll decide what's best," Mom was saying.

"That's just it." Mr. Marshall's gruff voice had that lifelong smoker quality. "It sure looks like he's home. His car's been here all day."

"I'm not sure that's any of your concern. I ought to know whether my husband is home or not."

"Who are ya talkin' to, Twinkie?" Aunt Jules joined the conversation.

"Well, now, who's this young lady?" The smell of Mr. Marshall's ever-present cigar wafted up the stairs.

"My aunt. Julie McGriffin, this is Joseph Marshall, our neighbor."

"Nice to meet ya, neighbor," Aunt Jules said.

"It's a pleasure Miss—or is it Mrs—McGriffin?" Mr. Marshall was uncharacteristically chatty.

Aunt Jules gave an impatient grunt. "A happily married *missus*."

"You don't say. And where's the mister?"

"Joseph." Mom sounded perturbed. "Thanks for checking on us. We're fine. Really. As you can see, we've got company, and we're rather busy. So, if you don't mind...."

"Sure. Sure. Merely being neighborly. I'll see ya soon. Nice to meet you, Mrs. McGriffin."

The door shut.

I looked at Brady and shook my head. "That was weird."

"Yep."

"Yer neighbor is a cheeky sort," Aunt Jules said.

"Not sure what got into him. He's always watched us from afar. I don't think he's ever checked on us. Even after an ambulance showed up when Nate had that seizure."

"Well, today seems to be the day for strange things, doesn't it, love?"

"Mmm-hmm."

"They say life is stranger than fiction, right?" my brother whispered, "whoever 'they' are."

I nodded. "I think 'they' are going to have to come up with a whole new category, especially for our family. Neither fiction or life is this bizarre."

Brady walked to the upstairs window that overlooked the front of the house. He parted the curtains enough to view Mr. Marshall's retreat across the street. The stout man let his fingers trail across Aunt Jules's yellow VW Beetle as he passed. He continued to his side of the street then stopped when he reached his yard, scuffing his foot repeatedly across a patch of grass near the driveway. Cigar smoke made a contrail down the road in the stiff breeze.

The old man turned in a slow circle, brushing his hands together. A white sedan approached, and Mr. Marshall tilted the bill of his cap in greeting. He wiggled the newsboy hat back into place and then, as if he knew he was being spied on, he jerked his head to where Brady stood watching.

Instinctively, Brady stepped away from the window. His palms were sweaty; his heart revved. Why did Mr. Marshall bother, today of all days, to take an interest in the Larcen household? Had the nosy neighbor actually seen something? Maybe Brady needed to do some neighborly observing for himself later this evening.

Mom planned an early dinner because Uncle Brent would be stopping by to pick up Nate and Nicole. She told us to keep the chit-chat about our trip on the light side for their sake. We munched on pizza and carrot sticks—an easy option in the midst of the commotion.

"This is the best summer *ever*." Nicole wrestled with a stretchy string of cheese, pizza sauce spattering her chin.

"Why is that?" Mom passed her a napkin.

Nicole wiped her face, smearing sauce across her jaw.

"First, Aunt Jules got to stay with us. Now, we get to go to Uncle Brent and Aunt Valerie's house. And we don't have to do any school."

"Hmm. I don't recall saying that." Mom used her own napkin on Nicole's colorful face. "A little math and reading for the summer isn't hardcore, kiddo. In fact, you can go ahead and take the math flashcards and your *James and the Giant Peach* book."

"Aw, Mom…" Nicole scrunched her face.

"Aw, seriously." Mom tweaked her nose. "Read it to Amanda and Felicity. They'd love to hear their older cousin read them a story."

"Well, okay." Nicole took a huge bite of pizza and seemed resigned to the prominent fate of homeschoolers everywhere: summer school. I knew kids who kept up with all of their classes year round, with only short breaks here and there. At least we had the bragging rights of doing the bare minimum for the summer.

"Oh my goodness." Mom shot out of her seat and snatched the phone from the counter. "I forgot to tell Dinah that Dad won't be in the office for a while."

She headed into the other room, phone to ear.

Someone knocked at the door and I jumped to answer it. "I'll get it." Through the peephole I spied Uncle Brent.

After unlocking all the deadbolts and the chain, I pulled the door open. "Hey, Uncle B!" Though his family lived but ten minutes away, we only hung out about a half-dozen times a year.

"If it isn't the beautiful high school senior, Sadie Larcen." After a hug he stepped inside. He looked to be on his way home from work, sporting his lab coat, a dress shirt with loosened tie, and khakis. His unruly blond hair was the only evidence that this pharmacist was a hippie at heart. That, and the fact that he'd much rather use the medicinal plants that he grew over anything the doctor might prescribe. The man had a prolific green thumb.

"What's with using all the locks?" He jerked his head toward the door. "I thought Brock was in Vituvia for the summer."

He knows. My mind sort of checked out. I stared at my uncle, amazed to hear someone outside my immediate family talk about the secrets we guarded so vigilantly.

"Sadie?" He snapped his fingers in front of my face.

I blinked. "Sorry. It's totally strange to hear you mention Vituvia. I didn't know that anyone else knew about it."

Uncle Brent reached an arm around my shoulder and leaned in. "I know. If you ever want to talk about it, that's cool with me."

"Thanks."

"I guess that means your mom never explained how I opted out of the 'family business.' She's never quite embraced the fact that I wanted to keep my life strictly topside." His arm dropped from my shoulder. "It's been a strain on our relationship, to be honest."

That explained why they weren't close. "I didn't know 'opting out' was possible."

"It came with a price. Certainly made me the black sheep of the family. I feel like everyone hopes I get struck by lightning or something."

"Oh, that's not true." I waved his notion away. "Mom only has good things to say about you. For real."

He grinned. "Well, that's a relief. Guess I can quit looking over my shoulder for lightning bolts."

We chuckled and walked into the kitchen.

"Uncle Brent!" Nicole catapulted herself into his arms. "I'm sooo excited to stay at your house."

"Wow, I need to stop by more often for epic hugs like this." He twirled her around.

Sophie stood and gave him an awkward hug. I remembered being her age and wondering if I was too old to show my excitement about seeing him. He might be Mom's only brother, but he was our favorite uncle. Dad had a younger brother, Jeremy, who we barely knew. A bigwig on Wall Street. "Too busy strutting about in expensive suits to mingle with us peasants," my dad sometimes remarked.

Uncle Brent kissed the top of Sophie's head while Nicole continued to cling to his middle like a monkey.

Mom came back into the kitchen. "Hey, big brother."

"How's my favorite, only sister?" He let Nicole slide down and walked over to Mom.

"Hanging in there." She wrapped him in a desperate hug that suggested she needed some of his manly strength to seep into her bones. "This is harder than when I was imprisoned with Liam."

He stroked her hair and gave an assuring wink to Nicole who looked confused by Mom's sudden emotional display. He pulled Mom back and gave her a penetrating look. "Anything you need, I'm here. You know that."

Mom stiffened. "Oh sure. As long as it doesn't require you to travel to certain places, right?"

Brent looked at the ceiling and pressed his lips together.

"Ahem." Aunt Jules cleared her throat.

Uncle Brent swiveled toward the sound. "Hey, Aunt Jules." He said her name with that awkward "thank you for the distraction" sort of enthusiasm. In two strides he was by her side, lifting her—chair and all—and landing a noisy smooch on her cheek.

She giggled. "Laddie, if ya don't put me down, I'll scalp those blond curls right off yer noggin."

My uncle lowered the chair, crossed his arms, and stood tall. "You'd have to be able to reach the top of my head. That's physically impossible."

"Me up. Me up!" Nate held up his arms and gave Uncle Brent a gleeful grin.

"Hang on, buddy." I led Nate to the counter. His Italian supper glazed his face and fingers. I grabbed a wet wipe and started scrubbing.

"Man, he's gotten big." Brent shook his head. "He's lost that baby look." He turned to Brady and offered his hand. "Brady Bunch. What's up, fella? They feeding you enough in this fancy cafe?"

"Most of the—"

"Brent," Mom cut in. "We need to speak with you alone."

The lighthearted niceties went kaput. Mom would not be playing the part of hostess this evening. Uncle Brent scooped Nate up and followed Mom and Aunt Jules into the living room.

I raised an eyebrow at Brady. "So much for keeping the chit-chat light."

"Really." He stood. "Well, I need to finish rounding up batteries and stuff to pack."

"Don't forget the bungee cords so we can strap the backpacks to our bodies—permanently." I socked him on the arm with my fist. Last time we traversed the tunnels, three of our four backpacks plummeted over the edge of a cliff.

Sayonara supplies.

"Not a bad idea." He laughed and headed toward the garage.

"Nicole, run to the schoolroom and grab your reading book and flashcards like Mom said." I offered her another napkin. "Also, pick out a couple of toys to bring. Or games. I only packed your clothes."

"I'm on it." She dashed out of the kitchen.

"Can I do anything?" Sophie stuffed her hands into her pockets and rocked back on her heels.

"Sure. I didn't get Nate's bath toys yet. Or the baby shampoo."

"Aye, aye, captain."

Standing in the empty room, I felt small. And alone. My uncle's proclamation about leaving the family business unsettled me. *So tempting.* Yet, I didn't think he had the misfortune of someone he loved being kidnapped and forced to the Tethered World. Twice. Surely Uncle Brent would do whatever it took to get a loved one back, if that were the case.

But wasn't his own kidnapped sister that important? In his defense, I didn't think to tell my uncle what happened when Mom and Dad disappeared earlier this summer. It happened so fast, and we left right away. Guess Mom filled him in after we returned.

Still, once things calmed down would I be willing to risk the relationships I valued and refuse to go back? I needed to process this idea.

I rushed to finish packing, grabbed my phone and earbuds, and headed outside to the late afternoon sunshine to sit and contemplate.

CHAPTER SEVEN

Since I wouldn't see blue skies or solar rays for some time, I knew I better soak them up. The perfect summer day seduced my senses, and the music offered a quick escape, which made my time of deliberation unproductive. With my head tilted back my and feet propped on a potted plant, I came dangerously close to dozing off.

That is, until something touched my leg. "Stop it, Ollie." *Nosy dog.*

"Sadie!" A whispered voice startled me.

"Wha—?" I nearly tipped over. Ollie doesn't speak human.

"Shh. It's me, Reiko."

I regained my balance just in time to be hit by a tsunami of shock. "What are you doing here?" My brain refused to comprehend that I was looking at the Gnome warrior who helped rescue my family with her stealth-fighting skills.

"Well, I didn't come for tea." She offered me a handshake, which amounted to grabbing two of my fingers with her entire petite hand. "How's the bravest girl in Washington state?"

I laughed. "You mean Sophie?"

"Okay, maybe there are two brave girls who live here. It's good to see you, Sadie." She offered a rare smile.

"You too! Wanna pull up a chair?" It hit me that this was the first time I'd seen her dressed in typical Gnome garb— tunic-style clothing—rather than miniature body armor. Her cone-shaped hat had an extra-wide brim that kept her face shadowed.

"Can we sit in the shade? Gnomes usually do their topside duties at night. Moonbeams are easier on us than sunshine."

"Okay, let's book it over to that tree." I pointed to the large evergreen that dominated the backyard. We dashed across the patio to the carpet of cool grass beneath its outstretched branches.

"I can't stay long." She parked herself on the ground.

"Well, it's my turn to surprise you." I settled beside her. "My family is planning to come back to the Tethered World as we speak."

She looked toward the sky. "Oh, thank the Maker! Today we found—"

"You won't *believe* what happened today," I went on. "This morning my dad vanished."

"Vanished? Like a Leprechaun?" Reiko removed her hat and ran nimble fingers across the stray, ebony strands of hair that escaped her braid. Her miniature Asian features derailed my train of thought. I never could get over how tiny Gnomes were, like human Shrinky Dinks.

I grimaced. "No, no. I mean he's missing. He said goodbye to my mom before leaving for work, but his car is still parked out front. We have to assume he's been taken below."

Reiko patted my leg. "Oh, Sadie, I'm sorry. I'll tell General Muggleridge the minute I return. We'll form a search party. But also, we came across—"

"There's more bad news. A lot more." I yanked up fistfuls of grass. "You know Queen Judith's twin sister, my great-aunt Julie?"

Reiko nodded.

"She showed up at our door late this morning, frightened so badly that she fainted. Someone ransacked her house. Thankfully she was taking a walk when they paid her a visit." I let the grass clippings fall from my hands. "But they left a note. A note written by her long, lost husband who she hasn't heard from in forever."

"And?" Reiko's unflustered face stared into mine. As head of secret ops for the Gnome military, she stayed as neutral as a garden statue most of the time.

"And..." I went on to tell her about the demands of the message, the subtle warnings, and the secret key.

Reiko's eyes were riveted to my face. "Did they find the key?"

I shook my head. "Nope. Made a mess and left her husband's note, which is beyond bizarre. Everyone thought the poor guy died in Vietnam. But, certain clues in the message make Aunt Jules think that some sort of Gargoyle creature had him in their clutches all this time."

Despite Reiko's porcelain skin, her face went pale. For the first time since we met, she appeared shaken.

I leaned in. "Reiko, what do you know about these beasts?"

She appeared to be using all her mental capacity to keep calm and carry on. She grasped my wrist. "Listen to me. Your family must leave tonight. You don't have time to wait for the fog necessary for Odyssey to whisk you away in secret. Tell your mother that tonight—*tonight*—I need to meet you at the bridge up at Moulton Falls. There's another way into the Land of Legend. Pack light."

"I don't know if—"

"Figure it out. I was sent here to convince you to come back. But the situation is more serious than we thought. The Sword of Cherubythe is in great danger. It must be protected at all cost. Go. I'll meet you at midnight. And make sure Brady and your mother come, as well—though it sounds as if that's already the plan."

I went inside to find Mom and the others hugging Nate and Nicole goodbye. I must have looked awful because my presence brought their warm-fuzzies to a standstill. Uncle Brent became all business and gathered up the luggage to load in his car.

Mom ushered me into the living room. "I said no one goes outside."

"I know." I placed my hands on my temples and shook my head. "I didn't even think about it. Sorry." Before she could gain momentum, I launched into Reiko's visit.

The rest of the evening ran together like muddy water. I managed to...manage. Emergencies aren't my strong suit. My dream job involved hiding behind a computer screen and making up my own realities. I would never pursue a crisis-management position.

With hyperventilation on my heels, I stumbled through the rest of the preparations. Reiko's shocked face kept broadcasting in my mind. It struck me that I never let her explain why she came all the way to our house in the first place. The only snippet I could remember was that she hoped to convince us to come back to the Tethered World. But, why?

Nervous energy flowed through Brady like an electric current. He channeled it with fifty push-ups on his bedroom floor. Though he wouldn't get a chance to figure out Mr. Marshall's overt attentiveness, Brady was stoked to learn they would head to the Tethered World, fog or no fog. He didn't even mind missing out on his driver's permit, though he still disliked the haircut. To think there existed another way into the Tethered World—besides a dragon's lair under cooperative weather conditions…sweet.

Brady collapsed onto the floor, panting. Though he'd kept up with the karate lessons he and Brock used to take together, he'd added his own home regimen to the mix. He may not be "high king in training," but Brady always assumed he'd revisit the wild, mysterious Land of Legend on less-than-friendly terms. He wanted to be prepared.

He never guessed it would happen so soon. But he welcomed it. Brady felt like he'd been in a state of limbo since they returned minus his brother. He hadn't quite understood the restless feeling he'd struggled with the last month or so, but it had dissolved as soon as his mom declared they would go back. And Reiko had specifically requested *him* by name. Why?

Maybe Brock missed him. Though autism kept most of Brock's emotions behind a mysterious veil, Brady occasionally caught a glimpse of his brother's feelings. The corners of Brock's mouth would twitch in amusement when he watched a funny movie. If their parents argued or one of their siblings was hurt or angry, Brock often stared at the floor as if he wished to disappear beneath the carpet. And when Brock immersed himself in water—whether a bath, shower, or swimming pool—he smiled.

Brady guessed his brother's somewhat stiff body felt a freedom in water that was more than skin deep. On rare occasions, Brock even hummed in the shower.

Perhaps Brock had asked to see him. Or maybe their dad's

disappearance and Reiko's request meant Brock was in trouble too.

No. Brady didn't dare let his thoughts linger on such a possibility. To allow the notion to even flicker through his brain left him anxious. He hated not being able to protect his brother. If something happened to Brock, even at such a distance, Brady would feel like he'd failed him.

Rolling onto his back, Brady spied Brock's pocketknife carefully placed in its plastic display stand. The carved, ivory-handled knife once belonged to Uncle Daniel, but Aunt Jules had passed it on to Brock for his tenth birthday. Brock soaked up any book or movie about Vietnam, even back then. Brady had been a little jealous of the gift at the time—after all, it was his birthday too. Aunt Jules had given him Uncle Daniel's pocket watch, but that wasn't nearly as cool as a knife.

Brady stood and swiped the knife from its stand on the dresser and shoved it into his back pocket. He should take it to Brock. His brother would appreciate the iconic reminder of home. And—who knows—maybe the knife would be reunited with its original owner at some point—if Uncle Daniel was indeed alive.

The half-hour drive to Moulton Falls felt like a three-hour swim through cement. No one spoke. It seemed much darker inside our minivan than it did outside, though clouds smothered the moonlight.

"Oh, great." Mom flashed on the high-beams and stopped the car. A chained gate prevented access to the parking lot. "Is there another way in?"

Aunt Jules looked back at Brady. "Ya know how to pick a lock, guppy?"

"Uh, seriously?"

"Well, either that or we take this-here minivan off road."

"Actually, that's probably the fastest option." Mom backed

up, and the headlights revealed a grassy drainage ditch on either side of the gate. "Here goes nothing."

She shifted into drive and hit the gas.

"Go, Mom!" Brady cheered.

I gripped the door handle and squeezed my eyes shut. We're off-roading in a minivan. On purpose.

My teeth rattled as we zoomed down and up the other side of the bumpy ditch—though the ride was, overall, uneventful. Fine with me since I knew I'd get my share of eventfulness soon enough.

Sophie clapped her hands. "Bravo, Mom. You're a natural."

Mom cut her lights and coasted across the empty gravel lot. She parked by the main trail that led to the bridge.

Before we clambered out, Aunt Jules whispered a quick prayer and reminded us that we had not stumbled upon this mission by chance. "Yer part of somethin' special. Somethin' big and important. This is the path the Creator assigned to our family. Let's make Him proud."

Backpack in hand, I climbed out of the vehicle. My heart shifted into high gear at the sound of the distant, thrashing waterfall. It thrummed in the background like our own epic movie soundtrack, ratcheting up the intensity.

Make Him proud. *Me?* It looked like I would have to wait until the end of this feature film to see if I could live up to such a lofty goal.

CHAPTER EIGHT

"How much you wanna bet our van gets towed?" Mom pressed the lock button on the key fob. The minivan winked its lights at us, saying goodbye.

"Why would they tow it?" Sophie looked from mom to the van.

"Because it says 'no overnight parking.'" She pointed to the warning sign. "No doubt they'll frown on the tire marks left in the ditch, too, and slap on a fine for that."

"I'll happily give ya me life savin's to get it out of the impound once the sword is safe and our men are free."

Mom clicked on her flashlight. "Small price to pay isn't it?"

"Absolutely, firefly." Aunt Jules tromped toward the graveled trail.

"Let me take the lead." Brady jogged to the front and turned on his headlamp.

"Thanks for being a gentleman." Mom held Aunt Jules's arm and let Brady pass. "Sophie, behind your brother. I'll help Aunt Jules maneuver the trails. Sadie, bring up the rear."

Sure. That way I can get snatched away and no one will notice. I went to the back of the line and told myself to shut up.

The trail sloped down through a series of switchbacks. The roar of pounding water made conversation impossible. The clouds parted enough for us to make out the arched bridge looming ahead, like a fortress spanning the Lewis River. A fortress made me think of castles. And Gargoyles.

I forced myself to focus on the path in front of me. A good idea since I nearly plowed into my mom and aunt. Despite her age, Aunt Jules was spry and energetic. She regularly strolled along the surf at her beachside home, combing for shells and picking up trash from careless tourists. Unlike the seashore, the woodsy trail we trekked changed inclines and traction. Wooden steps or leaf-strewn slopes meant she hesitated now and then, picking her way along. More than once my ankles tangled with broken branches as well.

We wound our way to the riverbank then up through the woods—which was super creepy from my spot at the back of the line. I didn't remember it taking this long to get to the top of the bridge when we visited Moulton Falls before. Of course, sunshine and dappled shade lend itself to a day of fun better than a cloudy, dark night.

At last, we turned onto the footbridge. Brady swept the beam of his headlamp between the railings and over to the other side. There, at the opposite end, waited Reiko. Preferred over Gargoyles ten to one.

She waved us across. I noticed she had changed from her casual tunic into chain mail and her usual pointy, metal hat. Without a word, she turned to guide us through another labyrinth of trees. She soon deserted the main trail in favor of a well-worn rut in the woods. My flashlight became my best friend. Trees and undergrowth surrounded me, reaching spindly fingers for every available body part.

Twigs snapped nearby, and my heart kicked into overdrive.

"Did you hear that?" I called.

"What?" Mom looked over her shoulder.

"A twig or something."

"Sadie, we're in the middle of the woods. Everyone's stepping on twigs."

"Yeah, but...yeah." It sure seemed like the noise came from behind me.

"Almost there, Larcens." I heard Reiko say from the front.

The thunderous sound of the now-distant waterfall had dulled to that of a low, continuous rumble. An owl hooted, followed by the swoosh of wings taking flight. I slowed and sniffed the air. A musty smell struck a familiar chord but it was too faint to place.

A few minutes later, we traipsed into a clearing. The woods encircled us and made a perfect spot for a picnic—under different circumstances. The clouds finally sailed away, and the moon drenched us in its iridescent glow. We could see without the use of our flashlights and shut them off.

Reiko took a moment to greet everyone. When she approached Aunt Jules, she removed her hat and gave a curtsey.

"What a pleasure to meet the sister of our dear Queen Judith." Reiko replaced her helmet. "You look so identical; I feel I'm in her presence."

Aunt Jules extended her hand. "The pleasure is mine, m'dear. I've heard so much about yer bravery and skill. I owe ya oodles of thanks fer protectin' me family while they were below."

Reiko steepled her petite fingers together. "I assure you that your family was equally brave and resourceful. We were in it together, and we all depended on one another to make it through."

"Looks like we're in it together yet again." Mom placed an arm around Auntie's shoulder.

Reiko nodded. "Yes. I'm sorry to hear about Liam." She turned back to Aunt Jules. "And your husband."

"Don't be sorry, pet. 'Tis the best news I've had in thirty-eight years. Daniel is alive, and we shall be reunited this side of heaven, Lord willin'." She winked at Reiko. "But it's not goin' to be an easy task. We need yer little people to help us."

"You will always have our assistance." Reiko bowed. "I've already sent word below to form search parties. And these developments have put us on high alert in regards to the sword."

She appeared to search for something in the shadows. "You will be transported to Berganstroud straightaway. The Meadow Faeries shall be here soon. This happens to be one of their favorite dells to frequent topside."

"Sweet!" Sophie clapped her hands. "It's like having some sort of superpower when we disappear with the Faeries. Though I'm sorta bummed we don't get to ride Odyssey again."

"Flying to Beacon Rock and traversing those tunnels would take too long." Reiko tugged at a dried leaf stuck in her chain mail. "We're extremely pressed for time and needed to expedite your arrival with some assistance."

"I've been ridin' around on Odyssey for years." Aunt Jules dismissed the notion with a toss of her hand. "Time to try somethin' new. Faeries sound extraordinary."

Yeah, 'cause dragons are so "last year."

"They're coming." Reiko pointed at a speck of distant light.

The breeze carried a soft chiming lilt. It also brought a whiff of the musty odor from earlier. Where *had* I smelled that before?

"Step inside this ring of toadstools." Reiko waved us to where she stood.

Mushrooms of various sizes grew in a wide circumference that I hadn't noticed in the moonlight. We shuffled to the center and clustered next to the Gnome.

Faint orbs wafted toward us. Their soft hue grew in wattage until a thousand glowing flecks of confetti exploded around our gathering and washed us with their lemon-lime brilliance.

Sophie nudged me. "The toadstools!"

I blinked at the sudden change in the mushrooms. They had become phosphorescent fungi.

Adrenaline made my extremities tingle. Despite my earlier reluctance, I thrilled at the sight of the Fey that had transported us to Vituvia once we made it through the tunnels on our first visit. Trying to zero in on one Faery was tricky. They outmaneuvered my ability to focus. One hovered a few inches from my face, allowing me to give it my full attention. Having a self-illuminating body made it easy to study in the dark. The silken wings fluttered at hummingbird speed. The butterfly-meets-alien face grinned at me, and a diminutive arm waved.

I wagged my fingers in return.

Aunt Jules giggled and clapped her hands. "It's like pixie dust. Exactly like pixie dust!"

Their chorusing chimes increased in volume. This was the Faeries' way of communicating. It started out like a charming jingle, but—I recalled—escalated to an earsplitting frequency.

The sound waves began to make a coherent sentence. "Circle up, Larcens. Circle up."

We clustered together. The little spheres of light started to rotate around our group. Sophie stood beside me, chin up. She looked ready to take on the world. The kid had moxie. And I wanted some of it.

Hair lashed across my face as the radiant fluff picked up speed, reminding me that I forgot to braid it. I pressed my bangs back with one hand and squinted ahead at the trees. The Fey moved so fast they barely obscured my view. The last time we traveled by Faerie I closed my eyes tight, fearful and unaware of what was about to happen. This time I hoped to watch the disappearance take place, if that were even possible.

Aunt Jules emitted a loud, "Woohoo!"

Sophie laughed with abandon.

Then someone—or something—stepped out of the shadows at the edge of the woods.

CHAPTER NINE

A BLACK HOLE TURNED ME INSIDE out.

At least, that's how it felt the instant the Faeries transported us from Moulton Falls. It sucked me in before I could figure out who, or what, had stepped into the meadow and ended before I could comprehend the sensation of my bodily molecules floating through space and fusing back together—if in fact that's how it worked. I found myself sniffing the roasted leather scent of pipe tobacco, squinting against a smoke-filled space. It brought to mind the smell I had noticed in the woods. Was I able to smell this place before I arrived? *Maybe...*

The haze kept us shrouded for a few moments. My eyes adjusted. The jitters subsided, and my insides warmed at the familiar sight. Gnarly Dwarves sat around a worn table puffing their pipes and poring over a large parchment map. In quick succession they noticed our arrival. A few jumped from their seats, obviously caught off guard. The two Dwarves who huddled at the far end of the table looked up, gave a welcoming smile, and hurried toward our group. Wogsnop and Lava!

I met the steel-blue gaze of my dear friend, Lava. His animal-skin cape fluttered behind his stout body, a dagger in his belt and sword at his hip. Wiry, gray hair sprouted from his head and beard, bouncing around his shoulders as he took on speed. I headed his direction, aware of a swelling sensation that stirred the fathomless space where emotions smolder, dormant and withdrawn—like waking from a long, laborious sleep.

"Roots and fruits! Look what the Faeries trudged up, would ya?" Lava's hearty laugh reverberated through my marrow and shook me fully—soulfully—awake. A deep breath. A jovial hug. A whiff of smoke and ale enveloped me. Strange but enchanting smells that crushed my lingering resistance with their familial comfort.

I took a knee and buried my face into his cascading, snarled curls and cried. This friend had been my rock in the tumult of our first visit, and I had missed him more than I realized.

"Sadie." Lava stroked my hair and patted my back. "I'm so sorry about yer father. We'll find 'im again. Never fear."

I pulled away, sniffed, and wiped my eyes. Tears were trapped in my lashes, and I blinked them free. Lava reached calloused fingers to wipe my cheek, his brows furrowed in concern.

"We will find 'im, sweet Sadie. I promise ya that."

My selfishness assaulted me. I shook my head. "I'm—I'm not crying about my dad." *Why do I make everything about me?* Lava offered me his handkerchief, and I mopped my face. "Of course, I'm scared for him and want to find him. But, I-I didn't realize until now how much I missed this place and you and—" I shrugged and laughed. "I don't really understand why I'm crying to be honest. It just feels *right* to be here. It's hard to explain."

His eyes glistened. He looked ready to cry as well, but the next moment he chuckled deep in his barreled chest. "It *is* right fer ya to be here, lass." He glanced at the others mingling nearby. "We've missed yer family and have talked about ya every day."

I swallowed and stood, squaring my shoulders. "Same here."

"Besides. the sword needs the Larcens like never before." Lava gave my arm a squeeze and turned to the other Dwarves before I could ask what he meant. "You blokes round up a dozen men and divide like we discussed. Looks like Wogsnop and I will be stayin' fer a bit."

Chairs scraped the floor and six grungy Dwarves filed by, tipping their hats. One of them caught sight of Aunt Jules and did a double-take. He nudged the others, causing a domino effect of blundering bows and confused looks.

Aunt Jules grinned and winked. "I'm not who ya think me to be, fellas. Queen Judith is me sister, though, so yer close." She gave a little curtsey. "Call me Aunt Jules. I already love ya like family. Pleasure to meet ya."

The burly Dwarves bumbled and bowed until they made it out the door.

I looked around the room trying to decipher where we had "landed." It seemed safe to say we were tucked into the rock fortress of Berganstroud, home to the Dwarves. My last visit brought me to their rugged dwelling twice, so it wasn't hard to recognize. But the torchlight revealed an unfamiliar space, cramped and cluttered with sundry weapons and crates. Add a multitude of hovering Faeries, mingled with a cloud of pipe haze, and it felt like the ceiling might smother us.

Wogsnop must have had the same sensation. He looked up at the glowing orbs, darting playfully in and out of the swirls of smoke, and cleared his throat. "Thank you, Spriggen Fey, for retrieving our friends. You're free to return to the meadow until further notice."

The specks of sparkles and wings spiraled together and vanished. The room seemed to expand a bit.

"Thank you for coming on such short notice, friends." Wogsnop removed his floppy leather hat and ran a hand through his coarse, salty-black hair. "Madame Julie"—he bowed in her direction—"it's a surprise and an honor to have you here, as well."

"Call me 'Aunt Jules,' if ya please, chipmunk."

"Aunt Jules, then." Wogsnop turned to Reiko. "Thank you for swiftly getting help. The patient had a rough day."

Reiko nodded. "You're probably wondering why I brought so *much* help."

The Dwarf lowered his voice. "With all the nasty reports about the sword's security being compromised, we're beginning to fear it is the time of the Great Upheaval. But prophecies aside, we're spread thin as butter at the moment. Of course, we're always glad to see the Larcens, and certainly glad for the help."

"Help? What do you mean, help?" Mom glanced from Wogsnop to Reiko. "I thought you guys were going to help *us*."

"Well—" Reiko began.

"Of course. Goes both ways." Wogsnop spoke over Reiko. "If you'll follow me to the infirmary, I'll show you the patient." Wogsnop turned for the door, Lava at his heels.

"Patient?" Mom wrinkled her nose. Confusion circulated

between us.

The Dwarves turned to find we hadn't moved.

Lava raised a bushy brow at Reiko. "Ya didn't tell them?"

"I did not." Reiko sighed. Her almond eyes were bloodshot and puffy. "A lot has happened since you asked me to retrieve the Larcens this morning."

"Very well." Wogsnop crossed his arms. "Fill me in. But make it brief for the sake of the convalescent."

"The convo-what?" Sophie whispered to Mom.

"It means 'patient.' The kind in the hospital." Mom stepped toward the Dwarf. "Who are you talking about? Is Liam here? Is he hurt?"

"No, no, Lady Amy. But I assure you we've got as many men as we can spare looking for him." Wogsnop shook his head and raised both hands. "Sounds like we both need an explanation."

"Exactly." Reiko's voice was terse. "Let me expound. When you sent me to fetch a Larcen or two, I learned from Sadie that they were already preparing to head to the Tethered World. Madame Julie—or Aunt Jules—found a note…"

I watched Wogsnop and Lava while Reiko's story unfolded. Their faces remained unreadable. *A patient?* My mind worked the puzzle.

"So, that's why they came," Reiko concluded. "The threat to the sword intensifies with each revelation. Between that, Liam's disappearance, and Daniel's, uh, reappearance, there's much to consider. Since the Larcens were planning to travel here, I didn't take time to explain about the topsider patient. After I spoke with Sadie about her father, my priority was to brief Vituvia and Berganstroud while the trail was fresh. Mentioning the patient would only have prompted questions and delayed my return."

"There's that word again." Mom placed her hands on her hips. "What patient?"

"We don't know who he is." Wogsnop shook his head. "We found someone in a remote area of the Berganstroud hills. Some of our spies were headed to an outpost near Ernest Peak when they came across a body—a human. They thought he was dead but found a weak pulse and rushed him back to the fortress. Doc Keswick has been tending to him. The man has improved."

"Mercy!" Aunt Jules held a shaky hand over her mouth.

"It's Daniel isn't it?" Tears tumbled over her cheeks and fingers.

"Well." Lava cleared his throat like he wasn't sure what to say. "He could very well be yer husband, ma'am—though I'm flummoxed that there could be a topsider here for decades without us knowin' about it. He's elderly. Quite frail and incoherent. I'd sure like to look at the note that Reiko referred to, if ya brought it."

"Take me to him. *Please.*" Aunt Jules clasped her hands together, pleading. "There's no need for the note if he's here."

"Yes, of course, Madame—er, Aunt Jules. We shall take ya to him. But, I must prepare ya for his condition. He's very thin. And pale. And scarred."

Aunt Jules pressed her lips together. I could tell she was trying to digest this information without losing hope.

I recalled how the Ogres had lashed my parents to torture devices, using them for sport. If we hadn't been able to rescue them, Lava could well be describing my mom and dad. My stomach clenched.

"This may not be your husband, ma'am. We don't know who he is or how he came to be here." Wogsnop situated his hat. "He only babbles, though he does speak English." He pointed to my mother. "We wanted Reiko to fetch you since you used to be a nurse. A virus has swept through our town and many a Dwarf is ill. We're short-staffed and unable to give the man as much attention as he needs. We hoped you might connect with him, maybe make sense from his words. Perhaps the company of another human would help him get strong enough to journey topside. And reunite him with his family."

"I've heard enough. Take me to him." Mom snapped into Amy Larcen, RN mode.

Wogsnop and Lava led us out of the room and down a long, chilly corridor. Dwarves rushed past, armed and tense. I wondered if the flurry of activity revolved around the new patient, or forming search parties for my dad, or something more. No doubt the latest threats to the sword sent a fresh ripple of panic through the fortress.

I wrapped an arm around Aunt Jules's narrow shoulders and hoped she could sense my desire to be brave enough for both of us.

An antiseptic smell greeted me outside a nondescript door.

Wogsnop nodded at a soldier who saluted and pulled the lever to let us inside. Above the door, engraved in stone, it said, "Infirmary."

We followed the Dwarves down a lengthy hallway peppered with numbered doors. They stopped at one marked number nine.

Lava reached for the knob and stopped, turning to Aunt Jules with a tender look. "If this patient turns out to be yer husband, I think ya should know one more thing."

Because Aunt Jules was still tucked beneath my arm, I felt the subtle shudder that quivered her bones. "Very well."

Lava shifted his weight and looked down. "The man inside is blind."

CHAPTER TEN

PAINFUL SOBS CARRIED FROM THE OTHER side of door number nine. I paced the hallway where I waited with my siblings. Mom said we should hang back while she and Aunt Jules ventured inside with Wogsnop and Lava. Whatever they'd encountered must have been awful, based on the cries I could hear.

Sophie cringed at a particularly piercing sound, and I stopped and took her hand. "You okay?"

Her expression told me she wasn't. "I've never heard anyone cry like that. Except in the movies."

"Yeah, doesn't sound like tears of joy. He must be in bad shape."

"Maybe it's not him. Maybe she's really disappointed."

I nodded. "Could be."

Brady sat on the floor next to our backpacks. He leaned against the wall, biting his nails. "Man-mode" seemed to have taken over: try to be stoic and act indifferent to any nearby emotional eruptions.

The door cracked and Lava slipped out. Brady hopped up.

"That didn't sound good," I said.

Lava shook his head. He looked shell shocked. "It was painful." He cranked a finger into his ear. "On my ears as well as yer Aunt. I knew it would be difficult."

I nodded as if I understood, but I didn't. I had barely survived a week in this hole-in-the-earth. Physically I fared fine, but on the emotional level...not so much. The thought of being here for decades, without human contact, felt unfathomable.

"So, it *is* Uncle Daniel?" Sophie hugged herself, rubbing her upper arms.

Lava nodded. "Best I can tell. She looked him over fer a bit. He's sleepin' and medicated so the little woman just stood there starin' hard. She appeared to be lookin' fer the man she remembered beneath the scars, and the age, and whatever else has changed. Then a jolt of emotion exploded. At full volume."

"Do you think he's gonna die?" Brady stuffed his hands in his jeans pockets. "Like for real, this time?"

My elbow met his ribcage. "What sort of question is that?"

"Um, a realistic one."

"Not a very nice one." Sophie scowled.

"I'm afraid we're needin' to deal with realities, not niceties." Lava scratched his chin. "Yer uncle nearly perished, but he's pullin' through. We've lost a number of our own to the same malicious virus he's recoverin' from. Now with yer dad disappearin' and the Trolls bein' uncooperative, there's plenty hangin' in the balance. Add to that the news of Gargoyles with their sights set on the sword, and the ransom note, demandin' the key..." The gruff block of a man trailed off and looked lower than a sinkhole. His usual gumption and tenacity seemed to have deserted him.

"Sounds so ominous." I wrung my hands.

He nodded. "I think the sword is in serious danger."

"What do you mean the Trolls are being uncooperative?" Brady asked.

"Ah, that's another story." Lava pulled his dagger from his belt and began cleaning his wide, flat fingernails. "Nekronok has altogether ignored the treaty he signed after his defeat." The Dwarf glanced up. "A couple of weeks after the battle, when we sent a delegation to meet with him, he refused to cooperate. Had more guards than ever patrollin' the Eldritch. In the past, the beasts rarely ventured beyond Ernest Peak. Now there've been skirmishes all the way to Vituvia. We believe they're spyin' on the security of the realm, scoutin' for vulnerability in regards to the Sword of Cherubythe. Gotta wonder if there's a connection between them and the activities of the Gargoyles."

We turned at the sound of the door opening. Mom tiptoed out. Her eyes were swollen and red, and she needed a Kleenex.

I put my arm around her, and she fought a new wave of tears.

"There's no way to describe how distressing that was." She sniffed. "I only know Uncle Daniel from pictures. There's absolutely no resemblance. It took Aunt Jules a long, hard stare to realize it's truly him. He looks like a POW."

"He *was* a POW." Brady grasped her hand.

Mom nodded. "True. Despite looking horrific, I think he's on the mend. His vitals are strong. What he really needs is to know his wife is by his side. That knowledge might be the ideal medicine for a full recovery. And they both need to experience a little joy after so many years apart." Her eyes brightened. "I'm very pleased—and rather surprised—by the excellent care he is receiving here."

Lava gave a curt nod. "Thank you, m'lady. Some Dwarves work topside to learn skills that we can utilize here in the Land of Legend. Medicine is very useful. Did the Doc come by?"

"No. He's busy with other patients. The nurse said she'd tell him we're here." Mom grabbed my arm and smiled. "Sadie, Joanie is his nurse."

My heart lightened to hear the name of the sweet woman who cared for Sophie and me like a mother on our first visit. "Can I see her?"

"No. You'd better let Auntie have her privacy. In fact, after I speak with the doctor, I'd like to get our search for Liam underway. There's not much I can do for Uncle Daniel at this point. We all know Aunt Jules can nurse anyone back to health, with or without a nursing degree. Especially the love of her life." She looked at Lava. "I know you folks wanted my help. But Daniel looks stable, and I have to find Liam. That's my first priority."

Lava's fingers twitched on the hilt of his sword. He opened his mouth as if to say something then pressed his lips together and shifted from one foot to another. "Yes. I understand. When we sent Reiko to make contact, we didn't know there would be more to the story. Ya certainly need to join the search fer yer husband."

"Thank you." Mom looked at my sister and brushed a tendril of hair from her cheek. "Sophie, I'd like to leave you with Aunt Jules. She needs moral support."

"Mo-om, I don't wanna be stuck in a hospital." Sophie's shoulders collapsed.

"I'll stay." I raised my hand and wiggled my fingers.

Sophie straightened and gave Mom an eager look.

"No." Mom slowly shook her head. "I don't think that's a good idea. You should come with me. Both you and Brady. It could be dangerous for someone Sophie's age."

"That's precisely why I should stay. Sophie is the one who thrives on danger. You three ride roller coasters and bungee jump." I patted my chest. "Remember—I'm the one on the ground snapping pictures. I'd prefer to stay and help Aunt Jules."

Mom pressed her lips together. That meant she was thinking. *Good sign.*

"Very well. Come to think of it, I feel better about keeping Sophie close by." She turned to my sister who frowned at that last sentence. "You *will* stay with me. You're not to run off with a band of Gnomes or something. Got it?"

Sophie nodded. "Got it."

"Lava, what's the plan?" Mom looked like she'd prefer to give the orders.

"Some of my men are going to scout for yer husband, some will spy on the Eldritch. Others are headed to enforce security in Vituvia." Lava peeked his head through Uncle Daniel's door then shut it again. "Not sure where Wogsnop got off to. Must've gone out the other door. Let me find him and see what he recommends." He trotted away.

"Guess I'd better tell Aunt Jules what we're planning." Mom left us alone in the hall right as Reiko rejoined us.

I looked at Brady and Sophie. *Deja vu.* "Looks like we're back to square one. Entangled with strange creatures and forming search parties for missing parents. All my favorite things rolled up in one."

"Hey, sis." Brady slung his arm around my shoulder. "You did great last time, and you'll be awesome again. Who knows, you might learn to like adventure—though I doubt you'll find much hanging around a hospital."

"Brady, may I have a word with you?" Reiko's tone reminded me that she'd requested him by name earlier in the day. Though curious, I stepped away, grabbing my nosy sister by the hand.

"Hey, what's the big idea?" She looked annoyed.

"It's called being polite."

Brady knelt, nodding as Reiko spoke in hushed tones near his ear. Why the secrecy? Brady's face morphed from pensive to animated while she spoke.

"What do you think she's saying?" Sophie whispered.

"How should *I* know?"

Brady stood and watched Reiko retreat down the hall. He turned, an eager grin plastered across his face.

"What was that about?" Sophie pulled me back to where he stood.

He raised his eyebrows mischievously. "Looks like Brock isn't the only one with a special assignment."

"Oh really?" I crossed my arms. "Do tell."

He looked around, like someone might be listening. "The Gnomes want me to train in their Special Ops." He leaned in closer. "They want to make me a Guardian of the Sword."

"Sweet!" Sophie bounced up and down. "Oh, I hope they've got a cool job for me too."

I offered my brother a fist bump. "Congrats. Sounds awesome."

He shrugged. "Mom has to agree to it first."

"Agree to what?" Mom stepped out of the door, as if on cue.

"Uh..." Brady glanced at me like he needed my moral support. "Reiko proposed a-a job for me." He laced his fingers behind his neck and gave Mom one of his I-hope-this-comes-off-as-a-casual, off–handed–remark–that–you'll–be–comfort-able–with look.

"She did, did she?" Mom offered back her best I'm-skeptical-of-your-attempt-to-act-indifferent look. "Do they need someone to flip hamburgers at their local Burgerville?"

Brady gave a nervous chuckle. "It's a little more exciting than that. They want to train me to—uh—you know, guard something."

Mom merely blinked.

"The Flaming Sword of Cherubythe, actually."

She pursed her lips and nodded slowly. "Oh, is that all."

Reiko and Lava turned the corner and walked toward us.

Mom rounded on the two of them. "So. You guys already have *one* of my sons in your employ. And now you'd like to keep Brady here as well? Surely you jest. Do I come across as a worn-out mother yearning for a break from her tiresome children or something?"

This was not going Brady's way.

Reiko and Lava exchanged an uneasy glance. The Dwarf's

bushy mustache stretched into a lopsided grin. "I understand your reluctance, m'lady. Truly. Let me assure you that it would be a temporary position until the danger has passed. Guardin' the sword was, until recently, a privilege only given to Gnomes."

"Well, that's different." Mom's tone was mocking. "If it's dangerous then *obviously* we should jump all over it."

"Mom." Brady sounded desperate. "I want to do this. Please. I mean, isn't this the kind of thing expected by our family's involvement here?"

Mom's eyes flashed. "You've no idea how long it took Dad and me to warm to the concept of Brock becoming king of Vituvia. We found out when he was ten and refused for the next three years." Her eyes rimmed with tears. "Our family was not supposed to get divided up and left to fend off monsters like this."

"Lady Amy," Reiko stepped forward. "If I may be so bold? If the sword is removed or Vituvia overthrown, no one you love will be safe. Not here. Not topside. Not ever again. Dwarf and Nephilim warriors have already been recruited for our new guardian program. We're leaking the news of this consortium to the Trolls for the purpose of deterring their interest.

"Rather than react defensively, we want to be proactive. Take the offense. Having the unity of our allies, both here and topside, makes a strong statement. Though we hope that it's more for show than out of necessity, events are rapidly escalating, and we want to be prepared. As you know, whoever controls the sword controls the Tethered World. In the wrong hands, the sword's power could be dangerous. Even deadly. Not to mention potentially plunging our underground world into darkness."

"As horrific as that sounds, you have plenty of trained warriors. Why do you need a fifteen-year-old topsider?"

Lava flicked his glance from Reiko back to Mom. "Because not every fifteen-year-old topsider is the spittin' image of the future High King."

Mom looked struck by the implication.

Uh-oh.

Reiko's words came out in a rush, like she hoped to douse the embers flaring in my mother's eyes. "Things—many things—are happening that point to prophecies of old. There are ancient writings that speak of 'kinship protecting kingship. Without the help of one son, Lady Amy, you may not be able to protect the other."

Silence pressed like gravity.

I tried to guess what my mother thought of this catch twenty-two, but she stared at Reiko as if she couldn't quite understand her language.

Lava took over. "We feel we must train Brady. It seems he is the one vital to protectin' both the sword and his brother Brock."

Mom's face hadn't softened, but she looked conflicted.

Brady grasped her hand. "Please, Mom, think about it. You don't have to say yes, but please don't say no. Not yet. It means a lot to hear I'm needed." He cocked his head. "Besides, I've been protecting my brother our entire lives. This really isn't so different."

My heart melted. How could Mom resist *that*?

She took a deep breath through flared nostrils. "I'll consider it."

Brady visibly uncoiled. "Thanks, Mom."

Reiko and Lava looked cautiously relieved.

"You'll have time to contemplate as we ride." Lava smoothed his beard with a calloused hand. "I know the hour is late. But we plan to ride through the night and get to Vituvia in the morn. Are you up to ridin' with us, or shall I have one of our men escort you tomorrow?"

Mom glanced at Sophie and Brady. "Kids?"

"Wide awake." Brady grinned.

"Me too." Sophie jutted her chin in the air.

"Well, I'm too wired to sleep." Mom put her arm around my waist. "I guess you can check on Aunt Jules and go to bed if you want. I hate the idea of leaving any of you behind. But the thought of Aunt Jules being alone at this time is even worse. She seemed relieved that you'd be staying."

I nodded. "I'll take good care of her. You guys get going. Sounds like you're in for a long night."

Brady and Sophie gave me a goodbye squeeze. We're not usually so touchy-feely, but a goodbye in this place held no guarantees of a safe—or soon—return.

Brady slipped his arms through the loops of the backpack, and Sophie followed suit. They fell into step beside Mom and trailed Reiko and Lava through the fortress. Brady couldn't suppress a hint of a smile.

When Reiko had mentioned that ancient writings spoke of kinship protecting kingship, it stirred Brady's imagination. It gave him a buzz to think that he, too, was someone God intended to use in this untamed land populated by legends. More than intended—planned beforehand—purposefully.

Brady Larcen: Guardian of the Sword, body double of the High King.

Had a nice ring to it. Pretty official. Although posing as royalty wasn't done for the fun of it. It meant Brock held a perilous position. He was a target. At the moment it didn't sound like he was in immediate trouble—but he might be in danger. Brady grimaced, knowing there was a difference. The latter gave him time to understand the situation and get prepared.

The way everyone went on about the sword made it sound as if *it* needed protecting even more than his brother. Maybe it did. But the Flaming Sword of Cherubythe could never hold a candle to family.

Of course, if the sword wasn't safe, neither was Brock. Nor anyone he loved. Which meant protecting the sword, his family, and his own life was one and the same. Intrinsically part of a whole. It made his mind spin to consider all the implications. So much at stake. So much he still didn't understand.

Brady shoved his hands into his back pockets as the four of them left the stone citadel and strode across a hard-packed, dirt road toward the stables. Brock's pocketknife met his fingertips, and his jostling thoughts were reined in by the familiar touch.

You're getting ahead of yourself. Work through it as you go.

Brady took a steadying breath and glanced at his mother's

profile. Her jaw was set. Her face reflected a mixture of worry and a dogged determination to get through the troublesome days ahead.

It was best to keep his musings to himself.

CHAPTER ELEVEN

ALONE IN THE PASSAGE, I STOOD with my hand on the door that led to where my great-uncle Daniel lay. I wondered if staying behind was the right thing to do. Maybe I should have been more protective of Sophie.

But I worried about Aunt Jules's well-being. That tiny woman held such a bold, bright spot in my life. She loved us fiercely. I wanted to be there for her, the way she'd always been there for us. She was practically my grandmother. My mom's mom, Grandmother Shannon—also Aunt Jules's older sister—passed away before my parents started a family. And Aunt Jules never had children of her own, which meant we all fit perfectly into one another's lives.

I didn't want to walk in unannounced, so I rapped my knuckle on the wooden door.

It opened slightly, then a cheery, familiar face split into a grin.

"Joanie!" I reached for a hug as she threw the door open and grabbed my middle.

"Oh, lovey, what a joy to see ya here! I've been missin' ya, and prayin' that the Maker would cause His face to shine upon ya every day."

We pulled apart enough to grin at each other. "I've missed you too. I hate that what brings me to this place is always bad news."

"M'dear, if it wasn't for the bad things, good things like meetin' each other never would've happened. The good Lord has a way of turnin' all the bad stuff on its head and redeemin' it in some way."

I swallowed a lump in my throat. "Wow. So true. I need to remember that." Between her accent and her optimism, she and Aunt Jules would get along splendidly.

"Live as many years as me and you'll learn a few worthwhile lessons." She winked. "C'mon in. I believe yer aunt could use a hug."

The atmosphere in hospitals must be universally identical. It amazed me that roughhewn rock walls could look so sterile and contain that antiseptic, discomfiting smell. The whitewashed stone gleamed as extra torches brightened the space. In the corner a squat, potbelly stove radiated orange warmth.

Sparse furnishings added to the sanitary feel. The hospital bed situated near one wall seemed out of place in this rudimentary setting. It was from an actual hospital bed with steel rails. It looked as if the Dwarves had placed a mattress and adjustable bed frame on top of two enormous tree trunks which substituted for the base. On my first visit here, I learned from Lava that Dwarves had mastered the art of dumpster diving topside. This bed must've been a trophy catch.

The patient made a small, subtle lump beneath the roughhewn covers. He faced away, so I only glimpsed the back of his balding head. Scars zigzagged his neck and the bare dome on top. Long grey hair from the lower half of his scalp sprawled wildly across the pillow. His pale, sallow skin—which hadn't seen sunlight in four decades—glistened with perspiration.

Of course, these observations hit within mere moments. My main concern was Aunt Jules crumpled in a chair against the opposite wall. She leaned over, elbows on knees and head bowed. From the way she shook, I could tell her tears continued.

She didn't look up when I shuffled over. Nothing I could think to say seemed remotely appropriate. I could only offer my presence.

Joanie disappeared through another door and came back with a wooden stool. Grateful to sit, I plunked down and reached a hand to Auntie's quaking shoulders.

She blew her nose on a well-used handkerchief, then grasped my hand with freezing fingers. I covered her hand with my other and tried to warm her.

"Nothin' like a good cry to chill ya to the bone, eh, sweet pea?" Her bloodshot, puffy eyes crinkled in a brave attempt at a smile.

"I'm sorry this hasn't turned out like you hoped." I rubbed her fingers in mine. "Really sorry."

"Don't be sorry, love. I'm pleased as peanut butter to have Daniel back in me life. He seems healthy enough, though he's not ready to travel home just yet. But all in God's good timin'. It's a mixture of sad and happy tears fer me. Joy is overflowin' right now on the inside. It's a miracle to have him back. Even if he's not in his right mind and doesn't know me. Course, selfishly I pray that he will know eventually."

"Of course."

"I remember the first time I laid eyes on Daniel." Aunt Jules smiled at the patient in the bed like she could see him transformed into the man she married. She giggled. "He carried a stack of books piled right up to his chin. Nearly dumped them on top o'me at my desk. I worked at the library in Dublin, y'know. Course I wasn't but a wee bit taller than the countertop. His books started slippin' and slidin' and tumblin' toward me." She reached over her head as if to shield herself. "He fumbled, tryin' to catch the confounded books and apologizin' all the while."

Aunt Jules's gaze reengaged with mine. "I've never felt such an electric shock. *Literally.*" She laughed—a lovely sound after hearing her cry. "In the midst of us tryin' to contain the avalanche, our hands clasped together. We exchanged such a jolt of electricity, we startled and the rest of the books toppled to the ground."

"Wow! Sounds like a memorable introduction."

"Oh, yes." She wagged her finger and gave a sly grin. "I'd already noticed the young soldier browsin' through the books on medieval history and Irish folklore. He visited every few weeks. Most of the men in uniform wanted to read dime novels. Easy escapes from their difficult life. But this young redheaded man—whom I'd have sworn to be a fellow countryman had he not been wearin' an American uniform—looked at books that interested *me.* So, I had me eye on him. And I noticed him a-watchin' me too."

"Did he ask you out?"

"After that jolt he asked fer me name. Before I could answer, this other fellow, also a soldier I'd seen before, swaggered up beside him. He leaned over, real smug-like. 'Don't waste your time on this stiff, doll,' he says. 'You can see he's a clumsy oaf. Whaddya say we catch a picture show tonight?"

"What?" I laughed, surprised by her perfect imitation of an American and that some goofball would speak to her like a gangster. "That's awfully cocky. What'd you say?"

"Why, I didn't even give 'im the satisfaction of an answer. I looked right back at the first soldier, the cute one with the freckles, and introduced meself. The second one didn't like it one bit. After that initial meetin' I saw both soldiers regularly—whenever they had a pass to leave the military post."

"Both of them?"

"Yes, both. See, they were cousins. More like brothers because William—the cocky one—had been orphaned as a child, and Daniel's family took him in. William had a twisted way of lookin' at the world. And he was very competitive, always tryin' to outdo Daniel."

"And jealous that Daniel got the girl."

Auntie grinned. "I suppose. Growin' up he always wanted to be faster, stronger, funnier, and better. Daniel purposely joined the Marines when he heard William intended to join the army. But ol' William changed his mind at the last minute and joined the Marines too. Though Daniel couldn't get away from his cousin's competitive spirit, he learned to be thankful fer havin' him nearby. Seems the military had a buddy system. which kept the two young men together. Nothin' like havin' someone ya know close at hand in a foreign land and the heat of battle. Even if he can be a scoundrel."

"Sounds like Daniel is an optimist. Like you."

"He was ever the gentleman and always took William's teasin' with a polite chuckle. Wasn't until our honeymoon that he admitted to bein' weary of havin' an extra shadow. Daniel took the opportunity to distance himself from his cousin even more by takin' me last name. *That* was somethin' his cousin couldn't compete with."

"What?" I stiffened in surprise. "I guess I assumed you reverted to your maiden name since Uncle Daniel wasn't around. That must've raised some eyebrows."

Her eyes twinkled. "Certainly unconventional. I told ya once that Daniel always believed in the lore and the legends. See, his grandparents came to America from Limerick, Ireland. Best I can tell that side o' the family had some sorta knowledge of the Tethered World. But they called it the Land of Moored-below."

"Moored-below. I like that."

"Me too." She patted my hand. "Daniel hadn't any qualms about me family history. He was merely thrilled to have found someone who understood his childhood fascination with Moored-below. When he learned I hadn't any brothers to carry on me family surname, he offered to change his to McGriffin. Otherwise I'd have been Julie Delaney."

"Wow. Had no idea. Guess once you and Uncle Daniel tied the knot, William had to back off. Sounds like quite a character."

"Oh, yes. His true colors emerged soon after we wed. All that machismo and smooth talk was merely a cover up for a wicked heart."

"Wicked?"

"*Wicked.*" Aunt Jules exhaled the word like it tasted as vile as what it represented. "After our honeymoon, the two shipped off to Vietnam. William's desire to be better than Daniel led him to delve into dark and forbidden things. Whereas Daniel loved the good Lord and was fascinated by the tales of Moored-Below, William consorted with the powers of evil. Things the Good Book warns us to keep ourselves far from. Daniel wrote letters, expressin' concern. Sayin' he didn't trust Will. So many letters—all growin' in suspicion and alarm. When Daniel was reported missin' in action, I never quite believed it."

She seemed to stare right through me. "Always wondered if William was involved with Daniel's disappearance, but he went missin' as well."

I stared at the stalwart woman of loyalty and faith sitting beside me. Today was the first day she'd laid eyes on her husband since her honeymoon? What kind of woman could keep hope kindled in her heart for thirty-eight years when the flame of love had glimmered so briefly? What kind of love had she found?

I couldn't wrap my brain around it. "You haven't seen this man since your honeymoon?"

Auntie nodded. A tear slid down her cheek. "And he will never look at me again, thanks to those monsters."

"Maybe it's only cataracts. Mr. Layton at church used to be blind. Then he had cataracts removed and could see, good as new."

Sadness engulfed Auntie's face. Her chin quivered. "It's...it's not cataracts, pet." Her eyes darted to where her husband lay. She gave a nod in his direction and opened her mouth as if to say something. Another tear dribbled down her cheek, and she turned away.

Her distress brought a sting of tears to my eyes. "It's okay. Take your time."

A sob wracked her shoulders. "You might as well l-look fer yerself. Get it over with."

I didn't follow. "Look at what?"

"His eyes."

"Okay." Circling around to the far side of Uncle Daniel's bed, I shifted until I could see his face.

I gasped and covered my mouth. My stomach thrashed. I spun away and leaned against the wall.

It took a few moments and a lot of willpower to avoid conjuring up the sight I witnessed. An atrocity lay on that bed, apparently asleep. I say apparently because there was no way to know for certain beyond deep, steady breathing.

One of his eyes was opaque. No better than a glazed marble bulging from its socket. The other eye was missing. A melded crater of skin—freshly blistered and blackened—left in its place.

CHAPTER TWELVE

With so many Dwarves heading in different directions, Brady and his mom needed to share a chestnut draft horse, while Sophie doubled with Lava on his paint. Riding across the prairies at dusk made the landscape look much different than Brady remembered. The domed, golden "sky" dimmed like a giant nightlight, casting an ember-like glow which silhouetted the chain of jagged mountains that reached from Berganstroud to Vituvia and beyond.

Brady pressed his legs against the horse's flank, spurring it through the fog that drifted from Whitt Lake. He didn't want to lose sight of the others, and the mist was thickening by the minute. Reiko led the way on her toboggan—a creepy-cool creature with a lion-like body and a fanged mountain goat sort of face. They were officially called *clovenboars*, but their manner of skimming across the landscape had a similar feel to a toboggan traversing the snow.

Lava and Bennett, another Dwarf who Brady had traveled with previously, rounded out the group. Chief Wogsnop left Lava in charge of those journeying to Vituvia, while he commanded the espionage crew that would surveil Craventhrall.

They rode in silence, though Brady felt the anxious undercurrent that converged on them like the fog. The Land of Legend seemed to be in a tangible upheaval. The rhythm of normal life disrupted so that no one knew exactly what to expect or how to react.

He'd braced himself for an ongoing lecture from Mom. After all, she had a captive audience. But instead of ruminating about potential dangers or thinking—out loud— about all the reasons why Brady shouldn't train with the

Gnomes, she kept quiet. It made him a little nervous. At least a lecture would've meant that *she* remained predictable. Even quizzical Sophie kept quiet.

They had been traveling for several hours, and Brady's adrenaline had long since dissipated. His eyes burned for sleep. The monotonous, flat terrain took a sudden downward plunge, jolting him out of his stupor. The mist somehow thickened, which made the steep descent all the more precarious.

"Hang on." Brady leaned back in the saddle as the horse picked its footing down the treacherous slope.

"Goodness." Mom tightened her grip on his ribcage, leaning along with him. "I think I dozed off."

The other riders appeared in the mist at the bottom of the hill. Gurgling water reflected the dull, amber light above. Brady's horse skidded to a stop.

"Good time to water the horses." Lava dismounted. "Let's stretch our legs and hope the fog lessens."

Everyone enthusiastically followed his lead. Brady took a noisy gulp from his canteen and passed it to his mom. "I think this might be Brodger Creek where the Water Nymph saved Sophie from the snakes."

"Yep. None other." Bennett paced a small circle nearby, stretching his arms above his floppy, worn hat.

"You think the Nymph is still here?" Sophie's voice carried through the mist.

Brady squinted, looking for signs of the mysterious water sprite, or the horrifying vipers that covered both land and water a mere six weeks before. "I've no idea. Let's hope those Sleeping Serpents are definitely *not* here."

Lava emerged from the fog chuckling. "I heard about your little adventure last time around."

"Not sure why that's funny." Amy stepped beside Brady, arms crossed, face crosser. "Sophie could have been bitten— could have died—when she fell in the water with those serpents."

The Dwarf sobered. "Very true, m'lady. Sometimes we must laugh at memories that might otherwise defeat us."

A snorting sound interrupted the discussion. The thick haze wafted enough to reveal Reiko's toboggan sniffing along the creek bank. A low growl idled in its chest.

"What is it, Thrym?" Reiko scurried alongside him.

The creature stiffened and jerked its head up.

The mist enveloped Brady again so that he could only hear a sudden commotion.

Reiko hollered, "Thrym!"

"What's going on?" Amy grabbed Brady's arm.

"I don't know. I hope it's not the Sleeping Serpents. I'm going to check."

"Well, I'm not staying here." She groped in Sophie's direction. "Stay with us, Soph."

They followed a muddle of footprints along the water's edge, then nearly ran over the others shrouded up ahead. Lava, Bennett, and Reiko stared at something hidden from view.

Brady strained to see what was right before him. At the same time, a series of snorts and screeches ripped into the night. The fog waned again and provided a glimpse of the toboggan lowering his curving horns like a bull ready to charge. He lunged at seemingly nothing, but a painful wail ensued.

In and out of the feathered fog, a small body catapulted. Another snort, another screech, and another body went flying.

Sophie squealed in amazement.

"Blasted Leprechauns!" Lava shouted. "That's what ya get fer sneakin' around where ya don't belong. Go back to Nimmickdell, or next time we'll finish ya off, ya hear?"

Yells and yipes and curses rained down from on top of the hill, followed by a few rocks.

"You better scram while you can." Bennett called.

"Way to go, Thrym." Reiko walked toward the creature. "Any more vermin?"

"What happened?" Amy squeezed Brady's arm.

Lava swiped the hat from his head and turned to the Larcens, scratching his scalp with a vengeance. "Weasley Leprechauns. Up to no good, I guarantee. Toboggans are able to see the invisible imps, thank the Maker. Otherwise they would've likely spied on us or robbed us, or who knows what."

"You think we stumbled on them here, or did they follow us?" Brady gently peeled Mom's hand off his arm.

Lava shrugged. "Couldn't say."

Reiko stepped beside Lava. "I can venture a guess. I found

this by the bridge."

She held out her hand and everyone stared at a pocketknife with a carved, ivory handle.

"That was in my pocket!" Brady pointed at his brother's knife. "How—"

"Pilfering pickpockets!" Reiko switched the blade closed and shoved it at Brady. "Taking our things and using them against us." She pointed at the rope bridge. "One of the four suspension ropes that support the bridge has been severed. Thrym caught them just in time."

I paced along the wall in the hospital room, chewing my fingernails. My eyes roved from the apparition in bed to my brokenhearted Aunt Jules. She curled in the chair, weeping. The job description for *moral support* didn't have a clause for this harrowing situation.

Joanie bustled in and looked from me to Auntie, hands on hips. "Time fer some vittles."

This sounded like an ideal diversion, but Aunt Jules refused.

"You need to eat." I crossed to her, grasping her hands. "If you don't take care of yourself, you won't be much help to Uncle Daniel. C'mon." I pulled her gently out of her chair. "He's asleep, I think."

We followed Joanie into a room farther down the main passageway. A table for two nestled beside an inviting fire. A black, sooty pot hung suspended over the flames, wafting a tantalizing fragrance. The rest of the room appeared to be used for storage. Bed linens, towels, and wooden utensils stocked a series of low shelves. *Staff lounge?*

Joanie snatched two bowls and ladled them full of green-hued broth from the pot in the fireplace. "Moss soup. Me own secret recipe."

"Oh...moss? Really?" I feigned enthusiasm.

"Yes!" Her round face beamed with a proud smile. "Very

nutritional. Eat it all. Doctor's orders."

"Speakin' of the doctor." Aunt Jules scooted closer to the table. "When might he be free to stop by and discuss Daniel's condition?" She glanced at her soup but didn't look eager to eat.

Joanie patted Aunt Jules's shoulder. "Soon. I do apologize. He's yet to come by. We've had a nasty virus making its way around Berganstroud. Doc Keswick has more than his share of patients to tend. He's positively exhausted."

"Is he the only doctor?" I blew ripples across the surface of the steaming green muck.

"Yes. Until recently, he's managed fine. Dwarves are hardy folk and illness is rare. We're more likely to deal with a broken arm or stitches here in the infirmary. The doctor has an apprentice, but the chap is too new to treat patients on his own. Fer now he shadows Doc and follows orders."

"I see." The aroma of the brew in front of me outweighed any doubts about moss and muck. With no silverware in sight, I assumed that drinking from the bowl would be the means of consumption. An introductory sip warmed me, throat to belly, and made my taste buds dance. "Mmm. This is amazing."

We slurped in silence for several minutes, content to listen to Joanie hum a tune as she tidied up the shelves.

A stout topsider stepped into the room and sniffed at the air. "Lemme guess. Moss soup?"

Correction...a tall Dwarf. I deduced from the scrubs and stethoscope that he must be the doctor. He strode over and offered me his hand.

"Doc Keswick." He pumped my arm and inspected us through rounded spectacles. "Pleasure to meet you both. My, you do look like our lovely Queen Judith! Ssspit-ting image! Pardon my delay. Crazy-busy the last few weeks. Dreadful virus making its way 'round these parts." He patted his trusty nurse on the back. "I believe Joanie has taken great care of you, though. How do you find the moss soup? It's the best in these parts. Am I right?"

Whoa. I stood, staring. This Dwarf did not fit his surroundings. Though the scrubs made him look doctor-like, they were too modern for this setting. And standing a head taller than any Dwarf I'd met made him seem much less Dwarf-like. That and his very American lingo.

"Yes, delicious. No need to apologize fer doin' yer job." Auntie pushed her chair back and stood. "Thanks fer takin' such wonderful care of Daniel. He seems to be doin' well—considerin'."

"Considering he was sick, dehydrated, starving, and blind, I'd say he's doing great. Two out of four ain't bad, anyway." He chuckled.

I blinked, dumbfounded.

Joanie jumped in. "Doc's always lookin' for the bright side." She laughed nervously and elbowed her boss in the ribs.

The doctor draped an arm around Joanie's shoulders. "Oh Joanie, did I stick my foot in my mouth again? Good thing I have you here to smooth over my bungling bedside manners."

Aunt Jules shook her head, her expression horrified. "That's me husband yer talkin' about."

"Well, it's good to find out who our mystery patient is, madam." He adjusted his spectacles. "Seems to be stabilized now. May be well enough to travel topside in a couple of weeks, with assistance of course. Daniel, did you say?"

"That's correct. Daniel McGriffin."

"Well, he's bouncing back. How is it he came to be in these parts? And was he blind in one eye the last time you saw him? I'm assuming whoever plucked out the other eye did so recently as a means of punishment."

Joanie elbowed the doctor again, but he merely fingered the beard on his chin. Unlike most Dwarves, he kept both his wiry salt and pepper hair and beard about an inch long. It contributed to his almost topsider appearance—and probably the sanitary conditions.

Auntie looked like she wanted to take the doctor's stethoscope and wrap it around his neck a few times. She pressed her lips together and drew in a deliberate breath. "No. He was *not* blind. I'm still unsure how he came to be 'in these parts' but it's been thirty-eight years since I've laid me eyes on him."

Doc Keswick shuddered and stepped back. "What? Thirty-eight years? You must've thought the poor man to be dead and gone."

"If ya don't mind me sayin', doctor, you've got quite a way with words, and it's not workin' in yer favor. Thirty-eight years *is* a long time to be separated, but I've never given up hope in me soul, and with me Maker, that somehow I'd learn the truth." She stepped toward the doctor as she spoke, and he took another step back.

"That's the sweetest thing I've ever heard." Joanie wiped a tear. "Keeps me hopin' that I'll see my papa again. He disappeared when I was a wee tot."

"Yes, that sort of faith is rare." Doc nodded, his face serious. "Justly rewarded today."

"Indeed. Now how 'bout tellin' me his prognosis?"

Doc Keswick folded his arms across his broad chest. "Scouts discovered him two days ago. Pulse barely perceptible. Low body temperature. He clearly had contracted the same virus that many of our people now suffer from. Bright pink spots, much like your measles, covering the torso and limbs. His spots were faded and flattened, indicating he'd been through the worst of it. But without food or water he wouldn't have lasted another day."

Aunt Jules wrung her hands. "Joanie said he's been incoherent. Ya haven't been able to understand a word?"

The doctor wobbled his head from side to side uncertainly. "Mmm, not exactly. He says things in English, but they don't make sense. He babbles about a cleft in the rock. And a key. Says he's lost everything. That's about it."

"When I'm able to speak to him, things will improve, wait and see." Aunt Jules placed her hands on her hips. "I have to believe that a part of him was hopin' and believin' fer me, like I hoped and believed fer him. That's the part I intend to talk to."

Doc turned to Joanie. "Sounds like you're out of a job. At least with this patient."

Joanie laughed. "I'll gladly pass it on to Lady Jules if it means that poor man will pull through and these two lovebirds can reunite."

"Tell ya what." The doctor walked to the shelves and picked up a mug. "You two finish your supper and get a good night's rest. Our patient is on heavy tranquilizers and won't be waking anytime soon. Tomorrow we'll hope that your voice will be the remedy needed for him to begin to piece his life back together."

Aunt Jules crossed her thin arms. "I don't care to leave Daniel. If ya have a cot or even a blanket, I'll be stayin' with him."

"Sorry, can't allow that." Doc ladled soup into his mug. "We're not equipped with ultra-sterile surroundings like your hospitals. We just had two new viral patients arrive, and I won't risk exposing you. Joanie will take you to your room and show you our procedure for disinfection."

Before anyone could argue, he left.

"I'm not certain I like that man." Aunt Jules raised an eyebrow. "He's brusque. And uncouth."

Not sure what that means, but I'm not crazy about him either. "He's right, though. You need to rest while Uncle Daniel is resting."

Joanie clasped her hands together. "Doc often speaks before he thinks. Please don't take it personally. He's good as gold, he is." She walked to the door. "Let's get ya both cleaned up and settled in."

She led us out of the infirmary and through a hallway to a small guest room with two beds and a fireplace. A female Dwarf knelt in front of the hearth trying to kindle the logs. Not nearly as sumptuous as the room Sophie and I stayed in the first go-round. But this room sat in close proximity to the clinic.

"Trinny here will be taking care of ya since I'm helpin' the doctor. But I'll get ya settled while she gets yer fire a-blazin'." Joanie turned down the covers on both beds. "And I'll be back to check on me favorite topsiders as often as possible."

She made a shooing motion with her hands. "Now, into the bathroom with ya both. I'll show ya how we deal with germs in these parts."

The little lady demonstrated the method to cleanse our arms, hands, and face—any exposed skin. Jars of dried herbs were to be mixed with bottles of oils, rubbed on our skin and rinsed away. She also provided us with clean sleepwear then gathered our clothes for decontamination. She showed us where topsider-sized tunics and pants were kept, then wiped down knobs and anything else we'd touched with some of the oil and herbs on a cloth.

She and Trinny snuffed out the torches and wished us sweet dreams, leaving us beneath mounds of covers. The snap and sizzle of the fire sounded like a lullaby. Though every ounce of my body wanted to escape the day, sleep hovered out of reach. Too many thoughts tangled themselves up together, and I couldn't push them away.

Aunt Jules sighed and wriggled around, sounding equally restless. I rolled onto my side and peeked across the room to where she lay. Her green eyes were open and glimmered in the firelight, though her goose egg looked bigger than ever in the flickering shadows.

"Sadie?" Her voice muffled against the blanket.

"Yes?" I wondered why she called me by name. Highly unusual.

"There's something I want ya to know."

"Okay."

She blinked three times before she spoke. "When the time is right, I'm passin' the key to you, m'dear."

"What!" I sat up on my elbow. "*The* key?"

"Yes. The key to The Flamin' Sword of Cherubythe."

"No, no, no." I shook my head for emphasis. "You need to try plan B. I'm not the person for the job." I plopped back onto my pillow and yanked the covers up. *End of story.*

"It's to be yers, cupcake. Of course, only if I'm nearin' death's door." She yawned. "Don't worry, I'm not plannin' on goin' anywhere. Not now that I've gotten Daniel back in me life. We've plenty o' catchin' up to do."

"I hope you're right about that." I peeked my head out of the covers. "But you're wrong about passing me the key. I'm the last member of our family that should have that responsibility."

"I disagree. And this isn't a decision I came to on a whim. I've been prayin' about it long before anything happened to yer parents this summer." The fire spit embers onto the hearth. "Yer the one who's been chosen."

The knot in my gut left me winded. "Seems like I should have some say in the matter."

"There are things that just *are*, dovey. Like the color of yer eyes. You've no say in that, and you've no say in this either, I'm afraid."

"Those are not the same sort of things, Aunt Jules." I rolled over and faced the wall. "I most certainly have a choice in the matter. You can't give me something that I'm not willing to take."

CHAPTER THIRTEEN

MY MIND STUMBLED OUT OF A dreamless sleep and landed in a muddle of confusing sensations. Something pressed against my face. The blanket? A hand? I needed oxygen. Panic throttled me. And then...

My body felt like a sack of sand. Nothing but deadweight. *Why can't I move my arms or legs?*

I became aware of friction on my backside. Scraping, like my body was a block of cheese being hauled across a grater. A monotonous huff of breath pricked my ears. Darkness surrounded me, but I couldn't say for certain that my eyes were open. I puzzled at what these things meant, feeling like a decapitated head floating along, aware of myself in a third-person sort of way.

Memories jutted into my brain fog. Shards from a broken mirror reflecting snippets of the recent past. Reiko visiting. Uncle Brent in his lab coat. Traipsing through the woods at Moulton Falls. The pieces fell into place, and I remembered Uncle Daniel in the hospital bed and talking with Aunt Jules.

But what was happening now?

My state of confusion and numbness seemed to point to one thing: I'd been drugged. Knocked out cold. And now I was at the mercy of *someone*, or *something*, dragging my limp limbs *somewhere*.

Oh, Lord, help!

My breath warmed my face. I registered that I was trapped inside a type of sack, scrunched into the fetal position. I squinted and could perceive pinpricks of dim light through the rough, woven fabric.

The kidnapper suddenly released the cloth bag, and my legs and torso plunked onto the ground.

"Ugh!" I couldn't suppress a yelp of pain as my head landed like a melon.

"You're awake. Good." The nasal voice ricocheted off of what sounded like an enclosed space.

With uncoordinated effort, I clawed my way out of the sack as a torch sputtered to life behind me. Footsteps approached. Despite my newfound headache, I recognized my captor as a Dwarf. He walked past. I tested my balance and sat up, rubbing a swelling lump on the back of my head.

"You're from Berganstroud," I said.

The Dwarf, busy lighting another torch, kept his back to me. "Your point?"

"Why did you kidnap me? Or did you rescue me? Was I in danger?"

He stiffened. I didn't recognize this particular bloke, but Berganstroud was a densely populated place. He looked a good deal younger than Lava and Wogsnop. Under different circumstances I would've complimented his auburn hair.

"Listen, topsider..." The Dwarf held the torch in one hand and put the other fist on his hip.

"I have a name."

He grimaced. "You think I don't know who you are, O Princess Sadie?" He said my name with a bitter sneer. "Sit there and shut up, and maybe I'll let you stay conscious, *Your Highness*."

"Do *you* have a name?" It seemed to me that if he needed to be a jerk, I needed to make it personal.

He gave a grunt. "Let's just say I'm the Dwarf who sees the future of the Land of Legend with clarity." He thumbed himself in the chest. "I'm the only one in Berganstroud who perceives that doing things like we've always done them means we make zero progress. We stagnate. It's time for a revolution of thought, but my kinsfolk are too set in their ways. *I'm* going to be the instrument of change."

"So, you're a traitor."

He kicked at a crate beside the door, pummeling a wooden slat with his foot until it splintered. "I'm not a traitor," he seethed through clenched teeth, "I'm a revolutionary." He strode over and stood above me. "Listen. This is about the Tethered World getting caught up with the 21st century. We cannot continue to huddle in our little, protective pocket in the earth, clinging to how we've always done things. I refuse to get overlooked while the world moves ahead."

I shifted my weight in an attempt to stand, but the two-legged tank shoved me backwards.

"I'm only getting started, *princess.*" He chuckled. "Or maybe I should call you garbage girl." He laced his fingers together and popped his knuckles. "You see, no one in Berganstroud wants to listen to my ideas. Why, I'm but the rubbish collector. Practically invisible. So I found others who *will* listen."

"So what? You smuggled me out in your garbage sack?"

He made a sour face. "No one's interested in trash. Or the one who disposes of it."

"Aren't you clever," I said flatly. "And what do you want with me?"

He ignored my question. "I'm tired of being part of a legend. I'm no longer content to be identified with a realm of people who are presumed to exist only in Middle Earth or Disney World."

"So, this is about your need for attention."

"Shut up!" He smacked one fist into the other palm. "I'll knock ya out, little girl. And this time I won't use chloroform."

I bristled at his bullying but kept quiet, taking in my surroundings. Crates and barrels lined the walls of a low-ceilinged room carved into the granite. I recognized it as a supply chamber burrowed into the Hills of Berganstroud. Brady, Sophie, and I made a pit stop in one like it when we were headed to Craventhrall on our first trip.

"The Dwarves of Berganstroud must join with those that have a vision beyond our world below, or they shall go the way of Atlantis. There are others here who have strategized for years. They've laid the groundwork for transformation. A few more pieces need to fall into place—like gaining access to the Flaming Sword—and everything will be ready."

The *sword.* It all seemed to come back to that powerful, illusive piece of weaponry. The faster I grasped this, the sooner I'd quit being shaken and shocked by every plot twist thrown at my family. Everything in this land pivoted around that mysterious sword.

While the Dwarf blabbed on, my senses returned with a distracting vengeance. Everything began to itch. The Dwarf kept his diatribe in high gear and looked oblivious to my sudden spasms of scratching.

"...along the way they've taken notice of other forward thinkers like myself. There are those from all walks of life who have connected and plotted and waited patiently for the signal." He took a knee and stared into my face. "Betcha can't guess what the signal is." Big cheesy grin. "It's something very specific. Foretold." He wiggled his fingers beside his head. "Prophetic sorta mumbo-jumbo stuff, ya know?"

Whatever.

He jutted his chin so close I held my breath for fear of tasting his. "The sign we've been waiting for is a regime change. A new ruler." He snickered. "And a beautiful, young maiden who is part of the royal family."

I swallowed and looked away.

"This isn't about *my* need for attention." He grabbed my face and forced me to look at him. "You see, Princess Sadie, this is actually about you. You and your brother are the signal for revolution."

CHAPTER FOURTEEN

Though part of my brain recognized the speech I was listening to ought to make me nervous about my future, the present became much more paramount. It took every ounce of self-control not to fling my body against a splintered piece of wood and attempt to scratch my skin off. This brought the Dwarf's bizarre ideas to a rather anti-climactic climax.

Still inches from my face he gave me a cruel smile, obviously expecting a reaction from the verbal bomb he just dropped.

With as much subtlety as I could muster, I raked my nails across the opposite arm. "Me? A signal? That doesn't seem likely." I couldn't stand it another moment. With a spastic jump, I landed on unsteady feet and did a series of squirms and scratches that surely gave the impression I'd lost touch with reality. "I'm so itchy all of a sudden, I can't stand it. What's going on?"

My captor's face changed from shock toward my wild gestures to dread when he heard my complaint. "Oh, blast it! Come here. Pull your sleeve up."

Between flails I gave my pajama sleeve a yank.

Swollen, fiery lumps polka dotted my skin. *This can't be good.* I jerked my sleeve down.

"Great." He threw his hands up. "Terrific. You've come down with the virus. Which means I'm probably going to get it as well." He lifted his leather hat and scratched at his ginger hair. "How am I going to lead a revolution from a hospital bed?"

"Sounds like a personal problem." I glared at the traitorous shrimp and fervently rubbed on various body parts.

Said shrimp walked to the doorway and looked down the passage, then came back. "Look." He lowered his voice and leaned in. "When they get here, don't tell them you're sick, okay? It'll only...uh...put you in greater danger."

"When *who* gets here?"

"Shh!" Finger to his lips, he looked back at the door. He exhaled and gave me a pleading look. "Listen. I'm sorry about how all of this personally affects you. Really. I'm a good guy. I merely want to see Berganstroud, and my fellow countrymen, move up in the world. Literally up. Topside. Unfortunately, there are casualties in war—"

"*Casualties?*" I glowered at him, my fingers curling into fists.

He rolled his eyes. "No, no. Not *that* kind of casualty. I mean there will be inconvenient circumstances for each of us. The fact that you are an important part of the plan is, no doubt, very inconvenient for you."

Between scratches I gave a cynical laugh. "You could say that."

He shrugged. "If I catch this virus from you, it's but a small price to pay for the greater good."

"Consider it my gift to the greater good, Dwarf."

Voices and footsteps carried into the room. The Dwarf stiffened and turned toward the entrance.

Two Dark Dwarves—Stygians as they were referred to in Berganstroud and Vituvia—shuffled inside and elbowed each other at the sight of me. Their beady eyes, like black marbles, gawked from putty-colored skin that looked clammy and lifeless. They shifted their gaze to my captor and offered a curt nod.

"Grimpenhauser?" asked the plump one on the left.

The Dwarf nodded back.

I scratched my arm. Grimpenhauser, eh? I would remember that.

"Hand over the prisoner," said the other Styg. He had an enlarged forehead which gave him an alien appearance.

Grimpenhauser turned and reached for me.

I flung his hand away and stepped back. "You really expect me to waltz off with Dumb and Dumber here? You should be ashamed of yourself, working with these creeps."

"Shut up, infidel!" wheezed the alien Styg.

"Infidel?" Anger roiled up and managed to overpower my itchiness. I clenched my fists and squared my shoulders. "Do you know who I am? I'm sister to High King Brock of Vituvia. You mess with me, you're messing with the entire royal family, some very deadly Gnomes, and a horde of Nephilim and Dwarves."

"Is that supposed to scare us?" The plump one stepped toward me.

"Well, if that doesn't, this ought to..." I grasped my sleeve with dramatic flair, intending to scare them with the threat of an epidemic. The next thing I knew, Grimp-the-Shrimp knocked me flat and smothered my mouth with his hand. A familiar smell took me right back to the panic-stricken moment of waking in much the same way from my bed in Berganstroud.

The instant I smelled it, I attached one word to the odor: *chloroform.*

Then the darkness swallowed me whole.

CHAPTER FIFTEEN

UNDER THE GLOWING LIGHT OF A new day, five weary travelers rode into the countryside of Vituvia. Brady revived at the sight of the distant city nestled into the mountainside. Its domed palace gleamed like a pearl inside an oyster split wide. Angry thoughts about thieving, hitchhiking Leprechauns subsided for the moment. Still, Brady patted the pocketknife, now tucked into the top of his boot, for the hundredth time since Reiko found it by the bridge.

The tidy rows of vegetation made Brady's stomach growl. Water, stale biscuits, and raw potatoes consumed on their last rest stop had left his taste buds stranded. Unfortunately, the devious little Leprechauns also snatched Sophie and his backpacks from their saddles after they dismounted. He tried not to fantasize about beef jerky and granola bars.

Storybook cottages cozied themselves at intervals along the path. Though the buildings within the city walls of Vituvia were built for visitors of all sizes, these rural Gnome homes were Gnome sized. They looked like dollhouses with picket fences.

Brady nudged his mom. "Wake up. You don't want to miss this." She hadn't been through this part of Vituvia on their last visit.

Amy groaned and pushed away from his back. "Wha...oh! Oh my, these are *adorable*." The rambling roses and blooming hollyhocks reached to the rooftops, shading the houses like a grove of trees. "I wish I had a camera."

Lava came to a sudden stop, drawing his sword. "Someone's comin'."

In the distance, a cloud of dust announced the approach of a rider from the direction of town.

"Probably a Vituvian, but ya can't be too careful these days." Lava adjusted his grip.

When the billowing dirt drew closer, Brady made out the wild, gnarly mane of a toboggan with a petite warrior on its panther-sized back.

Lava replaced his weapons as the nimble beast came to a stuttering stop. The toboggan snorted, apparently disappointed that its jaunt had come to an end.

Reiko trotted past Lava on Thrym. She and the other Gnome exchanged a salute. "Muscle, what's the problem?"

Sophie flashed Brady an excited grin. Muscle had been one of their personal bodyguards during their last visit. He'd grown a goatee since they'd seen him last.

"The Meadow Faeries delivered your message about the Larcens' arrival." Muscle tipped his metal, conical hat toward the family. "There was another attack, overnight, on the guard post along Forest Ridge. Colonel Muggleridge says it's too dangerous to let the Larcens stay here. With the exception of Brady remaining in Vituvia to train, he wants you to escort the remaining Larcens to Calamus. By way of Lake Alethia."

"That's the long way around. The Dwarves and I can take down a few measly Trolls on Forest Ridge, and it'll save another day of riding."

"Excuse me." Amy leaned out from behind Brady. "I'd much prefer that we stay together."

"I'm afraid it's already been decided for you, Lady Amy." Muscle offered an apologetic bow. He turned back to Reiko. "And this goes for you as well. Muggleridge was clear that you need to take the long way. As of now, we don't believe the Trolls know that all the Larcens are here. If you run into Trolls on the ridge, and one escapes to Craventhrall, Nekronok will know for certain."

"Understood." Reiko nodded.

"Forgive my impertinence." Amy tried again. "I trust that such decisions are made with the best interest of the sword and the safety of the kingdom in mind. But I'm concerned for the welfare of my family as well. An attack on Vituvia means I'm placing both of my sons in harm's way."

"*Mom.* I want to do it." Brady glowered, glad his mom sat behind him, unable to see his face.

"Lady Amy." Lava trotted up beside them, sounding a little

too jovial. "A boy Brady's age needs the opportunity to prove he's a man. In Berganstroud, a young Dwarf would've already had a year of apprenticeship with his chosen occupation."

Sophie winced from behind Lava, knowing he'd said the wrong thing.

"He's obviously *not* a Dwarf!" snapped Amy. "Where we live, he's considered a minor. I'm his parent. Don't force your ways on us."

"It's not a matter of forcing anything." Reiko nudged her mount over to the Larcens. "It is what your family is destined to do. By way of birth. You know this better than we do, Lady Amy. Please don't make it more difficult than it needs to be."

Brady could feel his mother shift behind him. He wished he could see her face and get a feel for whether anything made a difference. For several long moments, Brady could only perceive her steady breathing. He looked at Sophie for an interpretation of the silence. She bit her lip and shrugged uncertainly.

"Very well." Amy sounded resigned. "Though my motherly instincts say otherwise, my faith in God—in His purpose for the sword—and in what we, as a family, were created for is what I choose to rely on."

Brady swiveled awkwardly in the saddle to look at her, relieved by her implications.

Mom gave a weighty sigh. "Though I've understood our calling includes potential danger, I never expected to face such a continuous onslaught of it, I guess. We've endured kidnapping and torture. Separation from Brock. And now, Liam is gone again. It's been more difficult than I ever imagined." She looked from Brady to Lava. "But if such difficulty and danger is the right way, if it's what the Lord requires of us, then the Larcens will soldier on. No looking back."

Lava reached a fatherly hand to Amy's knee. "Oh love, I hear ya. I do. There's much that's been thrust upon yer family. Probably too much. When I think of how everything here has unraveled—and so quickly—it feels like too much for me. Too much for the Land of Legend. All we can do is continue with what the Maker places before us, and do it with all our might. He doesn't ask fer more than that. And that much we can each manage. By His strength."

Mom glanced at Sophie and smiled. "I believe my wise,

eleven-year-old daughter recently said something about our being here for a reason. And that 'just because our reason is dangerous, it doesn't mean God isn't with us.' Did I get that right, hon?"

"I think so." Sophie looked pleased with herself.

Brady squeezed his mom's hand reassuringly, his ribcage cramping uncomfortably from his twisted position. "Thanks, Mom. I'll make you proud."

She ruffled his hair, eyes gleaming. "You couldn't possibly make me more proud than I already am. Manhood has been thrust upon you this summer. Ready or not." She smiled wistfully. "And you've stepped up to the plate. Impressively so."

She looked at Muscle. "Train him well."

CHAPTER SIXTEEN

"SADIE, CAN YOU HEAR ME?" DAD'S tender voice peeled back layers of incoherency.

Unable to recollect why I felt so drained, I turned toward the sound to tell him I wanted to sleep. My lips interfered with my brain. They felt like two blobs of clay left out in the sun. It hurt to peel them apart.

"Ergh," was all that came out. My eyelids felt too heavy to make any effort at eye contact.

"Shh." Dad stroked my arm. "Don't speak. You've been very ill. I'm so relieved that you're coming around." He patted my shoulder. I heard his footsteps recede and my bedroom door close.

No wonder I feel like a human speed bump. My mind whirled through shreds of memories and soundbites. A kaleidoscope took me from Aunt Jules fainting on our couch to Aunt Jules crying in front of Uncle Daniel's maimed body.

It must've all been a dream brought on by delirium. But it seemed so real.

With effort, I willed my eyelids open. They burned and refused to focus, but eventually I could make out eggplant colored drapes. The light outside shimmered in a gold ribbon where the two lengths of fabric didn't quite meet.

I don't have purple curtains.

Rolling onto my back, I grew more perplexed to find myself in an ornate, canopy bed draped with impossibly sheer, gossamer fabric. *Toto, I have a feeling we're not in Kansas anymore.*

I reached for the billowy material. It swooped from the center of the bed and dipped down, toward me, before disappearing behind the headboard. The pale pink fabric slid across my fingers like water. My gaze skimmed from the material to my arm. I jerked it down impulsively.

Round scabs speckled my forearm like crimson craters. My stomach turned at the sight. I held my other arm up for inspection. It looked equally gruesome. Though I dreaded what I might find, I explored my face with my fingertips. Thankfully, it felt clear.

I wanted to call my father and get some details, but I must have gargled with sandpaper at some point, because my throat felt ravaged. With heroic determination, I sat upright to inspect the state of my legs and torso. In the process, a glass—or really, a goblet—of liquid on a bedside table caught my attention and screamed my name. I stared at the pale pink contents, wondering if it might be lemonade. A small sip told me otherwise, but I couldn't place the taste. Though I only managed a few mouthfuls, it felt sublime going down.

Several layers of luxurious blankets molded around my body. To my weak arms they seemed to weigh fifty pounds. I resorted to kicking my legs in slow motion to free myself. The pajama bottoms had scrunched around my knees, revealing pale skin and more nasty lesions along with deep scratches.

"Gross," I managed to say. Unable to tolerate the sight, I pulled a blanket back over my legs. In that instant, the memory of being insanely itchy and rubbing myself raw, flashed through my mind.

My pulse revved as further recollections fell into place. I looked around the strange room, hoping for a clue to where I might be. It didn't look similar to any room I'd seen in Vituvia or Berganstroud. Calamus, maybe? Yes, that must be it. Xander must have rescued me.

The next thought shot through me like a miracle cure: Dad was safe! And we were together. Joy zinged from my brain, down to my heart, and busted from my face with a smile that cracked my dry lips so that I tasted blood. I barely noticed.

All I could do was flop back on my pillow with a satisfied sigh and a fervent prayer of thanks. Despite my elation, sleep wasted no time pulling me back into its embrace.

"Wake up, Sadie, you need nourishment." The comfort of Dad's voice drew me from my cocoon.

With effort—though not as much as earlier—I forced my eyes open and managed a weak smile. Dad looked rather out of place in his polo shirt and jeans, perched on a tapestry cushioned chair in the fancy bedroom. But he was the best part of the view by far.

"You think you can sit up?"

I nodded, not trusting my voice.

He helped me get the pillows arranged so I could rest against the headboard. The smell of soup was like a siren's call, and I cupped the mug he offered with both hands and took a sip of what I discovered to be plain broth. Apparently I needed to start slow.

Questions contended with my hunger, and after a few marvelous mouthfuls I spoke in a strained voice. "I'm so happy you're okay. We were worried sick. What happened? Mom's here, right? Wherever we are."

Dad chuckled and gave me a look I couldn't quite interpret. "There's plenty of time for all that, Daughter. You need to recuperate."

I blinked. Had he just called me daughter?

"There's medicinal balm in that little pot on the bedside table. You should put it on your lips and your sores. It will help with the scarring. A princess shouldn't have scars."

"Sure." I reached for the medicine and smeared it on appreciative lips. "You have to at least tell me where we are. Is this Calamus?"

Another odd look. "No. This isn't Calamus." He slipped his hand in mine and leveled his gaze on me. "I wasn't kidnapped, Sadie. I came to prepare a place for you."

I could only stare back. Not kidnapped? And did he just throw in scripture as part of casual conversation? My mind felt too muddled to be trusted.

"It'll take time to explain where we are and how we came

to be here. But it'll also take time for you to fully recover. Why don't you work on that for now, since you're still weak? One thing at a time." He gave my hand a reassuring squeeze. "Okay?"

"Okay."

Something about the way he said it made me feel like things were definitely *not* okay.

CHAPTER SEVENTEEN

BRADY STOOD BESIDE MUSCLE AND WAITED for Colonel Smarlow, Chief of Covert Reconnaissance, to unlock a polished granite door leading into a part of Vituvia Brady hadn't yet visited. The Garden Dome. Residence of the legendary Flaming Sword of Cherubythe. When he arrived, the Gnomes had wasted no time escorting him here to view the spectacle that he would be guarding.

Smarlow rattled the skeletal key into position and turned it with a clunk. The guard on duty pulled open the door using the lower of two handles—most doors in Vituvia included one knob for Gnomes and another several feet higher for others.

"After you." Muscle gestured Brady to follow Smarlow through the doorway.

They immediately came to another door, this one without a guard, but requiring the key once again. The three walked through in silence, then Smarlow turned and locked the door from the inside.

Smarlow pointed to the ceiling. "If this door is left unlocked, and someone opens it again, a set of spikes will impale them."

Brady looked up, barely able to perceive the jagged skewers in the shadowed recess beyond the torchlight. He cringed. "Ouch."

Muscle chuckled. "Probably nothing you need to worry about. The key is always a Gnome's responsibility."

"But you better hope whoever last unlocked the door remembered to turn around and lock it again." Smarlow brushed past Brady. "We've lost a few Gnomes simply because the sequence of unlocking and locking were not followed. Distracted dolts."

Brady smirked, remembering Smarlow's short fuse during his last excursion. The Gnome was like a missile with feet.

They continued down the corridor, footsteps echoing off the stone walls, shadows taking on a life of their own in the flickering light. Another door crouched in the murkiness at the opposite end. Brady spied more barbed spears ready to strike.

The Gnomes had gone to great lengths to ensure the security of the Flaming Sword. It looked like a good storyline for a new Indiana Jones movie.

The door opened into a circular room lined with dark burgundy, cushioned benches. A tapestry rug stretched from the singular door to a set of tarnished metal doors opposite. Stationed on each side were two guards outfitted with chain mail and bayonets. The weapons appeared too big for their petite stature.

The guards saluted. Smarlow unlocked the door on the right. The two soldiers pulled both doors open in unison. Brady stepped onto a balcony where another Gnome stood motionless, outfitted with bow and arrows and sword.

They could go no farther. Brady wondered if he'd missed something. All that security for a mere viewing platform?

But what a view! Almost too much to take in. They stood on a railed balustrade thirty feet off the ground, the wall continuing another fifty feet or more to the ceiling. Torches blazed at intervals, and three more platforms jutted from the surrounding walls, soldiers on guard. The ceiling soared to a crystalized dome overhead—a replica of the golden expanse that encased the Tethered World. The arched, geode surface lit the stadium-size space with its amber hue.

Below him, a gleaming pearl floor met with azure water in an enormous semi-circle. The body of water quickly plunged from shallow turquoise to deep-blue depths. At least a dozen guards marched in synchronized formation along the water's edge and onto an ornately carved bridge that spanned the wide swath of water. It joined with the cobbled surface of what appeared to be an island on the other side.

The smooth, round rocks grew in size, becoming large boulders that mounded up like a thickset pyramid fifteen or twenty feet high. Ferns and other greenery sprouted between the boulders. Stout, gnarly roots intertwined with the stones like greedy fingers. The rocks abruptly melded into an enormous wall made from smooth, polished granite. Its distant top loomed as high as the balustrade and stretched around the perimeter of the island, smooth and unscalable. It created a formidable barrier to what lay beyond, sectioning off nearly half the cavernous building.

The focal point of the resplendent scene came from the pinnacle of the mound of boulders. Inexplicably thrust into the topmost rock, and obscured by flickering tongues of fire, blazed the Flaming Sword of Cherubythe.

Brady gaped, taking it in, unable to form coherent words. Whatever he had expected, this wasn't it.

"You're the first human, outside of our monarchs, to view this most valuable treasure." Smarlow placed his hands on top of the low railing and looked at the pageantry like a proud father. Then a shadow crossed his face. "I'm still not on board with allowing outsiders to participate in the duties charged to us by our Maker." He sighed and leaned his elbows on the railing. "Unfortunately, it's being forced upon us. We must take an offensive stance with this show of solidarity rather than wait for the enemy to strike the heart of the Tethered World. We must do everything within our power to protect the sword."

Brady studied the guards marching below and the others stationed about. Where did they plan to use him? What about the others? He had yet to meet his compatriots, but eight-foot Nephilim working alongside Gnomes—less than two-feet tall—seemed an unconventional combination.

"So...that's *the* sword. Pretty hard to fathom." Brady stared into the flames, trying to catch a glint of steel—or whatever heavenly swords might be made from. "It's such a vast chamber for such a small item." He gestured around. "I mean, yeah, it's on fire and all, but this, is so enormous."

"It's complex for a reason." Muscle nodded toward the spectacle. "Let's just say there's more here than meets the eye."

"Like what?"

Smarlow shot Muscle a disapproving look then leveled his gaze on Brady. "Patience, soldier. You'll learn about it soon enough."

My recovery came at a rapid pace over the next two days. Made possible by long naps, bowls of broth, goblets of the pink stuff, and the pot of ointment which I smeared head-to-toe. By day two of coherency, someone deemed me ready to enjoy a few vegetables in my soup. Outside contact was limited to brief visits from Dad, followed by a roly-poly female Dwarf who wouldn't speak to me. Rather, she came after dinner to pump the bathtub full of warm water in the attached bathroom and deliver clean clothes. She ignored my questions like she was stone deaf. Which I doubted.

Though grateful to be on the mend, concern continued to gnaw anxiously in the background. Where was the rest of my family? Why did Dad feel the need to be so tight-lipped? And why did my door need to be locked from the outside? I told myself that it must be for my own safety.

Perhaps I needed to be quarantined due to my illness. It was obviously quite contagious, since I was in Berganstroud but a single day before it attacked me. The lingering effects continued to make things feel murky and distant, like I was hovering beneath the surface of the water, watching life unfold along the shore.

After a miraculous soak in the tub and a set of clean clothes, fresh air sounded like the perfect thing to shake the brain fog that managed to come and go. I picked up the goblet and crossed to the purple, velvet drapes. My thirst seemed insatiable.

French doors hid behind the curtains. Beyond them sprawled an inviting balcony, outfitted with potted, flowering plants. The doors were locked, but I tried to see what I could beyond the baluster.

From the mellow glow in the sky, I knew we were still in the Tethered World. But the land that lay in the distance was unlike anything I'd glimpsed in my earlier travels. Towering trees and lush hills made me yearn to get a closer look. I tried the bolted doors again, then pressed my face to the cool glass, wishing to be less confined. With a sigh I gave up, already worn out from my short excursion.

I padded toward the four-poster canopy and stopped mid-stride, sloshing the liquid from my glass. A lifelike oil painting hung on the wall beside the bed—which is why I hadn't noticed it from beneath the canopy.

It was like looking in a mirror. Chill bumps raced across my arm. A painting of myself wearing a peacock gown stared down at me. How could this be?

Before I could work myself into a panic, the door opened behind me.

"The artist truly captured your beauty, don't you think?" Dad's voice swelled with admiration.

I swiveled around, spilling more of my drink. "How can you say that? Doesn't it bother you that some creep made an over-sized painting of your daughter without her knowledge?"

Dad cocked his head. "Well, good to see you're feeling better." He gestured toward a table and two chairs near the French doors. "Join me, won't you?"

I glowered. I hated the portrait as well as his reaction to it. Stumbling to a chair, I realized my mind felt crowded with cobwebs again.

Dad rested his elbows on the table and laced his fingers together. "Listen to me, Daughter—"

"Since when do you call me *Daughter*? That's totally weird." I sat the goblet down forcefully.

He looked a bit perplexed but nodded. "Fine, Sadie, whatever you wish. Now, remember the other day when I explained that I'd come to prepare a place for you?"

"Yes. Also weird."

"Well, it's true. I came here ahead of you, to get several important things set up, specifically for you. That portrait, for instance, is something I commissioned an artist to do for your bedroom here."

"A painting like that would take months to complete. Not days." I shook my head, which made me lightheaded. "There's no way someone could paint such an enormous, detailed picture just like that." I snapped my fingers.

"Remember that things in the Tethered World don't always operate the same as things topside."

Apparently my brain is one of them. "You're telling me. And what do you mean about this being *my* bedroom. I don't live here, and neither do you. Or have you forgotten about our other life? Our *real* life. You're scaring me with all this bizarre talk." A few tears sauntered down my cheeks, against my will.

Dad bristled. He cleared his throat and reached for my hand. "I think we're starting off on the wrong foot. Forgive me?"

I took a deep breath and nodded.

"Good. Between learning the part our family plays in the Tethered World and the stress of traveling here to rescue Mom and me, I know there's been a lot of new information thrown at you." He leaned toward me. "And although you're still coming to grips with everything, I have a secret to share. It would mean a lot to me if you will decide ahead of time to be agreeable. Can you do that?"

I pulled my hand away. "I don't know."

He looked disappointed. "Fair enough." He dipped his head. "Okay, here are some things that I *do* know. I know you aren't thrilled with the arrangement we have with helping the creatures down here. I know you miss Brock now that he must stay in Vituvia. And I know you don't like having to keep your life below a secret from the topside part of your life."

"Yeah, so?" I grasped my necklace. In the back of my mind I rehearsed the speech Dad gave me about my desires coming to fruition one day. Where was that side of my father hiding?

"So...what if I told you that we—you and I—could change those things *and* change history?" He shrugged. "With the right people on our side, and the right plan, we might even change the world." He gave me an odd smile which I greatly disliked. Was it more than cloudy thoughts that made me feel this way?

I looked at him for a long moment, chewing my lower lip. "I feel like I don't really know who you are right now." With my index finger I traced a knot in the wood-grained surface of the table. "Where's Mom? Does she know about this secret?"

Dad stood and paced between the table and the bed.

I crossed my arms and watched, noticing that the mental fog had thinned. "I'll take that as a no."

After a moment he returned to his seat and gave me that disturbing smile. "Sadie, Mom wouldn't understand if I told her about this right now. Work with me. Help me get plans off the ground and she'll come around. I know she will. But Mom is so emotionally involved—with her family's lineage being part of the history of this place—that she would be prejudiced to any plan that varied from her own."

"Dad, listen to yourself. You're talking like a traitor."

"Wait!" He took a deep breath, nostrils flaring. "Hold on. I'm *not* a traitor. I love our family. But don't you think there's been enough secrets kept for the last, oh, six to eight thousand years? Don't you think that the creatures down here are tired of being a secret as well?"

My heart pounded in response. I'd thought that very thing many times over the summer. "But you're asking me to keep another secret. From Mom."

"Yes, but that's temporary. Eventually we can tell Mom and everyone else." He raked his fingers through his hair. "Think about where we'd be as a society without forward thinkers. People used to be suspicious of vaccinations, right? Yet they've saved millions of lives and have wiped several diseases off the face of the planet."

"Dad, *we* are suspicious of vaccinations—ever since Brock was diagnosed with autism."

He looked confused. "Oh yeah, yeah, right. Well, you see my point, don't you? Change isn't something to vilify. Change is good. But change takes people with vision and courage. I'm a visionary, Sadie. Are you?"

My thoughts veered back to being lectured by Grimpenhauser after he abducted me. He called himself a visionary as well.

"So, the bully who knocked me out and kidnapped me, dragging me through the tunnels and passing me off to a couple of Stygians...he did all of that with your blessing?" I narrowed my eyes and cocked my head. "I suppose that's your idea of a *good* kind of change?"

Dad looked crushed and anxiously reached a hand across the table. "For that I am sincerely sorry. I couldn't figure out another way to get you here. I knew you wouldn't come without alerting others, which would've been dangerous. But I admit...it was a rough introduction to the revolution."

I did not reach my hand to his. "If you want me to remotely consider what you're saying, you need to find a better word than revolution. That sounds like we're starting World War

III or something."

He looked relieved and sat back in his chair. "That's my girl. And if it makes you happy, I'll call it something else. A new direction, perhaps?"

"Whatever." I shrugged. "So, where does this vision of yours leave Brock?"

"What do you mean? He'll go along with whatever we ask him to do, I guess. I'm still his dad. He'll listen to me."

"But you've always told us that Brock's autism was no accident. He's unique for a purpose. And I'd say being chosen to be ruler of an ancient kingdom is a pretty important purpose. So, if our Sovereign God chose Brock to rule Vituvia, are we not opposing God Himself by trying to upset the order of things in the Tethered World?"

Dad's face contorted. He obviously worked hard to mask whatever he really wanted to say. Perhaps his recent schemes had tainted his mind and shifted his heart from his role as father and protector. His subterfuge could not have come to fruition in the few days that he'd been missing. He must have been plotting this for some time. I guess running a cosmetology school is a good cover for clandestine activity.

At long last he said, "How do you know what I'm proposing *isn't* the new direction the Maker wants to take His creation?"

"How do you know it *is*?"

He smacked the tabletop, and I jumped. "Because I do!" He gritted his teeth as he went on. "I know because there are prophecies." He stood and leaned over the table onto his knuckles. "Prophecies about *you*. Think about it, Sadie. What kind of rulership can we expect out of Brock? An impressive ability to speak to Gnomes and solve complex equations? You, on the other hand, are eloquent, you're beautiful, and you'd make a wonderful liaison for talks between the Tethered World and those topside."

I could only shake my head in disbelief.

"What is it? What did I say?"

"Let's see. You insulted your son, who is absolutely brilliant in his own way. He is more suited for his job than the one you're offering me, that's for sure. Do you honestly think some world superpower is going to take me seriously when I offer to introduce them to my friends the Dwarves, like I'm Snow White or something? I think *you're* the one who's been ill."

He straightened. "I understand that it's a lot to take in. We've talked enough for today. I'm afraid I may have set you back in health by upsetting you. I should've waited. I'm sorry."

"Oh, I think it's better to get all these secrets out in the open, as you said."

He drilled me with his eyes like we were in a staring contest. I looked away.

"Goodnight, Daughter. Get some rest." He turned and left the room.

The lock on the door *clunked* into place, imprisoning me yet again.

CHAPTER EIGHTEEN

Get some rest? Sure, Dad. Conversations about insurrection and family mutiny are the best of sleeping tonics. I plummeted onto the bed, burrowing my head into the pillow, wanting to suffocate all the emotions that churned.

Nothing that Dad explained felt right. *He* didn't feel right. Not that things didn't make sense from certain angles. Over the summer, I'd questioned why all of the creatures needed to remain such a mystery. Why not bring the legends topside and end the speculation? At least there would be something interesting on the news for once.

Then I'd remember the sword, recalling what I'd learned of its power and importance. I'd think about the greediness of humankind. The Tethered World would be plundered. The sword might remain intact in order to keep the lights on downstairs, but the powers that be would charge a small fortune to travel below and another fortune to view the rare, celestial weapon. After they kicked out the Gnomes and enclosed the sword in a glass case, installing a proper alarm, of course. Nope. I couldn't imagine any sort of happy ending coming from such a scheme.

Which meant I could never agree to help my father. And that felt wrong. Yet agreeing to do what he suggested did not, by any means, feel right.

"Ugh!" I pounded the pillow. The thought of explaining that I believed he was misguided didn't do much for my immune system. My body felt drained and spent. I questioned whether I had the wherewithal to argue with Dad and stand my ground. Confrontations weren't my forte. Maybe I'd be rescued soon.

Yes! Of course. Search parties must be scouring the countryside by now. If I could put him off a bit longer, there would be no need for an awkward confrontation.

But they'd been looking for Dad days longer than me and hadn't found him yet. From the looks of this unfamiliar locale, and the great pains taken to get me here, he didn't want anyone to discover either one of us. A lump swelled right where I needed to breathe.

What now? Despair liquefied the lump with tears. My options appeared non-existent. My only comfort came from knowing my father loved me. Though misled, he wouldn't force me to do something against my will, let alone something that would endanger the sword. Surely not. Yet the interaction tonight felt especially peculiar. Several moments became tense in ways we'd never experienced. I didn't have a grid to place some of the vibes I sensed. Before tonight, Dad always respected my ideas and would weigh my input, especially in areas that directly affected me. He encouraged me to "own my choices."

The irony of it all: choices of my own no longer existed.

In regards to the Tethered World, life yanked me along with no option to disembark. I imagined myself to be a minuscule speck afloat on a tumultuous sea. The surrounding wind and waves dictated my direction. Until now, I always assumed that taking the path of least resistance equaled the safest route. The best way to hold onto my identity.

But truthfully, I had no idea who Sadie Larcen might be anymore. What I thought I knew about myself and my family seemed to have leaked into the atmosphere like air from a punctured life raft. I was powerless to stop it, which left me stranded in the ocean currents.

Somehow, I needed to stop being the Sadie who bobbed around shark-infested waters with toes curled, clinging to the deflated raft and shooting up flares in the dark.

A wicked crick in my neck pulled me from the bliss of sleep. I hadn't changed positions since I face-planted on the bed to wrestle with my emotions. It took a minute to flip over and work out the kink, but I managed to focus on the physical pain in order to avoid the mental.

By the dim light, I spied an apple and a bowl of steaming oatmeal placed on a bedside tray. Shuffling out of bed, I pulled the big drapes open to brighten the space. On a whim, I tried the French doors for the second time in as many days, hoping I might sit on the balcony and eat.

Since, of course, they remained locked, I settled for the table and chairs near the window. At least I had a decent view of wherever for breakfast. Happy to have something besides soup, I dug into the hot mush. My eagerness for "real" food screeched to a halt, spoon in mouth. The cook obviously didn't believe in seasoning. *At least I don't have to chew it.*

Insert. Swallow. I did that until I gagged, knowing I needed the nourishment. My eyes roamed my arms and legs, noting how nicely the sores were healing, and that I only had a few scabs left. Not the most appetizing thought. I grabbed the goblet to wash the goo down but stopped in alarm.

Today was the first time I woke without guzzling the pink liquid first thing. Ridiculous thirst assaulted me after I slept. Followed soon after by cloudy thoughts.

I'm being drugged!

Anger tempted me to throw the blasted glass across the room.

The locked door rattled. I scrambled to gain composure, unsure my dad should know my discovery.

"Hope you're feeling optimistic about the future today." Dad's smile told me he was testing my disposition.

My pulse revved. *How do I handle this?*

"When you become Ambassador of the Tethered World, you'll understand the future holds vast promises and opportunities." He walked up beside me.

"Ambassador?" I shook my head. "Not me. I'm not cut out for politics. And I honestly can't support the things you're asking me to stand for. I've thought about it a lot but I can't." There. Quick and forthright.

Dad's eyes flashed. I feared I wouldn't be able to stick to my convictions if he pressed me. Mercifully, his look melded into a smile. He leaned in and kissed the top of my head, making me feel safer than I had since my arrival in this strange place.

"Sadie." He guided me by my elbow over to the French doors. "Come here."

Dad reached for the twin knobs, and I gasped to see them turn and open beneath his grip. The doors swung onto the balcony. Dad turned and gestured for me to join him.

My mouth gaped.

"What's wrong?"

I pointed at the doors. "These doors were locked. How did you do that?"

He chuckled and shrugged. "There are always surprises in this place, or haven't you noticed?"

I raised a skeptical eyebrow. "Oh, I've noticed. But I haven't expected quite this many surprises from you." Tentatively, I stepped outside.

"*This* many? I opened a door. That's one thing and not very impressive at that." Dad threaded his arm through mine and drew me to the stone railing.

"Well, your disappearance, reappearance, and change in philosophy all count as surprises in my book." I stole a sidelong glance, wondering if he would spark again.

He remained unfazed. "Look at this view. Isn't it magnificent?"

For the first time, I had a sweeping scope of the landscape. Though the same crystalline glow lit up the sky, the scenery made me question if this could really be part of the Tethered World. The veranda towered several stories tall. Part of an enormous palace nestled into the mountainside.

To my left, the hill dropped down and away, sweeping into a lush valley fitted with jeweled bodies of water. Clusters of cottages speckled the slope near and far. To my right the knoll rose, but leveled off enough for a garden to flourish with rose bushes in bloom. It was a courtyard, actually, with benches and a marble statue carved with the likeness of an angel.

"Like nothing you've ever seen, is it not?" Dad whispered.

"It's lovely."

"Don't you think the world would benefit from finding a sliver of paradise like this?"

"Maybe."

"Think about all of the ways those topside could help

others down here. It would be a very beneficial partnership."

Last night's thoughts trickled in. Mankind had a lousy track record when it came to exploring new civilizations. War. Disease. Greed. Pillaging. There was nothing mutually beneficial in these things. I sighed, wanting to choose my words with care.

Dad must have misconstrued my silence for acquiescence. He put his hand on my waist and gave it a little squeeze. "Yes, yes, m'dear. You see, don't you? There's so much that our two worlds can offer each other. What a haven this place would be for earth. The last, true utopia."

I wanted to cover my ears so I wouldn't have to hear another twisted word. How long had my father been entertaining such ideas? Did Mom suspect anything? It certainly blindsided me.

"Take it in, Sadie." He pointed in each direction with gusto. "From the gleaming valleys below to the heights of these mountains, there's a fantastic world waiting to be discovered."

He turned and took both of my hands in his. My breath caught, anticipating something important by the way he looked at me.

"If you, my beautiful Sadie, will do what I'm asking. If you will become the ambassador for the creatures here and to people topside, then..." he turned back toward the vista and swept a hand across the horizon, "then all of this will be yours. I have the power to give it to you, if you will cooperate."

He turned and gave me a penetrating stare, squeezing the hand that he still held.

I swallowed and withdrew from his grasp. No longer did I recognize my father behind that gaze. It sucked the air out of me to realize he could not be trusted. And why did it feel like we just reenacted the temptation of Jesus on the temple mount? *"All this will be yours if you'll bow down to me..."*

To steady myself, and put some space between us, I reached for the rail. *Oh Lord, what do I do?*

He took a step toward me, drilling me with his eyes. I did not recognize those eyes.

An idea whispered into my soul. A singular thought that spiked me with both dread and relief—a confusing emotional concoction.

My mouth moved but nothing came out.

He leaned in. "Yes? What is it?"

I pulled back, thinking better of my notion. But the idea pressed me like a vise until it spouted out in an unsteady whisper. "Even the devil can appear as an angel of light. Or in this case...as my father."

CHAPTER NINETEEN

THE TIP OF A SWORD JABBED Brady in his Adam's apple, pinning him to the ground. On the other end of the weapon, a Dwarf peered down his enormous nose, smirking victoriously. "Checkmate, mate! But that was a good round." He removed the dull practice sword from its fleshy target and offered Brady a hand. "You're catchin' on quick, m'boy. You're a scrappy one."

Brady grasped the Dwarf's hand and stood. "Thanks. I think." It was his third defeat of the day. He'd lost count of how many in the week since he arrived, and it was getting harder to accept each loss with grace.

Wicklow, his brown-bearded opponent, chuckled and smacked Brady on the back. "You'll get there, son. You've got good instincts." He gestured around the courtyard where other Guardians were training. "Remember that all of us, no matter if we're Dwarf or Gnome or Nephilim, have had a sword in our hand since birth—so t'speak."

"I guess years of fencing classes aren't quite the same." Brady sheathed his weapon.

"Not entirely. But there's a lot of crossover in the technique. No doubt it's given you a jump on learning our style of combat. Go grab some vittles and rest a spell. You've earned it."

"Yeah, nice consolation prize," Brady mumbled to himself. He looked around for Brock, hoping to spar with him at some point.

Brock's technique had become proficient over the six weeks that he'd been in Vituvia training to be High King. His brother had morphed from rigid combatant to a fluid-moving machine. He'd memorized a complex series of movements, and in typical Brock fashion, didn't like to stray from the combination. But Brady and he were the most equally matched, in skill as well as stature. Often it was the only time Brady spent with his brother, though they'd enjoyed a reunion over dinner on Brady's first night in Vituvia. Apprenticing as king made for a busy schedule.

"Your skill is comin' along, lad." Queen Judith approached the table where Brady now sat, popping grapes into his mouth.

"Thanks, Aunt Judith. I'm not noticing much improvement, but everyone else says otherwise. Or they're good liars."

"No liars on my watch. Wouldn't tolerate it." She shook her auburn curls. "And everyone knows it." She leaned over and elbowed Brady. "Whatcha need is a rousin' melody to get yer feet a movin'. A good sword fight is like an intricate dance."

Brady chuckled, remembering the feverish dancing his aged aunt cranked out when given the opportunity. The woman danced circles around everyone. "I'll keep that in mind."

Aunt Judith's hand flew to her temple, and she supported herself on the table with her other one. Her face was pinched with pain, eyes closed.

"Are you okay?" Brady shot his hand to her shoulder. "Do you need help?"

The queen shook her head slowly and exhaled. "I'm fine." She blinked and straightened. "Sometimes I get the worst headaches. Thankfully, they're short lived."

"Wow. That looked intense." He withdrew his hand.

"So how's me sister?" The queen brushed her fingers together as if sloughing away the painful episode. "Have ya spoken to Jules lately?"

Brady pressed his lips tight, reminding himself that his aunt really *didn't* remember asking him this question every day since he arrived. "Actually, she came with us this time, remember? She's in Berganstroud." He purposely left off the part about Uncle Daniel after day three of the question. It made for too much explaining.

"She is?" Queen Judith looked genuinely surprised. Then, like a lightbulb switching on, she nodded. "She is! Oh, I do hope we can find a time to meet up soon."

"Me too." Brady spotted Brock coming across the lawn,

sword at his side. "I know she's anxious to see you as well." He stood and extended his fist to his brother. Brock preferred minimal bodily contact. Fist bumps were about right.

"Well, I best check in with Sir Noblin and see how preparations are goin' fer the ceremony tonight." Queen Judith offered the brothers a curt bow. "I shall see ya both, and the rest of our Guardians here, at the initiate dinner."

"Thanks, Aunt Judith. It's an honor to be a candidate."

His aunt smiled and clasped his hand, covering it with her other one. "I hope ya continue to think so when yer placed in harm's way. Rumors abound that Brock is a target fer our enemies. We're countin' on ya to be a decoy until the danger passes."

"Are you calling me a devil?" My dad, or whoever he was, stiffened, and I saw that strange look flicker again.

The accusation sounded ludicrous but rang true. I didn't trust myself to answer.

"I asked you a question, *Daughter.*" His mouth contorted to a snarl.

What I saw in his face confirmed what I sensed. The person in front of me could not be my father. Though that realization again washed me with relief, it left many dangling questions. *Where is Dad? Where am I? And who is this impostor?*

The nerve of someone trying to pass himself off as my dad—to manipulate me—spurred me to push back. "You are *not* my father. You're not Liam Larcen. Of this I'm sure."

The man glared. He appeared to recalculate his approach.

I crossed my arms and glared back. "Which means that I am definitely *not* your daughter."

A chill permeated the limited space between us. The muscles in his face flexed, and the charade that was my father seemed to dissolve. At the same time a blast of air descended, like a downdraft in a storm. The amber light of the Tethered World dimmed behind a sudden burst of smoke and ash. It obscured my view of everything for a merciful moment.

As the dust settled, my internal world quaked. Before me stood a coal-skinned Goliath. Charred, flaking hide covered a hulking body. A scar beneath his left eye forced the jaundiced orb to protrude, slightly, in an unsettling glare. Some sort of half-human, half-bat torso, clad in ebony leather vest and pants worthy of a rock star, stood there on twisted, taloned feet. Glossy black wings spread from his shoulders like a cape, completing the Beelzebub effect.

My vision swam, and I battled to hang on to consciousness, despising my weak constitution. The spectacle huffed a sulfurous breath into my face. The putrid smell revved my senses back to life. With full faculties and a fresh rush of fear, I stared up into my enemy's face.

Actually, I believed he must be the enemy of my very soul. Maybe I was staring at Satan himself. My mind screamed *run,* but I didn't trust my unsteady legs. I squeezed my eyes tight, praying in desperation. *Help me, God!*

A rough jerk on my head made me gasp. He gripped my hair in his hands. I blinked against the remaining haze that swirled above me in an ominous dance.

"You still think you're clever, Sadie?" His smooth, deep voice defied his monstrous appearance. "Betcha didn't know Daddy-dear had such a nasty temper."

A nefarious chuckle rattled his chest. He tilted my head enough to look me in the eye. I contemplated spitting in his ugly face, but the thought of what he might spit back kept me in check.

"It's too bad you wouldn't agree to my very generous offer. Now I must force you to do it anyway, minus the perks of pretty palaces and fairytale scenery."

"You can't make me do anything." I hoped I sounded braver than the quivering mess on my insides.

"Well, she's got spunk, doesn't she?" A cynical, sideways grin allowed one of his fangs to slip from between his lips.

Something began to press against my ankle and wrap across my shin. *Someone's tying me up!* I tried to kick it away, but the pressure rapidly increased, drawing my knees together as the rope slinked around and scaled my body.

My mind raced to identify the sensation—for I knew it

wasn't a rope. The mental picture made me whimper. I couldn't move my head to confirm what I imagined was coming up. The mere idea made my knees buckle, which warranted a yank on my still-captive hair. I squeezed my eyes shut, as much to block out the demonic face above me as to erase the image of what I guessed encircled my body below.

Another sulfurous snicker expelled into my face. "Betcha want a peek at your visitor." He jerked my chin to my chest.

Though I hated to look, I had to confirm my suspicions. Sure enough, I met the silvery glint of reptilian skin, a golden-eyed glare, and a forked, foraging tongue. A new spasm of flailing commenced, and a horrible screech escaped my throat.

The serpent now approached my middle, its intense stare riveted to my face. My breath came in shallow gasps as sanity retreated to a small corner of my mind. This must be happening to someone else.

Like a straight-jacket, the snake swirled its body around my waist. Then slinked to my back. *So, this is how I'm going down. Constricted by a serpent. Squeezed to death. Or bitten. Or both.*

The darting tongue probed the air and—I recalled from science—smelled me. *Me.* Its prey. With wild abandon, my fists punched against the scaly lasso around my waist. I barely noted that the iron grip on my head had been released when the coiling snake wedged both arms to the sides of my body. Hysterical screams racked my chest. I fought to wriggle my arms out of their entrapment, but the impossibly long viper held fast.

Here it comes. I braced myself for the inevitable, constricted, then swallowed whole.

When the snake summited my shoulder, the slinking creature cooed a disturbing, shh, shh, between flicks of its tongue. I fought to hang on to reason and consciousness. Both seemed ready to ditch me.

"Now, Ssssadie," the serpent hissed, "do you ssstill want to be ssso unreasssonable?"

An inky fog blurred my vision. Snakes don't speak! I no longer fought the urge to pass out but welcomed such an escape. Instead, the black beast huffed another nasty breath my way. Rotten smelling salts brought me back from the brink.

"Ansssswer me!" The snake bared its fangs, inches from my face, while the length of it encircled me, shoulder to foot, like stripes on a barber pole. "Prince Malagruel will not asssk again. He will only relishhh making you sssuffer."

What were my options? I couldn't go along with such a plan, but perhaps I could pretend. At the right time I might be able to escape or get help. Guilt swarmed like angry bees. How could I consider such a treacherous idea? I had to do the right thing.

No matter what.

"I-I will *never* help you." My voice sounded smaller than my little sister Nicole's.

"Ssso noble of you. Too bad no one will ever know that you died clinging to your sssself-righteousss idealsss."

My feet were yanked from beneath me. I landed with a yelp. The snake jerked my torso backwards, smacking my head on the ground. My body plowed across the floor, still bound by the reptile.

A headache blared between my ears. The serpent kept its beady slits trained on my face. I could feel its rope-like body being caught and jerked free beneath me across the floor. My gaze roved to avoid the fanged face hovering above my chest. Fettered by the serpent, I was dragged from the balcony, back into the bedroom.

The beautiful space no longer held any fairytale enchantment. Rather, it looked like a primitive room, complete with cobwebs and a large, dirty cot. On the wall, near the head of the bed, hung an empty frame with a large "X" scratched into the rock where my portrait once hung.

The striding form of Malagruel, whom by now I'd guessed to be a Gargoyle, pulled the snake and me out the bedroom door. His leathery, cape-style wings draped behind, reminding me of Darth Vader striding away. As he turned down the passageway, his wings separated enough to reveal a gruesome reality.

Rather than the Gargoyle gripping the lengthy serpent by its tail and tugging it along behind him like a rope...the snake *was* his tail. A tail that could encircle me, speak to me, and probably swallow me like a rat for supper.

My heart tolled a rapid staccato. *This is wrong on so many levels.*

With eyes squeezed shut, I tried to blot out the living

nightmare that had become my life.

CHAPTER TWENTY

Brady felt like the odd man out at the enormous banquet
table, surrounded by different sized chairs. He chuckled at
the irony—he wasn't merely the *odd*-man; he was the only
hu-man seated at the table. At least until Brock showed up.

Two Nephilim warriors sat on one end, Typhel and Holt.
He didn't much care for Holt, a cocky blond with a handlebar
mustache, but he'd met Typhel on his last visit, and he
seemed nice enough. At least he didn't gloat about wiping the
floor with Brady, the way Holt did.

The Dwarves, Wicklow, and Anton "the Brave", as he was
fondly referred to, rounded out the new recruits to the
Guardians of the Sword. Together with Brady and the other
Gnome Guardians, they formed a solidarity of allies, in
defense of the Flaming Sword of Cherubythe. At least that
was how General Muggleridge phrased it. In the history of the
sword, such a conglomeration of Guards had never before
been tested.

Brady shifted in his seat and realized the empty chair on
his right was now occupied. "Hey, Brock! Didn't see you come
in." He smiled to himself, pleased that his brother hadn't lost
his knack for silently approaching unsuspecting people.

Though Brock wasn't training to be a guard, Brady was
glad for a chance to hang out with his brother in this relaxed
atmosphere. It hadn't happened since his arrival dinner. He
reached into the front pocket of his black, Gnome-issued
trousers and removed Brock's knife.

"Bro, I brought you something to remind you of home." He
opened his fist, palm up, to reveal the ivory pocketknife.
"Thought you might like to have this."

Brock stared at it as if it might involuntarily stab him.

"That shouldn't be here."

"It's fine. You can put it next to your bed, here in Vituvia, and it'll remind you of home."

Brock shook his head in a rapid-fire motion. "No, no, no, no. That belongs in my room at home. Not my room here. That shouldn't be here."

With a sigh, Brady returned the knife to his pocket. He'd experienced enough of Brock's OCD moments to know there was no convincing his brother otherwise. He should've seen it coming. "It's okay. I'll take it home."

Brock continued to look horrified by the out-of-place object, staring at Brady's pocket with a scowl.

Thankfully, General Muggleridge cleared his throat from a podium positioned in front of the Vituvian flag. "Let us ask the Creator's blessing on our meal." He removed his pointy hat, revealing a bristly head of greying hair. "We ask, oh Mighty Maker, that you will lead us, unite us, and bless this meal prepared for us. Give us Your wisdom in these dark days. Protect us as we seek to protect the sword. So be it."

"So be it," the recruits repeated.

A team of Gnomes in crisp, black-and-white uniformed tunics delivered platters of food. Since a Gnome's arm span could only manage a human-size plate, and they planned to feed eight-foot tall Nephilim warriors, among others, there were many platters. Portable steps were placed on either end of the oval table. The Gnomes marched up the steps and onto the table, placing the food in the center. Brady had to admire the ambitious little folks. They found a way to do anything they deemed necessary.

While the hungry trainees mauled plates of spiced meatballs, stuffed mushrooms, and ginger-garlic potatoes, General Muggleridge explained about the next aspect of the program.

"Now that you've learned the routine of our tactical training, we shall move to the second phase. You'll continue to go through the rigors of physical conditioning in the morning, followed by marching formations and security protocol in the afternoon."

He grabbed the edge of the podium, his voice impassioned. "Remember, the sword is guarded with the ceremonial dignity it deserves. You will be expected to adhere to the formality of your station, or we will request replacements from your superiors. We prefer to see each of you succeed, enabling us to add to our numbers. Furthermore"—he gazed directly at Brady—"some of you may be selected for specialized instruction."

Self-conscious, Brady glanced around the table, wondering if anyone noticed. The others remained engrossed in their meal, some with their backs to Muggleridge.

"Our noble queen would like to share a few words of encourage—"

"General! I need a word with you." Muscle interrupted from one of the doorways.

All eyes turned to him trotting to the podium. Queen Judith, already making her way to the front, was intercepted by one of her Gnome bodyguards. He escorted her from the room as Muscle and General Muggleridge conferred.

A dark-skinned soldier approached Brock and Brady. "Your Highness and sir, follow me. We must get you both to a safe place. Immediately."

Brady and Brock stood. Curious murmurs percolated at the table and among the servants. Muggleridge pounded the podium with a mallet right as Brady made it to the doorway. He stopped and listened.

"Warriors! We need you for an urgent task. Report to Special Ops immediately for instructions. Dragon fire has scourged Forest Ridge, killing our guards. Evil has taken to the sky above Vituvia. The Banished are upon us."

My neck protested the weight of my head, which I strained to keep off the bumpy stone ground. If I didn't lift it up, my skull would resemble a bludgeoned pumpkin.

Creatures milled about. Whispers and snickers followed our sick parade. Peeking—while trying to look like I wasn't— I caught glimpses of other leathery-looking feet in a variety of shapes, as well as some enormous hairy ones in an earthy array of colors. Gargoyles and Trolls. Oh, and a few putty-colored, calloused feet with thick grey toenails poking through leather sandal straps—Stygians.

I recognized my prison. I'd been here before. The enchantment that had veiled my sight from this Gargoyle had also managed to display a serene façade that hid a very evil—and familiar—hunk of carved rock.

I was in the Eldritch. Palace of Chief Nekronok. Center of politics. Temple of mysterious rituals.

Though I dreaded being in the clutches of the Trolls—and trapped by the tail of this Gargoyle—a sense of relief settled inside. The Dwarves and Gnomes could get to me. And Chebar was here too.

The hope of spotting Chebar—the Troll who secretly served Queen Judith and helped her escape from the Eldritch on our first trip—made me open my eyes and gaze at the creepy cast of characters. It resembled an exhibition of freaks from a horror movie. Of course, I found the beady-eyed glare of the reptile to be the distracting star of the show. He hovered menacing and close, baring his fangs.

I spotted many Trolls, but I didn't notice Chebar among the onlookers. As one of Nekronok's sons, he probably had some sort of official duty to tend to. The knowledge that Chebar was somewhere nearby assured me of my ability to survive. Surely he was devising a plan or alerting the Dwarves and my family. I only needed to hang on a little longer.

The hulking Gargoyle stopped in front of two imposing carved doors. "Tell Nekronok I'm here with the prisoner."

"That's Chief Nekronok, if you p-please, Prince Malagruel," the Troll guard replied, visibly shaking.

"If Nekronok wants to remain *chief* then you better announce me on the double, imbecile."

"Yes, sir." The guard disappeared inside.

"It'sss time for your big debut in court, Sssadie."

I refused to look at the serpent.

"Prince Malagruel isss the judge and the jury. Thisss isss not a democracsssy."

I stared at the ceiling.

Fangs and a yellow-slitted stare broke into my line of sight as the snake stretched enough to look down on my face. It made me gasp as he squeezed my body tight in order to lengthen his own. "You will cooperate one way or another,

Princessss."

I gritted my teeth and tried to conceal the pain in my constricted chest. My breath was shallow, and my heartbeat thumped inside my eardrums. Something wet dangled from the snake's fangs. I turned my head right when two droplets fell. They landed on my cheekbone with a ferocious, burning sizzle.

"Stop! Please." Scorching heat swept across my face.

"Chief Nekronok will see you now." The door creaked, and I opened tearful eyes enough to see the guard step aside. The snake eased its grip around my middle when we began to move.

Though I'd intended to grasp the layout of this place, it now felt like someone had drilled a hole through my cheek with a lit cigarette, making it hard to concentrate or even hold my head off the floor. Perspiration beaded across my scalp. An intense face-ache left my eardrums buzzing from pain. My resolve to scope the layout wilted. I could only perceive an underwhelming amount of torchlight flickering against enormous, stone walls.

"What is the meaning of this, Malagruel?" Chief Nekronok's fiendish voice boomed. I remembered him from our last, terrifying encounter.

"The prisoner is uncooperative." Malagruel stopped a few feet from the Troll.

"In other words, you failed." Nekronok barely glanced my way. He crossed his arms, drumming his lanky fingers on his salt and pepper fur. "I thought you said your plan was foolproof."

"She's a greater fool than most, it would seem. I told you we should've nabbed the old lady too, for leverage, but your Dwarf on the inside did not follow orders." The Gargoyle leered down at me, and so did the snake. "But I shall enjoy employing other means to force this one to cooperate."

The snake suddenly squeezed me so tightly that my shoulders lifted from the ground, followed by the upper half of my body. I yelped. Malagruel's snake-tail had muscled me to an upright position, then all the way to my tottering feet. Thankfully, the serpent unraveled from around my torso as I straightened, which allowed me to catch my breath. I resisted the urge to coddle my pained face in my hands and attempted a stoic expression.

"A single insider cannot smuggle out two people at once. Quit shifting the blame."

The Troll and Gargoyle stared each other down, ignoring me. They didn't look too fond of one another.

"What needs to shift is your attitude." Malagruel's rotten-egg breath made me suppress a gag. "You can't pull off this coup without me. You need my shapeshifting prowess. You need my soldiers to do your dirty work. Thus, you need to show more respect."

"You're here on *my* invitation, Malagruel. If not for me, you'd still be experimenting with useless weaponry in your giant cave with that old bag of bones from topside. So let's not lose focus. If you want a position in my new regime, you'll show proper respect. When I control the sword, I will control *all* of the Tethered World. Including your measly kingdom. Keep that in mind."

Nekronok grabbed my hair and jerked me close to his ape-like face. "You listen to me. You're going to wish you would've agreed to cooperate with your *daddy* here, by the time I finish with you. You'll wish you could go back to your bewitching world with its fancy four-poster bed. Things aren't going to be quite as pleasant from here on out."

He shoved me away. I fell backwards, landing on my elbows with a jolt, the snake still twisted around my lower legs. Malagruel stiffened like he was unprepared for the sudden thrust to his slithering tail. *What a shame.*

"Magog! Take this insipid human to a holding cell." Nekronok kicked my ribcage. "Find Chebar and tell him to prepare the elements. Alert me when everything's ready."

I gasped and clutched my ribs, blinking against the resurgent sting of tears. Pain shot through my torso. I grappled for hope in the knowledge that Chebar would come. That hope flecked the darkness with a hint of light.

A bulky shape stepped from the shadows behind Nekronok—the darkest Troll I ever remembered seeing. His ebony fur glinted in the torchlight. He sported a gladiator-style leather vest and loincloth, a curved saber sheathed at his side. He stepped past Nekronok, then turned to face him. On the back of his left shoulder sat a nasty-looking sore, scabbed and obscured by fur, where some sort of symbol had been branded into his hide.

"As you wish, Your Excellency." He gave a curt bow and

turned toward me.

The snake unwound itself from my legs, forcing me to flip over face down in the process. The soldier stepped beside me and placed a vise grip on my head, as if he were palming a basketball with the span of his massive hand. I scrambled to get my feet under me and relieve some of the pull on my scalp as he dragged me along beside him. It would've been difficult enough without trying to cradle my sore ribs too. Why couldn't these creatures simply tie my hands and force me to walk like a dignified prisoner?

We left the room the way I'd entered with the bat-man. I still struggled to see beyond the floor and legs of everyone we passed. However, keeping my hair attached to my head seemed more vital than memorizing where we went. Between Magog's grip and the pain of the burns, I would've been happy to detach my head like a lizard separates from its tail. I bit my lip and tried not to cry, especially when my feet slipped out from under me. Onlookers mocked and murmured as I fought to keep up. Finally, the big ape stopped at another door and waited for the guard to pull it open.

It offered a brief chance to catch my breath. A stone staircase descended deep into the Eldritch, and we careened faster than my feet could match.

"Please! Slow down!" I grabbed the soldier's wrist in an attempt to push my head toward his hand and alleviate the pressure.

His wicked, amused laugh echoed through the stairwell, and he picked up the pace.

Mercifully, the stairs ended a few seconds later. My legs jostled to get steady as the creep yanked me down yet another hallway.

"Open the gate!" he hollered.

The piercing pitch of metal grating against stone made me wince. A tawny-colored guard scrunched down to stare curiously at me, eye to eye, when I passed. His shoulder displayed the same seared symbol as Magog's.

Barred chambers lined the passageway. In one cell, a nappy-haired Troll ran to the bars and shook them like a rabid chimpanzee. He screeched, baring his yellow fangs and swiping at me. He gave a catcall sort of whistle.

"Shut up, Grelk, or I'll have you flogged for the fun of it."

Magog stopped and released his grip. I rubbed my head and straightened my back, happier than I thought possible to do such a simple thing.

The guard approached with a set of keys. He was shorter than the other Trolls. Maybe six feet tall, but broad-shouldered and thick-necked. He lurched in a funny way when he walked, due to a serious set of bowed legs. It gave him a menacing swagger.

He unlocked a barred door and gestured for me to go inside. I was more than happy to put some space—and even bars—between myself and Magog. To be left alone for a while would be a welcome relief. As I stepped through, one of the brutes shoved me, and I found myself splayed on the floor, eyeballing a pile of dung left by a previous prisoner.

I rolled away from the disgusting deposit and glared up at the Trolls. I had a few choice words in mind but hoped my silence would quickly usher them away.

"Prepare to face the elements, oh high and mighty human." Magog spat distastefully at my feet. "I look forward to the show."

He sauntered away. The guard gave me his version of the evil-eye before locking me in the bare cell.

Face the elements? That comment would've made sense topside. Being abandoned out in the desert or in the snowy mountains would be a test of survival in severe weather. But there were no temperature changes or weather-related activities in the Land of Legend.

This made me nervous.

CHAPTER TWENTY-ONE

Brady, Brock, and the guard veered into a chaos-filled passageway. Like fish swimming upstream, they waded through soldiers and servants in an uproar. Brady felt every nerve in his body straining to get a sense of the unfolding drama. An undercurrent of fear was all but tangible.

The guard turned into a narrower, less populated passage and stopped before a set of doors flanked with busts of dignified Gnomes on marble pedestals. Brady helped the Gnome heave one of the wooden doors open, and the three scrambled inside.

A half-dozen torches blazed from the concave walls in the well-appointed room. Cushioned couches in graduated heights formed an octagon near the center around a low wooden table. Three enormous oil paintings hung between four more Gnome statues nestled against the curving wall opposite the door. Brady decided they must be in the palace parlor. A place for the queen to receive visitors.

"This way." The soldier walked to the framed painting in the center. A prolific family of Gnomes filled the canvas. Three life-sized children sat on a grassy lawn. A mother and father stood in the center, holding a swaddled baby between them. Four more young Gnomes stood on various sized boulders behind the parents.

The bottom of the frame hung at eye-level to the guard. He ran his fingers along the underside of the gilded wood, which produced a soft *click*. The entire portrait swung wide, hinged on the opposite side.

"Whoa..." Brady peered into the gaping hole in the wall.

"Step inside." The Gnome jerked his thumb toward the opening. "Don't wander away. It's easy to get lost in the secret passageways that crisscross the castle. Of course, there are other ways to get in and out, but I'll come back to retrieve you when the danger passes."

Brady hesitated. "I thought I was supposed to be helping protect the sword and my brother."

"Yes, of course. You've only begun your training, however. Until you're ready, we must protect *you*. Now, if you please?"

Brady understood but hated to miss the action—though he was relieved that his mom and Sophie were far from the trouble. He glanced at Brock, hopeful that the dark, confined space wouldn't provoke a meltdown. His brother had never been a fan of tight quarters—but much about Brock's personality had mellowed in the Tethered World.

The twins stepped inside.

"Until later." The guard bowed deeply and returned the portrait to its place over the hole.

Brady blinked against the darkness. Getting to explore a hidden web of tunnels would be awesome—but standing in this confining space for who-knew-how-long sounded tedious. He felt for the wall behind him. The cold stone met his fingertips, and he leaned against it.

"Pretty cool, huh?" Brady nudged his brother. "Did you know there were secret passageways in the palace?"

"Yes."

"Have you been inside one before?"

"No."

"Then how did you know about them? Did someone show you?"

"No one showed me. We learned about them in medieval history. All castles have hidden tunnels. A safety feature."

Brady chuckled. "Of course! How could I forget learning that in the sixth grade?" He shook his head, amazed by Brock's impressive memory.

"I can see," Brock said.

"Whaddya mean?"

"Holes. I can see through the holes."

Small circles of light could be faintly made out, now that Brady's eyes had adjusted. The circles were in pairs, all over the canvas in front of them. He peered through a set of nearby spheres. Though they weren't empty circles, the fibers in the canvas were sparsely woven, allowing one to see through the grid. "Cool! These are peepholes."

"Peepholes?"

"Yeah, like the one on our front door. We're probably looking out of the different Gnome faces that were painted on the front of this picture. Too bad, there's nothing to spy on out there." Brady shifted to the next set of "eyes," trying them out.

A cold and restrictive hand suddenly clamped over his mouth. "That's because *you're* being spied on in *here.*"

I pressed my body into the corner of the cell. The stone walls offered cool comfort to the burns on my cheek. Thankfully, the pulsing pain had mellowed to bearable aftershocks. My eyelids needed no coaxing to close—which conveniently removed the pile of poo from my line of sight. The solitary silence tempered my ragged mental state. My fingers grasped at the little, silver book around my neck. Zipping it back and forth on the chain evoked a familiar measure of calm—and a twinge of amazement that it had survived everything I'd been through.

I was grateful for time to collect my thoughts and courage, although Grclk, my neighbor a few cells down, disturbed the quiet with throaty howls and the occasional taunt. But hey, compared to talking vipers and demonic-looking Gargoyles, he seemed like an overgrown, grouchy teddy bear.

If I had ever questioned the reality of good and evil, such doubts had long since disappeared after my first visit to the Tethered World. And now, *now* I had to cling to what I knew about battling evil. That it wasn't an even fight. I've read the ending, and I know which side wins.

Though I had the ultimate victory in the war over my soul, I didn't feel so confident about the battles I might face in the belly of the earth. Didn't know what to make of—or how to prepare for—'the elements.'

There would be no majestic Lion directing Father Christmas to my side. No gifts of daggers or magical medicine to be bestowed. Neither a wise wizard nor an Elven lord would come to offer direction or aid. The great God-like characters that materialized in books could offer no hope.

Yet, I knew I had reason to hope.

I knew it was time to stop letting outside influences direct my destiny—time to stop bobbing helplessly in the ocean of circumstance. I couldn't afford to hold out for a superhero rescue or even insider help from Chebar. My eyes fluttered open and took in the desolate, depressing cell. I had to admit that the defensive strategy hadn't worked in my favor.

Time to be proactive.

Though being on the offense scared me almost as much as Malagruel and Nekronok, it would at least feel like a plan.

I gave a wry chuckle. What sort of a plan did I now possess? Only a mental one. A switch, like on a train track, that meant I would head down the rails marked: *endeavor,* rather than the ones that read: *react.*

It did not change one iota of my situation. No one could possibly look at me and know that I wanted, for once, to *try.*

In all honesty, I didn't know if I had what it would take to weather the storms—or the elements—rolling my way. But I did have hope. That commodity came from beyond myself, from Someone. Someone who knew how weak and cowardly I really was...even with the best of intentions.

Someone who remembers that I am fragile and made of dust.

The sound of scraping metal roused me from sleep. I shifted my head so I could peek from nearly closed eyelids and fake off whoever the visitor might be. Maybe if they thought I was asleep they'd leave.

Yeah, right. This wasn't the maid service looking for a do-not-disturb sign. The rattle of keys and a fresh round of shouts from Grelk were too much to pretend not to hear. I watched with drowsy curiosity as the guard swung the door open and tossed a burlap sack into the room.

"Put this on. They're coming for you."

After the guard left, I walked over and picked up the rough fabric. It was a touch more refined than burlap. Sort of a heavy, drapery cloth. Brown braids trimmed it on two opposite sides and continued past the edge of the fabric, one much longer than the other. There was a narrow hole in one spot. Only one hole? I had two arms, last I checked.

It took creative maneuvering, but after some trial and error, I figured out how to wrap the garment around me like a full-length sarong. The longer braid threaded through the hole and wrapped around my middle. Then both braids crisscrossed below my collarbone, like halter straps, before tying behind my neck. Only then did I slip out of my clothes, a rather awkward accomplishment beneath the burlap curtain. I wondered why they wanted me in such primitive attire and what the "Ceremony of the Elements" would involve.

The knowledge that Chebar had been the one ordered to prepare things was my singular solace. Surely he had a plan.

And if he doesn't?

The question poked me squarely in my conscience. It reminded me of my earlier resolve to quit being a victim. No more crossing my fingers in the hope of outside intervention. How that decision would play out in these upcoming events didn't inspire confidence, but I said a silent prayer that I would be strong when it counted.

I propped myself into the corner again, hopeful sleep would return. Instead, my mind wandered topside. How were Nate and Nicole doing at Uncle Brent's house? Did he and Aunt Val expect to have my brother and sister stay with them for this length of time?

What about Dad? Had Mom and he been united yet, or were she and Sophie and Brady still searching for him? Surely he'd been located by now. Perhaps we'd all be home together soon. I only needed to get out of this zoo, right?

Something deep down told me that things would not be so simple. Getting back with my family was only half the battle. Protecting the sword and securing the realm would take everything else and a miracle or two.

Before I could throw an all-out pity party, the guard returned with a female Troll that looked young. Maybe because she didn't tower over me by more than a few inches. Perhaps she hadn't finished growing. She sported the same recycled curtain clothing as me, and I felt a twinge of pride to see I really *had* put the thing on correctly.

"Turn around. Hands behind your back." The guard twirled his lanky finger.

I did so, happy to be tied up like a normal prisoner. He tightened the rope, and it burned my wrists. My hands were certain to look like fat, purple sausages soon.

The silent female grasped my upper arm and led me past the ogling eyes of Grelk. Her long fingers encircled my scrawny bicep and wrapped back onto her hand.

I caught her staring at me several times while she guided me through the dingy halls of the Eldritch. Whenever I responded with a grin, she looked away as if embarrassed. But I detected a shy smile on her leathery lips and decided she might be nice to know under different circumstances.

We crossed paths with Trolls and Stygians and several Gargoyles. The Gargoyles particularly terrified me with their bizarre appearance—some with features like hideous men and bodies of beasts, others with faces like a fiendish cartoon, bodies stooped and gnarled. Most of the onlookers had some sort of jeer or insult to spout, but I tried to keep my focus farther down the passage and ignore them.

At last we came to another set of doors, which two guards opened upon our approach. We stepped into a torch-lit staircase that spiraled up through the rock. When the doors closed behind us and we made it around the first curve, the girl stopped and untied my wrists.

"No need for these, is there?" Her voice confirmed what I thought about her age. Young. "They act like you're a dangerous threat, but I think you're smart enough to know you're outsized and outnumbered."

"Thank you." I rubbed my wrists and blinked back an embarrassing tear. I hadn't been treated with genuine kindness for days, and I appreciated the gesture. "Don't worry, I'm not about to take on the whole of the Eldritch."

Her hazel eyes grew round, and she shook her head emphatically. "Don't let anyone hear you say that. That's what our enemies call our sanctum. It's an insult."

"Oh, sorry. I'll be careful."

She smiled and offered me her hand. "Keturah."

"Sadie." I grasped her hand, and we studied each other's face.

"Sorry that we encountered each other under these conditions. I've always wanted to meet a topsider. But not like this." She pointed up the stairs. "We better keep going or they'll come looking for us."

"What exactly are 'these conditions'?" I tried not to sound winded. The stairs seemed to go on forever, and I had been sick in bed for the past week. "What sort of ceremony am I supposed to take part in?"

Keturah didn't respond right away. Finally, she stopped—which I welcomed—and faced me with a somber expression. "The Ceremony of the Elements is a ceremony of devotion. I'm quite sure your devotion does *not* lie with our Worshipful Master Nekronok. But…but perhaps you'll reconsider." Her eyes looked glassy. She turned and continued up the stairs, revealing the same symbol burned into her left shoulder. Her scar was much older than the ones on her male counterparts, but fur made it hard to decipher.

I pondered her words and followed. Surely they didn't expect me to pledge my allegiance to Mr. Bigfoot himself? Forget it.

"I'm here with the prisoner," Keturah called through a set of doors at the top of the stairs.

They swung inward. We emerged into a long hallway bordered with curtained openings. Another set of guarded doors stood at the opposite end. Keturah stopped at the first curtained entrance on our right and held one panel open.

"In here."

The room smelled of musky incense and held few furnishings. A long, narrow table stood against one wall, with two wide-mouthed bowls perched on either end. One bowl brimmed with water, a towel rolled neatly in front of it, the other piled with an array of flowers, from lilies to orchids to baby's breath. A smoldering twig of incense stood in a marble base between the two bowls. Its sapphire smoke spiraled into the air and mingled with the smoke from the torch mounted on the wall above the table. Several embroidered cushions lay scattered on the floor.

"Cleanse your face and hands in the bowl," she said.

I bent over and saw my reflection in the torch-lit water. It flickered in and out, like a television with weak reception.

Puffy eyes and a burned cheek were exactly what a teenage girl loved to notice about herself.

The image of my book charm winked in the light. I scooped my hands into the cool water and brought it to my face, daring to take a little sip because it looked clean. The wounds on my cheekbone stung, but I didn't allow myself to react.

The water dripped from my chin into the bowl, and I blinked my lashes free. Keturah handed me the towel, and I dabbed my face, thankful to a feel a bit cleaned up—though I knew the Trolls weren't concerned about my personal hygiene.

"So..." I hoped I might get a little more info from the girl. "You said this ceremony is about devotion?"

The young Troll nodded. "Now, lean over the incense and inhale, deeply."

That sounded absurd. "Why?"

She pressed her lips together and pointed at the scented stick.

"Not until you answer my question." I stood my ground. "You said yourself that I wouldn't pledge my loyalty to Nekronok, and I won't. What happens then?"

Keturah swallowed and stared at the floor.

"C'mon." I strangled the towel in my hands like it would wring an answer out of her too. "You've got to give me some idea of what I'm about to face. Please!"

"There are only two options in this ceremony." Her gaze slowly slid up to my face. "Devotion...or death."

CHAPTER TWENTY-TWO

MY STOMACH CINCHED INTO AN INSTANTANEOUS knot. Those were not the alternatives I expected to hear, though—honestly—what *should* I have expected? A get-out-of-jail-free card?

"I see." My voice slipped out in quiet terror.

Keturah nodded, her gaze a mixture of pity and helplessness. It was evident she hated my options as well.

"Here." She bobbed her head toward the incense and pulled the towel from my grasp. "They're expecting us soon."

Minus any bright ideas, I numbly stepped to the burning perfume and leaned into the smoke. I felt silly and gave a halfhearted sniff.

"No. Breathe deeply." Keturah gently pressed my back and waved her other hand through the haze, making it dance around my face. "It will help relax you."

I stiffened. What exactly was this stuff? I feigned a few deep breaths, lifting my chest somewhat while I held my breath.

"That's good." She patted my back. "Ah, yes. Do you feel it working?"

I nodded and acted pleased. The problem was I *did* feel different. No doubt the smoke diffused through the room had a bit of an effect on me anyway. Still, I wasn't about to let them drug me into submission.

"Now, have a seat on a cushion, and I'll make a garland for your hair." Keturah selected several flowers from the bowl and nimbly braided their stems together. Nice to know I'll go out in style.

In about two minutes she had created a lovely crown of flowers which she solemnly placed in my hair. Her finishing touch was a sisterly kiss on my forehead. Like a pinprick in a water balloon, her tender heart won me over, and I let anxious tears drip onto my lap. It meant so much to discover kindness in the midst of hopelessness.

"Oh, no. Let's not be sad." She handed me the towel, and I dabbed at my face. "You look lovely. Please don't cry. I'm so sorry you're in this position." She offered me her hand and helped me up.

I didn't know what to say. My head felt fuzzy.

"You know, Master Nekronok treats us well." Her eyes pleaded with me. "The idea may take some getting used to, but considering the alternative..."

"Thank you for your help and your honesty." I fingered the flowers on my head. "And for this beautiful garland."

She nodded and walked to the curtained doorway. A distant horn broadcast a sorrowful wail which permeated the air. "It's time."

I followed her into the hall and to the other set of guarded doors. The two Yetis looked me over but remained grim. Another blast on the horn and they pulled the doors open.

Buttery light enveloped me. I squinted and welcomed the change from torchlight to daylight. Even though the glow wasn't from real sunshine, it finished a close second. I found myself standing on the right-hand side of a sweeping balcony. It stretched before me in a semicircle, edged with a bannister that stopped halfway around and then picked up again about four feet later. On my left, a smaller, raised semicircle extended out, forming a platform or stage.

Keturah whispered, "When the horn blows again, walk to the symbol between the two bannisters."

I spotted the symbol etched into the ground in front of the space where the two railings stopped. Beyond the bannisters I could only see more of the golden light of the domed sky. The Eldritch had been chiseled into the stone of Mount Thrall, and I decided this veranda must be positioned near the top.

Someone stepped out of the shadows on the stage. An armor-clad Troll lifted an enormous, polished animal horn to his mouth and blew long and low. My heart revved off the charts, and I deftly put one shaky foot in front of the other, heading for the emblem.

As I rounded the curve, I met the proud gaze of Nekronok seated on the opposite side of the raised stage. He commanded an ornately carved throne, a golden scepter resting across his lap. He now wore a white tunic and trousers with gilded embellishments. A silken, purple cape rested on his shoulders, tied across his thick neck with gold braids. Between his heavy brows sat a polished, triangular emerald in an unusual setting, affixed to a narrow gold band encircling his head.

He looked like he'd escaped from a traveling circus.

On either side, stationed on shorter, less impressive chairs, sat a panel of dignitaries—or so I presumed. A female Troll, who gave new meaning to the term "big boned," sat on Nekronok's right, looking like his circus sidekick in her patchwork sarong dress. Beside her, a pasty-faced Stygian slouched under a turban-wrapped head, feet sticking out like a child in an adult's chair.

On Nekronok's left sat a pewter-colored Troll with the same heavy brow bone and deep-set eyes as him. The two were surely related. Next to the new Troll, the slithery figure of Malagruel radiated contempt. His wings encompassed his shoulders like a pleated, plastic cape, while his tail slithered menacingly around his taloned feet.

Murmurs and grunts drew my attention to the nearby railing. My careful steps wobbled a bit when my gaze fell on a large crowd of creatures that had been out of sight moments before. Out of sight because they stood on a platform built much lower than the balustrade, which meant I could only see the outer fringe of the masses as I approached. A mixture of Trolls, Stygians, and Gargoyles swarmed the enormous, curved area. Some pointed up at me. Others punched their fists in the air and snarled.

My mind felt oddly disconnected from what my body was doing, thanks to the incense no doubt. *If only I was watching this happen to someone else.*

The unsavory assortment of dignitaries seated across the veranda roused my curiosity in a way which kept my fear in check. What were their bigger plans if I agreed to help them? Did they really think a teenage girl could be taken seriously as an ambassador? What would happen to their lofty ambition when I refused to participate?

My feet met up with the emblem carved into the granite floor. I dropped my gaze from Nekronok and company long enough to recognize that it was the same shape I'd noticed seared into the fur of some of the Trolls. In fact, it was the same shape as the setting on Nekronok's crown. It reminded me of mountains, or teeth, something sharp and zigzagged. Still, I couldn't say for sure what it represented.

A hollow *boom* resonated from the recesses of the stage to my left. A large drum had been struck. The crowd behind and beneath me fell silent.

"Sadie Larcen." A familiar voice spoke my name from the back of the platform.

Chebar drilled me with his dark eyes as he crossed the stage, stopping front and center. Like his father, he gripped a gilded scepter, holding it at an angle across his tawny-brown body. His stern face held no recognition of the clandestine experiences we shared on my first visit. Not surprising since anything he did on behalf of the queen would cost him his life. Chebar was a mole living among the sewer rats of the Eldritch.

He also wore a shimmery purple cape edged with gold rope and matching drawstring pants—sans tunic. On his head stood something akin to the tall hats worn by the Pope, made from stiff gold fabric inset with jewels. He looked ridiculous, but the penetrating gaze he directed my way snuffed out any humor.

Two enormous, bowl-shaped pits flanked Chebar. Their appearance echoed the wide mouthed bowls in the preparation room, but these two were easily five feet across. One bowl brimmed with water; the other held hot coals. A bearded, shrunken creature stood on the far side of the smoldering coals and prodded them into a heap with a metal poker. I instantly recognized him to be the two-timing Leprechaun, Skoon—thief and blabbermouth from our first trip. I imagined myself roasting him over the coals like a marshmallow on the end of that poker. He studied me with an impish grin, and I glared back.

"As Overlord of the Elements, it is my duty to confer on you the elements of fire and water, or the elements of air and earth." Chebar turned and bowed toward his father, who now stood in front of his throne. "At your command, O Worshipful Master, I will begin administering the Rites of Devotion."

On my right, Nekronok took long, deliberate strides to the rail overlooking the horde below.

The frenetic crowd behind me, now favored with his

attention, began to chant, "Nek-ro-nok! Nek-ro-nok!" I remembered that same mantra from the last time I lay tied and helpless on the battlefield.

The chief raised his scepter and peered down at the crowd with a self-satisfied smile. He looked so smug and full of himself that I wanted to shove him overboard.

The chanting quieted. The mob's crazy anticipation penetrated the air as they waited for their revered tyrant to speak.

"Regardless of the outcome of the Ceremony of the Elements...today the United Dynasty of Thrall shall make history!"

The United Dynasty of Thrall? Seriously?

The masses grunted and snorted and cheered their approval. Nekronok turned to the other dignitaries and raised his scepter. Malagruel and the turban-headed Dark Dwarf joined the Troll at the railing, much to the deranged delight of those below. Nekronok and Malagruel faced each other, grasping one another's shoulders with their right hands. They bowed slightly, foreheads close to touching. Malagruel's tail took the opportunity to slither toward me and hiss, fangs bared.

Nekronok repeated the gesture with the Stygian, then returned his attention to the crowd and waited for silence. "With symbolic timing, we launch our foray onto the world stage. This ceremony will officially declare our refusal to silently submit to the tenants of the Land of Legend any longer. It manifests our first step toward world domination. Today, we have King Brock's sister. Tomorrow...the sword!"

The throng launched into a maniacal cheer. Nekronok soaked it in for a moment then raised his hands. "This ceremony serves as a milestone in our relationship with those topside. Whether it proceeds for better or for worse lies in the choice made by the maiden Sadie Larcen." The overgrown, over-egoed ape pointed at me but continued to stare out at his adoring fans.

Shouts and cheers and a few snarls of disapproval, swelled from the masses. Thankfully, I faced away from the creepy crowd.

He hushed the creatures again. "Let us enter this next phase of our alliance with solemn anticipation." He glanced at the Gargoyle and the Styg. "Let the Ceremony of the

Elements begin."

The three returned to their seats. Nekronok remained standing, holding his scepter toward his sixth son, Chebar.

Boom.

My heartbeat walloped in response to the drum, which seemed to wake my senses from isolation. Chebar raised his staff toward his father.

I felt small and vulnerable, like a speck of unwanted dirt. Although I hoped Chebar had some sort of plan B—still having no idea what plan A might entail—I also knew he could not risk exposure.

Perhaps I was the collateral damage they talk about in war movies. Expendable.

Boom.

Another thump on the drum, and Chebar lowered the scepter so that it crossed his chest again. He lifted his free hand toward me. "Kneel before the Overlord of the Elements."

I lowered myself onto trembling knees. My gaze locked with his, probing for a sign of recognition. Inky marbles looked through me in response.

Any hope of a plan B evaporated.

"Sadie Larcen, a generous offer from his Worshipful Master Nekronok and Prince Malagruel was extended to you, which you refused." Chebar sounded cold and biting. "You are hereby ordered to cooperate and pledge your devotion, or suffer the consequences of insubordination."

He lowered his hand and extended the scepter in its place. "Rise and make your choice: fire and water, or air and earth."

Boom.

I stood, unable to disguise my quivering limbs. "The choices have not been explained." Miraculously, my voice came out steady and strong, even a bit defiant. I grasped the charm around my neck. Though I didn't believe in luck, I was glad for the reminder that God had plans for my life.

Chebar leveled his deadpan gaze on me. "You will be branded by fire and cooled by water—or surrendered to the air and succumbed to the earth. Devotion or death. You choose."

It was then that I noticed that the end of his staff sported the etched symbol at my feet. His scepter was an ornate branding iron.

I swallowed.

Chebar walked to the bowl of white-hot coals and plunged the end of the staff beneath them. The hiss made Skoon jump back.

Chebar looked at me. "You are ordered to turn and walk to the ledge between the railings to contemplate your decision. When the drum strikes three times, the scepter will be ready. I shall walk toward you, prepared to place the mark of loyalty on your shoulder. But if you decide to remain dissociated from the United Dynasty of Thrall, you shall step off the edge, into the air, and plunge to your death. Devotion or destruction. Choose carefully."

Boom.

The first strike of the drum had expired before I even turned toward the railing. My mind reeled while unsteady legs moved me into the space between the bannisters. The restless crowd whispered and gestured at me, but the only thing that registered was the giant chasm below, ready to swallow me and spit me out on to the rocks. I could now see that the large veranda on which the monster mob stood was actually two separate semi-circles, with a wide gap between. That gap would be my trajectory—if I jumped.

In that mingling sensation of panicked thoughts and surreal emotions, I rehearsed the reasoning laid out for me by Malagruel disguised as my father. In the span between drumbeats, I thought about the history of this secret realm and the connection it had with my family. The Garden of Eden, the sovereignty of God, the freewill of man, and the bondage of the will. Every theological term seemed to converge on my brain. Did I actually have a choice...or had the choice been made for me by my being placed in this situation?

Boom.

Rather than leaving me in a state of confusion—for I certainly had little grasp of such lofty subjects—an inexplicable calm washed over me. Whatever the reason, this situation was far beyond my ability to grasp. It would be laughable to try. Looking out from the heights of the Eldritch and seeing the primitive settlement of Craventhrall in the distance below, I tried not to think about willing myself to step off the ledge. The only thing I knew was what I could not do.

I could not pledge my loyalty to Nekronok and his

nefarious plan.

Boom.

"It is time to choose," Chebar said from behind. "Whom will you serve? His Worshipful Master, Chief Nekronok and the greater good of the Tethered World? Will you boldly advance into the future with the United Dynasty of Thrall? Or will you die serving yourself and clinging to your narrow ideals?" His voice grew in volume, and I could tell that he approached as he spoke.

I looked at the wicked leaders that sat on my left, watching my torturous predicament with pleasure. Malagruel's reptilian tail swiveled between his legs and flicked its tongue at me.

"Think about it, Miss Larcen," Nekronok called. "You can make history with us," he gestured toward the miscreants beside him, "or die standing for a secret family history the world knows nothing about." He nodded in a condescending way. "Though you may, in the end, have a touching and respectable obituary."

Heat radiated from the branding iron. It skimmed my shoulder and warmed my cheek. I stared out at the expanse of nothingness that was to be my destiny. I prayed that I wouldn't scream but die bravely, standing for what is right.

"You either jump from the ledge into oblivion, or kneel down and brace yourself for the cleansing seal of devotion to a new age in the Tethered World."

Despite the calm that hovered around me, as invisible and real as the air itself, my pulse thudded in my ears and amplified the wounds on my cheekbone. My forehead prickled with perspiration.

This is it.

Though I expected some deep revelation or poignant, final thoughts, my brain felt numb. Unplugged.

"Choose now," Chebar barked, authoritative and fierce. "If you do not willingly kneel or jump, I shall push you to your death with this searing scepter of justice when the drum is struck a fourth and final time."

He sounded so hateful.

Then in a barely audible whisper he breathed, "*Jump.*"

Had I imagined that?

I dipped one foot into the air, as if testing invisible water. I brought it back to the ledge, and then...I jumped.

CHAPTER TWENTY-THREE

BRADY TWISTED AGAINST THE HAND THAT covered his face. He *had* to urge Brock to run for help. Instead, his brother searched the shadows with bewildered eyes, trying to make sense of the commotion. Brock's karate training prompted him to strike at the intruder, but the shoulder-width corridor made it a useless gesture.

At last, Brady opened his mouth enough to get a toothy chomp on the fingers pressed against his face. The hand slipped away with a shriek from behind, though a wiry arm held Brady in a headlock.

"Run! Jump out and get helfff." Brady's words were smothered out.

Brock popped the frame open and disappeared.

Brady couldn't get his footing. His captor dragged him backward, the darkness swallowing up their contentious tango. The narrow passage closed in, serving to press the confining arm tighter when Brady writhed against it. Breathing became difficult behind the clammy hand that smelled faintly of skunk. His mind raced for a solution. Even if he had his sword, he couldn't wield it without risking his own limbs.

It was so blasted dark! How could his kidnapper maneuver through the passageway without bumping the occasional obstacle? The black void encompassed everything, including which way was up.

At long last, the constraining walls fell away, and Brady sensed they'd entered a cavernous space. His captor hesitated, which gave Brady the opportunity to stabilize his feet beneath himself. Brady straightened his legs while simultaneously grabbing the arm beneath his neck with both hands. He bent forward with a thrust. His assailant flipped over Brady's back but retained the headlock, bringing Brady down with him. The two wrestled in the dark. Brady flailed and grappled blindly. His opponent, it seemed, landed every fist right where it hurt.

One particular jab bounced Brady's head off the stone ground. His brain went as black as the darkness surrounding him.

A wretched stench brought Brady back to his senses, gagging, followed by a headache of monstrous proportions. His face felt fat. Swollen. His right eye swelled so badly it obstructed his view.

But he could see! Faintly, at least. Anything beat the all-consuming black hole from earlier. Taking inventory, however, intensified his fears. His hands were lashed together above his dangling, heavy head. His kidnapper pulled him along by the rope that bound his wrists. Brady's ankles were held by another restraint. His legs were submerged in something wet, leaving him bone cold. It smelled like sewage. Sewage and vomit. Brady gagged and retched from the odor, turning his head awkwardly to expel.

Using light to his advantage—and dim light at that—he tried to make sense of things. Tilting his head back gave him an upside down view of his captor. He worked to interpret what he saw. Not a Troll. Not a Dark Dwarf. Not an Ogre.

Not human.

Brady had never seen such a creature. But the ebony hide that glinted in the dismal light left him with an educated guess. "Where are you taking me, ya big ugly Gargoyle?"

The dredging stopped. Brady plopped into the muck with a sickening splash and fresh jolt to the head. The Gargoyle straddled him and grasped Brady's neck, lifting him out of the disgusting brew. Yellow eyes glared fiendishly into Brady's own. Unblinking, reptilian eyes with black-slitted pupils.

"Good. You're awake. This will be more easily accomplished without your deadweight." He hauled Brady to his feet by means of Brady's neck. "*Walk*."

Brady coughed when the Gargoyle's lanky fingers released him. The brute stood no taller than Brady, but the Gargoyle's excessive strength trumped anyone Brady's size.

He shoved Brady's shoulder and sent him spinning into the sewage face first. Brady caught himself with his elbows, groaning from the impact.

The Gargoyle yanked him up by the collar. "You stinking human! Look at you." The creature walked around until he faced him again. A shaft of the dim light fell across his face, highlighting scaly skin, a sloped forehead, and a snub nose with a slit for nostrils. This dude was a walking, talking snake. "Filthy excuse for a king. Now move it."

The creature grabbed a loop on the rope around Brady's wrists and dragged him like a dog on a leash. This time Brady stumble-stepped to keep up. The rope around his ankles had enough slack for him to take small, rapid steps.

So...he thinks I'm Brock. Brady doubted the Gnomes planned on using him for Brock's body double quite this soon.

They tromped through the sludge in silence. Brady tried not to think about the reality of walking through a sewage system—or how much of it managed to splash into his various orifices. He assumed they were under the streets of Vituvia, traveling through enormous aqueducts that connected to the castle. Intermittent, perforated holes in the ceiling allowed a stale ray of light to seep into the darkness. With no body of water nearby that Brady knew of, he wondered where the gunk eventually ended up.

His captor stopped at an intersection of several tunnels, studying each shadowed option with a flick of his tongue. His *forked* tongue. Brady shuddered and stared into the nearby sludge where a gleam of light fell onto the brown surface. He absentmindedly studied the vibrations that disturbed the top of the water. The ripples grew, and a distant thrumming jerked Brady out of his stupor.

The Gargoyle appeared to have the same revelation. He stiffened and glanced at Brady. Water! Rushing water, likely headed their way.

"We need to get out." Brady hoped the Gargoyle would

agree.

"I know. Shut up and follow me."

They went through the closest opening. The snake-man hurried, either oblivious or indifferent to Brady's captive state. Brady lost his footing and careened into the sewage again, eyes and mouth squeezed as tight as possible.

"Get up!" The Gargoyle continued on without him.

Brady struggled to get his tied legs beneath him in the slippery slime. By the time he tottered to his feet the creature had returned.

"Wrong tunnel." He grasped the rope, and they trudged back to the intersection.

The churning, charging water sounded uncomfortably close. They sloshed into the next tunnel, which looked exactly like the other. How could this creature know which one was correct?

Behind them, the water pounded. Brady's heart hammered equally hard, urging him on. He found he could manage a faster pace if he walked on his tiptoes.

A crash from behind told him that the expulsion of water now converged into their tunnel. Thankfully, the Gargoyle seemed intent on getting out *with* his victim.

"Blast it! We're not going to make it waiting on you." The creature scooped Brady over his shoulder with ease.

Brady instinctively recoiled. Despite the relief of moving faster, he didn't like the idea of pressing his face against the beast's scaly back. The musky, skunk-like odor assaulted his nose.

The Gargoyle took on speed, jostling Brady with each footfall. The surging flood spewed mist onto Brady's face. He craned his neck, trying to glimpse the distance. Ten yards, perhaps?

His captor stuttered to a stop and dropped him. "Get up, I can't carry you out." He yelled to be heard over the roaring wall of water, yanking Brady's rope to expedite the process.

A faint glow radiated from a sizable opening ahead, while a providential shaft of light illuminated precariously narrow steps carved into a ledge in the side of the tunnel. The Gargoyle easily scaled the first few, pulling Brady along with unnatural strength.

The stairs were slick, and Brady's feet failed to find purchase. He slipped and dangled off the side. The Gargoyle cursed but held fast. Frothing water drizzled Brady from head to toe, the tsunami closing in. With a fierce grunt he curled his legs against the rock face. The Gargoyle struggled up another step causing Brady to swivel toward the liquid locomotive.

He had barely enough time to take a deep breath before water and darkness consumed him.

CHAPTER TWENTY-FOUR

FREE-FALLING TRUMPS ROLLER COASTERS IN their fear factor any day. The rocky surface of Mount Thrall blurred past my flailing body. A whoosh of air inflated my lungs and made breathing difficult. The ground approached at a ghastly speed, magnifying one coherent thought: *I can't believe this is how it ends.*

My consciousness wavered.

"Hello, Princess." My skydiving nightmare came to an immediate and unexpected halt.

Disbelief zinged through my senses. Prince Xander had caught me in his hulking arms. His ebony braids, charcoal cape, and silvery wings billowed like flags of freedom as he maneuvered away from the Eldritch. Indignant shouts from the disappointed crowd faded into the distance.

I clung to my Nephilim superhero, squealing with joy and relief. My real-life guardian angel. I spied Gage, Commander General of the army of Calamus, trailing at a distance.

Four flying Gargoyles rapidly approached. Malagruel led the flock of these fiendish birds of prey.

I would have to relish my extraordinary rescue later. "Xander, hurry. Gargoyles!"

The loathsome lizards hurtled our way. Sword in one hand, claws extended on the other, Malagruel matched our speed and then some. Xander shot toward the foothills surrounding Mount Thrall, his wings undulating in powerful arcs, seemingly unaffected by my added weight. My pulse continued to rattle my chest at Mach speed.

Over Xander's shoulder, I watched Gage run interference. He made a sweeping circle toward the Gargoyle at the back of the pack. The creature veered into his path but Gage, quite literally, somersaulted above him through the air. With his sword, the Nephilim timed a forceful whack on the Gargoyle's wing mid-somersault, severing it from his body. The big bat spiraled down, unable to control his direction. His screech alerted the others while he lost altitude.

Malagruel continued to pursue Xander and me. I held my breath, willing Xander to greater speeds. The other two Gargoyles turned their fury on Gage. The seasoned warrior pulled up short, treading the air with his wings. He held his ground—or airspace—with lithe, martial art skills deflecting the two flying demons.

The gap between Malagruel and us continued to shrink. "Faster." My tense body stiffened even more. "He's getting close."

We flew into the countryside surrounding Craventhrall. The Trolls' village sat in a valley surrounded by rolling hills, hemmed on one side by Mount Thrall. The lower knolls morphed into a ring of foothills that stretched up into jagged cliffs. Xander needed to turn, or gain altitude, or we would go out like Kamikazes.

Xander opted for swinging wide and curving back in the direction of Gage. I twisted around to view the two-on-one fight. One gristly Gargoyle received a lobotomy. The other took a stab at Gage but met with the metallic clank of the warrior's sword. Repulsed by the carnage, I buried my head into Xander's neck only to pull away, self-conscious.

A black blur approached Xander's side. Malagruel's glinting gaze focused on me, oozing hatred. Fear detonated through my insides. Had my life been spared only to end moments later at the hands of this beast?

"Xander, nine o'clock."

My guardian angel barrel rolled. I screamed. He pulled up short. The Gargoyle shot beneath us and Xander flew in the opposite direction. It didn't take long for the monster to redirect himself. Meanwhile, I had the pleasure of seeing Gage take down the third blackbird. Though not a fan of violence, I found an acquired taste for it under the threat of death.

Gage extended his sword and gained on Malagruel—who continued to gain on us.

"Hurry." I dug anxious fingers into Xander's back. My erratic heartbeat throbbed in my ears.

The Gargoyle foamed at the mouth and snarled, pouring on speed. He was so hyper-focused on us, he didn't notice Gage swooping in from above. Gage managed to catch the tip of Malagruel's wing with his sword.

The oversized bat spun around, out of control. He righted himself and charged at Gage, weapon swinging. But Gage anticipated it. He blocked the blow, but not before Malagruel's other hand clawed across the soldier's forearm. Gage cried out and landed a well-placed kick on the enemy's ribcage.

The Gargoyle swiveled and came back around with sword flattened. Gage ducked. The bat overshot, off kilter. Gage took advantage of the miss and sliced clean through Malagruel's snake-tail.

I cheered to see that nightmarish viper nose-dive into oblivion. This sent the Gargoyle into a lather, and he screeched after Gage, bleeding profusely. Xander swooped lower, and I lost my direct line of sight. Treetops rose around me as my rescuer came to a soft landing in a scrubby space between trees.

"Sit here, Princess." He placed me against ancient, twisted vines that encircled a massive trunk. "Don't move."

He zoomed away, sword drawn. Through the boughs of the tree I only caught snatches of the assault. Two-against-one seemed like odds I could bet on. In fact, the Gargoyle retreated in a hurry once Xander showed up minus one human being to lug around. The bat flew back toward Mount Thrall and the Nephilim prince, and his commander touched down in front of me.

Xander brushed his hands together several times. "I think we're rid of that vermin. Maybe for good. Gage gouged through his wing and dismembered his tail. I embellished his wings with a few perforations of my own."

The adrenaline buzz subsided, and my ribcage roared back to life. Though I'd been blissfully unaware of it while we streaked across the sky, Xander had squeezed me good and tight while he dodged the demon. I bit my lip and drew deep breaths through my teeth, not wanting to complicate things further.

Gage wiped his sword on a large patch of weeds. "Don't care to have Banished blood tainting my weapon."

"Here. You better put pressure on that wound." Xander

tore a strip of cloth from his cape and wrapped the bleeding claw marks etched across Gage's left arm. near the wrist. They looked deep and painful.

I turned away from the gash, tired of the brutality. "Thank you. Thank you both." I tried to mask a painful gasp. "I'm in total shock that I'm not smashed to smithereens at the foot of the Eldritch. That was miraculous timing."

The two giants knelt on either side of me. They continued to heave from the exertion, glistening with sweat, their wings now folded beneath their capes, out of sight. Xander's dark skin melded with his dark clothes and leather armor, reminding me of a muscular, chiseled rock. The weathered, freckle-flecked arms and pale skin of Gage would never offer much camouflage in the landscape of the Tethered World— especially against his charcoal uniform and silver chain mail. But both made me feel like a frightened animal that had found refuge between two stalwart boulders.

"Well, thank the Maker for such miracles." Xander examined his sword then stabbed it into the dirt. "And for Chebar, who alerted us to your predicament."

"What?" I stiffened against the tree, incredulous. "So he *did* intervene." I slumped again. "Wow. I knew he couldn't blow his cover, so I figured I might be expendable, y'know? But at the last second, I thought I heard him say *jump*. Everything happened so fast, I just—wow—it's hard to process."

Xander placed a hand on my shoulder. "You will never be expendable. That's preposterous."

An awful rush of warmth flooded my face. The extra blood caused the burns on my cheek to throb, reminding me of how dreadful I must look. My fingers flew to the wounds, and I mumbled an embarrassed, "Thanks."

Xander pulled my hand away and kept it clasped in his fingers. "Ever since Chebar returned to Craventhrall, he and Wogsnop have secretly shared information. Chebar gave the Dwarf several possible scenarios you may have had to face in captivity. Wogsnop alerted Calamus and Vituvia. The Gnomes sent Reiko, Mighty, and a few others to the Eldritch—on the lookout for such developments."

Xander nodded at Gage. "Guess you could say that Gage and I were only there in case all other options failed." His thumb rubbed small circles on the top of my hand that seemed to match the tempo of my pulse. "And, obviously, the other opportunities never presented themselves, so here we are." His crystalline eyes searched my face. "Now tell me what those monsters did to you."

I slipped my hand from his grasp—fearing I'd give him false hope, fearing I might take a helping of it myself—and folded them in my lap. The memories made me shudder. "That last Gargoyle you chased away tried to deceive me. He enchanted me or something. When I wouldn't cooperate he roughed me up. Nekronok helped."

I turned away, tasting bile.

"I cannot believe the Banished are returning to the Land of Legend." Xander punched a massive fist into his other palm. "As much I dislike the Trolls, I would never have guessed that they'd work with those devils. No one in the last several generations has had any dealings with them. Many assumed they were extinct."

"Did you?" I studied his brave face.

Xander's eyes narrowed. He shook his head. "No, not entirely. The idea made me feel better, especially when I was young. But knowing their history and being in line for the throne, I've had to assume they still lurked in the recesses of the Tethered World and could pose a threat one day. There have been rumors of travelers coming across Gargoyles in the hinterlands, but those tales usually came from less-than-stellar citizens with a weakness for gourds of ale."

"But a soldier should never underestimate their possible enemies." Gage raked calloused fingers through his graying, red hair.

"Exactly."

"That last one you chased away calls himself Prince Malagruel. He's working with Nekronok on some sort of plan to connect the underground world with life topside—after they take possession of the sword, of course. They wanted to force me to cooperate. To be their ambassador."

Gage scoffed. "A prince, eh? I doubt it." He tightened the bandage across his hand. A dark stain steadily blossomed across the fabric. "They're grasping for something way out of reach. There's a reason we've all survived for thousands of years here. The system works."

"The rest of the Tethered World is not going to stand for such insubordination. They've either overestimated their own prowess or underestimated their enemy." Prince Xander shifted closer. "What else did they say? Do you feel up to talking about it?"

Great question. What *did* I feel? "I'd rather wait and tell everyone at once." I shuddered. "It's not something I want to keep repeating."

Xander smiled understandingly with his eyes. "Of course. What matters is that we have you back. Safely."

I sighed and relaxed against the tree. "I'm seriously amazed that I'm alive." I shook my head. "All thanks to you two and Chebar. Now, I only want to get back to Berganstroud and Aunt Jules and eat. A lot."

The warrior prince stood and gave me a chivalrous bow. "Your wish is my command, Princess Sadie." He extended his hand and helped me to my feet. "Anything for you. Even food."

CHAPTER TWENTY-FIVE

MY AIR-TAXI TOUCHED DOWN IN the courtyard of the fortress at Berganstroud. Grateful relief made my knees buckle and I hit the ground. It swept like a powerful, emotional undertow, draining away the anxiety that had wired me for days. It left me exhausted and ready to hibernate like a bear.

Xander knelt beside me, his hand on the small of my back. "You okay?"

I nodded and considered kissing the ground—but didn't have the energy to explain such a topside gesture. My legs refused to straighten, and I remained crouched in the middle of the courtyard among the antiquated weapons. Wasn't I the latest relic from a battle? *Guess I'll make myself at home. No need to get up.*

Guards shouted orders. The massive wood and iron doors opened, and Dwarves flooded the courtyard. Lava was first to reach my side. In my stooped position, he easily placed a protective arm around my shoulders. "Oh, thank the Maker you've returned." He brushed hair away from my face. "How's my brave—roots and fruits! What happened here?" His fingers alighted on my cheek. "Let's get you to the doctor, m' lady."

I gave the stalwart man a feeble pat on the back. "I'm fine."

"Sadie." Xander still crouched on my other side. "You need to have that looked at."

I nodded, slow and deliberate. My head felt stuffed with cotton. "I will. Give me a chance to get my bearings." I straightened with measured care. "The adrenaline rush has officially evaporated."

Against my will, my legs gave out again, and I crumpled against the prince. He swept me up in one fluid motion. "Take us to the doctor."

"Out of the way, mates!" Lava bellowed orders.

I floated through the crowded corridors of Berganstroud in Xander's arms.

Dwarves milled about and eyed our mismatched group with a mix of curiosity and relief. Tension felt thick and oppressive.

Lying on an examination table made it hard to stay awake. I morphed into one of those dolls whose eyes automatically close when you tilt them back.

Lava went to fetch Doc Keswick, while Xander and Gage conferred in the corner of the room, hands clasped behind their backs, heads together. I wondered if Uncle Daniel was improving and hoped Aunt Jules would come by and tell me everything.

"Well, well! I hear *somebody* had quite an adventure at the haunted house down the street." Doc Keswick's booming voice startled me.

I grinned.

"I don't find that humorous." Xander stepped beside me.

The doctor raised an eyebrow. "Hoping to lighten the mood, Your Highness."

"Besides, it was funny." I chuckled.

Doc started doing his thing, listening to my heart, looking at my pupils. He inspected the wounds on my face and let out a low whistle.

Lava came back with Wogsnop and Smarlow in tow. The room felt cramped. Nothing like getting examined in front of a crowd. While wearing a burlap toga, I might add.

"All right, everyone's here." Keswick stepped back and crossed his bulky arms. "Normally I'd tell the powers-that-be to leave you alone until you've properly recovered. But since you appear stable..." He coughed and mumbled into his fist. He snapped his head up and winked. "And since I've been told how to do my job, go ahead and spit it out. Starting with those burns on your face. I can treat them while you give us a rundown of the last eight days."

"*Eight days?*" I sat up. "I've been gone *eight days?*"

"Yep." Nods from around the room confirmed it.

I eased back and pinched the bridge of my nose. "That's hard to fathom." I shook my head in denial. "Though, in some ways, I feel like I've been gone a month, but—wow—that's crazy. The first few days are a total blur, so I guess that makes sense."

The doctor pulled jars and tubes off the shelf against the wall. He had a small propane tank and Bunsen burner that he lit beneath a pot of water. "And those burn marks? You were about to tell me how you got them." He dumped a vial of liquid into the water. It turned gray.

"Yeah." My fingers sought the swollen, tender spots near my left temple. "They're from some sort of snake venom."

The faces around me contorted with a mixture of confusion and concern.

"Do you know what species?" Doc Keswick crossed back to me and zeroed in on the wounds.

"Actually, I don't even know if it was a real snake."

"Meaning?"

"Meaning...it happened to be attached to something." I glanced to where Xander leaned against the wall. "A Gargoyle."

Lava and Wogsnop took a step toward me, disbelief plainly on their faces. The Gnomes mumbled something to each other in frantic whispers.

"The snake was actually the tail of a Gargoyle." I shivered. "It wrapped around me, like a rope, literally tying me up. It-it spoke to me." Tears came tumbling down again. I wasn't ready to talk about the ordeal but needed to push aside my feelings for the sake of everyone's safety.

Smarlow marched to where the Nephilim stood. "What do you two know about this?" He jabbed a tiny finger at the mountainous men.

Xander gave the squat Gnome an amused smirk. "I know we maimed or killed four of the beasts. What's your little problem, Smarlow?"

Wrong thing to say.

Smarlow put his hand on the hilt of his sword. "You really want to go there, ya big bird? A quick slash at your Achilles will put you out of commission and take you down like Goliath."

"Gentlemen!" Wogsnop spun to face them. "Let's not allow the enemy to divide us without even being present. Be civil. That's an order."

"Maybe our enemy is disguised as an angel." Smarlow still had his hand on his weapon.

"What's that supposed to mean?" Xander no longer looked amused.

"Enough!" Wogsnop ordered.

The doctor blocked my view, examining my face again.

"It didn't bite me. Something dripped from its fangs."

"Colonel Smarlow, another word out of you, and I'll ask you to leave." I heard the frustrated footfalls of Wogsnop cross the room. All I could see was the salt-and-pepper beard and nostril hairs of the doctor. He tilted his head back and squinted at my face through his glasses. Not the best of views, so I closed my eyes.

"The peace of our realm, of life as we've known it, is in jeopardy, Commander." Rage seeped through Smarlow's words. "Don't you think it's the least bit unusual that the Nephilim have developed a sudden interest in aligning themselves with us?"

"We've always been aligned with you." Xander's voice boomed and startled me. "Is your memory as short as your stature? We lost men right alongside you in the last battle."

"How dare—"

"Smarlow, I meant what I said. *Leave.*" Wogsnop sounded livid.

The doctor stepped back to the counter. Smarlow strode to the door. He turned, hands balled into fists. "Think about it, Wogsnop. Since when have the Nephilim been concerned enough to insert themselves into the affairs of others in the Land of Legend? And why now?"

"Smarlow, there's been no reason to involve ourselves with anything for several hundred years." Xander massaged his forehead, looking weary of the conversation. "Things have been relatively peaceful."

"We've come to your people in difficult times." Smarlow's face bloomed red. "You've always acted too high and mighty, quite literally, for the likes of us." He glared at Xander like he was every inch his match. "Now, suddenly, you take pity on us? And at roughly the same time as the Banished dare to show their devilish faces again?"

"It would seem like the ideal time to lend our might to the cause. You need us more than ever."

"Maybe. Or maybe you've really joined forces to subvert the cause." Smarlow raised an accusing finger at the Prince. "After all, they're *your* distant cousins."

CHAPTER TWENTY-SIX

BRADY SPEWED WATER, GASPING FOR AIR with greedy, desperate gulps. The dawning reality of life—his life—being spared settled on him with astonishment. He blinked and looked around without moving his aching head.

Bright light made him squint, reminding him he also had a swollen eye. He saw that his kidnapper—and, ironically, his rescuer—moved about near the narrow slice of light up ahead. The Gargoyle's silhouette sat crouched, head close to the ground. Brady guessed the creature must be looking out from the inside of a cave.

If only he had the energy to run, or attack, or do something brilliant and bold. But his limbs were still bound, and he felt like a waterlogged mop—though at least he was no longer coated in sewage. He wondered if the Gargoyle would have allowed him to drown had he known Brady wasn't the high king.

Water trickled somewhere in the distance behind him. The silhouette approached.

"Time to get moving." He yanked Brady up by the arm and shoved him roughly toward the entrance.

Brady stumbled but managed to stay upright. Thankfully, the Gargoyle had lengthened the slack between his ankles. The entrance to the cave reminded Brady of a gaping mouth. Holding the rope, his captor slid between the lips of rock. Brady followed, blinking at the golden-hue visible between the branches of a willow tree that draped like a curtain in front of the opening.

Two heaps of cloth near the base of the tree made Brady step back in alarm. Two Gnomes. Dead. Their necks unnaturally twisted.

"D-did you do that?" Brady pointed a shaky finger.

"How do you think I got in? Now move." He pointed in the direction opposite of Vituvia, which Brady spotted about a mile away. "The fire has provided a distraction. But they'll soon be scouring the countryside for their little boy king."

The Gargoyle kept to the shadows along the foothills. Brady wondered if there were other caves that led underground, which would make it harder to distinguish which one they escaped from. He noticed their feet left prints in the dirt. Good. Although dusk would be arriving soon, making them difficult to track.

"Where did all that water come from?" Brady asked.

"Underground aquifer." He jerked on the rope. "No more questions."

Brady was left to ruminate to himself. It sounded like the fire was a means to an end. *His* end—or Brock's anyway. Which meant the Gnome who brought them to the hiding place behind the painting must be in on the subterfuge. Rotten backstabber. Still, the Gnome knew which of the twins were Brock. Did he intend for Brady to be nabbed instead? Last minute change of heart?

Too many questions, Brady decided. He prayed desperately to stay alive long enough to see the answers come to light.

Smarlow stormed out of the hospital room, but his accusations against the Nephilim hung in the air like pollution. Xander and Gage looked tempted to chase down the hot-headed Gnome.

I was curiously confused. The Nephilim and the Banished...related?

"Forgive that impulsive, angry Gnome, Your Highness." Wogsnop gave Xander a curt bow. "I'm learning that he's quick to pop off his opinion, but he's a good warrior nonetheless."

Xander nodded, visibly decompressing. "Not that I don't

want to shake some sense into him, but we've got a bigger problem on our hands than short-tempered Gnomes. We fought four Gargoyles when we rescued Sadie. Gage managed to take out three and dismember the snake-tail that did this damage to her."

The pot of water above the Bunsen burner bubbled. Doc Keswick plopped a strip of cloth into the cloudy water then removed it with tongs. It steamed and dribbled back into the bowl.

"A problem indeed." Doc's round glasses fogged. "One to be solved with others better equipped for war than me. Now then, mind if we get back to the story at hand? Sadie needs rest." With another pair of tongs, the doctor squeezed the cloth then waved it a few times to cool.

"Of course. Or we can come back when she's feeling better." Xander's eyes flashed to my face and softened when they met mine. "Whatever is best for her."

"Thanks." I gave him a weak smile. "But I'd rather get it over with."

Wogsnop yawned. "Fact is, we're all tired. I appreciate you soldiering on. We need your information to assess the threat level."

"This will sting." Doc Keswick approached with the folded, sweltering cloth and pressed it against my wounds. "But you're obviously a tough wad of gum, so you'll survive."

I sucked in my breath, closing my eyes tight. After the initial sting, it felt soothing. "Wad of gum? Thanks. Dream come true."

He chuckled and flipped the cloth to a warmer spot.

"What did Smarlow mean," I asked through gritted teeth, "about the Nephilim and the Gargoyles being related?"

"A history lesson for another day." The doctor glanced at the Nephilim. "Such a ridiculous claim it barely qualifies as an insult. What we need is information about the present situation, if you please."

"Okay." Though my interest was piqued, I laid it aside and launched into my horror story. Beginning with Grimpenhauser dragging me from bed in a garbage sack, I ran through what I could remember about the last week— still in shock that I'd lost that amount of time. Between revelations of my kidnapper, contracting the virus, and Malagruel disguising himself as my father, everyone appeared shell shocked at one point or another.

Doc Keswick remained all business, disinfecting my wounds, assessing the last few signs of the virus, and applying ointment where needed.

"When I jumped from the heights of the Eldritch, I really thought it was the end," I concluded. "Until my guardian angel caught me in midair." My gaze met Xander's. A tear escaped. "You saved my life. Thank you." My voice came out in a raspy whisper, but he heard it and gave the subtlest of nods.

Gage shook his wounded hand like it was asleep.

"Oh my goodness. Gage! Your fingers." I pointed.

He quickly hid his arm behind his back. "It's nothing. I'll have it looked at when we return to Calamus."

"Nonsense, you're in a hospital. Let me see it." Doc Keswick walked over, hand extended expectantly.

My stomach fluttered, knowing that what I'd glimpsed had been much worse than I guessed my face to be.

All eyes drilled the old soldier. He stared back, non-compliant.

"Come on, Gage, let the doctor look." Xander nudged him. "That's an order."

Gage swallowed, his face revealing a deep dread as he brought his hand out from hiding.

The flesh extending past the bandage looked blackened and charred. His fingers like burnt hotdogs. The doctor removed the bandage. The incisions oozed an inky fluid that looked like poisoned blood. The top layer of skin closest to the cuts had turned white and flaky. The layers underneath were charcoal black—leathery looking like Malagruel himself—and extended into the surrounding skin, the color fading as it traveled up his arm.

I cringed at the gruesome sight but couldn't help but stare.

Doc let out a low whistle. He turned the Nephilim's massive hand, palm up. It was already a pasty grey.

"Though I've no experience treating Nephilim, I'm guessing this is *not* how your skin normally reacts to a wound?"

Gage seemed angered by the question, though it may have been more about the reality of his condition. His temple flexed with the set of his jaw. "I bleed red, exactly like you. Normally."

"Doc, may I speak to you outside?" Xander nodded at the doorway.

"Certainly."

"Anything you have to say can be said in front of me. I've seen the worst of battles and battle wounds. I can handle it." Gage spoke like the words tasted bitter.

"Really, Gage, it might be better to wait until—"

"Speak, Your Highness." His teeth were set.

Xander didn't appear intimidated. More like he was unsure how to say what needed to be said. Hands behind his back, it only took three enormous strides to walk to the other end of the room. He turned, opened his mouth, then closed it.

"*Xander.*" Gage dipped his head. "Your Grace. Don't spare my feelings. What is it?"

The deep olive skin on Xander's arms and face glistened with perspiration. He pressed his lips together. "As a dutiful prince who must know history—so Calamus is not doomed to repeat bad decisions—I've had to study the early accounts of our people."

He dropped his eyes to the ground and resumed his pacing. "It's true. There's a connection—albeit a very distant one—to the Banished." He looked at me. "You've heard the story, no doubt, in Genesis, in which the 'sons of God' bore children with 'the daughters of men.' Both the Gargoyles and the Nephilim are descendants of this line."

My skin tingled across my scalp, aware that I was hearing things of which topsiders have no knowledge.

"The children of these unions were strictly human in their abilities. In other words, they did not have access to the spiritual realm like their angelic ancestors. Yes, they were large and powerful—some even born with wings—but mortal in every other way."

He leaned against the wall. "Yet there were those that wanted to possess supernatural abilities. They turned to false gods and the dark arts. They tapped into forbidden magic and began to change into the devilish beings they sought out. Those wicked Nephilim transformed into the Banished. They were worshipped by some in Greece and, of course, the Druids. They became known as *Gargoyles* when Templars practiced their masonry rites and called them up from their banishment. They appeared in pagan ceremonies and became symbols that Masons replicated on their buildings or fountains. Dark powers that ruled over cities, even cathedrals."

Gage looked Xander up and down. "This isn't anything new."

Xander nodded. "Yes, that was for Sadie's benefit. But there are details you may not know—unless you were forced to learn them because your future kingdom may depend on such knowledge. There are several stories involving the Nephilim encountering the Banished. Those tales come with various endings. I don't know which ones are the truth because there's not been an occasion to find out for certain—until today."

"Let's hear it." Doc lifted Gage's arm for further inspection.

"One is that a wound from the Banished has the power to turn a Nephilim into stone. Like a statue of a Gargoyle. The other is...that it will eventually turn a Nephilim into a Gargoyle."

No one spoke. Gage took deep breaths of air.

"Of course, neither option is acceptable." Xander's voice was quiet and wavering. "Though I don't know which theory is true, I can say for certain that something is happening to your arm, my friend, and it must be stopped."

Gage looked pale and unsteady. He glanced at his graying arm. "And how, exactly, do we make it stop?"

Xander glanced at Doc Keswick, then back to his commander and friend. "There's only one certain remedy." He swallowed. "Amputation."

CHAPTER TWENTY-SEVEN

Many things happened at once. Gage flew into a rage at the preposterous idea of a one-armed soldier. Lava and Wogsnop dismissed themselves so they could speak to the council about the information I shared. Doc Keswick decided that Gage needed immediate surgery, as he could already see the grey flesh spreading.

He also declared me properly patched up and ordered me to bed. As I walked out the door, Doc sank a hypodermic needle into the neck of the frantic warrior while his commander-in-chief held him down.

The history lesson left me unsettled. The thought of a bunch of Gargoyles invading the Land of the Ancients—the portion of the Tethered World inhabited by the Nephilim—sounded like a Zombie apocalypse. Something worth preventing at all costs.

Back in my room, I eased onto the bed then realized I still wore the ridiculous toga outfit. Before I could scrounge some clothes from the wardrobe, Trinny bustled into the room.

"Princess Sadie." She curtsied then clasped her hands together. "Thank the Maker you're safe! We were worried sick. As you know, we've had enough sickness around here already. Now, how can I make you more comfortable?"

"Getting out of this crazy outfit for starters." I made a distasteful face. "Bad as I need a bath, I can barely keep my eyes open, so I'll worry about that tomorrow."

"Of course." Trinny rummaged through the folded tunics.

"Where's Aunt Jules? She'll be coming to bed soon, won't she?"

The Dwarf stiffened, then continued to look at the clothes, obviously ignoring me.

Uh-oh. "Well, won't she?"

She draped a mustard-colored pair of drawstring pants over her arm with a maroon tunic on top. Her movements were slow and deliberate.

A foreboding fist landed in my gut. I should be getting used to this feeling.

Trinny turned a somber gaze on me. Her silence blared a deafening alarm. Once she spoke, I knew I wouldn't like what she had to say. She extended the clothes to me. I laid them on the bed.

She licked her lips. "Aunt Jules is in Mr. McGriffin's room."

"O-*kay*. Not surprising."

"Your uncle is doing much better. Lady Jules has barely left his side, and he's responded to her presence quite favorably."

"But?" *Get to the point!*

"But your dear aunt has come down with the virus. She's ill. Terribly ill." The Dwarf kept her gaze on the floor.

"What?" My recent bout with the nasty virus sat fresh upon my list of things I wanted to annihilate. "Where? Take me to her." I pulled off the toga and worked my way into the tunic and pants, abandoning modesty.

"She's not to have any visitors." Trinny busied herself taking away the dirty dress. "She's in your uncle's room, since he's immune. But only Joanie and the Doc may go in or out, as they've been inoculated."

"But I've had the virus!" This suddenly became a *good* thing. "I'm immune too."

Her eyes grew round. She nodded. "Okay. Yes! I still need to check with Doc Keswick. He's given strict orders, and I dare say I'd get my head surgically removed if I make such a call myself." She pointed to a bowl of fruit and nuts on the bedside table. "Have something to eat, and I'll locate Doc and ask. Be back in a jiffy."

I sighed. "All right."

Trinny hurried out without closing the door.

Snatching an apple from the bowl, I stretched my legs across the bed and leaned against the wall. Exhaustion pressed down on every inch of my anatomy, but I needed to see Aunt Jules. Needed to assure myself that she would pull through. Mainly, of course, because I loved her. But a selfish corner of my mind needed to prove there was no way that fateful key would end up in my possession anytime soon.

The sound of footsteps and voices carried from down the hall. I stopped crunching my apple so I could make out what was going on.

"You can't just leave, Smarlow. We're in the middle of strategizing."

The footsteps stopped nearby. "I'm not leaving." That was Smarlow. "Not yet, anyway. I'm walking off steam. No one is taking my concerns seriously."

"Maybe because they're unfounded." I recognized Lava's frustrated voice. "Yer harpin' on the Nephilim seems quite an overreaction. They have shown they're loyal to us. We've no reason to be suspicious. There's enough to worry about with the Banished, Trolls, and Stygs gangin' up together."

"Exactly why what I said is not so far-fetched." Smarlow was losing volume, and the footsteps picked up again.

I slid from bed and crept to the door.

"Look, I'm asking you as my friend to keep your eyes open to the possibility. It's not completely outlandish."

Lava grunted. "Well, that depends who ya ask. Though I personally cannot fathom the two becomin' allies, there's been an awful lot of surprises of late, hasn't there? I promise not to rule anything out."

"That's all I want."

Their voices continued to recede, and I dared to creep down the hall after them. I wasn't normally an eavesdropper, but Smarlow's suspicions unsettled me. Especially in regards to Xander.

"If the Nephilim ever decide to switch their allegiance," Smarlow was saying, "we wouldn't stand a chance. We'd be surrounded by muscle on every side. The sword would be lost to the enemy."

"Perish the thought, my friend," Lava said.

The two turned the corner, and I tiptoed closer.

"No. Keep that thought at the forefront and stay watchful." Smarlow's voice was low and wary. "Or we all may perish."

CHAPTER TWENTY-EIGHT

"BREAKFAST!"

Someone was *way* too chipper for me, breakfast or not. I cracked an eyelid to see Trinny placing a tray on the nightstand. Wait...when had I gone to bed?

I sat up, trying to pinpoint my most recent memory.

"You're looking a mite better today." She picked up a metal cup. "Here, drink some water. Fluids are important to get you going again."

"Uh...I don't remember getting in bed. Did I collapse?"

"Oh yes, you collapsed, all right." She placed a fist on her hip. "In a heap in the hallway." She shook her head. "I came back after talking to Doc and found you crumpled on the ground. Scared me half to death."

"Oh." The memory of following Smarlow and Lava returned. I smacked my hand to my forehead. "Sorry about that. How did I get here?"

"No worries, dear. I ran to fetch help. Pop helped me get you to bed. Doc came by and took a look at ya. Said you were plumb tired, that's all."

"Pop? Who's that?" I took a big gulp of water.

"My father, Lava."

I blinked. "Lava is your dad?"

"Sure is." Trinny crossed to the fireplace.

"Oh, he's the best." I smiled. "I missed him and Joanie the most when we went home last time." The smell of biscuits became too much to ignore. I snatched one from the tray and let a bite melt in my mouth.

"He talked plenty about you too." She leaned on the fire poker and looked at me. "When Joanie couldn't tend to you because of all the patients flooding in, I jumped at the chance to help so I could get to know this topsider my father grew so fond of."

"I'm glad." I smeared the biscuit with jelly. "Not glad about the virus, of course, but glad to make a new friend."

Trinny blushed. "Never thought I'd meet a topsider, let alone call one a friend." Her eyes widened. "Roots and fruits! I need to stop visiting and let you get ready."

"Get ready?"

She swept the ashes and embers back into the fire. "Xander has orders to take you to your family in Calamus. Chief Wogsnop wants to put as much distance between you and the Eldritch as possible. And as soon as possible. Doc will be by in a few to look you—"

"Wait a minute." I held up my hands. "What family in Calamus?"

"Oh, no one thought to tell you, did they? We received word that your mum and sister were taken to Calamus. A safety measure."

No mention of Brady made me hopeful, for his sake, that he was permitted to stay in Vituvia. "Wow. Okay. Good to know."

She nodded and replaced the fireplace tools on their proper hooks then headed to the bathroom.

"What about Aunt Jules? I can't go anywhere until I see her."

Trinny turned from the doorway, her face somber. "I'm afraid you won't be permitted to, Miss Sadie. When I found you in the hallway yesterday, I was bringing back a very firm *no* from the doctor. I'm sorry."

She disappeared in the bathroom, and I could hear the water pump filling the tub.

We'll see about that. My eyes burned with tears. Tears that seemed too eager to flow these days. I'd never been a crier so this was becoming a source of irritation. But not nearly as irritating as the helplessness I felt in regards to Aunt Jules. I *had* to see her. Wanted to assure her that I was okay and confirm that she would be okay.

Trinny must have sensed my displeasure. She left clean clothes on the foot of the bed and excused herself.

A warm bath worked like a tonic on my nerves. Every ounce of the Eldritch was scrubbed from my body—with extra care taken around ribs and goose eggs. The burns on my cheekbone felt better. I hadn't given them a thought since I woke. Nor had I looked at them yet.

When I finished bathing, I leaned into the cloudy, old-fashioned mirror to inspect the damage. They looked better than expected. Two oblong sores that were starting to scab over.

Before I finished changing, someone knocked. "Hang on." I threw on my tunic and swished water in my mouth. *What I wouldn't do for a toothbrush.* I settled for sucking on a hunk of cinnamon bark which, surprisingly, did a decent job of refreshing my mouth. Joanie swore by it.

I opened the door to Doc Keswick's smart-aleck smirk. Trinny stood beside him, carrying the doctor's bag.

"Taking a vacation, I hear." He stuffed his hands into the pockets of his lab coat.

"Is that what you call it?" I opened the door wide and stepped aside. "I thought I was being forced to leave against my will."

Trinny busied herself making the bed while the doctor poked and prodded and made curious noises. "Mmm-hmm. Ahh. Oh, yes." Dark circles framed his eyes behind his spectacles.

"Since I've had the virus, I'd like to know why you've refused my request to see Aunt Jules." I winced as the doctor smudged ointment on my scabs.

The amused look on his face made me feel like he wasn't taking me seriously. I stepped back and folded my arms. "I'm not going anywhere, with anyone, until you grant my request to see her."

"Is that what this is? A *request*?"

"Hey, it's not like you're Mr. Thesaurus, always choosing precisely the right word."

Trinny giggled. "She's got ya there, Doc."

He held up his index finger. "Unless I'm telling you how to get well or take care of a wound." He placed his hands on my shoulder. I stiffened. "Or, if I'm telling you that your aunt is in isolation, and you can't visit her right now."

"But I've already had the virus." Tears revisited my eyes.

He looked at me regretfully. "Your aunt is in a fragile state. I've no idea what kind of germs you may have brought with you from Monkey Mountain over there." He jerked his thumb at the air. "Too many unknowns. You wouldn't be heading off to Calamus this soon under normal circumstances. You should be kept under observation. Unfortunately, you're on the Troll's Most Wanted list, so the danger outweighs my preference. Distancing you from the Trolls is what's best for you. I also must do what's best for your aunt."

Trinny picked up my breakfast tray. "Is there a message we can convey to your Aunt Jules on your behalf?"

A message? I had pages of things to say, questions to ask, and conversations that needed finishing. Would I ever get that opportunity? "Tell her I love her. And I can't wait to have tea with her soon."

Doc put his things back in the leather pouch. "Once the ointment soaks in, you should be good to let your sores air out and scab over completely. I think you'll be fine for your journey to Calamus with Superman. But promise me you'll get plenty of rest once you're there."

I nodded and walked behind them to the door. Smarlow's warnings about the Nephilim roused a bit of anxiety, but I dismissed it.

"Don't worry about your little redheaded relative. I'm the best doctor in these parts." He winked.

I gave him an exasperated glare. "You're the *only* doctor in these parts."

He waved me off and turned to go. "Don't give me semantics."

"Hey!" I reached out to stop him. "How is Gage?"

"Good as new." Doc shrugged. "Minus an arm, of course. Good thing he has another one for backup."

Lava and Trinny escorted me to the courtyard where Xander waited. Seeing father and daughter together made me wonder how I could've missed the resemblance. She looked like his female clone, minus an inordinate amount of facial hair—which is probably how I missed the resemblance.

Xander rushed to greet us, taking my hand. "How are you

feeling?"

My concerns felt foolish. "Okay, I think." I shrugged. "Better than I've felt in over a week, actually." I slipped my hand from his. "How's Gage?"

"Angry as ever. Still in pain. I hate to leave him here, but there's much that needs to be addressed without delay."

"Your Highness." Lava shifted and cleared his throat. "Might I suggest stayin' low to the treetops and huggin' the foothills as ya travel? Don't want to draw any undue attention to yerself or yer cargo."

"Goes without saying, but thanks." Xander looked annoyed by the suggestion.

The thought of being carried in his hulking arms—while not under threat of falling to my death—seemed a little close for comfort. "Guess there's no chance I could ride Sonnet?"

Xander stiffened, his expression wounded.

"Well..." Lava scratched his head. "I hadn't considered that, but Sonnet is currently in Vituvia. A bright, white Pegasus would be an obvious target, anyway. You'd be safer with Xander."

I shrugged. "Spontaneous idea."

Much to my relief, Xander suggested I ride piggyback. Standing on the low end of a rusty cannon, my arms encircled his tree-trunk neck.

Lava insisted he belt the two of us together as a safety measure. "No tellin' who or what ya might encounter. It's a long flight across the mountains." He wrapped a wide leather strap around the two of us. "No survivin' a fall from that height."

"Careful of my ribcage." I helped guide the belt around my waist. Right then and there, *awkward* took on a much deeper meaning. But Lava had a point.

Xander took a literal flying leap, and Lava and Trinny waved goodbye.

I managed to ride comfortably between Xander's powerful wings, his cape fluttering around my legs, braids whipping me in my face—though I used most of them as a pillow. Soaring above this quasi Middle Earth made the awkwardness melt away. Left me feeling free. Victorious even. I'd turned a corner and survived the lions' den, both internally and externally. By some miracle, maybe I had left most of that self-protective, scaredy-cat Sadie back in

Craventhrall.

Maybe I've sprouted wings of my own.

We hugged the tops of the trees, tracing the curve of foothills until I lost track of time. Branches sprouted higher than others, making Xander dodge to the side or shoot over the top, revisiting the roller coaster sensation I tried so hard to avoid. It also made me mentally thank Lava for his foresight with the human seatbelt.

My personal air-taxi banked to the right unexpectedly. "Someone's heading our way." He touched down on a sizable jut of rock on the side of a cliff.

Going vertical on his back meant I dangled painfully from behind until he unbuckled the belt. Once free of our bonds, I spotted two distant figures approaching. It looked like more Nephilim.

"Who do you think it is?" I rubbed my tender ribs.

"Pretty sure it's Mother dear. And her bodyguard." He sounded suspicious. The end of the belt drooped in the dirt. He whipped it back and forth like an annoyed cat twitching its tail. "This is quite out of character for her."

Oh joy. Queen Estancia was not my favorite person. I had a few mental nicknames for her high-and-mightiness—that was one of them—along with the Ice Queen and the White Witch. Not to say she's evil like the infamous Queen Jadis of Narnia. But she's cold. Brutally cold and biting. The exact opposite of my mom.

In no time, her imperious figure alighted beside us, followed by a Nephilim warrior who looked like a Native American giant.

I suppose standing beside any woman who's close to seven-feet tall would be intimidating. Add to that her muscular, burnished skin and masses of braids, and it was like being in the presence of a female warrior from a video game. All she needed was laser-shooting eyes.

"Mother." Xander bowed while I attempted a curtsy. "I can only assume you bring foreboding news."

"Well, well, how fortuitous to meet you here." Estancia folded her silvery wings behind her broad shoulders. "Miss Larcen." She nodded at me. "Looks like you've had a rough go."

"You could say that." *Thanks for the confidence booster.*

The woman gave him a severely disapproving stare. "What

are you doing flying around with *her*?"

Xander placed a hand on my back. "I was bringing Sadie to Calamus to join her family. And you? You're not one to take a leisurely flight."

"I went to Vituvia to meet with Queen Judith. When I arrived, I found the forest scourged by fire and the Gnomes in an uproar. The Gargoyles attacked."

My hand flew to my mouth.

"No!" Xander used the belt like a bullwhip and snapped it against the stone. "What happened?"

"My visit was brief. Long enough to grasp what took place. I volunteered to alert Berganstroud."

Xander paced the rock platform. "Did you see any of the Banished on your travels?"

"No, I did not. The attack happened yesterday, before dusk."

"Did you see either of my brothers?"

She ignored my question. "The consensus seemed to be that the fire was merely a stunt. A way of announcing the return of the Banished to the Land of Legend. They did not invade the city. At least not yet."

My nerves relaxed a little.

"I say it's an act of war." Xander stopped pacing and crossed his arms. "Sadie was held captive in the Eldritch by both the Trolls *and* the Gargoyles. This is very serious."

The queen didn't bother to look my way. "Agreed, my son. Listen..." she glanced at her imposing bodyguard. "Allow us to take Sadie to Calamus. You should return to Berganstroud and warn the Dwarves. You may be needed to help defend their fortress. I'd like to get back to your father so we can discuss a strategy of our own."

Oh no. Emphatically no. I didn't want this woman to take me *anywhere*.

"Very well. Perhaps Vincent should accompany me." Xander gestured to the warrior that stood a half-foot taller than himself. "Berganstroud has been hit with a devastating virus. Their resources are strained with many sick soldiers. Also, I had to leave Gage there to tend a wound inflicted by the Gargoyles."

Both Estancia and Vincent blinked at the news.

I scrambled to come up with a legit reason to refuse their plan.

"Gage fought a Gargoyle? How did that happen?" The queen looked as if such a meeting sounded absurd.

"We were rescuing Sadie. I'll fill you in later. We should get going."

"*You* should get going." The queen lifted her chin. "Vincent will stay with me. The Queen of Calamus should not travel alone in such perilous times."

Xander flexed his jaw then dipped his head. "Of course." He offered the belt to Vincent.

My mind screeched a resounding *no,* but I couldn't come up with a reasonable protest. I needed to get to my family.

Vincent took the belt without question. Perhaps the contraption was not a new concept.

"When I return to Calamus, I shall dispatch a small regiment of soldiers to Berganstroud for insurance."

"Very well." Xander turned to me. "Sorry to desert you like this, Princess. But I leave you in capable hands."

Ice cold hands, unfortunately. "It's fine."

Getting strapped on Xander's back only *seemed* awkward compared to being buckled to a total stranger. But it could've been worse. Getting tethered to the Ice Queen may have given me frostbite.

We took to the sky, and I found it impossible to relax. The whole experience occurred way outside my comfort zone. Thankfully, Queen Estancia zoomed ahead in typical self-importance so I didn't have to make eye contact and act like everything was groovy.

These two didn't feel the need to hug the treetops. We soared freakishly high, and I found consolation in the broad shoulders that blocked my view. The exertion of the flight brought on a strong whiff of body odor from Vincent that I tried to avoid by breathing through my mouth. He kept his silky black hair in a thick braid down the middle of his head. After a few good whacks in the face, I captured it in my hands, hoping he wouldn't mind.

About an hour into the flight, we banked in a wide circle. Clinging to Vincent's back at an angle made me appreciate Lava's foresight once again. *Seat belts save lives.* The three of us spiraled down. Queen Estancia leveled off close to the treetops, and we landed on a grassy clearing high on the hillside. A rest stop sounded terrific, even though I wasn't the one exerting any energy.

I had to admire Vincent's precise landing. My feet landed precisely on a boulder behind him. Once unbuckled, I hopped off and noticed a cave nestled on the opposite side of the glade, where the hill swelled into the Berganstroud mountains.

"This way." Queen Estancia strode toward the opening. She didn't appear to have a casual respite in mind.

Vincent grabbed my wrist. My internal alarm blared.

I had to scramble to keep up with his huge strides. "Hey, you're hurting me."

He ignored me. I stumbled on a rock, and he yanked me upright.

Out of the yawning mouth of the cave stepped a Troll.

CHAPTER TWENTY-NINE

"WELL, THIS TOPSIDER IS AN UNEXPECTED bonus, Your Highness." The pewter-colored Troll bowed, torch in hand. I recognized him as the one sitting beside Nekronok on the platform of the Eldritch.

Something was rotten in the state of Denmark.

"Indeed. What a shock to run into my son gallivanting across the mountainside with this mammal."

"Mammal?" I tried to wrestle free from Vincent, the Nephilim-vise. "You're a lying, traitorous Medusa." And Smarlow is a genius!

"Shut up!" Her hand flew to my face with a fierce slap. I tasted blood. Vincent kept me upright. "Have the others arrived?"

"Everyone's here except the worm."

"We can start without him."

The seismic activity of my heart would probably have registered on the Richter scale. Vincent dragged me inside. An eerie glow emanated from a curve in the recesses of the cave. We turned down a narrower tunnel that spilled into a candle and torch lit room. A singular hole glowed from the domed center of the high ceiling, forming a primitive chimney through which the smoke drifted up and out. The shaft of dim light from the opening highlighted the center of a crude stone table where six fat candles burned and flickered on top of a mound of wax—evidence of candles past.

Three hulking figures lurked in the shadows behind the table. They stepped up to the slab of stone which allowed their forms to be illuminated. When I saw Nekronok and Malagruel glowering at me like hungry animals, aftershocks rippled through my body. Chebar was the third figure, but his presence brought only a sliver of comfort to the uncertain atmosphere.

Before my eyes, Skoon and another brown-headed Leprechaun materialized. They sat in dark coattails and knickers next to the candles. They wiggled their knobby little fingers through the flames. Skoon glanced at me with wicked satisfaction.

It looked like I'd walked back into the lions' den. Or viper pit. Too many fitting descriptions.

A throaty chuckle resonated from Nekronok. "My, my. This *is* a fascinating turn of events." He leaned his large knuckles on the table, the candlelight enhancing his menacing snarl. "Did you miss us, princess? Perhaps you had a change of heart? Or maybe you wish for a second opportunity to plunge to your death? That can be arranged."

"What is going on?" I turned hateful eyes onto Estancia.

"Let's discuss it, shall we?" The Ice Queen swept her hand toward the table.

Vincent released my aching wrist. I massaged it, trying to rub his sweaty stench away with the pain.

Tree stumps cut in differing heights hemmed the perimeter of the table. Estancia grabbed my elbow and steered me to a tall hunk of wood.

"The worm, Ophidian, has arrived with the prisoner."

The queen swiveled to face the entrance, yanking me off balance.

The silver Troll stepped to the side. Two figures emerged from behind him.

"Brady!" I wrenched myself free before Estancia could react.

My brother reeled back on his heels as I ran to where he stood beside a slender Gargoyle. Brady looked terrible and wonderful all at once. I flung my arms around his shoulders with a sob.

"*Brady?*" Queen Estancia's indignant shout resounded in the cavernous space. "I thought we were expecting Brock. What did your pet-idiot do, Malagruel?"

"Are you okay?" I whispered in his ear.

I felt him nod. "Better now."

A hand wrapped around my arm and pulled us apart. "Back to the table." The Troll shoved me to the ground.

"*Hey.*" Brady yelled like he was channeling all of his anger into the one word. "Don't treat her like that."

"I'm okay." I stood up and rubbed my knee. My gaze sought my brother's face, pleading with him to play it cool. "Really. I'm fine."

Back at the table, I used a foothold notched into the stump to haul myself up under Estancia's hostile sneer. Brady scuffled over, his hands and feet roped together. The black, shriveled-up excuse for a Gargoyle slunk beside him. The creature had reptilian features and was puny and unimposing.

Malagruel strode over to Brady and his captor. I couldn't help noticing his wrapped stump of a tail with a victorious smirk. Brady's eyes widened and his mouth gaped open, staring up into the demonic form of Malagruel.

But the Gargoyle next to Brady appeared more terrified than my brother.

"How could you make such a stupid mistake?" Malagruel snatched the quaking Gargoyle off the ground by its neck. "Without the future king, we don't have the leverage we need."

"Th-they said the king had shorter h-h-hair than his twin." The writhing minion wheezed the words out. "His was shortest."

Malagruel flicked his gaze at Brady and tossed the creature like a piece of trash. "I'll finish with you later." He turned on his taloned feet and stomped back to the table.

"All is not lost, gentlemen." Queen Estancia commanded the space with her presence. "Let's sit. It's been a long flight." She flipped her braids over her shoulders and slid onto a stump. "We're still missing one."

The sound of a match being struck sizzled from the shadows, the flame obscured behind a hand. Or maybe a paw. Then a puff of smoke blurred the glowing nub of a cigar.

Mr. Marshall sauntered up to the table.

Brady and I gasped.

"Howdy, neighbors." He bit the end of his cigar and offered a Cheshire grin.

The pungent, musky smoke assaulted my nose. My mind reeled back to the strange odor I noticed when we traipsed through Moulton Falls. Mr. Marshall had been following us. It was *him*. He must have been the one who stepped into the clearing an instant before we disappeared.

My brain wrestled with a flood of implications.

Brady caught my eye. We exchanged looks of disbelief and disgust.

"What are you doing here?" my brother asked through clenched teeth.

"Oh, we'll come around to that eventually." Marshall chuckled and climbed onto his seat beside Brady, across the table from me. He wore a rumpled, navy suit and had exchanged his newsboys cap for a fedora.

I tried to recover my shock and put on a facade of confidence. If these creatures smelled fear, they used it against you. Rubbed your nose in it. Spooned it into your mouth until you gagged on it. My nerves revved into high alert, ready to use whatever secrets I could acquire against these fiends. With a look of what I hoped to be cool indifference, I grasped the charm on my necklace.

"Enough theatrics." Nekronok sat down and folded his arms. "Must you puff on that stinking thing while we're meeting?"

"Listen here, Chief Monkey-man." Marshall flicked his thumb across the cigar and released a spray of ash. "You want what I can bring to the table? Then you better get it in your furry little head that this here cigar comes with me. Everywhere."

Nekronok appeared to use all of his mental powers to take the insult without retort. He blinked. "I'll allow it for now."

"That's what I thought." Marshall gave the Troll a caustic sneer and puffed a fresh cloud into the air.

The Leprechauns twirled their arms through the smoke, making it billow in different directions.

Malagruel snickered. "Rather entertaining to watch an old man push around the feared Chief Nekronok."

Nekronok laced his long, nimble fingers together with slow deliberation. He stared straight ahead. I had to give the big beast credit, he certainly showed diplomatic restraint. "Enough with the petty remarks. There's much to discuss, so let us lay our egos aside for the greater good." With one swipe of his arm he knocked the two Leprechauns off the table like bowling pins. "What alternative plans do you have, Estancia, since Malagruel's *worm* failed to deliver the goods?"

Skoon and his cohort scrambled into the shadows.

The Wicked Witch—her new, fitting nickname—sat erect,

looking around the table with superiority. "We still have the goods. We may not have the one trophy catch, but we have his family members. Surely their multiple lives are equal to his one."

"Whether we have the king or his false-lookalike here, I believe the *princess* shall now reconsider her position in our favor." Nekronok regarded me through angry slits. "Looks like you've been given another opportunity to work for us. Maybe if threat of your own life isn't enough, you'll find your brother's life to be motivating."

"My brother would not want me to work for you. Ever."

"That's right." Brady placed his bound wrists on the table. His fingers were swollen.

"Certainly not. Yet a girl with such self-righteous ideals would not send her brother to death if it was within her power to prevent it. I'd say all for one and one for all. Because if you refuse me again, I'll kill you both."

"We'll see about that." I glared across the table at the Yeti. "Is it necessary to keep my brother tied up? We're obviously outnumbered."

"Tie her up too, Rooke." Nekronok jerked his head to the silvery Troll.

"With pleasure, Father."

"Oh, c'mon!" Brady smacked the tabletop.

Father?

Skoon scurried to the Troll and tossed him about a yard of rope. Someone had planned ahead.

It was pointless not to cooperate. With a contemptuous grin, I thrust my hands toward Rooke. Brady obviously wrestled with a few choice words, making contortions with his mouth.

Estancia cleared her throat. "I see several advantages to this situation. It may be more providential than having King Brock. It provides a subtler way to work things in our favor. Less demanding."

Her eyes cut to me. "We all want something here." She fanned her fingers around the table. "We represent the majority of the beings in the Tethered World. Yet, we have much less of a voice. Rather, Gnomes—the puniest, weakest creatures—make the rules. The Dwarves of Berganstroud, as their cohorts, help enforce the will of the few onto the will of the many. The 'many' will stand for it no more. It would behoove you to listen closely to the offer we now confer on you."

"I've already been presented with the offer. Asked and answered from the balcony of the Eldritch." I glanced at Brady. He gave me an encouraging nod. But if it came down to it, could I really send him to his death?

"The things we delineate *will* come to pass." The queen steepled her hands together. "The power of the sword will be ours with or without your cooperation. The benefit of your assistance, however, is that our plans will succeed more peacefully. With less bloodshed. You may think I'm an outright fallen angel for how I'm handling this, but I truly do have the best interest of the Tethered World in mind. We all do."

"Oh, really?" I raised a skeptical eyebrow. "Too bad God isn't in the business of striking liars dead with a lightning bolt."

"*Sadie.*" Brady shot me a warning look.

Malagruel laughed. "Guess you would die along with us." His sulfurous breath wafted across the table. "He who is without lies, cast the first lightning bolt." He leaned on his elbows and gave me a fanged smile.

"Gag her. Gag them both." Nekronok nudged his son.

Oh, great.

Estancia sighed. "I'd prefer to be able to discuss this in a civil manner."

"Ask yes or no questions," Nekronok said.

I glanced at Chebar, who sat on the other side of his father. He did not return my gaze. But I thought his jaw flexed a few times in the candlelight. Rooke—who I was beginning to think was his father's henchman—was offered two strips of cloth from the other Leprechaun. The Troll dutifully wrapped them around Brady and me. It hurt to have my mouth yanked open and drove me nuts to have the cloth against my tongue. Salivating commenced straightaway and swallowing became close to impossible.

"As I was saying," Estancia went on. "We all want something here. Even you and your little brother."

I shook my head vehemently. Other than our freedom, these reprobates could offer nothing of interest.

"Oh, yes." The Ice Queen leaned in. "Yes, you do." She snapped her fingers. "Vincent, please retrieve our special guests."

Her bodyguard left the room. A sick feeling settled in the pit of my stomach. I felt certain she had my father. I glanced at Brady. His eyes smoldered back. My brain unleashed an angry flood of thoughts.

From the array of curious looks, I guessed that the other reprobates were not aware of Estancia's special guests.

Footsteps preceded Vincent's return. He stepped into the chamber and bowed. "Here are your prisoners, my queen."

My mother and sister stumbled into the candlelit cave.

CHAPTER THIRTY

Brady dove off the chair toward his mother and Sophie. He heard Sadie's muzzled screech behind him. Rooke wasted no time hauling him back to his seat, but Brady made it close enough to see their tear-streaked faces. They were gagged and had their hands tied behind their backs.

"Here they are!" Estancia's singsong voice made Brady want to throttle her, female or not. Surely social protocols didn't apply to seven-foot-tall women.

The two prisoners stumbled forward, propelled from behind by another Nephilim guard that was surely related to Vincent. Sophie fell. Amy knelt beside her, unable to help with her arms bound behind her back. The pair staggered to their feet.

"That's far enough." The queen held up her hand when they neared the table. "We've no more seats. And I don't care to hear their sniveling."

Amy's eyes changed from heartbroken to hostile. She shot poisonous arrows at every non-Larcen in the room. Sophie had the look down pretty well herself.

Brady took deep, deliberate breaths. His heart pulsed so loudly he had a hard time hearing.

"Afternoon, Amy." Mr. Marshall tipped his hat.

Amy and Sophie blinked in wide-eyed astonishment.

Wham. Brady landed a forceful elbow into Mr. Marshall's shoulder, knocking him from his stump of a chair. Amy gasped. Malagruel laughed.

The old man groaned from his landing spot. Sadie caught Brady's eyes and gave him a subtle, encouraging smile. But he realized that such a small victory wasn't enough. It would take pummeling the roomful of barbarians into the dirt to make him feel better.

Rooke helped Marshall to his feet. The man released a torrent of curses on Brady and brushed the dirt from his rumpled suit.

"My, my." Estancia gave Brady an admiring stare. "Maybe we can use you after all. A shame you're so scrawny."

Brady unleashed a frustrated yell through the gag in his mouth.

The Nephilim queen fingered the bracelets on her wrist and sighed like she was bored. "As you see, the list of Larcen captives keeps growing." She glanced at Sadie. "What a stroke of fortune when they showed up in Calamus. Surely they provide a wee bit more motivation for you to cooperate."

Sadie trembled. A tear plopped onto the table. She turned from Estancia's icy stare and looked at her mom and sister. Amy stepped toward Sadie, and the guard wrenched her back in place.

"Excellent strategy, Estancia." Nekronok sounded impressed.

"It gets even better." Her voice dripped with syrupy sarcasm. She stretched her full lips into a cruel smile and gestured dramatically at the Larcen's neighbor shrouded in smoke. "Care to sweeten the deal, Joseph?"

Mr. Marshall lowered his cigar and smirked. "Of course, of course." He looked from Brady to Sadie, to the others. "I've imagined this moment, for years. Planned for it. Wondered how it would play out." He chuckled. "Gotta say that the reality trumps the crazy scenarios this ol' brain conjured up."

"Spit it out, for Thrall's sake," Nekronok grumbled.

Marshall must have felt pretty confident. He stared at Chief Nekronok and took a long drag from his cigar. He turned back to the others, blowing a smoke ring.

"As I was saying. Today has been a long time comin'. Thirty-eight years, I think it is."

Sadie stiffened.

Thirty-eight? Brady narrowed his eyes. *Why does that sound familiar?*

"See, I had to track down your aunt—back before there was such a thing as the Internet. Took years." His beady eyes crinkled in a look of self-amusement. "Had to watch the little lady and figure out what she was up to. Since she and Daniel never started a family, I figured she'd need to get her extended family involved sooner or later."

Sadie's eyes grew wide. Brady felt like he must be missing something important.

"Sounds familiar, eh?" He eyed Sadie and flicked ashes onto the table. "Yeah. Changed my name, even. How 'bout that for dedication? William Joseph Delaney became Joseph Marshall." He pulled at his lapels with both hands like some big shot. "Finally tracked down your oddball, homeschooling family and waited for a house to hit the market. One near enough to keep an eye on things. Landing the house across the street was nothing short of miraculous, by golly."

Queen Estancia expelled a loud breath. "Time is of the essence. We have plans to implement. Soon."

Marshall held his hands up in surrender. "All right, all right. So listen, kids. There's one more thing you should know." He pinched the cigar in his teeth and wheezed out a laugh. "I've got your dad in my basement." He clapped his hands together. "Yep! A little insurance topside."

CHAPTER THIRTY-ONE

Tears drenched my cheeks and dripped into my open mouth. Brady reached his tied hands across the table, and we clasped fingertips. His body trembled like my own, though his appeared to come from a deep, molten rage. I shot hateful darts at Marshall while trying to swallow things that needed a tissue.

Mom and Sophie cried and protested, but I couldn't bring myself to look at them. The physical power of emotional pain left me numb.

Estancia laid a patronizing hand on my arm, clamping hard when I tried to pull away. "Now the picture is complete. I have your mother and sister. Nekronok and Malagruel are sure to keep your brother in a cozy dungeon. This gentleman has your father topside." She twisted my wrist. "I assume *we* have your attention."

I cried out and heard my mother pleading from where she stood. What did this woman expect me to say—if I could speak?

"That was a yes or no question, princess." Malagruel smacked his talon-like hand on the table, making me flinch.

With an unsteady nod, I agreed.

"*Goood*," Estancia purred. "My associates have already offered you a powerful position within our new alliance. Opportunities like this don't usually come around a second time. You'll accept their generous offer, yes?"

Though I heard objections from my family, I nodded.

Nekronok leaned on the table with his elbows. "Before you get any grand ideas about backing out once you return topside, let me explain that your brother stays with me in Craventhrall until some sort of coalition between the United

Dynasty of Thrall and the leaders topside can be formed."

Brady and I jerked our heads to the Troll. That could take months!

Nekronok gave a nefarious chuckle. "Don't worry. I'll make sure he has food and water."

All I could do was glare.

"Excellent." The Ice Queen laced her fingers together. "Though I'm still not on board with calling our alliance by that ridiculous name. United Dynasty of Thrall? Much too exclusive."

"We can discuss the wisdom of the name later." Nekronok stared contemptuously across the table. "Let's finish with business."

Estancia rolled her eyes then looked at me. "Now then, the other little favor involves the welfare of your mother and little sister. I plan to personally escort you back to Vituvia, under the pretense of having warned Berganstroud about the attack on the Gnomes and pulling you out of a dangerous situation. That should set me in their favor. You will not breathe a word of anything to anyone, or else Vincent sends word to his brother, Wasik," she pointed to the warrior standing beside my sister. "He's got a nasty temper. Clear?"

My chest heaved with unsteady breaths. I didn't know I was capable of such a swell of anger. Brady buried his face against his palms. I gave another begrudging nod.

The queen laughed with wicked amusement. "This is going splendidly, gentlemen! In the interest of time, I'll discuss my plans for Vituvia with our new *ambassador* along the way. But there's one little thing I think everyone here would like to confirm." She pressed my shoulder so I had to face her. "You *do* know where the other key is, correct? The key that releases the sword?"

I shook my head, thankful that I didn't have to disguise the truth.

Estancia had my throat in her fingers before I knew it. I gasped against the gag, arms flailing. "You'd...better... not...lie...to...me." Her voice was low and menacing.

Coughing and gasping against her grip, I attempted another shake of my head. I could hear Brady and Mom trying to protest. Sophie cried.

The Wicked Witch's fingers yanked my head toward her face. She drilled me with a stare that seemed to gut me like a fish with cutting mistrust. "The *key*! Do you know where it is?"

I shook my head rapidly and hoped to look sincere before I died of a lack of oxygen.

She shoved my head away. "I believe her."

Wheezing and lightheaded, a fresh round of tears commenced. *Oh God, I hope You have a plan. And that You'll shout it loud and clear.*

Nekronok grabbed my wrist from across the table. I whipped my head up and stared with glazed eyes. "Then there's one more thing you must assure us of—and deliver on—before your family sees the light of day." He squeezed tighter. "You will find out where the other key is hidden. When it is in our possession—whether you turn it over to us or help us acquire it—and once the other conditions are met topside, your family will be freed. By then, you'll be in too deep to dig your way out. You will be the face of the Tethered-World-meets-topside alliance."

Behind me, someone tugged at the cloth gag around my head.

"We won't need this on our journey to Vituvia." Estancia pulled the fabric away.

I wiped my face with my sleeve and took cleansing breaths, relieved to use my mouth again.

Estancia slid from her seat and lifted me like a child from a highchair, placing me on the ground. "We accomplished what we set out to do." She straightened her Centurion-style clothing. From a pouch attached to her belt, she withdrew a folded piece of paper sealed with wax. She glanced around. "Where are those impish Leprechauns?"

Skoon and his companion appeared on top of the table. I wondered how long they'd been there.

"I need one of you to deliver this to the Ogres of Skellerwad." She brandished the paper in her fingers. "You'll be permitted to ride back with Wasik as far as Calamus."

Skoon's friend leapt from the table. "Thistle, at your service." The brown-headed Leprechaun removed his hat and bowed.

"You fail to deliver this to the Ogres and I will hunt down every male in your family and disgrace them by shaving off their beards." She stretched the note his way. "Understood?"

Thistle nodded, a fearful look on his face. He snatched the

letter from her, sliding it into his dark-green jacket.

So, this evil woman was going to insult my family further by befriending the big, nasty Ogres—the brutes that used my parents for sport in a torturing contest. I stared at Estancia, half expecting horns to sprout from her head.

Instead, she straightened and pointed to Skoon. "You will accompany me."

He bowed and tipped his hat, revealing reddish hair. "It shall be an honor, Your Grace."

Looking forward to strangling you with my bare hands, shrimp.

"You'll do everything I ask, exactly as I specify, or your family meets the same fate I warned Thistle about." Without giving Skoon time to respond, she looked at the others. "Now then, we move ahead with our plans. It seems the Maker has worked things out differently than we planned. But it's for the better, I believe. King or no king."

I stared at her incredulously. "You really think you're doing something for *God?*"

She pasted on a smile. "Absolutely. He's shaking the Tethered World from its complacency. He is moving. Taking us in new directions. The Stonecipher has given me a Word from the Maker confirming my plans."

"Oh, please." I rolled my eyes.

Estancia lifted her chin, closed her eyes, and recited,

"The scepter's passing signifies
A regime change that shall defy
Traditions bound and much revered
Once youthful beauty draweth near.
The world above shall reach its hand
To those within our cryptic land.
With female fair upon our side
And power of the sword to guide
The wings of change shall then unfold
And secrets hidden shall be told."

The Wicked Witch opened her eyes and leveled me with a cold, remote stare. "Frankly, I'm not a fan of having to rely on others to carry out my business." She shrugged. "But I believe my Stonecipher possesses divine insight."

"Yeah." I nodded. "I'd say *possess* is the right word."

"Remember, *Daughter*," Malagruel walked around the table, towering above me like he had at the Eldritch. "I told you there were prophecies about you."

I glowered at him. "Sounds like they came from a false prophet. I believe he should be stoned." My hands balled into fists. I turned to Estancia. "You are a desperate, wicked woman. You're willing to stoop to blackmail, kidnapping, and child abuse to get what you want. Please don't insult God by slapping His approval on your selfish tyranny."

Her nostrils flared when I used the word "wicked" so I chalked that up as a small victory.

"Lisss-ten." The word hissed from her teeth. "There's an unfortunate cost to change. One I am prepared to pay. One I am prepared to answer for." Her glance flickered bitterly around the room. "On my coronation day, I fancied myself with the good I could do for my people. I love my subjects. I love the Tethered World. And, yes, I even care for the good of Vituvia and Berganstroud. My visions for the Tethered World are inevitably frustrated by tradition." Her eyes darted to Malagruel. "Sometimes you have to dance with the devil in order to grasp your goals."

A deep, throaty chuckle emanated from him. "Love you too, cousin Nephilim." He waved his fingers in her face.

She narrowed her eyes. "Shut up." Her expression changed to patronizing when she looked back to me. "So, let's just say you're not the only one put in a compromising position. But if it means we gain control of the sword and finally implement effective plans, it'll be worth every concession I had to make."

I clenched my teeth in anger. Oh, how I wanted to smack her pretentious face. Instead, I sprinted for my mom and sister before anyone could stop me. We huddled together the best we could. I ran my fingers over their faces. Their eyes pleaded with me, a mixture of fear and despair. An instant after I reached them, Brady was there too.

"I love you. So much." Our foreheads pressed together, desperate to touch one another.

"Get back." Vincent yanked me away.

Rooke shoved Brady to the table.

With his iron grip, Vincent dragged me through the tunnels. "I love you guys." I yelled over my shoulder.

"Keep quiet." Vincent jerked my arm.

"We're going to be okay. Have faith," I yelled louder.

Estancia remained inside, speaking to the others.

When we emerged from the cave, I squinted in the bright light. A Nephilim soldier stood guard, saluting Vincent.

"What does Prince Xander think of your allegiance to this traitor queen?" I asked.

Vincent stiffened. "Affairs in Calamus are none of your concern."

"Did you not hear that little 'prophecy' the queen recited? Sounds to me like your affairs are definitely—and officially— my concern." I leaned into his personal space. "Therefore you might do well to fear for your soul if you or your brother lay a hand on my family." I sounded much bolder than I felt.

"Oh, really?" He snickered.

Estancia marched out of the tunnel and snapped her fingers. "Cut her bonds. Let's go."

Vincent withdrew a dagger from his belt and slashed the cords. I rubbed my wrists, happy to separate the twins.

"Stand on the rock." He pointed.

I froze. Two Hippogriffs grazed in a scrubby clearing beyond the rock. Their freakish features—an eagle's head and talons in front merging with a horse's hind end— snapped me back to our last journey. The bizarre creatures were used by the Trolls in battle, one of which had eyed me like a tasty morsel. I assumed that these Hippogriffs belonged to the Trolls inside the cave. I spotted another beast near a distant grove of trees but couldn't make out its features.

"Move it." Vincent pushed me toward the rock.

Estancia crossed her arms and waited impatiently for me to get situated on Vincent's back.

My mind buzzed with a powerful concoction of emotions while we winged over the mountainous terrain. Mr. Marshall—no, Mr. *Delaney's* revelations unsettled me more than almost anything else. The depths of his deception made my stomach somersault. He *had* been spying on us, all these years. Ugh! What a creep.

I couldn't shake the tremor of panic that sprouted up now that both Estancia and Nekronok had mentioned the other key. This news did not bode well for the safety of the sword, let alone those that I loved. Whether or not the prophecy was true, my family had unwittingly become pawns in a chess game of monstrous proportions. And the monsters were playing us like absolute geniuses.

Checkmate, Larcens.

CHAPTER THIRTY-TWO

As we approached Vituvia, I spied the blackened, scarred tree line on the hills above the palace. It sickened me. What a ploy. The tentacles of manipulation were far-reaching indeed.

Fresh anger simmered inside. I glanced at Estancia, intending to glare her down. Instead, I shuddered as Skoon materialized on her back with a condescending sneer. He'd been there all along, invisible. The Leprechaun cackled at my shocked face, obviously amused.

The Nephilim descended. Vincent touched down outside the protective walls of the city. I wondered if they chose to avoid flying over the wall unannounced because it might result in a rain of arrows from soldiers stationed along the top.

The Wicked Witch adjusted her clothing and crossed to where I stood, Skoon at her heels. "We will walk through the gate to a hero's welcome." The imp disappeared again. "Ugh, you look utterly horrid after all your blubbering." She whisked her fingers through my hair and across my clothing, as if it might improve the situation.

"Guess I have you to thank for that."

She grabbed my chin and jerked my face close. "Remember, *princess*, behave. One word from me and Vincent heads back to Calamus. Furthermore, I have spies everywhere, including our invisible friend here. So if you so much as murmur in a questionable manner, your family will pay."

"Understood," I practically spat. She withdrew her hand.

Turning on her heels, she strolled away. "Come now. We must discuss my expectations. There are things I require from our little arrangement."

Even a strolling Nephilim makes for a hurried human. I attempted to keep pace with quick strides, dreading to hear her outlandish stipulations.

"The reason for the fire"—she waved her hands toward the distant hills—"besides the Gargoyles heralding their return, was to provide grounds for me to come to the aid of the Gnomes. In return for my gracious offer to personally warn Berganstroud, I'd earn the Vituvians' trust. Trust that will, I hope, put me in their good graces."

We skirted the back side of a large, fenced garden. A Gnome worked between leafy rows of vegetation, wielding a hoe. He swiped the hat from his head and waved it in our direction.

Estancia and Vincent gave an enthusiastic wave in return.

"Wave," the queen barked. "You're happy to be here, remember?"

I flipped my hand up and down halfheartedly.

"As I was saying"—she skirted a large rock in time for me to trip over it—"what I shall propose to Queen Judith is now practically guaranteed by our fortuitous meeting today. My bringing you to Vituvia and your unwavering support on my behalf will *finally* get me what I want."

"You always get what you want, no doubt."

She stopped long enough to look down with a condescending sneer. "Of course. I also want you to speak to me with proper veneration. Particularly in Vituvia." She moved onto the main road leading to the city gate.

"What do you want from the Gnomes?"

"For them to permit me to see the sword...among other things."

The gate loomed straight ahead. "So the sword is totally off limits? What other things could you want besides that?"

Estancia pulled up short. "The sword is absolutely off limits to almost everyone but Gnomes. They have never allowed anyone to see the sword. Not even at the annual Festival of the Sword, which is why we never attend. And, yes, there's something else that interests me. I'll leave it at that."

"I thought the Gnomes invited a selection of the Nephilim and Dwarf warriors to train as Guardians of the Sword. They asked Brady, as well."

"It's all a show." She waved it off and continued to walk.

"They want to put on a united front to impress the Trolls and the Gargoyles. And they may well station our men near the Garden Dome. But I'd wager shaving my head that they'll not allow them to stand guard inside the sanctuary where the sword resides."

"The Garden Dome?"

"Oh, good gracious." The queen stopped and gave me an exasperated look. "Have you learned nothing of the goings on in Vituvia? The Garden Dome is the largest of the three domes gracing the palace, see?" She pointed to the gleaming castle that commanded the distant hillside, visible between the wooden planks of the gate.

Four Gnome guards stationed outside the gate approached us.

Estancia grabbed my hand and looped it into her arm. "Remember, the Gnomes adore you. I need them to feel the same about me so I can get into the Garden Dome."

It would help if I at least found you tolerable. "I hope you don't expect me to lie for you."

The queen reached her opposite hand to mine and squeezed my fingers like a clamp. "I expect you to do whatever it takes to keep your family alive. If that means persuading your little friends to come around to my way of doing things, then you better do just that. Convincingly. The prophecy implies that I must have you by my side to get near the sword. Make it happen or your family pays." She held her head high and smiled lightheartedly at the approaching warriors.

"Princess Sadie, Queen Estancia. Welcome back!" An African-looking Gnome removed his pointy, metal hat, and the others followed. They bowed.

I attempted a curtsey, but the Ice Queen jerked me upright. "Royalty doesn't return obeisance," she said through smiling, clenched teeth.

"Oh."

"My good Gnome, I trust there were no further injuries fighting the fire?" Queen Estancia looked every inch the benevolent ruler.

"Not that I'm aware, Your Highness." He replaced his metal helmet. "It did not spread into town."

"And the young man? The king's twin. Has he been located?"

I pressed my lips tight and dug my fingers into her muscular arm.

"I'm afraid not." The Gnome shook his head.

"So tragic. I'll be sure and put my men on it when I return."

Ugh! You wench of a woman.

"Thank you, Your Majesty." He bowed then turned toward the gate. "If you'll follow me, I'll signal to raise the gate."

I tried to slip my hand from the queen's arm as we walked, but she latched on with her own hand again. "Keep it there and look pleasant." She spoke through a pasted smile.

Two could play at the talking-through-your-teeth game. "Tell me, where does Xander stand on the issue of opposing Vituvia's leadership? Or is he even aware there's an issue to consider?"

The Gnome removed a small animal horn from his belt and blew it long and low, twice. From somewhere on the other side, soldiers worked to lift the heavy gate with a series of ropes and pulleys. The enormous structure groaned, lifting its spiked wooden beams from the ground. They looked like trees that had been fashioned into enormous toothpicks.

The queen increased her pressure on my hand "First of all, you will refer to him as *Prince* Xander. Better yet, Prince Alexander. Secondly, I don't answer to my son for my decisions. And thirdly"—she dug her long nails into my flesh—"you need to drop any fanciful ideas you might have about marrying him, because I will never allow it."

"*Marriage*?" I laughed despite the pain of her grasp. "Being a part of *your* family is the last thing I want from life. Don't worry." A tiny corner of my brain—or was it my heart—scoffed at such a blanket assessment of the prospect. "Besides, I'm sixteen. No one gets married when they're sixteen."

The gate stopped halfway, which allowed plenty of headroom.

"You're not too young in the Tethered World. I was betrothed to King Aviel at age twelve. We married three years later." She patted my hand in a motherly way. "Now be a good girl. *Behave.*"

I bit back several sarcastic remarks and walked through the gate. Strolling arm in arm with the Wicked Witch left me hoping that Dorothy might land her house squarely on top of her once we walked into Munchkinland.

A handful of soldiers bowed in greeting. The dirt beneath our feet soon became the cobblestones of the main road. It led straight ahead, more or less, through the charming market and shops of Vituvia and on to the palace. The buildings within the city were built to accommodate guests of all sizes. Some store fronts had two or three different sized doors. Some doors had knobs set in multiple places. A slatted walkway stretched along the storefronts, like a boardwalk in an old western town.

I couldn't help but notice the lack of activity. Few Gnomes milled about. The ones I spotted seemed to be headed away from us, in the direction of the palace. We were all but ignored.

"Where are your adoring fans?" I yanked my hand away and clasped it behind my back before she could react.

She flared her nostrils and cut her eyes to me.

"Not much of a hero's welcome." I smiled sweetly at her.

Estancia stiffened and opened her mouth. Before she could unleash on me, a couple of Gnomes and a Dwarf jogged past.

"Up ahead. Bella said it happened in the park." One of the Gnomes pointed up the street.

Two Gnome children zoomed out of a store sporting a "Petite Sweets" sign, leaving the door ajar. Four more kids ran from between two buildings and scrambled over the cobblestone.

"Looks like we made it in time for something important, Your Grace." Vincent took to jogging up the slight incline.

"Vincent! Royalty does not run."

He slowed, but I noticed Estancia had quickened her enormous stride. This, of course, meant I was running, royalty or not.

The road leveled off and forked around a grassy, circular park. It appeared that all of downtown Vituvia had crowded onto the lawn. Here and there, Dwarves frustrated the view of the Gnomes caught behind them. Some Gnomes stood on benches, or climbed onto statues to get a better view.

When you're as tall as a human, however, a crowd of Gnomes and Dwarves is nothing. I could see the main attraction perfectly.

I froze. Disbelief and triumph jolted every nerve ending in my body. "Dad!"

CHAPTER THIRTY-THREE

BRADY PEERED DOWN AT THE HILLS of Berganstroud from the back of Chebar's Hippogriff. He decided this ride must be the single perk of being Nekronok's prisoner. Sitting astride the creature, with Chebar behind him, Brady stroked the feathered neck of the eagle where it transitioned into horse fur. This beast was the epitome of an enigma.

Nekronok and Rooke escorted Chebar and Brady—the chief slightly ahead on another Hippogriff, big brother slightly behind riding a Griffin. Brady did not recall seeing these half eagle, half lion legends the last time he visited. But he was learning that the Tethered World harbored continual surprises. Case in point: the Gargoyles. What next? The Loch Ness monster?

Sitting with Rooke and looking a tinge green was Mr. Marshall—or Mr. Delaney—or whoever the man considered himself to be. *Mr. Scumbag* was Brady's new nickname for the guy.

Malagruel accompanied them across the sky, darting round about like an annoying horsefly. Without his reptilian tail for balance, the Gargoyle flew with an erratic rhythm. The Trolls appeared to find the big bat an annoying showoff, doing their best to ignore his antics. Somewhere down below, the Gargoyle's failed "worm," Ophidian, slithered his way back to Abaddon, the place the Banished called home.

Somewhere else, Brady thought with a pang of sadness, his poor mother and little sister were headed to Calamus as prisoners. His sorrow gave way to guilt at the thought of allowing them both to be there in the first place while he stayed behind in Vituvia. He should have insisted on taking them himself—should have been more protective. Instead, he barely looked back in his eagerness to join the Guardians of the Sword.

That didn't exactly turn out the way he'd hoped either.

Malagruel shot in front of Brady, startling him from his thoughts. Brady hadn't seen anything in the Tethered World to rival the hideous figure of the Gargoyle. He felt squeamish every time the thing looked his way. But the demonic brute lost his evil edge when Brady glanced at the stub of a tail poking through the hole in his black trousers. The foot-long nub, wrapped in a dirty white bandage, reminded Brady of a flag of surrender waving nervously back and forth.

Still, Brady couldn't quite put a finger on the relationship between Nekronok and Malagruel. He sensed constant tension between the two. A common lust for the sword appeared impetus enough for them to overlook their differences.

Mount Thrall loomed ahead, jagged and claw-like. Brady regarded the oppressive structure of the Eldritch chiseled into the mountainside. His stomach lurched, knowing this would be home for an indefinite amount of time. What would he have to endure?

He looked at his swollen, roped wrists and guessed things would only get worse. The ropes etched crimson circles into his skin, raw and bleeding. Brady grinned thinking about a country song he knew about how "chicks dig scars." By the time he left Craventhrall he might be a real heartbreaker.

The flying enigmas soared in a wide circle, spiraling toward the Eldritch. Brady closed his eyes and inhaled his last taste of perceived freedom, praying that a way out would present itself sooner rather than later. With Chebar secretly on his side, surely something would come to light.

A spacious ledge of rock jutting above the roof of the Eldritch made for an ideal landing pad. The creatures touched down, trotting a few feet to a stop. Malagruel zoomed past, zipping down the face of the structure, out of sight.

Brady reluctantly slid from the Hippogriff and paced to regain circulation in his legs. Once the Trolls and Mr. Marshall dismounted, the creatures took flight, heading to wherever flying freaks of nature go. Brady watched his scumbag neighbor and the three Yetis, wondering about the plural form of Bigfoot. Would that be Bigfeet?

"Take him to the dungeon." Nekronok sauntered up to

Brady, looking him up and down. "Let's see how he does in solitary confinement."

Chebar stiffened. "I think the regular cells are sufficient to hold a human."

"I don't recall asking you to think. Do it." The chief leaped from the stony ledge onto the roof of the Eldritch. He strode to a large wood-planked door that sat flush with the granite roof. He jerked the hatch open and looked at his son expectantly.

Chebar grasped Brady roughly by the arm. "Yes, sir."

Rooke and Mr. Marshall chuckled as they walked past.

Brady stopped and looked back at the old man. "You better sleep with one eye open after this. If anything happens to my father, it'll be my personal mission to make sure you regret it."

Marshall wasted no time in lighting another cigar. "Now, son, that's no way to talk to your elders." He huffed smoke, and Rooke turned away coughing. "But rest easy, boy. I'm going back shortly to check on your pop. Once we gain control of the sword and get your sister working on our behalf, I'll release him in pristine condition. That's a promise."

"Let's go." Chebar stepped past Brady and descended a few stairs.

Brady took one tentative step down. "Your word means nothing to me. But I'll be true to my threats if anything happens. *That's* a promise."

The narrow stairs spiraled into the rock. The light from the door above didn't illuminate far. Nekronok followed Brady into the hole then closed the door. Everything disappeared into the void, and Brady reached for the wall. Claustrophobic thoughts crowded in. Behind him, the chief breathed heavily, sounding like the animal he really was. Brady felt like hunted prey.

"Put your hands on my shoulder," Chebar barked. "I don't need you tumbling on top of me."

A dozen more steps and they came through a door and into a dimly lit hall.

"This way." Chebar grabbed Brady's upper arm. "Don't try anything stupid."

Mercifully, Nekronok headed in the opposite direction. But not before he promised to pay Brady a visit in hades.

Chebar steered Brady through a labyrinth of halls and staircases. Releasing his arm when they were alone, acting like a bully when others approached—several passersby struck at the prisoner as well. Brady despaired of memorizing his way around. Stone passages, as it turns out, tend to look alike. One thing he couldn't mistake: they were always headed down.

"Through here." Chebar opened a filthy wooden door. "I'm going to get you out as soon as possible," he whispered as Brady walked past.

Screeches and snarls echoed, faint but desperate. Perspiration trickled between Brady's shoulder blades and meandered down his temple. Torches were few and far apart, engulfing them in swaths of darkness. The stench of other prisoners made Brady nosedive into his shirt. Things were heading south at breakneck speed.

Every ten feet or so, a barred door appeared on Brady's left. At the end of the hall sat another Troll. He snored softly, slumped in a chair, head lolled to the side.

"Minchess!" Chebar's shout made Brady jump. "I don't believe you can get demoted any lower than the dungeon. Unless you'd like to be locked up in solitary yourself."

The guard sprang to his feet, panic stricken. He straightened to attention and saluted. "Yes, sir. Sorry, sir. Won't happen again, sir."

"You must think me a bigger idiot than yourself if you believe I buy a word of that." Chebar shoved Minchess so hard he fell back into his chair. "Now take this prisoner to an empty cell."

Minchess looked Brady up and down, as if only now realizing a human stood before him. "Who is this? How'd we get a topsider?" He removed a set of skeleton keys from his belt.

"All you need to know is that he's valuable. Leave him in one piece. Got it?"

"Yes sir." The Troll nodded emphatically. "One piece."

Minchess led them back down the walkway while Brady wondered how many "pieces" the other prisoners might be in. By the sounds of the growls and groans, they weren't in great shape.

The guard unlocked one of the middle doors. Brady walked to the opening. Stone steps dove into bucketfuls of darkness, leading who knew where.

Chebar removed the ropes that bound Brady's wrists. "Get in there."

"What's down those stairs?" Brady swallowed.

"Your guest room." Chebar pressed a hand against Brady's back.

Brady stepped uneasily across the threshold hoping his eyes would adjust as he descended. It didn't happen. To make matters worse, the wall on the right abruptly ended just beyond the reach of the paltry light spilling through the cell door. He kept his hand pressed against the left wall, not interested in discovering how steep the stairs were by stepping off the other side.

The door screeched shut, a piercing sound that amplified in the small space. Brady glanced back at the barred door and saw that Chebar had left. Minchess turned the key, sealing Brady's fate.

Impulsively, Brady crept back up the stairs and started counting how many steps to the bottom. Couldn't hurt to know how far it was between the black hole and freedom.

Seventeen steps down. Deep steps for large feet. *Seventeen* reminded Brady of Brock. As much as he despised his current predicament, he was glad Brock hadn't been the one captured. Brady had his recent, undesirable haircut to thank for the mistaken identity.

He couldn't bring himself to explore the inky expanse at the foot of the stairs. Not yet. Instead, Brady wadded himself against the wall at the base of the steps and gazed at the rectangular patch of light between the bars.

Would anyone be able to find him in this sliver of darkness? He felt so lost and utterly insignificant.

But…his haircut!

Cutting it had seemed like a waste of time—not to mention a loss of good-looking hair. What was the point of cutting it if he couldn't get his driver's permit?

All along—it occurred to Brady now—God had other plans for this haircut. Major plans.

Which meant God knew all about this sliver of darkness.

CHAPTER THIRTY-FOUR

BEFORE I COULD CATAPULT TO DAD, Estancia had her icy hand wrapped around my arm, gluing me to her side.

She leaned in. "This changes *nothing*."

Dad was sprinting my way, hopping over Gnomes and dodging Dwarves. My heels were dug in, ready to run. "Understood." I nodded. "Let me go!"

"One hint of trouble and you know what happens." The queen shoved me forward. "How wonderful. Your father has been found!"

The queen's lying enthusiasm did nothing to dampen mine. My body resonated with joy—my heart so full of the stuff, it threatened to explode like fireworks. The two of us slammed into each other on the fringe of the crowd. I pressed myself into his strong, protective arms and felt him heave with emotion. My pent-up anxiety liquefied into tears.

"You okay, love?" Dad whispered against my hair.

I nodded. Oh, how I longed to tell him everything—and almost did. I mean, he was my *dad*. He knew how to fix anything. But Estancia's warning outweighed the impulse. If I wanted to help my family, both in Calamus and Craventhrall, I had to tread carefully. *Wise as a serpent, harmless as a dove, right?*

The crowd cheered and clapped. We pulled apart. I smiled up at Dad, and he kissed my forehead.

"Queen Estancia." Dad stepped around me and bowed. "Pleasure to see you again, Your Highness."

"Mr. Larcen—or is it Lord Larcen here in Vituvia?" She gave Dad a teasing smile. "We have been searching the Tethered World for you. Glad to see you're unharmed."

Dad put his arm around my shoulder and squeezed. "I'm

glad to be unharmed. And back with my family." He looked down at me. "Where's Mom and the others?"

"Your wife and young daughter are under my protection in Calamus." The queen stepped in before I could respond.

"Are they in need of protection?" Dad looked from me to her.

Estancia pressed her lips together and gave a single, solemn nod. "Absolutely. There was an attack on Vituvia yesterday. Sadie was held hostage in Craventhrall prior to that. Things are quite unstable, I'm afraid."

Dad faced me, hands on my shoulders. "You were kidnapped? Did they hurt you?" His gaze probed my face. He touched the sores on my cheekbone with gentle fingers.

"I'm fine, Dad. Promise. I'll tell you about it later." I smiled. "I'm just glad you're here. Where have you been?" Figured I'd play innocent for the Wicked Witch.

"Let's talk about this while we make our way to the palace, shall we?" The queen guided me by the elbow into the crowd of onlookers. Dad kept pace beside me.

The Gnomes parted before us and applauded as we passed. Cheers of "He's safe!" and "Welcome back!" could be heard. Dad waved. So did Estancia, though no one addressed her.

I grabbed Dad's hand. The road to a happy family reunion lay long and difficult ahead, but his arrival meant a reunion was possible. Hope lived on.

"You're not going to believe my story." Dad smiled in the amused, eye-crinkling way that I loved. His chestnut hair had a smattering of gray at the temples I hadn't noticed before.

"Try me." I squeezed his hand. *Can't wait to hear more about our personal family stalker.*

From the corner of my eye, I saw Estancia stiffen.

"This entire time I've been chained up in Mr. Marshall's basement." His eyes grew round. "Yeah, handcuffed to some pipes. I could only kneel on the ground, arms overhead. Tormented for information."

"*What?*" I didn't have to pretend to be shocked about torture.

"I know. Crazy!" He shook his head. "We've always joked about how suspicious he acts. Turns out it was more than nosy-old-man syndrome. He's been spying on us. Knows about this whole place." He gestured at the scenery with his free hand. "Can you believe it?"

"Yes—I mean no. No, I can't believe it. But, yes, it's pretty crazy."

"He wants to get his grubby paws on some sorta key. Convinced I know where it is."

The ornate gates of the palace loomed ahead. I would be extraordinarily happy to get inside and see Brock and have a sense of safety—regardless of the giant leech and her bodyguard beside me.

"What did he do to you?"

"Ugh!" Dad threw his head back. "First, he refused to bring me food. But his wife, Abigail, snuck me things here and there." He chuckled. "Poor woman is much too nice for that man. Anyway, he went from one strategy to another. Sleep deprivation. Kicking me in the gut. Zapping me with a cattle prod. He became progressively violent."

"That's terrible!" I made a fist and imagined plowing it into a certain cigar-smoker's face.

"And how did you manage to escape, pray tell?" Estancia sounded bored.

"Well, yesterday—at least I think it was yesterday—Joseph had to leave. Said he had some important, secret meeting. And guess who, or rather what, played babysitter?"

I cut my eyes to him. "Um, I'd say Mrs. Marshall, but she's more of a 'who' than a 'what.'"

"True. It was definitely a 'what.' A seven foot, hairy 'what.' This big ol' Sasquatch comes down to the basement and stares me down like I'm his first meal in weeks. Some grunt who smelled like wet dog."

The guards stationed at the palace noticed our approach and hollered orders at the soldiers behind the gate. The arched barrier split in two and slowly opened.

"How did you get away?"

Dad chuckled. "Seems we all underestimated timid, frail Abigail. She knocked on the door and announced dinner. Said her hands were full. The Yeti opened the door and was greeted with a bullet in the chest."

"What?" My mouth gaped. "Mrs. Marshall shot him?"

He laughed again, shaking his head. "I was stunned. She unlocked my handcuffs, stuffed a wad of money in her purse, and said she was going to disappear. Suggested I do the same."

"Whoa. Sounds like she's watched a lot of crime TV."

"I ran home, figuring you guys wouldn't be there. Changed clothes, headed to Beacon Rock. And *then...*" He rolled his eyes with exaggeration. "there was the matter of contacting Odyssey, the dragon, so I could access his lair and tunnels—but that's another story. Once inside, I bumbled my way down then asked the Elves of Willowmist to summon the Faeries...and, voilà, here I am."

We approached the gate as two Gnomes came into view across the courtyard. They were running as fast as their tiny legs could carry them. I recognized the pair as Sir Noblin and Revonika, part of the queen's advisory council.

"Welcome back, Larcens. Welcome!" Sir Noblin huffed to a stop in front of us, Revonika on his heels. "Oh, thank the Maker you're both safe. And *here.* My goodness, this is indeed a miracle. We've been searching and praying and scratching our heads in confusion. Not to mention the frightening attack on Vituvia." The elderly Gnome always had plenty to say.

Freckle-faced Revonika looked from Dad to me, eyes wide and questioning. "Were you captive together?"

"No." I shook my head. "We have two entirely different stories."

"*Ahem.*" Queen Estancia cleared her throat, and the two Gnomes seemed to notice the giants in their midst for the first time.

"Your Highness, pardon our impertinence." Sir Noblin removed his hat and bowed, exposing his head of thinning gray hair. Revonika curtsied. "Everything is out of sorts. Including our manners. Do we have you to thank for the safe return of our royal family members?" He replaced his hat.

The queen showed a hint of a smile. "Sadie has returned to Vituvia under my protection."

Sir Noblin bowed again. "We are truly in your debt. Please"—he gestured toward the palace—"come inside and refresh yourselves. I shall speak to Queen Judith about freeing time in her schedule to allow everyone to give a full report."

The palace halls trembled with excited whispers and scurrying feet. The queen acted synthetically mother-like, fawning over me like I was her long, lost daughter. Everyone, including my father, found her convincing.

"It's good to see this side of Queen Estancia," he whispered to me. "We didn't spend much time with her on our last trip. She's not what I expected."

I smiled and nodded under her watchful eye.

"Is there any way I can see Brock?" Dad craned his neck in all directions.

"Of course. I'll take you to his quarters." Sir Noblin waved them forward. "If he's not there, you may relax while I locate him. His room is quite comfortable. More than adequate."

The conversation trailed as the two of them walked away, leaving me alone with my parasitic shadow. I wanted to see Brock too, but it seemed better to wait. Great. Looks like misery really does love company.

Revonika led us to a parlor room, replete with statues and paintings of famous Gnomes. At least I assumed they were famous since they'd been immortalized in plaster and on canvas. I made a point to sit in a chair as far from Estancia's selected seat as possible. The less idle chitchat the better. Vincent remained outside the door.

"I shall send refreshments your way to hold you until suppertime." Revonika curtsied again. "Please make yourselves comfortable. I'll return when supper is ready, unless Queen Judith wishes to see you before then."

The Ice Queen perched on the edge of a cushioned sofa, looking rigid and much too large for the furniture. "Very well."

I had the impression she was not accustomed to waiting for others. The Gnome left us alone, much to my discomfort. Estancia didn't appear thrilled by the prospect either, with hands clasped in her lap and nostrils flaring.

I looked around the room and took in the furniture collection. Though the Gnomes had made an effort to include items for larger visitors, they hadn't quite scaled the size to Nephilim proportions. Perhaps they didn't have many visitors from Calamus until recently.

I curled in the chair and closed my eyes, not needing to feign being tired. It had been a long day. Though my body managed to adjust to the longer daylight hours and shorter nights when in the Tethered World, my recovery time after the Eldritch hadn't prepared me for all I squeezed into this particular day. Sleep swept me away with ease—I didn't even have time to grow mistrustful about the conniving queen on the other side of the room.

Stupid mistake.

CHAPTER THIRTY-FIVE

My eyes snapped open. Skoon sat on the table opposite Estancia. The two toyed with something the queen held between her fingers. Something long and silver.

I lunged for it. "That's my necklace!"

She shot to her feet and easily held the jewelry out of reach. Skoon disappeared. "This trinket?" An evil smirk stretched across her full lips. "Let's call it extra insurance. It's obviously important to you, though I can't imagine why. I'll hang on to it until I'm sure everything is in motion."

My body trembled with impotent anger.

A knock on the door forced us into civility. The Wicked Witch palmed my necklace, and I stepped back to the chair.

"Here we are." Revonika pushed the door open, and six Gnomes swarmed the room with trays of food. Tons of food.

I took deliberate breaths, trying to calm myself. Estancia dropped the necklace into her pouch and returned to the sofa.

The food kept coming. Two more Gnomes entered, pushing carts with utensils and beverages. I eyed platters of chicken and vegetables. This looked like an all-you-can-eat buffet rather than a snack.

"Queen Judith, King Brock, your father, and a few others have decided to take their dinner in here to meet privately." Revonika clapped her hands twice, and the servants stationed themselves against the back wall.

Sir Noblin came in with Queen Judith. She looked resplendent in a simple sapphire gown, a silvery cape draped around her shoulders. Dad and Brock followed behind. I sprang from my chair and rushed to Brock, stopping short of a huge, smothering hug that wouldn't be well received.

"Hey, Brock!" I extended my arms and tried to detect his current state of mind. "Did ya miss me?"

He grinned and shifted so I could give him a side hug. I complied—at first. Then besieged him anyway. It had been too long. He tolerated me for an entire second then stiffened. "I don't like that."

My hands flew up in surrender. "Too bad, little brother. I missed you something terrible." I smiled. "Won't happen again, though. Not today anyway."

Dad chuckled. "Poor guy. He had to deal with my suffocating embrace too."

Sir Noblin, Revonika, Smarlow, and Muscle rounded out the group. Servants scurried to bring extra chairs into the parlor.

I crossed to Queen Judith and curtsied. "Great aunt Judith, it's wonderful to see you again."

"Get over here, sweet pea." She extended her arms to me. "I'm quite comfortable with a good, old-fashioned hug. And I'm workin' on wearin' down yer brother here. Heaven knows that when I first arrived I had me own idiosyncrasies too."

We embraced, and my mind flitted to Aunt Jules with a twinge of pain in my chest. Did Aunt Judith know about her sister's illness? This didn't seem the time to ask.

Queen Estancia looked humorously out of place. Her oversized body amidst the flock of Gnomes brought *Gulliver's Travels* into the realm of non-fiction.

Her mouth drew to a frown. "This is highly unconventional."

"No time to get caught up in conventions and protocol." Queen Judith seated herself in a chair beside Estancia. No one sat beside the Nephilim queen on the couch, though there was plenty of room.

Dad pushed a chair beside mine, and a Gnome slid another chair next to Aunt Judith. Apparently Brock needed to be on the *official* side of the room.

Servants dished up food and placed it on the tables in front of us—several of which were brought from elsewhere to accommodate.

Dad grasped my hand, and I glanced at him. His eyes were rimmed red.

"You okay, Dad?"

He swallowed. "I heard about Brady. It sounds like he's in

danger."

Queen Estancia suddenly slid to the end of the sofa closest to me. Her not-so-subtle warning, no doubt.

Dad blinked at the obvious intrusion. "Do you have something to add about Brady?"

She stiffened and lengthened her neck. "Not at all."

My dad squeezed my hand as if to say we'll talk later.

Her watchful eyes made my anger prick. A swift kick to her shins would make me feel so much better about now.

Food won out over retaliation. I dove in to potatoes with mushroom gravy and cheese-stuffed mushrooms—fungi were always on the menu since they grew prolifically in these parts. Estancia ate with stilted effort, making a point of picking at her food and clicking her tongue disapprovingly. Throughout dinner I deliberated about how to alert Dad to what was really going on—without getting caught.

"Ah! Delicious food always paves the way fer productive conversation." Queen Judith brushed her hands together and straightened her skirt.

Queen Estancia immediately dropped her forkful of chicken and sat up straight.

"Oh, now!" Queen Judith waved a hand toward Estancia. "I'm not much for formal pishposh. No need to stop eatin' because I'm finished. Go on, enjoy. I'll talk."

Estancia was the picture of mortification. "I've had plenty. Thank you." Her eyes roamed the room, taking in the travesty of the rest of us with our mouths full of food. "Queen Judith, I've something I'd like to discuss with you."

Queen Judith smiled with her eyes. "And I with you, my friend."

Once again, Estancia flared her nostrils. "I would appreciate it if you would address me by my proper title."

Aunt Judith arched her eyebrows and gave a slow nod. "Very well, *Queen* Estancia, you may have the floor first."

The icy woman glanced at me then laced her fingers together. "As you all know, when I heard the news of the attack I felt it imperative to warn your friends in Berganstroud."

"They are *your* friends too, are they not, Your Highness?" Sir Noblin pushed his plate away and dabbed his beard with a cloth napkin.

"The Dwarves are our allies, yes." She pressed her lips

together as if such questions were absolute tedium. "But it's no secret that we are less—uh—intimate with the Dwarves than yourselves. Until recently the Nephilim have kept mainly to themselves."

"Which I find curious." Smarlow crossed his arms and glowered.

"Hmm. In what way?" The smirk on Estancia's lips showed her feeling of superiority.

"Smarlow, this is not an appropriate time for your brooding." Muggleridge placed a hand on Smarlow's shoulder.

"Fine." Smarlow continued to stare at Estancia. "Answer me this, O Queen. Why did you pay a visit to Vituvia on the very day we were attacked? To my knowledge, your realm has never initiated contact with us first. At least not in the last hundred years or more. I was en route from Berganstroud when you came and would like to hear the account for myself."

Preach it, Smarlow! He was a perceptive little Gnome.

Estancia fluttered her eyelashes and looked toward the ceiling. "I suppose the perilous times in which we live make for paranoid denizens. I shall choose to overlook your ridiculous innuendo." She smiled sweetly at Queen Judith. "As I was saying...I felt compelled to offer my services to you in your hour of need. Being able to fly *does* have its advantages."

"I'm sorry." Queen Judith scooted to the edge of her chair, brows pinched. "What was the reason for your visit? I don't recall hearin' an explanation, come to think of it."

Estancia swallowed but didn't lose her pompous demeanor. "I...I never had the chance to expound due to the attack. But I wanted to personally see how the search for Sir Liam, here was going." She indicated my dad, "I-I wanted to present something to him as soon as he was found."

I studied her nose to see if it might be growing like Pinocchio's.

"It was such an important proposal I could not entrust it to anyone else." She gave an innocent shrug. "But when I arrived, as you know, Vituvia was in a panic. I only did what was right."

What a load of nonsense!

"I see." Queen Judith grasped Estancia's hand. "We are

very thankful." Apparently, Auntie was buying it. "Let us not put off yer business any longer."

I could see the victorious glint in Estancia's eyes. She really thought she had everyone fooled. Maybe she did. But I was determined to find a way to expose her true character without endangering Mom and Sophie. Somehow.

The Ice Queen shifted in her seat and looked at my dad. "What I wanted to ask Sir Liam was about his daughter. Of course, it would be preferable to speak to you and your wife together about such things." She glanced at the others. "But I've placed Lady Amy and Princess Sophie under my protection in Calamus."

Dad looked at me questioningly. I shrugged, equally curious. What excuse for her visit was she pulling out of the air now that she was on the spot?

"My son Xander has taken quite a liking to your beautiful daughter." She smiled at me with veiled condescension.

I did *not* like where I saw this heading.

"It would seem to be an advantageous alliance to betroth our children to one another in marriage."

My dad coughed. "*What?*"

The woman had ridiculous nerve. If she hadn't already scoffed at such an idea to me privately, I may have been worried. But she had only come up with this to save face when pressed. Still, I had to perform for her little show.

"Dad, you're not going to let her do this, right?"

"She's sixteen." Dad pressed his hands against his knees. "What an outlandish notion."

"Well"—she flicked her wrist in the air—"something to think about. We can talk timetables later."

"Like, never." I crossed my arms.

"Certainly a flatterin' and beneficial proposal," Aunt Judith said. "But we've more pressin' things to discuss, me thinks."

Estancia swiveled to face Queen Judith. "Certainly. There's the—"

"Which is what brings us to plans for retaliation," Aunt Judith interrupted. "With the Trolls alignin' themselves to the Banished, we're grateful to have the Nephilim as allies. We need to shift to the offensive. Craventhrall expects us to cower and allow them to walk all over us. Instead, we shall show 'em who they're messin' with." Aunt Judith raised her fist. "We shall not be bullied."

"Here, here, Your Grace!" Sir Noblin applauded.

Queen Estancia cleared her throat. "Yes, well. I hope we can assist you. However, there are certain conditions I'd like to establish in order to invest our troops in this retaliation."

"Conditions? Are ya not concerned about the Flamin' Sword of Cherubythe fallin' into the wrong hands?" Queen Judith gave an exaggerated shrug. "Well then, we won't be wastin' any more of yer time. Go on back to yer mighty city and prepare to live in the dark. Once the sword falls into enemy hands there's no tellin' what sort of chaos to expect."

"I wish for no such thing." Queen Estancia jutted her chin in the air. "As you know, the recent battle cost us many lives."

"It cost the Gnomes and Dwarves many more." Queen Judith leveled her gaze at the hulking monarch. "The unfortunate price of freedom."

"Yes. Most unfortunate." The Ice Queen steepled her fingers together. "And a price we are willing to pay once again, if we may first have some assurances from Vituvia."

"Such as?" Queen Judith raised an eyebrow.

"Assurances that what we are fighting for really exists."

The Gnomes sputtered and looked at one another.

Aunt Judith pressed her lips together and cleared her throat to signal for quiet. "You *doubt* the existence of the Flamin' Sword of Cherubythe? You've some other clever idea about how the light shines upon our underground world? Please, share it."

A pretentious smile settled on Estancia's lips. "It is not for me to put forth alternative theories. But before I agree to place more warriors in harm's way we would like the certitude that the sword is not merely a theory that's been perpetuated by the Gnomes for centuries."

Queen Judith looked incredulous. "I cannot believe what I'm hearin'. You've got a lot of nerve to doubt what all the Tethered World—both the Land of Legend *and* the Land of the Ancients—have believed and protected for thousands of years." She frowned disapprovingly. "Utter nonsense. We won't be bullied—not by the Trolls and certainly not by *you*."

"There's a difference between bullying and negotiating. If you want the help of our large, powerful army, then you will show us what it is that our men are dying to protect." She lifted her hands, palms up. "Quite simple."

"You honestly think we can't manage without you?" Smarlow stood, red in the face. "I beg to differ, Your *Highness*. Though we mistakenly expected that your kinsmen would fight for what is right, we will not grovel to please you."

Estancia balked at the bold Gnome. "Call it what you want. I don't see that you are in any position to argue. Look at the stature of your army in comparison to Trolls and Gargoyles. You need our size and strength to stand and survive."

Smarlow balled his hands into fists and trembled. He looked ready to launch and explode on impact.

"Colonel Smarlow, take yer seat." Queen Judith attempted to diffuse the little firecracker. She turned her penetrating gaze to the Nephilim queen. "Are you a poor student of history? Time and again the Maker has used the small, seemin'ly weak vessels of His creation to confound the mighty. I'd say He takes particular pleasure in such incongruence. You need to be choosin' yer words more carefully—and yer allegiance, fer that matter."

Wow. That oughta smart. It hit me that the Wicked Witch expected me to help sway the conversation in her favor. If things didn't go her way, Mom and Sophie would pay.

I cleared my throat. "I don't know why it's such a big deal." That didn't sound very official.

Estancia turned sharp eyes on me. From her reaction, I sensed she had forgotten about our arrangement in the heat of the moment. Recognition flashed, changing her expression. "Go on."

I blinked at her and then at the others who now stared back expectantly. "I mean, is there some law forbidding what she wants?"

Queen Judith looked at Sir Noblin.

He scratched thoughtfully at his beard. "Not specifically. There are certain conditions mentioned in our founding documents. But such a request is unorthodox. The Gnomes will not be strong-armed by threats." He pounded his fist on the table with the last sentence.

"I agree." Queen Judith looked her royal counterpart squarely in the face.

The muscles in Estancia's jaw flexed.

My mom and sister needed a different answer!

"I think you should reconsider." My gaze circled around the room. "Would it hurt anything—as long as the conditions are met? Shouldn't we forget pride and traditions and work together? During my dreadful days in the Eldritch I overheard the Trolls and Gargoyles collaborating and strategizing. Dangerous plans are brewing that would alert the entire planet to the presence of the Flaming Sword of Cherubythe. Their insatiable lust for power extends all the way topside."

The friction diffused a couple degrees.

"Thank you, Lady Sadie." Aunt Judith bent her head in my direction. "'Tis true. This is not the time for pride or assertin' our independence. Our Creator has endowed each of us with unique abilities and roles here in the Tethered World." She gave Brock a loving glance. "I wish to be an example of a benevolent ruler to our next in line."

She straightened and turned back to Estancia. "Though I deem yer request as borderin' on the heretical, it is not worth jeopardizin' our longstandin' relationship. However, I shall not violate our foundin' documents. Barrin' any surprise stipulations—for much time has passed since we've looked into the matter—you will be permitted into the Garden Dome."

Queen Estancia lost her edgy posture. "Very well."

"Sir Noblin will look into this straightaway." Aunt Judith stood and turned to General Muggleridge. "We've no time to waste in procurin' a battle plan. Meet with your leaders and report to me in a few hours." She pressed her shoulders back and returned her attention to the giant. "Was there anything else, Queen Estancia?"

The Ice Queen met Aunt Judith's steely gaze with her own. "I don't believe so."

"Then yer free to stroll the courtyard, visit the music chamber, or refresh yerself in a guest room. Revonika can escort you to any of these places if ya wish."

Estancia nodded once. "Thank you."

Aunt Judith swished out of the room, followed by the Gnomes. Servants began removing the dirty dishes. Revonika remained behind with us.

Awkward silence descended. Though I ignored Estancia, I felt her eyes on me—like she could bore into my brain and read my thoughts. Did she suspect I intended to tip off my dad about Mom and Sophie?

I grinned at Dad, who looked dreadfully tired. Brock walked intent on looking at the faces of a family of Gnomes on the center canvas, brushing his fingertips across their eyes.

Revonika wandered up beside him and pointed to the male Gnome in the center. "That's my great-great-grandfather Foster."

That's it! All the paintings and artwork brought to mind a museum. A museum made me think of code words.

"So...Dad." I drummed my fingers on my knees. "You know how Mom and Sophie absolutely love art?"

Dad wrinkled his nose inquisitively. Estancia moved closer.

"I think they'd *really* like this collection." I gestured around the room. "Mom would probably ask if she could be the—what's it called? Oh, the *curator* of all this art."

"Let's leave this suffocating, small room. I'd like to find the music chamber." Estancia stood and placed a viselike hand on my shoulder.

Dad continued to look puzzled.

"Do you have artwork in Calamus, Queen Estancia?" I batted my eyelashes at her. "Since my mom and sister are there, maybe they could be a curator of your artwork."

"What are you talking about?" Her gaze shot warning flares between us.

"A *curator* is an important job." I glanced at my dad. "Very important."

Recognition flickered across his face. "Yes. I *do* believe Amy would find that fulfilling." He stood and looked at Estancia. "Would you mention it to her when you return?"

"Don't be ridiculous. We've no need for a curator." She grabbed my forearm. "Let's go."

"I'd like for us to stay together." Dad grasped my free hand and searched my face. He looked conflicted.

I patted his arm. "You look tired, Daddy. Why don't you go. Go and...rest. I'm going to keep Queen Estancia company."

Estancia pulled my wrist. "Revonika! Lead us to the music chamber."

The Gnome narrowed her eyes but didn't balk at the rude woman.

Dad's eyes flashed at the giant. "I'll catch up with you later, Sadie. I'm going to spend time with Brock. And maybe take a lengthy nap."

I glanced over my shoulder and gave an urgent nod. *I sure hope you're thinking what I'm thinking!*

CHAPTER THIRTY-SIX

BRADY CRACKED OPEN AN EYE AT the sound of a particularly loud screech. The faint rectangle of light continued to glow at the top of the stairs. He wondered if the sounds and cries that punctuated the silence were prompted by the inmates' physical pain or mental anguish. Staying around long enough to find out was not something Brady wanted to consider.

His wrists throbbed. He gently probed the raw skin with his fingers then pulled away, cringing over the germs that surely lurked on his hands. He sighed and wondered how he'd survive the boredom—and filth—of solitary.

A small lump in one of his pockets made him sit up. He still had Brock's pocketknife!

His hands had been tied up for so long, he'd forgotten about it. The slim knife didn't weigh much. Apparently the Trolls were accustomed to disarming their enemies' visible weapons. Swords and daggers weren't something that could be concealed.

Brady thrilled at the prospect. This weapon had the potential to be his ticket out if he stayed alert for the right opportunity.

A door opened, scraping across the stone floor with an odious screech. Brady heard footsteps, snarls, and cursing.

"Shut up!" A gruff voice boomed. The pattern repeated.

Soon a dark figure shadowed Brady's doorway. "Here, topsider."

Brady rose to his feet. The hulking silhouette left Brady clueless as to the meaning of the visit.

"You hungry or not? Haven't got all day."

Food! Brady scrambled up the steps. The Troll stood

beside a cart piled with dinner rolls.

Brady slipped his hands between the cold metal shafts. The Troll plopped two rolls in one palm and handed Brady an empty wooden cup from the bottom of the cart.

"This is your only cup. Don't lose it in your pit." The big ape lifted a pitcher and splashed water into the cup. "Dinner is served."

"Just bread?" Brady stared at his meager meal.

"Whaddya expect? A well-rounded supper?" The Troll chuckled and pushed the cart a few steps. "Once a week, those with good behavior get half a chicken. Hasn't happened in months."

Brady sipped the water, not wanting to waste any by sloshing it on his way down the stairs. It had a bitter aftertaste, but at least it was wet. Seventeen steps later, he leaned against the wall, chewing the dry, tasteless bread and washing it down with a sip of water.

Before he made much of a dent in the second dinner roll, his stomach churned uncomfortably. He tried to keep his mind off the nausea that brewed. Though he couldn't finish the bread, he didn't feel that it caused his sudden sickness. The water was the likely culprit.

He stuffed the roll into his pocket, afraid something might nibble on it if he placed it anywhere else. Ugh…he didn't need to think about what might keep him company in this dark dungeon.

Shaking and lightheaded, Brady coiled into a ball and pressed his face against the cold granite for relief. He tried hard to think about nothing.

At long last, dusk arrived. It boggled my mind to think of all that happened in the past day. Fortunately, Queen Estancia was far too superior to have a slumber party with a commoner like myself. My Vituvian title of "princess" fooled her not.

The White Witch parted with a stern warning. "Remember, I have eyes and ears working for me *everywhere.*" After Brady's kidnapping in the palace, I didn't doubt it.

I desperately hoped that Dad understood my insinuating remarks. He hadn't made an appearance after dinner, so I felt optimistic. My mind made the rounds to my family members, both in the belly of the earth and topside, and I prayed for a happy ending to this real-life horror flick.

Brady passed the night expelling bodily fluids. He could not remember ever feeling this nauseated or having such severe cramps. A swift and sudden death sounded rather appealing. Minchess called him a "lightweight," rousing jeers and laughter from the other prisoners. Whoever came on duty next commented from the top of the stairs. "You shouldn't drink the water."

Understatement of the year, Brady thought.

Whenever sickness overwhelmed him, he counted four strides into the dark abyss, away from his self-imposed station at the bottom of the stairs. Four strides. If he found himself needing to plumb the depths of his prison cell in the future, at least he could avoid that toxic spot.

Any plans for the pocket knife seemed futile. Brady didn't want to go anywhere, even if he could. Except maybe to heaven.

A new spasm of sickness surged, and he bolted four steps and retched.

A day spent in forced companionship is about as fulfilling as a root canal. Estancia hovered close, her invisible talons clamped on my nerves while she masqueraded as an attentive mother figure. I had to wonder how Xander turned out so well. Maybe he had a terrific nanny.

Vincent looked as bored as I felt. He dutifully followed as the queen dragged me from one part of the palace to another, impatiently cursing protocol. My necklace mocked me from around her wrist.

"Your Highness!" Revonika scurried to where Estancia sat listening to me plink out a lame song on an out-of-tune piano in the music chamber.

Revonika curtsied. "I've come with news. Sir Noblin has reviewed the founding documents. Please report to the throne room to be briefed."

The queen stood with such triumph, Revonika jumped.

We followed the Gnome, and I kept an eye out for Dad. Thankfully, the narcissistic queen hadn't noticed his absence.

The guards denied Vincent access to the throne room. He looked peeved to have to take orders from such tiny creatures but stood to the side, arms folded across his muscular chest.

At the far end of the stately room, Queen Judith sat on her gilded throne, scepter in hand. Beside her, on a less-elaborate chair, sat my brother Brock, rocking back and forth in his subtle, familiar way. Either this "debriefing" was an official act or my great-aunt thought better of the casual interaction she had extended to Estancia the night before.

"You may approach the throne when Queen Judith extends her scepter." Revonika stood on her tiptoes—a useless gesture—and whispered up to Estancia.

The giantess narrowed her eyes. "I know how this works."

Sir Noblin came in through a side door, followed by an elderly Gnome in an official-looking black robe with purple tassels draped over his shoulders. I recognized him from our last visit. They crossed to the steps leading to the throne. The older Gnome held the wooden ends of a rolled-up scroll.

Queen Judith raised the scepter and pointed at Estancia. "Approach."

Hmm. Can that thing shoot bullets?

The Ice Queen took slow, deliberate steps. I half expected "Pomp and Circumstance" to start playing.

After three strides, Estancia turned and extended her

hand to me. "I would like Princess Sadie to accompany me."

Great. Revonika pressed my leg. I stepped forward and joined the march to the throne, keeping my hands clasped behind my back. We stopped in front of the steps, and the robed Gnome unrolled a portion of the scroll.

Sir Noblin cleared his throat. "Attend to the words of our founding document as interpreted by Sir Kittrick, Chancellor of the Vituvian Court."

Sir Kittrick nodded. "In the exposition of those who may attend to the Flaming Sword of Cherubythe, these are our findings." He held the scroll at arm's length. "The Flaming Sword of Cherubythe is hereby entrusted to the oversight of the noble citizens of Vituvia. Their—uh—duty is to protect the sword from en-em-ies. Yes! *Enemies* both domestic and—uh—abroad."

Estancia sighed impatiently.

The Gnome swallowed and looked from Estancia to Queen Judith. "My apologies. I'm translating as I go."

The Nephilim queen stiffened beside me. "How do I have assurance that what you're saying is accurate?"

Queen Judith propped the end of her scepter on the floor with a forceful *thud.* "What ya should already be assured of, is that Vituvians are true to their word and honest to a fault. That ought to be enough." She seemed every bit as formidable as Estancia when she spoke with such conviction.

The Wicked Witch turned her cool gaze back to the chancellor.

Sir Kittrick smiled nervously and scanned the parchment. "The Guardians of the Sword must attend to the sword's security with due diligence and proper ceremony. Anyone who presents themselves before the powerful sword is hereby—uh—exhorted to reflect upon their state of virtue. The un...un-wor-thy shall face judgment." He lowered the scroll and bowed.

Brock stopped rocking and looked at our aunt expectantly.

Queen Judith placed the scepter across her lap and steepled her fingers together. "As Chancellor of the Court, what is your official assessment in this matter?"

Sir Kittrick offered another bow. "Your Grace, it is my scholarly opinion that there is nothing in these documents to preclude a non-Vituvian from viewing the Flaming Sword.

Though the wording makes a point of exclusivity in regards to the guarding and oversight of the sword, it seems to allow for the presentation of others as long as that individual is worthy. Or as the document specifically states, 'has reflected upon their state of virtue.' As long as Queen Estancia understands and considers the inherent risks, I see no reason to deny her request."

"Thank you, Chancellor." Queen Judith leaned toward Brock and whispered something that made him grin. She straightened and looked at Estancia. "Are you of a sound mind in regards to your virtue? And are you willing to risk being misguided about your self-assessment?"

Queen Estancia looked at the two rulers seated before her with disdain. "My mind is quite sound. What is this *risk* I'm to assess?"

"The risk is simple. If you're wrong about your state of worthiness, you face judgment." Aunt Judith's face was unreadable.

"Then I'm ready to be given the honor of coming before the Flaming Sword of Cherubythe." She clenched a fist to her chest and raised her chin proudly. "I'm a good person."

CHAPTER THIRTY-SEVEN

I GLANCED AT THE CEILING EXPECTING lightning bolts to strike the woman dead on the spot. Nothing happened.

Brock briefly caught my eye. Such a gesture—initiating contact—is rare. I saw doubt on his face.

Growing up, Brock had an uncanny sense about others. As a child, he often came unglued around certain people. Although the person wasn't doing anything out of the ordinary, perhaps only making small talk, they revealed a different side of themselves if faced with one of Brock's meltdowns. Without fail, the episode exposed a shallow individual. As the meltdown intensified, the person in question became agitated and downright rude to Brock and whoever he was with. It became a good litmus test for babysitters when we were young.

The way Brock glanced at me now made me hopeful that he had matured past the meltdown stage. Regardless, life in Vituvia had definitely taken the edge off his self-protective shield.

Queen Judith stood and lifted her scepter. "It is hereby decreed that our ally, the noble Queen Estancia of Calamus, is to be brought before the Flaming Sword of Cherubythe. Once this request has been granted, Vituvia expects to have the full support of the Calamus military at our disposal. Do you agree to these terms, Queen Estancia?"

From my close proximity, I saw the glint of triumph in the Wicked Witch's gaze. "I find those terms agreeable, Queen Judith."

My aunt looked at the Gnomes before her. "Thank you, Chancellor Kittrick. Sir Noblin, please lead us to the Garden Dome."

Sir Noblin crossed to the door he had entered earlier and spoke to the guards stationed there. They conferred together, and he returned. "Smarlow will meet up with us. Shall we proceed?"

Sir Noblin and Revonika led the way, speaking to guards and others as we walked. My irritating chaperone and I, shadowed by good ol' Vincent, followed Queen Judith and Brock. A general buzz infiltrated the palace; wide eyes regarded us with interest.

"How soon can we return to Calamus after you lay eyes on the Sword?" Speaking to someone a foot-and-a-half taller than myself made it hard to judge how loud to speak in a private manner. "I want my family back together."

She cut her eyes at me. "Remains to be seen." A low chuckle emanated from her chest. "The sword might be the impetus for my request, but I have a greater goal."

"Why doesn't that surprise me?"

"Well, I suppose I could tell my future daughter-in-law where my real motivation lies."

"Ugh. Lucky for you I know you're lying through your teeth." I smiled condescendingly. "I really don't care what motivates you."

She laughed again. "Unfortunately, I've thought of a few scenarios in which having you and Xander together might be to my benefit." She shook her head. "But let's hope that won't be necessary."

"Oh, it won't."

We turned into a wide, lengthy corridor lined with nature tapestries and statues of humans—the closest of which I recognized as Great-aunt Judith. I guessed that the others must be former monarchs of Vituvia as well. At the end of the passage stood a single, arched door flanked by two guards. The Vituvian banner perched proudly above the doorway, its purple fabric a beacon of color in the gleaming, limestone hall. The flag displayed beams of light radiating behind the silhouette of a tree, whose trunk was obscured by the shape of a sword with a curved blade.

"That tree." Estancia nodded toward the banner. *That* is the real prize."

"Why?"

Soldiers saluted Queen Judith as we walked.

Estancia gave me a sidelong glance. "It's the tree that is

guarded by the sword."

"Fine. Whatever."

"Surely you *know.*"

Smarlow came scurrying past with a set of keys attached to a chain around his waist.

"I don't know. And if it's important to you, I honestly don't *care.*"

"Well, dear Sadie, allow me to give you a quick history lesson."

Brock and Queen Judith stopped several feet from the door. Queen Estancia pulled me back to her side.

"That tree is a specimen of *the* Tree." She leaned close and whispered into my ear. "Grown from a seed taken from the fruit of the Tree of Life. Straight from the Garden of Eden."

Whether it was day or night, Brady hadn't a clue. He only now began to care about such trivial things as breathing and thinking. The chills had passed with the last wave of nausea. The fever finally abated. His senses began to once again make sense.

He recognized the screech of the main door opening. A series of sounds replayed from the night before—or however long it had been since he drank the tainted water. Footsteps started and stopped. Trolls snarled and swore and rattled the bars. The guard growled back with a ferocious "Shut up!"

Must be mealtime, thought Brady. Though he couldn't be sure which meal.

A bulky shape appeared at the top of the stairs.

"What is rotting in this cell?" The Troll coughed.

"I've been sick." Brady's voice was raspy and weak.

"No kidding. Welcome to Craventhrall." Sarcasm dripped from the Troll's words. "Here. Special delivery. Straight from the boss."

The sound of something skittering down the stairs made Brady grope the steps. His hand fell on a lump of bread and then another hunk smacked against his cheek. The shadow moved on to another cell.

Brady held one roll in each hand and leaned his head against the stone corner, eyes closed. What he really wanted was water. Clean water. He felt certain he'd lost every ounce of bodily fluid. He couldn't scrounge up a teardrop if his life depended on it, let alone swallow dry bread.

"Hey, topsider."

Brady winked open an eye.

"Almost forgot. Chebar had me bring some boiled water to you. Guess he knew you weren't tough enough for Craventhrall water." He chuckled.

"Thanks." Brady eked out.

"You gotta come get it, your lowliness." The shadow of the Troll shifted, and Brady could hear water sloshing.

He didn't want to lay the bread on the filthy floor so he added them to the stash in his pockets. With a groan, he fumbled up the steps. Head whirling, limbs shaking. Water was the only thing worth the effort.

"Bring your cup."

"*Ugh.*" Brady crawled backwards down the half-dozen stairs he had scaled. Cup in hand, he traversed the long road to the top.

The Troll, who Brady could now see was a mottled grey-and-brown Bigfoot, lifted a small pitcher and poured it into the trembling cup that Brady extended through the bars.

"Do all topsiders smell as bad as you?" The big oaf hacked, expelling his own foul odor for Brady to deal with.

"If they've been puking all night." Brady didn't trust himself to make it back down the stairs with the water. Instead, he leaned against the bars, and took a tiny sip. As it leaked across his parched tongue, he feared the whole cycle of sickness might begin again. He decided to wait between swallows to see if anything happened.

The Troll left to the sound of inmates rattling doors and screeching like madmen. Brady exhaled unsteadily, allowing his thoughts to wander back to things that mattered. How was Sadie coping under all the pressure? It seemed unfair for everyone's fate to rest on her shoulders. She wouldn't have to do it alone if he could help it. He was supposed to be a Guardian of the Sword, and he intended to fulfill that calling. But...hadn't he succeeded at protecting Brock—sort of accidentally—which was also part of his new job description?

Brady raked his fingers across his buzzed scalp and grinned. He'd managed to play his part as body double rather well. He shuddered to imagine Brock being captured and getting sick as a dog in this black hole. Horrible! Brady would gladly relive the entire ordeal as long as his brother remained safe and could continue his training.

But Brady *had* to escape. He had information that those in Vituvia needed. Sadie wouldn't have an opportunity to alert anyone with that witch Estancia watching her every move. Even worse, both Nekronok and Estancia alluded to possessing one of the keys to the sword, interrogating Sadie about the other key. Which meant the sooner Brady could get back on his feet and out of the Eldritch, the better.

After several minutes, he dared to try more water, noting the lack of bitterness that had marked the liquid he drank earlier. This made him hopeful. Eventually, he downed half the wooden cup, and his body slowly revived.

Shifting to retrieve a roll from his pocket, he decided to brave a couple bites. With his shoulder pressed between two bars, he could see a sliver of the main door, along with the knuckles of a Yeti grasping the bars with his leathery fingers in the next cell.

The fresh roll smelled yeasty and, well, *normal.* Something Brady welcomed since life had turned inside out, along with his stomach. He was surprised that the Trolls had a flare for baking bread.

After a tiny nibble and a few watchful moments, the bread had the desired effect. Encouraged by the settling in his stomach, he took a big bite.

Or, at least, he tried.

His teeth clamped onto something hard and metallic. "Wha—?"

Brady pulled the roll apart and gasped. An item had been baked into the bread. He grasped the object, heart pounding at what he perceived it to be. The rest of the roll plopped onto his lap, and he cupped the prize in his hand.

CHAPTER THIRTY-EIGHT

MY BRAIN TRIED TO PROCESS THE latest headline: The Tree of Life Lives On. How had *that* tidbit of information been left out of the family history lessons thrown my way? And what were the implications of the existence of such a thing?

The entourage moved through the doors, interrupting my mental meltdown. Vincent was not permitted inside.

Another door blocked our way even as the first one closed behind us. Smarlow worked the key in the lock, while I tried not to feel suffocated in the tight space. I eyed Brock—who normally hates to be trapped like a pickle in a jar—but he stared ahead, cool and indifferent. *Guess that means I'll survive.*

Colonel Smarlow held the door open. As we filed into a narrow hallway, I heard him mumble something about "the guile of the Nephilim." He waited for us to pass then locked the door behind us.

The torchlight cast a creepy conglomeration of shadows on the stone walls. We glided down the passage to yet another locked door. Smarlow elbowed his way to the front, grumbling. He clearly disliked this turn of events.

From the dim, confining corridor, we spilled into an open, well-lit room. Red velvet benches framed the circular perimeter. To my surprise, two Nephilim warriors stood on either side of the next set of doors. Each stood beside a Gnome holding a lengthy spear. When the Nephilim caught sight of Estancia their eyes widened and, in unison, they bowed.

"Your Majesty!" The one on the right stepped forward. His blond, shaggy hair and droopy mustache made him look like a Viking.

"Holt." Estancia looked from the blond guard to the other. "Typhel. I see the Vituvians have put you to work."

Smarlow crossed to the Gnome guards and conferred.

"If that's what you want to call it, Your Highness." Holt looked around the room with disgust.

"Meaning?" The Ice Queen raised an eyebrow.

"Meaning we have no weapons, and we're stuck in this overgrown coffin for far too long each day. We've yet to see the sword. Two days on duty here, and you're the first visitors to grace those doors."

"You're on probation, soldier." Smarlow swiveled around, hands on hips. "There's protocol to follow."

"Exactly as I predicted." Estancia lifted her chin. "Our men haven't been allowed inside." Then, as if she thought better of jeopardizing her position, the contemptuous look melted into a smile and her head tilted. "But, no doubt a necessary procedure. We have our formalities in Calamus as well."

Holt pressed his lips together and stepped back.

Typhel nodded. "Yes, Your Majesty. And you should know that the Gnomes have treated us well."

"Of course we have." Smarlow stepped up to the double doors and inserted his key in the lock. "Let's finish our business, shall we?"

The Gnome guards opened the doors in unison. Queen Judith and Brock stepped through first. The two Nephilim warriors shifted closer and craned their necks to peek.

"To your posts!" Smarlow barked.

They both snapped to attention against the wall on either side of the doors.

Sir Noblin and Revonika stood across from each other in the doorway.

Revonika swept her hand toward what appeared to be a balcony. "After you, Queen Estancia." The Wicked Witch walked through in two long strides.

I looked from Revonika to Sir Noblin. "Am I allowed inside?"

"The Royal family is always welcome." Sir Noblin offered a curt bow.

With a quiver of excitement, I stepped into the Garden Dome.

The vast space felt like another world. Exotic, mysterious, and full of color, it hummed with life and smelled of orchids and gardenias. Other lofty terraces dotted the perimeter, a guard stationed on each. Below us, rows of Gnomes marched in a complex pattern across a shimmery, white floor that curved against a beautiful, turquoise lagoon.

But the *pièce de résistance* pulsated from a lush island on the other side of the swath of cerulean water. On top of a mound of rock that was covered with thick, contorted roots, a flame flickered brightly.

Astonished by the sight, I sucked in my breath. The fire frolicked in vibrant contortions, challenging me to spy what hid within its blaze. A glint of metal teased but refused to reveal much, especially from this distance.

I scanned the expanse of an enormous, glossy wall that stretched behind the sword from one end of the island to the other. It soared up, higher than our balcony. Then I noticed the golden quartz roof that vaulted over the entire scene—a miniature version of the sky that lit the Tethered World.

"Unbelievable." Estancia breathed beside me in the softest of whispers. She stepped up to the low balustrade that encircled our balcony.

She blocked my view of the Flaming Sword. *Don't mind me.*

"It's somethin' to behold, isn't it?" Aunt Judith stepped beside her royal counterpart. I couldn't help but notice how petite she looked next to the giantess. Inside and out, they were polar opposites.

"Oh yes. Be-*hold* is a good word."

In front of me, Estancia's wings shifted beneath her cape. Silver feathers slid free from the fabric. I blinked, taken aback. With swift movements the witch stepped on top of the low railing, wings unfurling beneath her cape.

The Nephilim queen leapt from the balcony, taking flight. But not before I lunged after her, wrapping my arms around her knees.

CHAPTER THIRTY-NINE

THANKS TO THE FRESH-BAKED KEY from Chebar, along with the knife in his pocket, Brady made a miraculous comeback. Sure, the water helped. As did the bread. But the lifelines he now possessed resuscitated him, body and soul. He had tools to tackle an escape. He only needed to bide his time and pay attention to his options.

Admittedly, those were limited. At least until he figured out the pattern of life in this pit. He tried to pass the time with laps up and down the stairs. On his second round he sputtered to a stop, exhaustion reminding him of how he spent the night sick as a dog.

Out of breath and energy, he sat down. So much for that. Now, dying of boredom seemed a realistic hazard. No wonder his neighbors screamed like insane animals.

The main door opened and Brady heard footsteps. Snarls percolated from the other cells. Was it time to eat already?

"Topsider!" A Troll stepped to the cell door, silhouetted.

"Yes?" Maybe he had earned half a chicken.

"You have a visitor." The Troll fiddled with the lock and stepped aside.

Blast the dark! Brady couldn't tell one Sasquatch from another. Was Chebar coming? Or his less-than-charming brother?

"Told you I'd visit." The fiendish voice of Nekronok sucked the wind from Brady's newly-revived sails.

He swallowed.

"Tell me, topsider." The chief Troll towered over Brady from a few steps above. "What do you know about the key?"

Before Brady could form a response, Nekronok hacked in Brady's face. "What in the name of Thrall have you been doing in here? Ugh! It reeks."

Brady smirked in the dark. Apparently, vomit could be a weapon of mass destruction. "Your water is disgusting."

"Listen." The Troll shoved Brady against the wall with a lanky hand around the neck. "I'd be happy to drown you in our disgusting water, which may be arranged if you outlive your usefulness. Now, tell me about the key."

Brady fought for oxygen. He clawed at Nekronok's spindly fingers and sputtered. Thankfully, the big ape loosened his grip enough for airflow. But Brady's mind grasped for reason. Was the Troll referring to the key in Brady's pocket or the one for the sword belonging to Aunt Jules? He assumed—and hoped—it was the latter.

"I didn't know a key existed until right before we returned to the Tethered World."

"Where is it, topsider? I need both keys to remove the sword." Nekronok's hand tightened again.

Brady shook his head and gasped. "I don't know. Honest."

His grip tightened. "Let's see if I can refresh your memory." The Troll lifted Brady off the ground.

"*Arghf.*" Brady couldn't sputter a word. He grabbed onto Nekronok's arm and tried to pull up against his own body weight to relieve the pressure.

A throaty chuckle rumbled from the Yeti. "You're making this difficult. Remember how this ended when I pay you another visit."

Brady's head slumped, and Nekronok dropped him in a heap on the stairs.

I squeezed my eyes shut and clung to the flying Nephilim. What was I thinking? What if I fell?

Estancia tried to kick herself free. Her tall gladiator sandals allowed for a decent grasp around her ankles where I now clung for dear life. At first my cheek was shoved against her calves, but it didn't take long for gravity to pull me lower.

The Gnomes shouted orders. I dared to open my eyes. Down below the soldiers aimed arrows toward us. Shouts of "Get down here!" and "Surrender!" and "Save the topsider!" were lobbed in our direction. The bright-blue water glistened into view.

Something clasped around one of my legs, distracting me. It felt like fingers digging into my flesh—*Skoon!* The invisible parasite had me in the same way I had Estancia.

"Get off!" the queen shouted while she tried to wriggle free. "You won't stop me from climbing over this wall and getting to the tree! I shall eat a piece of its fruit, obtain the power of the sword, and live and reign forever!"

Sweating hands and a moving objective meant my grip slowly deteriorated. My face was now planted against the woman's ankles, and my feet trailed behind like tails on a kite. I tried to kick Skoon off with my free leg.

An arrow zinged past me. Estancia shrieked in pain and tilted to the left. I couldn't see what had been hit, but it didn't slow her down much. Maybe her wing?

My hands slipped to the top of her sandaled feet. Dangling beneath her, I had a clear view of what loomed ahead.

The wall.

My weight must have affected her buoyancy. It didn't look like either one of us would clear the barrier. She tried to shake me loose, but my fingers found purchase in her laces and straps. Another arrow caught her left wing as she beat downwards. It sailed through her feathers without apparent damage.

A dozen yards from the wall, the Wicked Witch finally gained altitude. But not enough for me—which was certainly her strategy.

If I was going to be taken out by the towering slab of stone, I wanted us to go down together. With what little strength I could muster, I yanked at her legs, trying to disrupt her momentum. She cursed and stiffened, frustrating my efforts.

I flung my legs in wild contortions, Skoon and all. By twisting my body beneath her, I hoped to interfere with her trajectory. My swiveling limbs had the desired effect. Her legs pivoted with my weight, throwing her off course. She dipped lower, and I knew she wouldn't recover in time.

Bracing myself for the inevitable collision, I coiled up and swerved to allow my hip to take the impact against the wall.

"Ugh!" I hit with a painful smack. Skoon let out a wail and lost his grip.

"Get off me!" Estancia snarled. "I will have the fruit." Her upper body lay across the top of the wall. "I will live forever!"

My hands trembled and ached. The gravity of my weight yanked my knuckles from their sockets on several fingers tangled in her straps. I couldn't get free if I wanted.

Now that Estancia was an anchored target, the arrows began to fly. Two hit her thick, leather tunic. One bounced off, the other stuck feebly in her short, leather skirt that flounced above my head. The Herculean woman began to pull both of us over the top of the wall.

My left hand completely lost its grasp. I screamed, assuming I was going down. But the snared fingers of my right hand kept me bound to her foot. The Flaming Sword blazed below and to my left. Though I could see the sword better from this vantage point, I didn't have time to gawk. My fingers burned in their entrapment. Something would have to give, and the landing didn't look promising.

I heard the zing of another arrow. Estancia stiffened and screamed. A shaft protruded from the back of her leg—her hamstring had been strung. Writhing in pain, her grip faltered, and we both careened to the ground.

A large fern cushioned my fall—and I cushioned it for the Nephilim. That didn't mean I landed unscathed. Everything hurt.

The giantess rolled off me and clawed at the shattered stump of an arrow in her leg which had snapped in the fall. With a piercing screech, she pulled it free. I watched with morbid fascination, assuming she would give up. Instead, she grabbed my arm, dragged me close, and pointed the bloody tip of the arrow at my throat. "Get back or she dies!"

A line of Gnomes on the other side of the water kept their weapons trained on her while four more stopped advancing across the bridge.

"Get up!" she screamed in my ear.

I tried to push off the ground, but several fingers felt like uncooperative lumps of meat. Something painful barked at me from my ankle. Estancia must have lost patience because she hauled me up, using my body as a shield. Her arm wrapped around my shoulder, and the arrowhead pressed into the soft flesh beneath my jaw.

My hand flew up to her wrist, trying to pry it away. Her bracelet—which was my necklace—pressed against my palm. Yes! I yanked it free with a surge of vindication.

"Yer acting foolishly, Queen Estancia." Aunt Judith's voice carried through the tense atmosphere. "Yer outnumbered. Yer injured. Release Princess Sadie, and we shall give ya leniency in yer trial."

The Nephilim limped toward the mound of rock. I faltered along in front of her, wincing as I put weight on my foot. I could hear her grunting with each step, and I chimed in with moans of my own.

"There won't...be a...trial." Estancia's voice was labored. She began to trudge up the heap of rocks. "Once I get...my hands on the sword..." she said so that only I could hear.

"You can't do anything without the key," I huffed.

She stepped sideways onto a gnarly root and pulled me up after her. "That's what they want us to believe. I say we put their claims to a test."

The flames threw off a lot of heat, though the sword still perched a good four boulders away. Was she really going to stick her arm inside the fire and try to yank it free? Or worse, make *me* do it?

Though I doubted her theory, I couldn't bear to let her try. What if she released it? The sword in her control would have the worst of repercussions. I *had* to stop this giant. Somehow.

She yanked me up another level of rocks and roots. I wondered where Skoon might be lurking. Did he plan to help free the sword?

Flames flickered in my periphery. Estancia gained another foothold but I dug my heels in—one of them anyway— determined to make things as difficult as possible. But I was no match. She laughed and hauled me up again.

"Drop your weapons or the princess dies." The Wicked Witch deftly repositioned the arrowhead against my throat.

The Gnomes complied.

"Now step back. Against the wall!" Her voice had a maniacal edge. "All guards on the balustrade step inside and close the doors."

Though I couldn't lift my head to watch, I heard the sound of doors closing.

In an instant, Estancia shoved me onto a boulder, her

knee pressed against my chest. Flames billowed above my head. Jagged rocks protruded into my back. The blaze washed my face with heat.

Towering above me, the queen reached a greedy hand into the fire then withdrew it with an astonished gasp. She turned her hand over to inspect it.

"It doesn't burn!" She gave a wicked laugh. "Amazing."

I had a birds-eye view as she grasped the sword's hilt. She yanked hard, crushing my chest with her knee in the process. It hurt, but I didn't cry out.

"Nekronok is wasting his time chasing down keys. The sword is *mine*." She let the arrowhead slip from her fingers and clutched the hilt with both hands. She pulled. Hard.

My chest hurt. Badly.

Keeping my eyes trained on her delirious face, I groped for the discarded arrowhead with my swollen fingers.

"I think it moved!" She repositioned her grip and tried again.

With a guttural yell, I plunged the point of the arrow into her leg.

She screeched, releasing the sword and shifting her weight to swipe at the wound. I rolled from beneath her and shoved her leg away. Her hands flew up in an attempt to catch her balance.

She tumbled backwards with an indignant screech. The momentum caused her to summersault off the boulders and land with a splat on the cobblestoned ground—one leg dangling off the edge into the water.

The Gnomes snatched up their weapons. A half dozen scrambled over the bridge, bayonets at the ready. "Don't move!"

The soldiers across the water drew their bows taut.

Estancia's head pivoted to the warriors. A gash on her hairline bled profusely, staining the rocks crimson between the twisted braids that splayed around her face. She opened her mouth, but before she could utter a sound, a giant orange tentacle shot from the depths of the water. It spiraled around her leg and cinched tight.

I blinked. An octopus?

She screamed. Her body lurched toward the lagoon. Another tentacle split the water and wrapped around her other leg. The Gnomes lowered their weapons. Everyone stared.

Two more enormous tentacles—one on either side of Estancia—flung themselves to the cobblestone ledge, bracing against it. As I watched with shock and horror, the creature pulled the flailing, screaming woman into the aqua blue depths.

With a splash, the tentacles slipped out of sight. For a moment, the water churned. Then a few bubbles percolated the water's surface.

Just like that, Queen Estancia was gone.

CHAPTER FORTY

SOMETHING SCURRIED ACROSS BRADY'S FOREHEAD. HE sat up with a shriek, slapped at his face, and bolted up the steps toward the light. He smacked at his clothes, shivering with revulsion.

Convinced his visitor had skittered into the shadows, he sagged against the bars. What a way to wake up! The reason for his lying there in the first place came back in a rush. Nekronok made Brady's skin crawl as bad as any insect.

With the calming of his heart came the realization that Minchess must be back on duty. A loud snore carried from the end of the passage, mingling with disgruntled murmurs from other cells. It made for quite a clamorous symphony.

And seemed like a perfect time to escape.

No, he told himself, he hadn't been here long enough to recognize what an ideal time looked like. Besides, he didn't know his way around the Eldritch. Although it wasn't as if he would be given a tour of the place soon. Nekronok intended to keep him locked away.

Chebar expected him to use the key, right?

All of these thoughts sent his heart racing again. Could he really do this? Was he well enough? Clever enough?

There was only one way to find out. Standing on unsteady legs, he reached between the bars and felt for the keyhole. Should be relatively easy…

Brady snatched the key from his pocket and studied it. Unlike modern keys that had many teeth in a specific pattern, skeleton keys were simple and straightforward. Nothing special. Except, of course, this one would open his prison door.

He slid his hand back to the keyhole, thankful that his

arms were able to fit through the bars with room to spare. The awkward angle proved challenging, but during a particularly loud snort from the guard, Brady felt the *clunk* of the lock against the pressure of the key.

"*Yes,*" he whispered under his breath.

The door swung inward, and he stepped into the corridor. Minchess lay slumped in the corner, snoozing hard. Brady shut the door, hoping the guard would assume he languished somewhere in the bowels of that stinking cell.

He pressed against the wall between cell doors, sidestepping, to keep his eye on Minchess. Brady slid to the next doorway then fished out the pocketknife and flipped it open. The three-inch blade didn't look like it could do much damage to a seven-foot gorilla, but it beat heading out unarmed.

Key in his left hand, blade in his right, he shot across the doorway. So far, so good. Two more to go. He waited for a round of noise. A prisoner wailed loudly, and Minchess shifted in his seat. Brady's heart stuttered as he slipped into the shadowy part of the wall, away from the torch's limited reach.

Sleeping Sasquatch didn't wake. Brady drew a steadying breath then dashed across the next doorway. Light from the square, barred window on the exit door guided him through the darkness. Thankfully it was perched too high to silhouette Brady's escaping form.

He hoped the door was unlocked. If not, he'd need the key in his right hand to maneuver quickly. Switching the knife with the key, he took a tentative step. As he tiptoed in front of the last cell, a hand reached through the bars and grabbed his upper arm.

"Wha—?" Brady clamped his mouth shut and tried to wriggle free.

The Troll snarled. With his left hand holding the blade, Brady lashed awkwardly across the wrist of the beast. The leathery fingers recoiled, and the Yeti screeched. Brady lunged to the exit and grabbed the lever.

Locked!

Would the key work? With shaking hands, he rattled it in the latch. Another *click.*

The prisoners were now in an uproar. The door scraped across the rocky floor like a triggered alarm. Brady looked back as he stepped out—just in time to see Minchess place his hands over his ears and change positions. Brady shut the door and locked it.

Now what? He stood out like chum in a shark tank.

The current passageway hadn't much more light than the prison area. He looked around, certain that when he arrived with Chebar, they'd come from the left of where he now stood.

Brady headed right.

The door at the end of that hallway had gaping wooden slats, reinforced with perpendicular metal bars. Brady kept his back against the wall to keep an eye on the opposite door.

Between one of the slats he spied—big surprise—another passage. He shifted but couldn't make out any Trolls lurking about.

He tried the lever, slow and steady. Locked *again*. Brady slid the key into the hole and shimmied it around.

Nothing.

He knelt, keeping his ear alert for the sound of the mechanism cooperating. Behind him, a different noise swelled. It seemed someone had managed to wake the guard. The door to solitary shook on its hinges.

Brady fiddled with the key in hurried desperation. At last the lock gave way at the same moment the other door flew open. Brady dashed out and slammed the door, locking it again. This time it cooperated. Heart in his throat, he turned to run.

A wall of fur blocked his way.

I stared at the rippling water. My heart smashed against my ribcage like a wild animal trying to escape. Though there was no love lost in parting with the Wicked Witch, I couldn't process what I had witnessed. A giant octopus? Queen Estancia...dead?

The Gnomes shouted orders and dashed about. The four closest to me clambered up the rocks to my aid.

"Hang on." I held my hands up. "I need to catch my breath."

"Certainly." The redheaded Gnome beside me nodded. All four hopped down and stood at the water's edge staring at its glassy surface.

Between unsteady gulps of air, I looked at the rocks around me, taking stock of the situation. My swollen, shaking fingers couldn't resist brushing the nearby thick, contorted root. A root belonging to The Tree of Life! How was this possible?

The way in which the rocks and roots had entwined themselves was a beautiful melding of the immovable and the ever-changing. Moss, ferns and other fronded-plants had anchored themselves in the spaces. And—wait—was that a trickle of water among the rocks?

I shifted my weight for a better view. Sure enough, water meandered down the uneven surface of the boulders and in the crevices between roots. It spread across the cobblestones below, heading into the tropical lagoon.

I tracked the seeping liquid in the opposite direction. The ribbon of water appeared to spring from beneath the flames that billowed around the sword. It looked as though this sliver of liquid slowly fed the turquoise moat below.

The beauty of the flickering fire distracted me. I lost myself in the gleam of the weapon and the blaze of holy heat. A profound realization settled over me. In facing these challenges, strength had been coaxed out of hiding. Fear had been scorched, liberating me from its grip. My fortitude had been tested with fire, and it had survived. I no longer resented this real-life fairytale that consumed my family. Staring at this smoldering symbol of history and knowing that part of its narrative now included me, warmed me with an exhilarating peace. *My life is no longer my own, and I'm okay with that.*

"Sadie, are you well?" The carrot-topped Gnome touched my shoulder.

I blinked. "Sorry, were you talking to me? There's so much to take in..."

He smiled. "I know. Take your time."

"I think I've recovered enough to move." I tried to press myself up to my feet. "*Ow.* Um, maybe not. I don't think I can put any weight on my ankle."

He bowed. "No problem, Princess Sadie. We shall get you a stretcher."

The mental picture of a million Gnomes surrounding my giant, planked body was laughable. "No. Really...I only need crutches or a cane."

"With those fingers?" He pointed at my bulging digits.

I shrugged. "Okay. Maybe not. You know where to find me."

He turned to leave.

"Hang on!" I called after him. "Someone needs to know what's going on in Calamus—and Craventhrall too. I have vital information."

"Absolutely. I'll find Sir Noblin or General Muggleridge." The Gnome bounded away.

I lifted my leg and inspected my swollen ankle. It didn't look as bad as what Brady and Brock had incurred from karate. But I'd led a pretty athletically sheltered life. What did I know?

A silvery gleam in the dirt near my foot made my heart leap. My necklace! I plucked it up by the tiny book charm and smiled. To think it had survived that action sequence! Wow! God certainly was in the details.

Speaking of surviving. Where was Estancia's minion, Skoon? Panic resurfaced. This ordeal wasn't over yet.

Glancing for movement or *something* that might give away the Leprechaun's presence, I shifted the best I could, scouring the area. I was about to alert someone when I spotted the pitiful creature.

His body, no longer invisible, lay slumped beneath the fronds of a large fern beside the wall. Crumpled leaves obscured his form, but I spied his red beard and pale skin. Very pale. I had a feeling that the plant didn't break my fall as much as the Leprechaun did.

I swallowed and looked away, unsure of how I felt.

At ground zero, the marching formations had been replaced by extra guards along the water's edge and around the perimeter of the gleaming, pearl floor. At this level, a singular door led in and out of the stadium-sized space. The door opened about the time I spotted it.

In walked Brock and Queen Judith.

What a wonderful, calming sight to my eyes! They zigzagged around the soldiers and jogged across the bridge.

"You okay?" Brock asked from the bottom of the boulders.

I smiled at my brother. "Never better. Especially with you here."

"Oh, ya poor dear." My sprightly aunt scaled the rocks, defying her age. She sat beside me, putting an arm around my shoulder. "Goodness, look at yer fingers. What a horrible woman that Estancia turned out to be, eh? Never did have a good feelin' about her." She patted my back. "Yer such a brave girl, Sadie dear. Vituvia is in yer debt. Perhaps the prophecies that declared 'kinship shall protect kingship' were not speakin' of Brady as we assumed."

I shook my head vehemently. "Ugh! Prophecies are the *last* thing I want to think about right now, okay?" Adrenaline gave way to indignation. I was beginning to despise the "p" word.

"Ya can't run from yer callin', but I understand yer reluctance fer the moment." Aunt Jules patted my back.

I bit my lip, closing shop on a scathing comeback.

Brock picked his way up the boulders and sat near my feet. "Queen Estancia is dead." His face showed little expression. I had no idea if this was an accusation or a matter-of-fact statement.

"Yes. I didn't mean for that to happen, y'know." I glanced at the water. "Can either of you tell me about that sea monster? I guess it's an octopus?"

Queen Judith chuckled. "Sure is. That's our very elusive Guardian of the Garden Moat. He's very old and, yes, very large. We call him Levi, for short."

"Short for what?"

"Leviathan."

"What?" I stiffened. "Like Leviathan from the Old Testament?"

"Well..." She shrugged. "Not exactly. But he's a giant sea creature, so the name is fitting."

"I'd say." I touched Brock's shoulder. "Don't you think so? Remember when we were little and Dad read us that part of the Bible?"

"Yes. In the book of Job." He nodded. "Queen Estancia is dead."

Back to that pleasant subject. "Yep. Pretty horrible way to die. Even if she was a pretty horrible person."

He glanced at the water then back at me. "She wasn't worthy."

"What do you mean?"

Silence.

I looked from Brock to Aunt Judith. "What's he talking about?"

"Exactly what Chancellor Kittrick read from the foundin' documents." She laced her hands together and stared out at the water. "Queen Estancia obviously did not take time to reflect on her virtue as instructed. She was not worthy. How was it phrased, Brock, when Chancellor Kittrick read it?"

Brock closed his eyes. I knew he must be replaying the formal proclamation.

He looked at me. "The unworthy shall face judgment."

CHAPTER FORTY-ONE

THE TOWERING TROLL GRABBED BRADY'S SHOULDERS, snarled and shoved him against the wall. Brady gripped the knife, knowing he had one shot to disable the brute. A flesh wound would only irritate the Yeti and make him all the more unpleasant.

The nearby door shook on its hinges. "You're dead meat, topsider!" Brady recognized the voice of Minchess.

The Troll in front of Brady ignored the other guard. "What have we here?" Startling green eyes glinted from a brown face. Yellow fangs loomed so close, Brady spied a cavity.

"H-hello." He swallowed, hoping to buy enough time to be sure of his target. "They let me out for good behavior."

The lock rattled with the sound of a key. Brady became thankful for the uncooperative door.

"Wonder what sort of reward Chief Nekronok will give me when I drag your sorry body to him?"

"I don't plan on finding out." Brady plunged the knife beneath the jaw of the big ape and drew it across to the other side.

The Troll's pupil's dilated, eyes springing wide. He exhaled an awful gurgle and staggered backwards. The door sprung open right as the brown Bigfoot toppled over. He brought Minchess down with him.

The startled guard grappled with the falling body and ended up pinned beneath his comrade. Brady decided it was better to disable Minchess than to have the big ape chase him down.

"Sorry." Brady punctured the bottom of the guard's feet with a stab of his knife. They made for easy targets.

Brady dashed away, choosing his direction by how quickly

he could distance himself from the bloodshed and screams of pain. The hallway came to a T, and he peeked around the corner. To the left, the passage met up with another corridor. A Troll lumbered past. Brady ducked back, heart hammering. When he risked another look, the passage was deserted. The other direction led to a set of stairs. *Up* seemed like a good plan. He made a mad scramble to the stairway and took the steps three at a time. At the top of the first set of stairs, he stopped on the landing to catch his breath.

The stairwell was a shadowy cylinder with an underwhelming amount of light. Darkness seemed to be the theme down here. Maybe Trolls, like nocturnal animals, didn't need much light to see.

He shoved the key in his pocket, freeing his hand for whatever might come, but continued to white-knuckle the knife. The way his fingers felt in the cool air made Brady guess they were wet with blood. He shuddered and wiped the blade and his hand against his pants. Killing was not his thing. His stomach clenched thinking about what had happened. *No.* It would only debilitate him to replay it. He had to keep moving. Hesitations and second guessing would jeopardize his life. He would learn to live with his choices.

After three more flights of stairs, he approached an arched doorway. Backed against the wall, he glanced in each direction. The stairway fed into a wide passage, with three doors directly across the way. To his right, a dead end. To his left, as best he could tell, it stretched on, intersecting other corridors. At least there were more torches in this area. He prayed for good instincts—there wasn't time to deliberate.

Two Trolls and a Dark Dwarf ambled out of the farthest door and headed in the opposite direction, without closing it. The Trolls strode ahead while the Stygian waddled fast to keep up. The three turned into the first wide hallway and disappeared.

Sweat stung Brady's eyes. He wiped his face on the sleeve of his tunic, wincing at his pungent body odor. The doorway the creatures had wandered from looked like a reasonable place to duck and hide.

As he padded across the floor, Brady's leather boots squeaked on the stone. He cringed and hurried inside, berating his hyperactive heart. Freaking out was a disadvantage. He must remain calm and clearheaded.

His eyes adjusted, and he noticed a faint glow of candlelight farther inside. Large, black objects became visible. Rows of them. They were arranged in a semicircle around the lone light that flickered from atop a candelabra. Something tall and rectangular stood behind it. A table?

Brady crept closer. No, not a table—an altar. He was in some sort of ceremonial chamber. The rows of black objects were seats fashioned from boulders. His skin crawled. Evil felt tangible here. It pulsated from the glow of light wavering near the altar. He wanted no part of it.

Shuffling back to the door, he was about to peek out when he heard gruff voices. He pressed against the wall, every nerve at attention.

The sounds grew louder, accompanied by heavy footsteps. He guessed they were headed inside. Brady dashed behind one of the stone seats, crouching so he had a view of the entrance.

Two Trolls walked through the door. Despite the darkness, Brady felt sure they would notice him and tear him limb from limb.

"I say they will only add an element of uncertainty to our plans." The lighter-colored Troll was saying to the darker one.

Chebar! Brady recognized the Troll's voice.

The two Trolls meandered to the front row and selected seats in the shadows against the far wall.

"But Nekronok says the Gargoyles are good for his dirty work." The darker Troll sounded female. "The ones that fly, like Malagruel, can get places faster than he can get his Hippogriff to take him."

"They offer certain advantages, but I don't think the benefits outweigh the risks."

Chebar looked back at the door then leaned close to the other Troll. "The Gargoyles are unpredictable and power-hungry. They've been banished for so many centuries they're willing to agree to anything. They're desperate." Chebar placed his hand on the shoulder of the female. Was she his girlfriend? "I've seen the disdain in Malagruel's face when Father gives orders. Mark my words, the Gargoyle is only biding his time. He'll take us down when the opportunity arises."

The female straightened.

"Have you shared your concerns with Nekronok?" Her

shrill voice carried a little too well in the stone room.

"Shh." Chebar pressed a long finger to his mouth. "Not yet. I get the sense that Father doesn't trust the big bat. But he's in so deep, trying to get control of the sword, he doesn't see the bigger issues at stake. That's where I believe you can be of assistance, Gwendolyn."

Gwendolyn? Brady tried to recall where he had heard that name.

"Me? Oh, I don't know. Nekronok has barely spoken to me since that topsider was rescued in the Ceremony of the Elements. I've never seen him so angry."

"He's not angry at you, Stepmother. If anything, he needs your comfort." Chebar patted her shoulder.

"I'm not so sure. When he gets that way, it scares me."

"All the more reason he needs you." Chebar swiveled Gwendolyn toward him and placed one hand on each of her shoulders. "Have the cook fix Father's favorite meal. Invite him to your quarters. Pour some wine. Try to get him to relax and talk about his plans. It would be good for him to get his secrets off his chest."

"You really think I have such influence?" She sounded astonished.

"Absolutely." Chebar nodded. His hands slipped from her shoulders. "He could have any female in our clan, and he has chosen you. You've been the only one since Mother died."

Gwendolyn sighed. "You're right. I need to use my position to help him do what's in his best interest."

"Exactly. Just remember...tell me everything you learn. The only way we can truly help him is to work from your position on his private life and my position on the business side of things." Chebar offered her his hand. "We're a team, you and I. Right?"

"I've never been on a team." Gwendolyn giggled and shook Chebar's hand.

"Excellent—"

"Chebar?" A familiar voice spoke from the doorway.

Brady swiveled in time to see Rooke step inside. By the time Brady glanced back at the other two, they were kneeling in front of their seats, hands raised, rocking back and forth.

Chebar dropped his arms. "Can't a Troll pay homage to their ancestors? What do you want?"

Rooke snickered. "Since when do you care about paying

homage? It took me all evening to find you because this seemed like the last place to check." Rooke sauntered toward the other two, who now stood. "What in the name of Thrall are you doing here together? I thought you couldn't stand our dear stepmother, Chebar."

"What?" Gwendolyn placed her hands on her hips.

"Pay no mind to this big oaf." Chebar stepped toward his brother. "He can't stand the fact that I'm Father's favorite. The only thing Rooke has going for him is status of firstborn son."

"Don't flatter yourself!" Rooke shoved Chebar. "If you're not careful, you'll be Father's first *dead* son."

"Is that a threat?" Chebar stepped back into Rooke's personal space.

"Stop, you two." Gwendolyn pressed a hand on each of their chests. "You need to stop competing with each other and get along. For the good of Craventhrall. For your father."

The Trolls remained rigid.

"More like a guarantee than a threat." Rooke spoke first.

"You do realize, big brother, that if something were to happen to you, Father has the freedom to choose his successor."

"Please, can't we work together?" Gwendolyn clasped her hands.

"You expect me to work with someone who wants me dead?" Rooke lunged at Chebar.

Chebar blocked Rooke's attempted blow. He followed it up with a nimble kick in the stomach.

Gwendolyn shrieked and jumped away.

Rooke doubled over, and Chebar kneed his brother in the face, sending him flying backwards. Rooke whacked his head on one of the boulders on his way down. Brady heard a sickening *thunk*.

"Oh, no." Gwendolyn rushed over to where Rooke had fallen.

"He came after me first. You witnessed it."

"Yes, he did. Do you think he'll be okay?"

Chebar grunted and paced in a circle. "Unfortunately, yes."

"Chebar! You don't need Rooke's blood on your hands. Nekronok may not be so understanding."

"I know, I know." He held his hands up. "I'm venting. Go

get help. Find the Healer and bring him here."

Gwendolyn stood and nodded. "Okay." She strode out of the room.

Chebar sat on the closest hunk of rock and leaned his head into his hands.

Brady felt jittery from watching the exchange. But he saw a window of opportunity to have assistance getting out of the Eldritch. Though he wasn't entirely sure what Chebar was up to with his stepmother, he knew the Troll was the reason he had made it this far.

Brady stood and cleared his throat.

Chebar jumped up into a defensive stance.

"It's me. Brady." He held up his hands. "I escaped."

CHAPTER FORTY-TWO

I WOKE FROM A DEEP, SATISFYING sleep and tried to wipe the drool off my mouth. Catching sight of my bandaged hand, I stopped short. *Oh yeah, I've been mummified.*

Three fingers on my right hand and two on my left looked like elongated marshmallows with moldy spots—thanks to some sort of green goo smeared underneath the bandages. I shifted onto my elbows and stared at my equally fat and fluffy foot. Or ankle, really. The herbal salve had also oozed through its thick, gauzy bandage and stained it algae-green.

Though I couldn't see anything, my ankle felt better than when the Gnome's physician—an herbalist named Prilla— had poked and prodded and wrapped it up. I raised my leg and noticed the salve had leaked onto the sheets. Gross.

A clock ticked away on the floor beside my bed. Well, my *mattress*. In order for eighteen-inch Gnomes to check on my wellbeing, they needed me at floor level.

I did a double take. A clock? In all my travels around the Tethered World I had never seen a clock. The round retro face was encased in pale yellow metal, a set of bells stationed on top. My fingers fumbled against it but I managed to turn it around. A winding mechanism poked from its backside.

Anything vintage made me smile. Maybe they'd let me keep it. I sighed and dropped my head onto the pillow, my mind heavy with everything that had happened and full of questions about everything else. I hated the isolation I had experienced this trip. At least last time we were in the trenches *together.* This time I'd been moved and toyed with throughout my visit, like some diabolical game of cat and mouse.

The door to my small but tidy room opened. Prilla

marched in, followed by Revonika.

"You're awake!" Revonika scurried up beside me and placed a petite hand on my shoulder. Her freckled cheeks bunched into a smile. "How is our brave princess today?"

Prilla busied herself at a shelf of supplies.

"Feeling fashionable in my bandages, thanks." I grinned. "I was admiring this clock. And wondering why I'm worthy to have such an unusual item in my room."

"Ah, that." Revonika picked it up and studied it. "We have a small stash of these. Even a few on the walls in several of our meeting rooms. When Prilla gives you a clock, it means there's a timely protocol you're expected to follow."

"Yep, yep, yep!" Prilla carried a tray of bottles and bandages over. "Now that you're awake I shall leave you with two herbal tinctures to take every hour on the hour. But first—"

"Ouch!" I yelped at her none-too-gentle shifting of my leg.

"Oops. Sorry." She shrugged. "Not used to patients the size of small trees. Not sure how much force to exert."

I nodded, wincing.

"You want me to fetch more pillows so you can sit up?" Revonika replaced the clock. "And maybe a book?"

The normalcy of the question made me want to hug her. "Yes, please. That would make me the happiest person on the planet."

She curtsied. "Goodness. You're easy to please." With a giggle she left.

Prilla carefully unwound the bandage from my ankle. "Am I being gentle enough?"

"Yes. Thank you. How's it looking?"

"Hmmm. Let's...oh, wow!"

"What?" I perched on one elbow to get a better view. My foot and ankle looked like it belonged to an alien. Lumpy and purple with a disgusting green glaze. "That looks appetizing."

"I'm going to retract my earlier diagnosis of a sprain. It's difficult to judge with the swelling, but it might be broken. This salve is made from comfrey. A plant with bone-knitting properties. Though it's helpful, I'm not confident your ankle is properly set." She glanced at me. "Can you wiggle your toes?"

I tried. "Ah! Um, no." I took a deep breath. "They don't quite work."

She grimaced and shook her head. "That's not good. We need to get you to Doctor Keswick. Except..."

"Except?"

Prilla paced to the door and back, wringing her hands. "Except Berganstroud is probably under attack as we speak. After everything that happened yesterday, Queen Judith dispatched troops earlier this morning."

"I don't believe Berganstroud is in danger."

She stopped pacing and looked at me. "What makes you so certain?"

"Because Queen Estancia admitted that the attack on Vituvia was for show. Part of an elaborate plan to earn favor by volunteering to warn Berganstroud. Bringing me back to Vituvia was an unplanned bonus. She hoped all of her good deeds would grant her access to the Garden Dome."

Prilla looked like I'd slapped her. "Surely you jest."

"Nope. That's what she told me."

"*Ugh.*" She stomped the floor. "Do you know how many soldiers were injured trying to fight that fire? Guess that giant got what she deserved."

The door flew open, and a pile of pillows with legs scrambled into the room. "Sadie, you've got a visitor." Revonika's voice was muffled behind her load. She plopped the pillows down and ran back to the door. "She's in here."

Prilla and I exchanged curious glances.

The doorframe filled with the enormity of a tall, brooding warrior. Xander looked at me with a flint-like gaze.

My breath caught. Did he know? Or was I to be the one to tell him his mother was dead? "Hi."

"Hello, Princess." His eyes softened a bit.

The use of his typical greeting calmed my nerves.

Xander crossed to me and knelt, grasping one of my injured hands.

Even with wrapped fingers, my hand looked small in his. "Xander...listen. A lot has happened since—"

"I know." He swallowed and nodded. "I heard about my mother."

"Please. You must know how sorry—"

"Shh. There's nothing to say." He pressed a finger to my lips. "If anyone should be apologizing it's me. My gut told me that something was amiss about mother's little story. Her flying around to come to the aid of Vituvia was out of character. Since your first visit here, she's often been secretive and inaccessible. Her behavior has been suspicious for some time."

A tear slid down my cheek. "I'm still sorry."

He wiped the tear away. "Thank you. No need to be."

Another tear escaped. "I'm sorry for everything. Things have fallen apart so quickly. I feel like I'm in the middle of an apocalypse." I sniffed. "And it revolves around my family. Everyone was fine until we showed up."

Prilla smeared fresh goop on my injuries and set about wrapping my foot again.

"Why did your family come here at all? Because the Trolls captured your parents." Xander brushed a clinging strand of hair from my wet cheek. "Though I wish circumstances were different, it's provided a chance for us to meet."

I swallowed and looked away. My emotions were in an uproar. Humans don't fall for Legends. Time to change the subject. "You know, your mother told me some disturbing things."

"That's not surprising."

"About prophecies concerning me. From a stone-stone..."

"Stonecipher. He is—or was—Mother's personal seer." He shook his head. "Frankly, I don't put much stock in what he says. Though he claims to hear from the Maker, there are things that do not line up with the ancient Scriptures."

"That's a problem."

His thumb stroked one of my bandaged fingers. "Are you going to be okay?"

Prilla nudged the giant with her tiny palm. "If you'll give me more space to work, she'll be fine."

"Certainly." Xander stood.

The Gnome unwrapped one of my fingers. The knuckles looked like they belonged to someone Xander's size. Prilla made *tsk-tsk* sounds.

"Say..." I glanced from Xander to Prilla. "What if I could get back to Berganstroud in a hurry? So the doctor could look at me."

"In a hurry?" She raised an eyebrow. "Like horseback? You really think your beat-up body can handle that? You're bruised from head to toe."

"No. Not horseback. Angel-back." I smiled at Xander. "Or Nephilim-back."

"Oh!" She straightened and turned to him. "How does our Nephilim friend feel about this? I thought Berganstroud was under attack, but Sadie disagrees. What have you heard?"

"I'm on my way to Calamus *from* Berganstroud. My mother sent me to the Dwarves to warn them after the attack on Vituvia. When I arrived, Reiko and her crew had just returned to Berganstroud from spying on the Eldritch—you'll recall they were there with Gage and me to rescue you. They had overheard the Gargoyles bragging about the attack on Vituvia. Said it had been a mere exhibition, with no further plans that anyone was aware of." He grimaced. "I stopped here to see the damage for myself and get a report of what happened. What a shock to learn that you were in Vituvia instead of Calamus, as I thought. And that my mother had deceived us all."

"A shock indeed, Prince Xander. Sorry for your trouble." Prilla turned and cocked her head at me. "Well then, seems like it would be safe enough to send you back. I'd certainly like to see your ankle properly set."

I sighed. "Guess that depends on Xander." My gaze met his. "I imagine you need to be with your father in Calamus in light of the circumstances. Hopefully, my dad is there retrieving my mom and sister. Aunt Judith sent soldiers for backup as soon as I told her about their predicament yesterday. Your mother made them her prisoners. Said if I didn't cooperate—"

"*Ugh.*" Xander pressed his fists against his head in frustration. "That woman. I didn't know how deep her lust for power really ran."

"It's so complicated, it's exhausting." With a huff I plopped my head onto the pillows. "Somehow we need to get Brady out of the Eldritch."

"What?" Xander took a step toward me.

"Yeah. Everything's messed up." I squeezed my eyes shut. "It's okay, Smarlow is on top of it now. But there's so much uncertainty." My lashes fluttered, freeing a fresh round of tears. "Not to mention my aunt and uncle laid up in the hospital."

"Oh! That reminds me." Xander sounded anxious.

I peeked an eye open.

He unbuckled the leather pouch attached to his belt. "Joanie asked me to give you something. Said to find you as soon as I returned to Calamus—but the news about my mother left me blindsided." He withdrew a small, tan object. "Your aunt wanted you to have this."

My world shattered into a million pieces. I blinked, trying to make sense of what he said. Trying to understand why he was handing me a leather bundle tied with a cord.

"Sadie?" He stooped over me. "You don't look well."

Prilla stepped away.

"Did she say my aunt *wanted* me to have it—past tense—or my aunt *wants* me to have it?" I stared at the package, fearful of what it represented.

He shrugged. "I don't remember her exact wording." He knelt down. "Something about your aunt making Joanie promise to get this to you without delay. That it's personal and very important. When Joanie learned I was traveling to Calamus—where I assumed you to be—she entrusted it to me with those instructions. But I don't remember her exact words."

My hand trembled as I reached for the object.

"I think I understand." Xander laid it in my hand then brushed his fingertips across my damp cheek. "You're not sure if Aunt Jules is still alive."

CHAPTER FORTY-THREE

BRADY TOOK DEEP, STEADYING BREATHS FROM inside a pitch black closet. Once he had revealed his presence to Chebar in the ceremonial room, the Troll stepped forward, grabbed Brady by the wrist, and all but dragged him to the nearby storage closet.

Chebar had shoved him inside with a promise. "I'll return as soon as I can get you safely out."

Now, Brady leaned against the wall and stared into the void, willing his frazzled nerves to chill. Chebar's reaction had startled Brady. He thought the Troll might be marching him to solitary or even Nekronok. The closet came as a welcome relief to the momentary panic.

Before Brady could make himself too comfortable, Chebar flung the door open again.

"Follow me." The Troll turned into the stairwell that Brady had come up during his escape.

Brady hesitated. Was Chebar taking him back?

"Do you want to get out of here or not?" Chebar demanded.

Brady nodded and plunged down the stairs after him. At the bottom, thankfully, they went the opposite direction from which Brady had come. But the hallway stopped short. A dead end, except for a tall, narrow door.

The Troll grabbed the handle and gave it a frustrated jerk. "*Argh.* Locked! I made a point to unlock this yesterday."

"Here!" Brady fished the key from his pocket. It fell with a clatter. Chebar swiped it from the ground and thrust it into the keyhole.

Shouts of "Anyone see him?" and "Alert the guards!" electrocuted Brady's panic-button.

Chebar rattled the key in frustration. With a fierce grunt,

the lever busted loose in his hand. He and Brady stared in surprise. Chebar threw it aside and yanked the door open.

Brady dove into a dark passage. Chebar jumped in after him and slammed the door shut. The only light came from the shattered door handle.

"Hey!" A gruff voice bellowed. "What's going on?"

"Let's move." Chebar pulled Brady into the depths of darkness at a flat-out run.

Brady hoped the Troll had those nocturnal instincts he'd wondered about earlier. Behind them, the door opened with a *whack*.

"Who's in here?" The distant voice demanded.

Chebar maneuvered Brady with swift but terrifying precision. Brady felt certain he would either face-plant into a wall or be grabbed from behind. Footsteps echoed through the tunnel. By the sounds of it, there was more than one Yeti on their trail.

After what felt like eons—exhausting eons—Chebar yanked Brady up a set of stairs and into tight quarters. Brady guessed they were in another closet. He found himself sandwiched between the Troll's back and a mound of something soft and musty-smelling. Clothing or blankets perhaps?

"What are—"

"*Shh.*" Chebar hissed.

Footfalls stomped past their hiding place.

"We'll wait a few minutes to make sure we've lost them," Chebar whispered.

Brady felt the grueling night of sickness catching up with him. He slumped against the cushion of smelly fabric. "Thanks, Chebar. You're a real friend."

"You're welcome."

The air in the small space closed in on Brady. Between perspiration, body heat, and stale air, he felt a fresh twinge of nausea.

Chebar pressed the key back into Brady's palm, triggering a question. "Hey, what do you know about the key to the sword?" Brady asked. "The *lost* key. Is it true your father has it?"

Chebar stiffened slightly. Brady was close enough to feel it. "I'm not certain. Malagruel claims that one of his worms tracked it down topside. It's the only reason my father agreed to work with the Banished, so I know he's convinced of its authenticity. I have yet to see it myself. It cannot be tested until the second key is captured, and he gains access to the sword."

"Which is exactly why I need to get to Vituvia." Brady wiped sweat from his forehead with the back of his hand.

"Do you know the whereabouts of the second key?"

Brady hesitated. Though he could honestly say "no" to the question, he *did* know who had the key in their possession. Should he admit that to Chebar? No way. Family secrets stayed with family. "No, I don't. In fact, I only recently learned that such a key existed."

Chebar shifted. "If you find out its whereabouts…you can trust me, you know. I'll help you protect it."

"Of course." Brady stiffened and swallowed. But the sweltering, stinking coffin they were stuffed inside probably held sway over his senses. "Uh. Thanks."

The door creaked open. A waft of fresh air helped Brady shake his muddled thoughts.

"Let's get out of here." Chebar stepped from the closet.

"Hallelujah," Brady mumbled and crept forward.

Chebar grasped Brady's wrist. "This way."

They continued up the stairs at a more relaxed pace until a thunder of footsteps swelled from behind. Chebar shifted into overdrive. Brady floundered to match the Troll's stride, stumbling like a toddler trailing an adult.

Several flights later, the two burst through a door into a well-lit hallway. They fled to the end and turned the corner as their pursuers stumbled out of the stairwell. Chebar made a sudden turn into another corridor. Brady thought his shoulder might dislocate if Chebar kept this up.

Two doors barred the end of the passage, and they exploded through them. The bright light of the domed sky made Brady squint. He tried to make sense of where they were while Chebar propelled him forward. It looked like an outdoor stage. They dashed between two enormous bowls, one mounded with coals and the other brimming with water. They hopped off the platform and headed to a low balustrade that hemmed most of the circular space. There was no railing dead center. It was here that Chebar skidded to a stop.

Behind them, two Trolls lumbered through the doors onto the stage. When they recognized Chebar they stutter-stepped.

"Chebar! You've got the prisoner?" A dirty white Troll looked from Chebar to Brady.

"Yes, I've been chasing him down. Finally caught him." Chebar gave Brady a hardened sneer and twisted his arm behind his back. "Didn't know topsiders could run so fast. Thinking of throwing him off the cliff." He shoved Brady so that his feet teetered on the edge. "But I have a feeling he's more valuable alive." He jerked Brady a few feet back.

Brady yelped, truly in pain.

"He wounded Minchess and killed Rutledge." The matted gray Troll stepped off the stage and sauntered toward Brady. "Nekronok might prefer him dead once he—"

The Yeti stopped mid-sentence, eyes wide. Suddenly, something clamped Brady's shoulders like a vise. His body lifted off the veranda.

He flailed, screaming with shock and pain. Yellow feathers on a barrel-chested monstrosity filled his panic-stricken gaze. He was in the talons of a Hippogriff.

Chebar clawed at Brady's feet and conveniently missed. The three Trolls grew smaller, swinging angry fists at the air and cursing loudly.

Brady didn't know if his escape was part of Chebar's get-out-of-jail-free strategy, or if the Hippogriff decided he looked like a delicious, warm-blooded snack.

One thing for certain...the talons holding his shoulders *hurt*. A dark stain leaked across the filthy, black tunic shirt and hinted at injuries beneath. The creature veered away from the Eldritch, and Brady could no longer see Chebar and the others. He was at the mercy of this bird-horse.

The beating of the creature's massive wings made a deep whooshing rhythm, carrying Brady higher. Trees became small, green blobs. The disorganized township of Craventhrall looked like rubble.

Mount Thrall's foothills loomed close enough for Brady to do the math. The beast needed to gain altitude if they were going to clear the approaching swells.

Instead, the pressure on Brady's shoulders disappeared. Wind rushed upwards against his body, making it impossible to breathe, whistling in his ears. He looked up, horrified. The Hippogriff had released him.

Brady was skydiving without a parachute.

CHAPTER FORTY-FOUR

I SAT ON A BENCH OUTSIDE Brock's room early the next morning. Six AM to be exact. I knew the time, thanks to that trusty yellow clock in my hospital room. After a restless night spent tossing my aching body around in bed, I hopped up—with the help of Gnome-made crutches—to dress and ready myself to leave.

Once Xander learned that Queen Judith had dispatched dignitaries to speak to King Aviel about Estancia, he felt he could deliver me to Berganstroud. He asked the Gnomes to keep Vincent under lock and key until he learned his Father's preference: Lleave the traitor at the mercy of Vituvia or drag him back to Calamus.

We would depart after breakfast, so spending time with Brock was imperative. No telling when I would see him again.

But first I contemplated the small, leather package from Aunt Jules, wondering if I should open it. Somehow, I decided that if I unwrapped it and acknowledged its insertion into my life, it meant I accepted Aunt Jules's death. Since I refused to embrace such an unthinkable prospect, I refused to open it. Which, in my convoluted mind, meant she still lived. I'd spent the night crying my eyes out and wrestling with what it meant to be given the key to the sword—for that's certainly what it must be—and this unfounded theory was as far as I mentally traveled. Yet here I sat deliberating again.

Curiosity is a powerful thing. I allowed myself to feel the object. The cushioned outside padded something thick and solid and elongated in the center. The key that could unlock the Flaming Sword of Cherubythe was in my possession and likely as close to the sword as it had been in decades. Probably centuries. Maybe millennia. Were the two powerful items drawn to each other like Frodo's ring and Mordor from *The Lord of the Rings*?

Hopefully not. Especially if the other key was as close as Craventhrall. The possibility of both keys being drawn together by an unseen force could mean the sword was in more danger than ever. Even if my imagination was off kilter—a real possibility after everything that had happened—this ordeal wasn't finished. As long as Nekronok had one of the keys in his grasp, he wouldn't abandon his goals simply because Estancia bit the dust.

I gripped the leather package and smacked my leg. Why now? These two stinking keys had been content to fly under the radar since...*forever*. Now, here they were, practically throwing themselves at the sword. I shook my head. That would not happen on my watch.

With a *humph*, I stuffed the leather bundle into my pouch. Under no circumstance could Nekronok know its whereabouts. I would have to talk to Aunt Jules about the best way to secure it. And by some miracle, we needed to get the *other* key out of Nekronok's paws and back to its rightful key-keeping family—wherever they might be.

Crutches in hand, I wobbled upright and swerved toward Brock's room. He probably wouldn't like being awakened so early, but I didn't like how he had to stay here, away from the rest of us. Summer was coming to a close, however, so I hoped it wouldn't be long until we were reunited as a family. His apprenticeship was slated to end in September, then resume each summer until his eighteenth birthday.

I knocked on Brock's door and waited with doubtful patience. He and Brady both slept like residents in a morgue. Without a blaring alarm clock, a knock was laughable.

The door opened, and I blinked in surprise. *How can there still be things that surprise me?*

My gaze moved from eye-level to Gnome-level. Of course, High Kings in training didn't answer their own doors. Silly me.

"Princess Sadie!" A familiar looking Gnome bowed. "To what do we owe the honor?"

"Good morning." I dipped my head. "I wanted to visit Brock before I leave for Berganstroud. Revonika will bring breakfast to us here."

He nodded. "Certainly. Allow me to—*ahem*—wake him and

get him presentable. It may take a few minutes."

I laughed. "Of course it will. I'll wait."

The door closed. I grinned to overhear the Gnome attempt to wake Brock. Six times.

At last the attendant waved me inside. Brock stood by a table looking bleary-eyed and disoriented. At first he stared through me. I thought perhaps he was having one of his fake-awake moments, being the hardcore sleepwalker that he is. But a lightbulb switched on behind his eyes, and he straightened. "Hi, Sadie."

As he tolerated my hug, crutches and all, Revonika came in with a servant. Each carried a tray of food. In a moment I had my brother to myself for the first time since—since all of this crazy stuff happened the *first* time. That realization made me fight off tears and reach my hand to touch him way more than he preferred.

We enjoyed eggs and toast smothered in mushroom and sausage gravy. I did all the talking while he listened, exactly like old times. It was a gloriously normal meal—outside of eating with bandaged fingers in a palace full of Gnomes.

"So, little brother, I've got to go back to Berganstroud today. The doctor there needs to look at all my bruises and things."

He took another bite of food and blinked without expression.

"You gonna miss me? At least a little?"

He gave the slightest of grins. "I don't miss bossy girls."

"What?" I laughed at the out-of-the-blue comment. "You must be getting me confused with Sophie. She's the bossy one."

"Girls are bossy."

My cheeks hurt from smiling so hard. "Not all girls are bossy. Where did you get that?"

"Aunt Judith is bossy. Sophie is bossy. Queen Estancia is bossy."

"*Ooh* yes. Estancia was very bossy. But not all girls are like her."

"Aunt Jules is a nice person."

"See. There ya go." The mention of Aunt Jules brought all my earlier uncertainties back. I swallowed. "You know, I should probably tell you something." I reached for his hand, but he pulled away. "Aunt Jules is very sick. She's so sick that some people worry that she might die."

His eyes roved my face like he wasn't sure he understood. "She's sick?"

I nodded. "I know the Vituvians are protective of you. But if they would allow you to visit Aunt Jules, I bet it would make her feel better." *Because she has to be alive since I haven't opened the package.*

"Aunt Jules is sick."

Such statements perplexed me—though they were commonplace with Brock. I never could figure out if he was parroting what I said or processing it.

"Yes. So perhaps you can talk to Aunt Judith about letting you come to Berganstroud. She should come too. They're sisters, after all."

"Aunt Judith is sick." Brock swayed back and forth in his seat.

"You mean Aunt *Jules.*"

Brock shook his head. "No. Aunt Judith is sick."

I studied his face. Was he confused? "What do you mean?"

"She told me she's dying."

The treetops were rapidly approaching Brady's careening body. No sooner had he found himself free falling—which was long enough to watch his brief life zip across the movie screen of his mind—when the Hippogriff swooped down, catching Brady on its back.

Brady let out a yelp of shock at the sudden jolt, followed by a "*Yessss!*" as he wrapped grateful arms around the powerful neck of his fine-feathered friend. This creature surely had come to rescue him—rather than swallow him by the beak-full. Brady realized that the Hippogriff dropping him had been its way of getting Brady situated on its back.

Puncture wounds and all, Brady had never felt better.

The Hippogriff hugged the mountain-scape, veering over the trees like a heat-seeking missile. Though Brady didn't know where they were headed, he was happy that it was opposite from Craventhrall. But what if the beast was trained to take him to Calamus instead? Maybe it would deposit him on the front steps of Queen Estancia's palace.

The powerful creature banked to the left. Soon the spiked fence line above Berganstroud came into view. Brady pumped a fist in the air. This day had gone from the lowliness of pond scum to the heights of super-heroism. Was that even a word? Well, it was now, he decided.

Guards stationed at their posts aimed arrows at the flying legend.

Uh-oh! Brady leaned closer to the eagle head. "Bank sideways so they can see me." He hoped the big bird understood him.

Thankfully, the creature circled high above the fortress, above the reach of arrows.

He waved to the Dwarves below. "Heeey! It's me. Brady." It was like yelling into a vacuum that sucked sound into oblivion.

An arrow flew toward them but lost altitude short of its target. Friendly fire was an inconvenient hitch in the escape plan. Clinging tightly with his legs, he wriggled out of his tunic and waved it wildly above his head.

Soon the weapons were lowered, and the Hippogriff descended. Brady could hear shouts from one set of guards carried to the next. By the time the creature touched down outside the fortress, five Dwarves were jogging their way.

"Sir Brady!" Lava looked like he couldn't trust his sense of sight. "How? What?"

Brady slid from the Hippogriff's back. It immediately launched into the sky.

"Thank you!" Brady waved his tunic at the big bird.

The Hippogriff opened its beak, let out a screech, and flew away.

"Hey, Lava." Brady grinned. "Whaddya know? I happened to be escaping the Eldritch today and thought I'd drop in."

"You...what?" The Dwarf scratched his beard and looked confused. The other four Dwarves gathered around Lava and looked from him to Brady.

"I'm only messing with you." Brady leaned onto his knees and expelled a long breath. "Well, sort of. I really did escape. Somehow Chebar had that split-personality beast snatch me to safety." He shook his head. "My mind is officially *blown*."

Lava recovered enough to sputter some stilted laughter. "O-oh, okay. What a shock. We had no knowledge of yer situation." He stuck his hand out for Brady to shake. "Thank the Maker that He's got everything handled whether we know about it or not."

Brady grasped his friend's hand. "Definitely. It's been a bizarre couple of days."

"Looks like we need to get those wounds tended to straightaway." Lava nodded toward Brady's chest.

"Ah, it's just a flesh wound." He smirked. "I've never felt better."

The other Dwarves returned to their stations. Lava led Brady through the fortress gate, past the antiquated weapons, and into the citadel.

The weight that lifted from Brady's shoulders almost convinced him he could perform parkour—or at least a half-decent cartwheel—down the hallway. His life felt like an experiment in extreme emotions.

In the infirmary, Doc Keswick cleansed the puncture wounds while Brady bit his lip and grimaced. Lava looked on, frowning.

"Earning your manhood today, are we?" Doc chuckled. "You look awful, you know—and smell worse. What happened to your wrists?"

"Gee, thanks." Brady lifted his arms and turned his scabbed wrists around. "Well, guess I should start at the beginning..."

Launching into everything that had happened since he set out to join the Guardians of the Sword had a therapeutic effect. Bringing the peril and challenges into focus made him keenly aware that he could not take credit for his miraculous escape. Indeed, it was *miraculous*. The tale had Lava spitting mad from one point to the next.

Brady cocked his head. "So, Doc, that's why I look and smell so manly."

Doc Keswick chuckled. "I think I'm going to order you to bathe before I dress these wounds." He walked to a basin and ladled water into a cup. "Drink this. You're more than a little dehydrated if you spent the night vomiting and worse."

Brady took slow sips of water, relishing each drop.

"I'm going to find Wogsnop." Lava crossed to the door. "We

must free Sadie and the rest of yer family. Why is it that when one threat gets neutralized, another rears its ugly head? What's the Tethered World coming to?"

"Make sure your plans include me," Brady said.

"Of course. As long as Doc agrees."

Doctor Keswick shrugged. "Any young man who can take down Trolls and survive being Hippogriff bait is someone you want on your team. I'll get him fixed in a jiffy."

Lava offered a thumbs-up and left.

"Well, now." Keswick gave Brady a once-over. "You still stink, so first things first."

Brady stood, his tunic wadded in one hand. "Fine with me." He followed the doctor out the door. "When I'm done, I'd like to see Aunt Jules."

The doc stopped mid-stride.

"And Uncle Daniel too. I'd really like to meet him."

Doc Keswick slowly turned.

Brady couldn't quite read the look on the doctor's face. "Unless that's not a good idea."

"Uh, certainly." Keswick pursed his lips. "I'll make sure you get to meet your uncle."

"Great."

Doc opened his mouth as if he had more to say then turned and led Brady to a small guest room with a water pump and basin.

CHAPTER FORTY-FIVE

XANDER 'CARE-FLIGHTED' ME TO BERGANSTROUD after breakfast. Strapped once again to his back, I had plenty of time to wrestle with my thoughts and puzzle through the various situations.

Brock represented a bittersweet piece of my life that I'd left behind earlier this summer. I thought that part of my heart had scabbed over pretty good. But spending time with him this morning reopened the wound more than it had soothed it. Especially after the shocking revelation about Aunt Judith. Brock refused to expound on the bomb he dropped, saying he promised not to talk about her sickness. Apparently, disclosing her death was not the same thing in his mind.

Then there were those puzzle pieces in Calamus and the Eldritch. The uncertainty of it all made me want to cry. So, I did. Right there on top of Xander's long braids and cape. I gave him a thorough soaking.

From Xander's broad back it was hard to see much. When we lost altitude, I assumed we were nearing Berganstroud. Instead, he touched down on a cliff overlooking the Dwarves' town, placing me gently on top of a boulder. I balanced on my one good foot, holding his shoulders while he unbuckled the strap. Prilla had fitted me with a crude walking splint since the crutches couldn't travel with us.

"What are we doing here?" I took his hand and hobbled off the boulder, leaning heavily on him for support. He led me to another slab of rock that appeared to have fallen from farther up the mountain. It was flat on top and wide enough for both of us to sit.

"This is one of my favorite places to get away. You're one

of my favorite people. I thought you two should meet."

I laughed and patted the rock. "Nice to meet you, favorite place."

Looking across the landscape, I could see why he loved it. Berganstroud sat in the nea -distance on our left, the peninsula jutting out protectively, shielding the town. Though a cliff sliced the mountainside behind us, at our feet the land sloped gently away. Treetops covered the hillside and spilled into the meadow, becoming scarce as the distance increased. Brodger Creek and Whitt Lake reflected the amber sky, looking like a giant may have overturned his pot of liquid gold.

I smiled at Xander. "Thanks for sharing this. I've been so upset and stressed out about my family. This is a nice diversion."

His eyes searched mine. Penetrating and resolute. "I also brought you here to speak with you privately before we find ourselves in the middle of a fresh round of commotion."

Oh, goodness. What was I thinking, allowing myself to be alone with a guy? A tall, dark, handsome, flying superhero kinda guy at that. I looked away. *This is totally inappropriate.*

"Hey." He grabbed my hand.

I told myself to pull away, but my hand wouldn't listen to my brain. It stayed right there in his large, protective grasp, bandaged and bruised.

"Why do you start pushing me away when I try to have a meaningful conversation?" His voice was low and sounded wounded. "I get the impression that you return my emotions, at least in part. Or am I misreading you entirely?"

If I looked at his face, he would read the depth of feeling that swelled inside. I only wanted to let him see the tip of the iceberg. That's all I could allow myself to acknowledge. Things were much too complicated, and I was much too young to have love interfering with life.

Still, I couldn't lie. Nor did I wish to give him false hope. "No, you're not misreading me. I do have feelings for you, but..."

"But?" He squeezed my hand a little.

"But I cannot let my feelings guide me. Feelings can't think. They may help inform my decisions, but they can also be misleading—however good the intentions and wonderful the emotions."

"I'm not sure I follow." He scooted enough to sit sideways. "Would you mind looking at me? Things make more sense when I look into your eyes."

Great. I shifted so I could see him better. And pulled my hand away. I wasn't going to give him both my hand to hold and my soul to explore. "I'm saying that you're correct. There are feelings inside me that get...stirred up when you're around. But I have to look at more than that. I have to consider some pretty huge differences. Where I live. Where you live. That's one big issue. Not to mention I'm human and you're...what? Half angelic or something? That's an insurmountable problem if you ask me. Those two obstacles alone mean we have our own version of Mount Thrall wedged between us. That's too much of a mountain to move."

"The fact that we live far apart is not such an enormous issue. One of us can move."

"That would be me, right? You can't exactly strut your stuff topside, you know. I told you last time that you would end up being studied under a microscope or locked in a cage, so that's a no-go." I bit my lip, knowing he wouldn't like my next statement. "And I'm not willing to live here full time." Looking into his silvery-blue eyes made a small corner of my mind toy with the idea anyway.

"Given time and my fervent prayers, you might change your mind." He grinned. "And as to what species I am...let me assure you that I'm a genuine, boring human. Yes, I might have wings, but there's nothing supernatural about Nephilim any longer. For some reason, the Creator allowed this trait to remain in our DNA. My personal belief is that He has future plans for us that will involve the need to fly. Like He has plans for the sword and the tree. Do you realize what a gift you topsiders have in the Scriptures? Those of us down here are a lot less certain of our place in the order of creation. Though, overall, we have a much broader belief in the Creator."

Wow. What was I to do with these revelations? *Nothing.* Shut him down. "I'm sixteen. You can't explain that away. I don't even know how old you are, come to think of it. And if you're one hundred percent human, how do you explain what the Gargoyles did to Gage?"

Xander stood and walked away. "I don't know. It's been troubling me since it happened. On the one hand, I've been taught that I am human—in a segment of society that doesn't quite fit topside. Kind of like your brother Brock, except our uniqueness is our size. Having the trait of flight is part of our royal lineage—with a few exceptions to the gene-pool." He kicked a rock down the embankment and turned to me. "I'd never questioned it until that happened to Gage. Though I read about such things in our early history, I didn't believe it could happen now."

"That must be really unsettling." I shook my head, perplexed. "If only there was a way for me to help you."

He kicked another rock.

My heart hurt for him. "What you said about the Scriptures. If you're human then why wouldn't they apply to you?"

Xander pressed his lips together and shuffled back to his seat. "I choose to live like the Scriptures apply to me as an individual. But frankly, what Scripture mentions about Nephilim isn't exactly flattering. Then there's the matter of being quarantined below ground." He leaned onto his elbows, staring at his feet. "It's all ambiguous enough to make me wonder where I truly stand."

I placed my hand on his back. "I'm so sorry. I can see why you've got so much, uh, *angst* about it. Though what I think matters little in light of eternity, it sounds to me like you've made the right decision in regards to how you live and Who you live for."

He looked at me from over his shoulder. "Really?"

"Really."

"Thanks." He sat up. "Listen. I understand and respect what you're saying about the obstacles that stand between us. You're probably right. It won't work." His voice dropped to a whisper. "But please, do me a favor. Don't rule it out. Not yet. Maybe after everything settles down in this tumultuous place, things will look different."

Somehow, he managed to slip his hand back into mine while he spoke. I didn't trust myself to reply, so I nodded.

"Thank you." He stood and pulled me to my feet, drilling me with those irresistible eyes. "Twenty-three."

I cocked my head. "Twenty-three what?"

"Years. I'm twenty-three years old."

Of course. Seven years apart. Exactly like my parents.

I dropped his hand and shrugged. "I'm still only sixteen."

CHAPTER FORTY-SIX

Doc Keswick placed his hand on the lever of room number nine in the infirmary. "If your uncle is asleep, I'm not going to wake him. The more he sleeps the more his mind improves when he finally wakes up. Of course, having your aunt here has been the best medicine." He opened the door before Brady could reply.

A frail-looking man lay in one of two beds. His face was a mass of scars, all the way to one of his eye sockets *sans* the eye. Brady's stomach clenched at the sight. The other eye stared at the ceiling like an opaque piece of glass.

"He's asleep. Sorry," the doctor whispered. He stood over the balding man who barely made a lump beneath the covers.

Brady looked from his uncle to the doctor. "How can you tell?"

Doc pointed at the filmy-white eye. "Daniel's eyelid closes about half way when he's asleep."

Brady nodded. He found it hard to remove his gaze from the appalling sight. It made him feel guilty for having two good eyes to use in order to stare. "What happened to him?" He spoke softly.

The doctor walked back to where Brady stood. "Torture. Years and years of it." He shook his head. "Seems the Gargoyles tried to force him to make weapons for them. He's been rehearsing it in scattered conversations. Best we can tell, they tried to force him into smithing guns for their use. Sounds like he eventually made them a supply of sorts. But I think they all misfired—maybe on purpose, or else they didn't have any ammo. We can't quite get the totality of the story."

Doc removed his glasses and cleaned them on his lab coat.

"After failed guns, they moved on to swords, even wanting him to replicate the Flaming Sword of Cherubythe. Not sure how that turned out. Then they learned of the key and suspected he knew where it was." Keswick shook his head. "A lot of holes in the rambling story. I'd estimate his eye was removed before he came down with the virus. A punishment for something. Seems the Gargoyles abandoned him to the wilderness once the virus showed up—another form of torture that saved them the trouble of killing the man, no doubt. Your aunt got more out of him then any of us. She pieced his fragments together into what I've given you here."

"Speaking of Aunt Jules, when can I see her? Where is she?"

Doc Keswick replaced his glasses and turned away. He walked to the empty bed next to Uncle Daniel. "I'm afraid I've got bad news for you, son." He turned and placed a hand on the mattress. "Your aunt came down with the virus that's been ravaging Berganstroud."

Brady stiffened at the doctor's serious tone.

"Your aunt—"

Tap-tap-tap. Someone knocked on the door.

Doc Keswick shifted his gaze from Brady and made a beeline for it.

"My aunt what?" Brady stepped in front of the doctor.

"Hang on, we'll talk—"

"Doctor, are you in there?" A voice hollered through the door.

Brady crossed his arms and stood his ground.

He gave Brady a reprimanding stare. "I *am*," he called. "What do you need?"

"I've got Sadie Larcen with me. She just arrived and asked to see her aunt. And she's injured."

Brady sprang out of the way and opened the door himself. His sister's right foot and ankle were swaddled in a crude-looking splint. She leaned on a pair of metal crutches beside Joanie.

"Brady? Oh my goodness!" Sadie wobbled into his arms. "You're free!"

"I am." He laughed and pushed his sister to arm's length. "And so are you. No more giant nanny from you-know-where. How'd you get away?"

Doc Keswick held a finger to his lips. "Shh."

Sadie beamed at Brady and dropped her voice. "Long story. But I'm back. Xander dropped me off a few minutes ago. He's heading to Calamus after he visits Gage."

"Good to know *he* hasn't crossed to the dark side." Brady hugged her impulsively again. "We'll have to exchange escape stories later. Deal?"

"What happened, young lady?" Doc Keswick lifted one of Sadie's wrists and inspected her fingers then stepped back and gave her a once-over. "Glad to see we have crutches on hand that are your size. You and your brother are quite a pair."

Sadie grinned. "We try." She lurched into the room, followed by Joanie. "I've got a letter for you from Prilla..."

She stopped speaking and stared at the empty bed.

Brady glanced from his sister to the doctor. "Doc Keswick was about to tell me about Aunt Jules. Good timing, Sis."

The doctor scrubbed the bristly whiskers on his chin. "Yes. I was explaining to Brady about your aunt having the virus. Which...you already know." He nodded at Sadie then glanced at Joanie, like he needed help.

"Since when are you at a loss for words, Doctor?" Sadie took a step toward him, blinking back tears. "Just say it."

He cleared his throat. "Yes, well. Your Aunt Jules has slipped into a coma." With a catch in his voice he added, "I doubt she'll make it through the night."

Between the 'gift' from Aunt Jules in my pouch and the stark, empty bed beside Uncle Daniel, I had prepared myself for the grim reality of death. But Aunt Jules *wasn't* dead. With this knowledge, hope dared to cast fragile roots into the fragments of my heart. As I followed Doc Keswick to Aunt Jules's room, I walked with a spring in my hobble, swinging anxiously between the crutches.

He opened the door to a sterile, confined space that barely had the capacity for our four bodies to squeeze around her bed. Out of habit, I expected Auntie to be hooked up to monitors and oxygen. Of course, down here, that was an impossibility. Rather, her petite form lay peacefully beneath a blanket. The virus had left its mark on her pale, Irish complexion, but it appeared to be in the healing stage. Scabs speckled her neck and arms; a few dotted her face.

I walked to one side and grasped her fingers the best I could. "Aunt Jules. It's Sadie."

"And Brady." My brother stood on the opposite side of the bed holding her other hand.

"I'm so sorry you were sick and alone." Tears trekked down my cheeks. "I didn't mean to leave you by yourself. But you probably know that. I want you to know I've been brave. You'd be proud of me." I squeezed her fingers. "You need to wake up so I can tell you about it."

"Yeah. I have a pretty cool story too." Brady over enunciated, and his voice rose in volume. "Can't wait to tell you everything while you drink hot tea, with Uncle Daniel."

"Psst, you're yelling. She can either hear us or not, y'know?" I winked at him with wet lashes.

Aunt Jules's peaceful face didn't change.

"Do you think she's still contagious?" Brady dropped her hand and looked at the doctor.

"No." Doc leaned against the wall. "Once the sores scab like that the worst is over. Unless, of course, you slip into a coma."

Joanie elbowed him. "You need to get a filter on that mouth, doctor."

"More like a muzzle." Lava appeared in the doorway, smirking.

"That was goin' to be my next suggestion." Joanie pointed a warning finger at the doctor.

"Is there any reason she has to stay in this room?" It felt as spacious as a bank vault.

Doc looked thoughtful. "I suppose not, other than for observation. We separated her from her husband because he still has an unpredictable, combative side. We didn't want her in danger. The influx of new patients has slowed, thank the Maker. The virus seems to have run its course through town. All available rooms are occupied, however." He gestured around the room. "This was a storage closet."

I nodded. "Well, since I'm back, can we stay in one of the

guest rooms together? I want to be with her."

"I don't see why not. After I look at your injuries, of course." He shook his head. "First snake bites and now...what? What is all this?"

I grinned. "Oh, you know. I simply can't resist death-defying feats."

"Quit being vague." Doc Keswick crossed his arms.

I sighed then took a deep breath. "The short version is that I had to prevent Queen Estancia from getting to the Tree of Life in the Garden Dome. And from trying to release the Flaming Sword of Cherubythe. She-she sort of...died...in the process."

Four sets of eyes blinked with varying degrees of disbelief.

"It's true." I nodded. "She's dead. I didn't personally, you know, do the deed."

"Roots and fruits." Lava shook his head. "One thing after another in these parts."

Brady turned me to face him. "Did you say tree of *life*? As in the book of Genesis Tree of Life?"

"Yep. I'll explain later."

"Guess I was smuggled away from my guard training before *that* revelation."

Joanie looked pale. "What, pray tell, possessed that woman to do such a thing? I thought she was on our side. Have we lost an ally, or merely our ally's queen?"

"She admitted that some of the soldiers were loyal to her. But I got the impression King Aviel didn't know what she was up to. Xander certainly didn't. He's quite upset."

"I don't doubt she was schemin' without the knowledge of some of her subjects." Lava tapped his foot anxiously. "But I can't imagine her husband was ignorant. The king has his loyal servants and soldiers as well. I'm bettin' he knew. He allowed it because it would, ultimately, be to his advantage."

"What's your point?" Doc asked.

"My point is that we better prepare for the Nephilim army to pay us a visit sometime soon. Especially if the king blames Sadie for Estancia's death. Nothin' fuels the wrath of a ruler like the need for vengeance."

CHAPTER FORTY-SEVEN

AUNT JULES MADE IT THROUGH ONE night. And another. I ignored everyone else, only visiting with Brady if he came by. Beyond a catheter, which Joanie took care of, the primitive facilities couldn't offer much support for my aunt. Certainly not an IV with nutritional supplements. Joanie or Trinny came by a couple of times a day to help me spoon honey-water into her mouth to keep her blood sugar raised. Thankfully, her ability to swallow was triggered when we dribbled the liquid into her mouth. She also needed to get shifted around to avoid bedsores. A simple feat for me to manage on my own, due to her size. It was easier after removing the bandages from my still purple fingers.

I'd heard that people in a coma can hear what's going on around them. So I talked incessantly. Especially about Daniel. It seemed important to keep that hope aflame, if it did, indeed, still burn.

What I did *not* discuss was the dread that had leeched my optimism away. The dread that what Lava suggested might come true. King Aviel would hunt me down. He'd blame me for killing his wife, and in the process hurt others, many others. Beyond that—and worse than that—was a fear I had yet to admit to anyone. What might the king do to my mother and sister in the name of retaliation? Had Dad been able to extract them before news of Estancia's death reached Calamus? If not, that made three family members at King Aviel's mercy, a quality he may not be well acquainted with.

The fortress was abuzz with preparations. Brady loved being caught up in it, which I totally understood. But I was happy for the distraction of taking care of Aunt Jules. Besides, I was supposed to elevate my foot for several hours a day, though after Doc set my ankle he fixed me up nicely with a walking splint.

"Brady finally told me how he escaped the Eldritch, Auntie." I poked the fire and swept the ashes from the hearth. "Remember how Chebar helped Great-aunt Judith when she was there? Well, he not only did it for me, but he also did it for Brady."

I told her the story, even though he had shared it with me in her presence. Sometimes I couldn't come up with new things to discuss in this one-sided conversation.

"Sadie!" Brady's voice preceded his pounding on the door.

"Come in."

He flung the door open and stepped inside, eyes wild, sword strapped into place. "Gargoyles and Trolls are approaching, from both the sky and across the Hills of Berganstroud. Arm yourself but stay put for now."

Before I could respond, he dashed down the hall.

The news left me reeling. Big bats and Yetis were more terrifying than the Nephilim, though it was no surprise that they wouldn't give up without a fight. "You hear that, Aunt Jules? Big bats and Bigfoot are headed our way. Just what we need."

My Dwarf-issued sword and dagger lay beneath my bed. It seemed ridiculous to wear the sword in the bedroom, so I opted for sliding the compact dagger in my sash.

Normally I wouldn't bother with a belt while lounging around inside. But the contents of the pouch meant I needed to guard it and keep it close. And far away from Nekronok and his thugs.

My heart did an unsettling jig every time I acknowledged what lay inside the sack. Feeling the weight of its contents in my palm, I crossed to Aunt Jules. "There is one thing I haven't shared with you yet, Auntie. Because...I-I can't figure out how I feel about it myself. But you should know that I have the package you wanted Joanie to deliver."

Releasing the pouch, I grabbed her hand. "I haven't had the nerve to open it." I giggled nervously. "You know, I'm not the least bit superstitious, but I made a deal with myself that as long as I don't open it, you'll live long and prosper. Sounds goofy, I know. But I can't help feeling that accepting this key means letting go of you." Tears blurred my vision. "I'm not ready to do that."

Her fingers tightened around mine.

I blinked at our hands. "Can you do that again?" Even while I asked the question my mind declared, *I imagined that.*

She squeezed it again.

My heart fluttered with a mixture of joy and disbelief. "Oh, thank the Lord! Have you been able to hear me all this time? Squeeze once for yes and twice for no."

Another squeeze.

I limped to the door and yanked it open. "Joanie! Doc! Come quick."

Footsteps padded my way. Trinny came sliding to a stop. "What is it, m'lady?"

I waved her over. "She started responding to my questions by squeezing my hand. Can you believe it?"

Trinny grabbed my aunt's hand, not much bigger than her own.

"I told her to squeeze once for yes and twice for no."

"Are you in pain, Madame Julie?" Trinny cocked her head as if listening to the language in their fingers.

I saw Auntie press twice. "See. See!"

Trinny's face split into a smile. "I shall report the good news to Doc. He'll be thrilled." She sprinted toward the door then stopped and turned. "I'm guessing you've heard the bad news?"

"Yes." My joy deflated, and I patted the hilt of my dagger. "I'm prepared for anything."

"There seems to be no rest for the weary." She shook her head and left.

I snatched up Aunt Jules's hand, excited by the prospect of having a conversation with her.

"Let's see. We were talking about...oh. The key." I studied her face to see if anything else may be cooperating.

She squeezed my hand.

"I wanted to wait until you're better to open it."

She squeezed again. Twice.

"You don't want me to wait?"

Two more presses.

I swallowed. "All right." With shaking hands, I removed the item from the sack. The small wad of bound leather may as well have been a hand grenade.

I've faced serpents, Trolls, and a giantess. Open the tiny package, for Pete's sake.

I sighed unsteadily. "Okay. I'll do it."

My swollen fingers made it difficult to grasp the leather cord. Laying the package on her bed, I worked the knot with both hands. At last I released the binding and slowly unfolded the leather. Another layer of leather was cocooned underneath.

"Here goes nothing." I didn't take my eyes off the thing, as if it might jump up and bite me if I looked away. The second layer swaddled a stubby piece of wood, encircled by glimmering gold.

I recognized it immediately.

"Aunt Jules! Your *ring* is the key?" My wide eyes studied the familiar object. I slid it off the piece of wood and turned it over, trying to understand how this piece of jewelry could possibly be the key to the Flaming Sword of Cherubythe. "But...how?" I glanced up at her face.

She was watching me.

CHAPTER FORTY-EIGHT

Brady crouched beneath a chunk of overhanging granite that jutted from the mountainside. He squinted through the branches of a tree limb that he and Lava had dragged over to disguise the opening. Two more soldiers sat inside the shelter with them.

Dwarves had stationed themselves in strategic places—both across the plateau where Brady sat and on higher peaks and lower burrows. They had bows and arrows, swords, slings, and even catapults at the ready. Since Brady and the other three had gotten situated, the only sign of impending attack came from the half-dozen Gargoyles that patrolled overhead, too high to reach. Guards in the outposts had returned earlier with reports of Trolls, Gargoyles, and Stygians crossing distant hills en masse.

Brady did not like the term "en masse." The quantity of soldiers from Berganstroud embodied the exact opposite of such a description. He wasn't sure if their stealth could make up for the lackluster numbers.

A dark figure swooped low. Brady blinked as a large Gargoyle alighted on a rock that perched on the edge of the plateau. The leathery creature crouched, wings folded against his broad back, sword in hand, and peered down at the land below. Brady could almost convince himself that he was looking at an actual statue of a Gargoyle stationed on the pinnacle of a gothic building.

One of the soldiers beside Brady made a low growling noise at the sight. Lava reached a meaty fist his way and punched him in the shoulder to shut him up. The soldier glared back but held his tongue. With two fingers, Lava pointed to his own eyes, then out at the Gargoyle.

The pulse that pounded between Brady's ears made it hard to concentrate. He had never been faced with fighting multiple enemies. So far, his battles had been with one creature at a time. The prospect of a live-action fight sequence both exhilarated and terrified him. He was thankful the Gargoyle had his back to their hiding spot. He didn't feel prepared for anything yet.

While he stared at the beast, another form careened into view. It was a Nephilim. It caught the Gargoyle from behind with a swift kick to the head. The creature flew into a series of airborne somersaults.

It righted itself, but the Nephilim barreled toward it, sword drawn. Metal clashed and sparked as the two battled in the air. Within seconds, more Gargoyles and Nephilim intercepted each other in the skies above.

"Well, I'll be a Stygian's uncle." Lava shook his head. "The flyin' giants are still on our side, after all. Let's give 'em a hand, boys."

With a guttural yell, Lava and the other two Dwarves sprinted into the fray, slashing at the ankles and legs of any enemy that hovered low enough to stab. Other camouflaged Dwarves charged the battlefield. Several snarling Gargoyles alighted, swords drawn.

Brady stumbled out with much less flair. He felt like a lost little boy. He breathed out a prayer and rubbed his sweaty hands against his pants. Adjusting his grip on his weapon, he wondered how one jumps into hand-to-hand combat.

A Gargoyle landed squarely in front of him with a devious laugh. "Looky what I found. A scrawny little topsider." He sized Brady up. "You'll make a nice warm up for a *real* fight."

Brady swallowed, white-knuckled the sword hilt, and took the first swing.

Aunt Jules followed me with her eyes—those magical green eyes that always shimmered with a hint of mirth. She glanced from the ring to me, as if begging me to put it on.

"It probably won't fit my pinky finger." I stared at the golden band. Its series of waves and notches made it look like a faery crown.

From my peripheral vision, I saw movement. Aunt Jules lifted her pointer finger.

"Look at you! You're improving by the minute." I grabbed her hand. Her finger poked my palm. "What is it?"

Another poke.

"You want me to try it on anyway, don't you?"

She squeezed my hand.

"Seems silly, but okay." I released her hand and plucked the ring from my palm, directing it toward my little finger.

"*Mmm.*"

I raised an eyebrow at Aunt Jules. "Oh, now we're finding our voice and getting bossy, are we? So…you object to my pinky finger? Did you forget that there's a sizable difference between you and me while you were in Never-never land?"

"*Mmm,*" she repeated.

"Yes, ma'am. I'll squeeze it on a different finger so we can be sure and call the fire department once its properly stuck. Oh, wait! They don't have a fire department in these parts." I smirked and shifted to my ring finger, glancing at Auntie. "Is this the one?"

She blinked, slow and deliberate.

I pushed the tip of my ring finger into the wedding band. No—into the *key.*

To my amazement, my finger traveled through the circle of gold. The ring glided over my knuckle and came to rest like it had been custom-made for me.

I blinked and turned my hand over, inspecting it. "What just happened?"

Emerald eyes glinted mischievously.

"You're full of secrets and surprises, aren't you?" I shook my head, shocked that the key had been hiding in plain sight all this time.

Somehow it had officially claimed its new owner.

Brady wiped his bloody sword across a patch of weeds. He hoped no one saw the queasy disgust on his face. He had a ways to go before he'd be considered a battle-hardened soldier.

Two Gargoyles lay dead, and he'd suffered only a few shallow wounds to his extremities. Glancing at the bodies littering the top of the plateau, he picked out the two lifeless bats he was responsible for killing. Some of the other casualties were Dwarves—including the bloke who received the sock in the arm from Lava.

Catching his breath, Brady watched the skirmishes that remained. Three Dwarves and two Nephilim against two Gargoyles.

A host of Trolls and Stygs peppered the next hill over, marching across it like rows of industrious ants. The flying Gargoyles had arrived ahead of those on foot, so they were the only enemy Brady had contended with so far.

He took a deep breath, hoping to recuperate before the onslaught. Without others coming to the aid of the Dwarves, however, failure seemed certain. There had only been a couple dozen Nephilim fighting against the enemy. Were more on the way?

A shadow darkened Brady's space. He jerked his sword up, ready to strike.

"Whoa! It's me." Xander alighted beside Brady, glancing at the bodies. "You've had your hands full, I see."

A nearby sword fight ended with a lobotomy to the bat's ugly head. The remaining battle was now five allies against one enemy. While Brady and Xander looked on, it was suddenly five victors staring at a slain Gargoyle.

"So much for that miscreant." Xander looked at Brady. "Looks like you saw some action today too."

Brady grinned. He liked the sound of that. "Guess so. I took out a couple."

Prince Xander smiled and nodded appreciatively. His gaze

drifted to the distant hills. "Looks like we're *all* going to have our hands full shortly."

"I know. How do we stand a chance against so many?" Brady hoped he didn't sound as scared as he felt.

"Follow me." Xander nodded toward the edge of the plateau.

The two Nephilim that had been embroiled with the Gargoyle wandered up beside Xander. Brady walked with them to the ledge. Xander spread his arms triumphantly.

"Wha—?" Brady gasped at the sight.

The vast land that stretched in the direction of Vituvia swarmed with soldiers. From the meadow to the sky...help was on its way.

CHAPTER FORTY-NINE

"WELL, WELL. YOU CAN'T KEEP A spunky redhead down, can ya?" Doc Keswick shook his head and crossed to where Aunt Jules lay. He went to work taking her vitals.

Her ability to move slowly progressed.

"Are your vocal chords working well enough to tell me how you're feeling? Are you aching, chilled, lightheaded?" He placed his stethoscope to Aunt Jules's chest. "You can whisper, and I'll hear you clear as day through this."

I could see Aunt Jules's mouth move, but no sound came out. She hadn't tried to speak since her "*mmm*" grunt earlier.

"What's that?" The doctor moved the stethoscope and leaned in.

Her lips moved again.

"Daniel?" Keswick straightened. "Maybe tomorrow. I'd like to observe you for a while."

"Doctor!" Joanie bustled into the room. "Gage is gone."

"What?" He spun around.

"He left." She wrung her hands nervously. "I told him we were bein' attacked. Then I left to get a clean pillow coverin'. When I returned, he was gone. His hospital gown in a heap. His clothes missin'."

"Blast it!" Doc ran a hand through his hair. "You can't go telling a warrior we're at war. That's like telling the crows you planted corn."

"It's all my fault." Joanie pressed a hand to her forehead and paced in and out of the doorway. "What should I do? He's probably flown the coop by now."

The doctor let out a ragged sigh. "I guess we let him learn a tough lesson." He threw up his hands. "I'll be happy when I can get back to treating patients that are shorter than me.

All these others are too unpredictable."

"Doc Keswick!" Joanie placed her hands on her ample hips. "Shame on you. Sayin' such a thing in front of our friends. Take that back."

I covered my mouth to keep from laughing.

"Are you my mother or my employee? I'll do no such thing." The doctor waved her off.

The talk of war made me anxious. "While you check Aunt Jules, I'm going for a walk." I patted her leg. "Be back after a while. I'm gonna stop by Uncle Daniel's room and let him know how great you're doing."

I brushed past the feuding Dwarves and headed down the hall, playing with the band of gold around my finger. A thrill galvanized me every time I touched it or rehearsed the way it had adjusted to fit so perfectly. To think that the God of the universe encapsulated something miraculous in the creation of this ring...something that responded to the person who He had selected to wear it and guard it. It made my head spin and my faith grow.

I pushed the door open and peeked into room number nine. Uncle Daniel sat hunched in a wheelchair beneath a pile of blankets. He was situated near the glowing potbelly stove in the corner of his room. I watched from the doorway for a few moments. Someone had given him a much needed shave and haircut.

He looked so sad and alone.

"Can I help you?" His low, raspy voice startled me.

"Oh, hello." For some reason I felt shy. "I don't think we've been properly introduced. I'm your great-niece, Sadie." I took a few steps into the room. "Good to see you up and about. You look better."

He turned his face toward my voice. "My wife told me about you." He extended his hand, and I rushed to shake it. He maintained his grip, his thumb rubbing across the ring on my right hand. "I see you've come into possession of Jules's ring."

My mouth went dry. This was their *wedding ring*. A symbol of their love. He had barely returned to sanity and the sanctity of marriage, and here I was—a virtual stranger— wearing his wife's ring.

"Yes. Aunt Jules insisted on passing it to me." I withdrew my hand. "That's one reason I came by. To tell you how she's doing."

"She's sick, isn't she." He said it as more of a statement than a question. "I've missed her. She's the only reason I've been able to find my mind again." He grinned. "I've been told that I still lose it here and there. The good thing is, I don't ever remember it happening."

"You're definitely better than when you arrived. *Much* better. I'm so thankful." I crouched beside him and tried to avoid staring at his scarred face. It still made me cringe. "I've got good news for you. Aunt Jules has come out of her coma and is recovering. She should be able to visit you soon."

He grinned again. I could see a hint of the younger man that Aunt Jules must have noticed back in that library in Dublin. "This is good news, indeed. I've been praying for her. I don't recall when they took her away, though I've been aware that she's gone. If anything happened to her, I fear my sanity would desert me for good. I can't survive losing her twice."

I blinked back tears. What a love story! "I've never known two people could love each other the way you do." I chuckled and stood. "You guys have set the bar so high I'll probably never get married."

"Oh, now, there's someone for everyone. I believe that." He laced his fingers together and placed them on his blanketed lap. "Thank you for bringing me such good news. It strengthens my resolve to keep fighting for my own health to know she'll be by my side again."

"Aunt Jules is a special woman to many people." I squeezed his shoulder. "I'll come back later and visit, Uncle...Daniel." It seemed odd to use his name while speaking *to* him instead of *about* him.

"Excellent. I'll look forward to that."

I turned and walked to the door.

"And, Sadie..."

"Yes?" I looked back.

"It is *right* for you to have the ring now. May the peace of the Tethered World continue long enough for you to pass it on to your successor."

Brady made his way down the wooded mountainside. The trail had looked much easier from the top of the plateau. When Xander told Brady his parents and sister were among the advancing cavalry, Lava insisted that Brady reunite with them as soon as possible. "I'm a parent before I'm a soldier. After such a lengthy separation, they need to know yer all right." Lava pointed at a worn rut between trees. "Follow that footpath, and it'll spit ya out near the stables."

Xander offered to shorten the journey by taking Brady on a piggyback flight, but the mental image made Brady feel more like a kid than a soldier. He'd killed a Troll and two Gargoyles. Piggyback rides weren't for him.

Still, the Nephilim insisted on accompanying him through the woods.

"Does your sister ever talk about me?" Xander cast a sideways glance at Brady as they hopped a log laying across the path.

"Who, Sophie? Yeah, she talks about you and Gage sometimes." Brady chuckled inwardly, knowing that Sophie wasn't the sister in question.

"Not Sophie. *Sadie.*"

"Ha! Only joking." Brady was happy to spy flat land through the wooded embankment. "Yeah, she talks about you, but probably not the way you're implying."

Xander's face fell.

"Which, knowing Sadie, means she is busy *thinking* about you and trying to decide what to do with her feelings. She's an introvert, which means we have to guess what she's thinking most of the time because she won't talk about it."

"I see." The soldier grinned. "So you think she *does* think about me."

Brady shrugged. "I don't know. She doesn't say."

With that, Brady sprinted the length of the trail, hoping Xander would drop the subject.

Although Xander stared after Brady with a quizzical look,

he let it go.

Horses and toboggans and foot soldiers churned up dust in the expansive land stretching from Berganstroud. Black shapes on the horizon grew in size like approaching WWII bombers.

"Not sure how we're going to spot my parents in the middle of this cattle drive." Brady shielded his eyes as they walked to the periphery of the passing throng.

"They'll be with my father. Look for the Nephilim standard."

"Standard?"

"Yes. Our flag."

"Oh...yeah." Brady kicked himself for forgetting that lesser-used word. "Say, how did it go with your dad? Lava was certain your father would want to avenge your mother's death. But instead..." He spread his hands toward the army of Calamus.

Xander turned his head and spit. "It's complicated." He pressed his lips together, hesitating. "Let's just say my mother has always felt the need to get her way. Though my father is no pushover, there have been times he decreed one thing, yet another transpired because my mother got involved. Since it does not reflect well on his kingship to try and retract or fix such events, he let them slide. He resented her more each time."

One of the mounted Nephilim soldiers caught sight of Xander and saluted. Xander nodded.

"Before I made it back to Calamus," Xander said, "a horde of Ogres showed up at the castle. They carried a letter bearing my mother's seal. It requested their assistance in overthrowing my father—in exchange for a position in a new union between powers. As it turns out, Mother didn't know Ogres can't read. So, her underhanded plan failed by epic proportions."

"Whoa. Bet that wasn't well received."

Xander shook his head. "Not at all." He gestured to the army. "Hence, our presence here."

"Hey! Is that your flag?" Brady pointed to a horseman carrying a red flag with golden wings and a crown on the insignia.

"Sure is. Come on."

The two dodged horses carrying hulking soldiers and

toboggans with their tiny Gnome warriors.

"Father!" Xander jogged to a group of horses trailing the proud banner of Calamus.

King Aviel slowed his horse, and the others followed suit.

Brady ran past the king, waving his arms ecstatically. "Mom! Dad! Sophie!"

Before he reached them, the three Larcens had dismounted and were running to embrace him.

Tears flowed freely.

For a few minutes, Brady became a boy again. A boy that needed the comfort of his parents, at least for a while.

He knew that the future held more evil to face and monsters to slay...but for once he wasn't in a hurry to get there.

CHAPTER FIFTY

I WASN'T INTERESTED IN DANGER AND bloodshed, but I was awfully curious about the way things were going outside the fortress. If the Nephilim were coming from one direction, as Lava predicted, and the Trolls and Gargoyles from the other, the Dwarves would make easy prey for the likes of such a triple threat.

Having spent a lot of time in Berganstroud, I knew my way around with a degree of confidence. A set of stairs marked 'To the top' made me hopeful I could get to the crown of the rocky peninsula the fortress was carved into.

A young, clean-shaven guard stood beside the door, pretending not to see me—though I caught his glance several times as I approached from down the hall.

"Good day." I tried to sound official. "These stairs go to the top of the fortress, correct?"

A red glow warmed his cheeks. "Correct." He eyed my bandaged foot.

"Perfect. I need some fresh air. Be back in a bit." I stepped toward the door, but he shifted in front of it.

"I'm sorry, m'lady." He held up his hand. "I cannot let you pass. It's too dangerous."

"Oh, c'mon. I need a little fresh air. You know how long I've been inside these rock walls?"

He swallowed, and his cheeks flamed darker. "N-no. But you can't go up there alone. It may not be safe. Besides, you're injured."

"This is no big deal. I feel great." An idea struck me. "You're sweet to be concerned. That means you're a good soldier. What's your name?"

"Niffgy." He was sweating.

How cute. A Dwarf crush!

"Say, Niffgy. If you escorted me up there, then I wouldn't be alone, right? You would protect me, wouldn't you?"

"Y-yes." He nodded. "I guess it wouldn't hurt for a few minutes." He straightened and looked like he wanted to appear confident.

"Terrific! Thank you." I offered him a curtsy. *Take that Queen Estancia. I, Princess Sadie, curtsied.*

He led me up a spiral staircase. Torches stationed at intervals lit the cylinder. Dwarves certainly knew how to chisel their way through a mountain. At the top, some sort of dome sat like a lid on the staircase. A few pinpricks of light pierced through in slender shafts. Niffgy looked through various holes and declared it safe.

With a loud grunt, he heaved the dome up and over, exposing the top of the stairs. After climbing out, I realized that the cap used to conceal the staircase was actually a hollowed-out boulder. Truly impressive!

A couple of guards posted on the nearby ridge came jogging over. "What's going on? Is there a problem?"

"No problem." Niffgy held up his hands. "Princess Sadie only wanted to get some fresh air."

"And you *agreed*?" A guard with a braided black beard and equally dark eyes glowered at Niffgy.

"Well, I-I was trying to—"

"Get back into the fortress. Immediately!" The other guard, a dark-skinned fellow, pointed emphatically to the stairwell.

"Uh, boys..." I pointed to the sky. "Looks like you've got company."

The Dwarves turned. A legion of Nephilim approached, some gliding, others with undulating wings—all with swords drawn.

Niffgy unsheathed his weapon and shouted at me. "Get back down the stairs. Hurry!"

The other two guards gave Niffgy a condescending smirk. In fluid succession, the Nephilim landed on the nearby plateau. Niffgy started to charge the giants, but soon stopped and turned to the other Dwarves.

"Why are you standing there? Didn't Lava say the Nephilim couldn't be trusted?"

The dark-skinned guard shook his head. "Go back to guarding your door, Niffgy." He thumbed himself in the chest.

"We're the ones with current information. Turns out the Nephilim are still on our side. Now get back to your station."

Relief washed over me. The Dwarves and Vituvia needed the Nephilim. Especially if they were going to keep the enemies' hordes far from the sword.

Niffgy looked crestfallen. He walked back to the stairwell, head down, and motioned for me to follow.

"Hello, Princess." Xander was suddenly at my side.

I blinked, biting back an impulsive yelp. "Xander! Hi."

"Well, this makes my job easier." He grinned at me then looked at the Dwarves that stood staring. "Back to your posts, men. I've got orders to fetch Princess Sadie."

"Orders from whom?" The Dwarf with the braided beard strutted up beside Xander.

"From her mother."

"What?" I clasped my hands together.

"Trust me," Xander went on. "Amy Larcen is a force to be reckoned with. You don't want to keep her waiting."

The Dwarves looked uncertain.

"It's true." I nodded. "Very true. It's best if Xander takes me to her right away."

Niffgy, who had stopped with his head poking from the top step, looked at Xander with what appeared to be a hint of jealousy. The other two Dwarves shrugged and wandered back to their posts.

"My mom is *here*?" I grabbed Xander's forearm.

He snatched up my hand. "Yes. And your Dad and little sister."

I slipped my fingers from his grasp, not wanting my resolve to melt away the longer he held my hand. "Let's go. I can't stand it!"

"Your wish is my command."

Before I could protest, Xander scooped me into his arms.

Niffgy glowered, grabbed the ledge of the rocky lid, and—after several frustrated snarls—hauled it closed.

In two strides, Xander was airborne. From over his shoulder, I viewed the troops milling about on the peninsula. Winged Nephilim conferred with Dwarves across the top of the plateau. As Xander gained height, my breath caught at the sight of Craventhrall's army, soon to converge on Berganstroud. There were *so* many, and I felt certain they had help from their creepy cohorts, both the Gargoyles and

Stygs.

When I looked the other direction, disbelief and shock hit even harder. A multitude of soldiers spread across the plains. As Xander glided lower, I recognized troops from both Vituvia and Calamus. Horses, toboggans, and foot soldiers were bearing down on Berganstroud. A good number already ascended the foothills and were close to cresting the plateau. I spied their steady movement along the trails and through the tree branches.

Craventhrall didn't stand a chance. They'd lost their leverage with my family and had no ally in the Nephilim. Did they even know that yet? This could be a record-short battle.

Xander coasted down to the paddocks. Though most of the horses were headed into the fray, three large draft horses munched hay in a corral. Four familiar humans stood in a cluster talking and laughing. They were unaware of my admiring gaze, spiraling from the sky to join their party.

"Look out belooow!" I called.

Four heads jerked up and split into smiles. In no time, I was smack in the middle of my favorite people, all of us hugging and crying and blubbering. I was lightheaded with happiness. Though it had been harder than any of us would've guessed, the victory was sweeter than anything I'd experienced. Each of us had endured our own personal nightmare, emerging with gratitude and, no doubt, a fresh round of faith.

Xander cleared his throat. We relaxed our group hug enough to look his way.

"I'm going to join my fellow soldiers. But while I have you all here, I would like to apologize for my mother's unspeakable behavior."

"Xander." I stepped away from the group. "There's no need for—"

"Yes there is." He held his hands up to silence me. "My mother endangered all of you in one way or another. She has tainted the family name and brought shame to the royal crown and the Nephilim citizens. I only wish I had discovered her schemes before it came to this. Now, if you'll..."

He trailed off, staring above our heads. I turned to follow his gaze. *Is that—?*

"*Gage!*" Xander's voice boomed. He leapt up and greeted his commander with an air-born hug. "What are you doing here, my friend?"

"Looking for you." Gage touched down, and Xander followed.

"I thought the doctor said about two weeks before you'd be released." Xander clapped the rugged soldier on the back.

Gage's left arm came to an abrupt end a few inches below his elbow. From his triceps down, his arm sported a stretchy, elastic bandage—an obvious topside commodity.

"I don't give a cat's whisker about what the doctor said." Gage shrugged. "I'm not about to sit in bed while my fellow soldiers are at war right above my hospital bed."

"I would do the same thing." Xander laughed. "I was headed to the top of the fortress. There's a mass of creatures marching this way. I want to greet them with the point of my sword."

Gage jerked his thumb toward the Berganstroud stronghold. "That's where I came from, trying to find you. Representatives from both sides are meeting as we speak. Your father and others have congregated in the expanse between the two armies. Things are at a tense standstill."

"Are you serious?" Xander exploded into the air. "We don't want to miss this."

Gage leapt up and took flight after him.

The rest of us stood, blinking, trying to understand what we had witnessed.

"Is it possible that the war could end before it even begins?" I looked from Dad to Mom.

Dad shrugged. "Perhaps. Negotiations have prevented many wars."

Sophie crossed her arms like an authority on all things war related, "I heard King Aviel say that *he* was going to make sure the Trolls knew that Calamus was not on their side. If the Trolls and Gargoyles were going to attack the Land of Legend, they had to get past the Nephilim army first. On the land, and"—she poked her finger toward the sky—"in the air."

"I hope it's not over, I wanted to go back out and fight." Brady kicked the dirt.

"Excuse me?" Mom gave him an I-don't-think-so look.

Dad wrapped his arm around her shoulder. "What Mom is trying to say is that we're thrilled to have all of us back together. In one piece. Let's enjoy that unique aspect of Larcen life for a bit, shall we?"

Cheers roared to life from the distant hill.

"Sounds like that's that." Brady couldn't disguise his disappointment.

"Why don't we see for ourselves?" I looped my arm through his.

"Up there with that ruckus?" Mom pointed and looked dubious.

"Mom, they're cheering. That's not the sounds of battle." I hobbled to the gate. "C'mon, I know a short cut." I looked at my leg and flashed my dad a smile. "Mind giving your little girl a piggyback ride?"

CHAPTER FIFTY-ONE

BRADY PERKED UP A LITTLE ONCE he walked into the citadel with his family. Something about the rock fortress seeped into his bones and made him feel tough merely from being within its walls. By the time Sadie led them to a door marked 'To the top,' he had swallowed the bitter pill of disappointment. It helped to realize he liked the rush of preparing for battle better than the danger of battle itself.

A guard stood at the door and stepped in front when they approached.

"Sorry, Princess Sadie." The young Dwarf blushed.

Good grief, does that shrimp like Sadie?

"Listen, we've got to get up top. This is the easiest way with my foot." Sadie placed a hand on the guard's shoulder. "I really appreciate your taking me up earlier. Things worked out for the best! I'm reunited with my family."

Sadie turned. "Hey guys, meet Niffgy. He was super helpful to me earlier."

Brady and the others waved or nodded.

"So." Sadie shrugged. "Whaddya say? We have it on good authority that the Trolls and Stygs are going to retreat. Did you hear the cheers?"

Niffgy looked confused. "Nooo…"

"Well, aren't you the least bit curious?"

Brady had to admire how Sadie worked her adoring fan. The pink-faced Dwarf obediently led the group up a set of stairs, hefted a large, hollow rock out of the way, and helped the ladies out of the stairwell by offering his hand.

Sure enough, groups of Gnomes, Nephilim, and Dwarves were celebrating with songs, chants, and even playful sword fights. It was a happy mass of commotion, and Niffgy wasted no time joining the festivities. Brady and family walked into the middle of it like tourists enjoying a bevy of new and unfamiliar sights. On the distant hill, Brady spied the vast, retreating army from Craventhrall. After all the conniving and kidnapping, all the threats and imprisonments, how was this even possible?

Sadie hobbled along, leaning on Dad's arm, waving at the occasional Gnome or Dwarf who greeted them. Sophie ran ahead and found Lava, smothering him in a hug and talking excitedly. A group of Nephilim called Brady over and asked about the Gargoyles he'd slain. He felt proud and embarrassed to be included in such a macho discussion.

Up ahead, King Aviel, Chief Wogsnop, and General Muggleridge climbed onto a cluster of boulders in varying sizes. Each representative held a flag—or *standard.*

"Friends and countrymen!" King Aviel's voice boomed across the crowd. "May I have your attention?"

The excited banter slowly dwindled, and the warriors turned to the three leaders.

"Never in the history of our land have things been in such constant upheaval. The Flaming Sword of Cherubythe and the Tree of Life, have been the focus of-of..." The stoic, silver-haired king looked unsettled.

Muggleridge leaned in and whispered something, but Aviel shook his head. "Our most valuable resources have been threatened. A coordinated effort was made on the part of our enemies"—he took a deep, steadying breath—"and by some within our own ranks, to usurp the God-given place of the Gnomes, and expose the lives of all who dwell in the Tethered World to the probing eye of greedy topsiders."

The crowd booed and made sounds of disgust.

"Yes, it is most distasteful." The king nodded. "Incomprehensible. Today there was strength in numbers— and not with the enemies' faction like they hoped. Once again, we've seen that the sovereign plans of our Creator cannot be undone. May we all remember that in the days ahead, as our enemy will certainly regroup. Evil will not slink off into the shadows for long."

With creepy coincidence, a Gargoyle streaked overhead like a bullet. He released a bloodcurdling wail.

Warriors unsheathed their swords.

Brady recognized the stub-tailed troublemaker. Was

Malagruel really stupid enough to attack his enemy solo?

The bat circled back around. By now, several of the winged Nephilim soldiers had taken to the sky in pursuit. The Gargoyle returned to where the leaders stood and suspended himself above them long enough to shout, "This isn't over! We still have a key to the sword."

He made a hasty retreat, pursued by a half dozen Nephilim.

The throng shouted their disapproval, while King Aviel and the others tried to restore order.

"A timely reminder, my good folks," King Aviel shouted over the dwindling noise. "We've been granted a reprieve. But we cannot become complacent. If the enemy has a key, then we must continue to protect the sword with unwavering vigilance."

The warriors pumped their fists in the air. Some cheered the king's words while others cursed the no-good Trolls and Gargoyles.

Brady wandered up beside Sadie and put his arm around her shoulder. She smiled up at him. Way up. Brady couldn't help but notice how much taller he had become...but when? How long had they been here anyway? He couldn't guess. A month, maybe? No wonder he missed Nate and Nicole.

King Aviel continued to speak. It looked like General Muggleridge and Chief Wogsnop wanted to say something, but the Nephilim king barely took a breath.

While all eyes were glued to the leaders, another sight cruised into view. A flash of gleaming white wings and tail, the flick of a mane, and the snort of a horse interrupted the king's diatribe.

Not any horse. Not *even* a horse.

The beautiful Pegasus, Sonnet, circled the gathering with two regal riders on her back. The crowd around the boulders parted and allowed Sonnet a space to land and trot to a stop.

Queen Judith and Brock slid from the horse's back to the sound of wild, adoring cheers.

Elation sprang to new heights at the sight of my brother and Aunt Judith. My mother gasped, "Brock!" Dad pulled her back when she tried to run to Brock's side. The queen leaned to my brother and kissed him on the cheek. And he allowed it!

Wogsnop offered the queen his hand and helped her onto one of the rocks. Brock stood on the ground nearby. King Aviel looked disappointed that everyone's attention had shifted away, but he remained gracious. Xander stepped up beside his father, opposite the mound from Brock. The two Nephilim favored each other more than I realized. If I pictured Xander with a headful of silver braids, it would be hard to tell the two apart from this distance.

Queen Judith raised her hands to signify quiet. Allied soldiers continued to emerge from the mountainside trails and gathered around to hear the news. The six Nephilim that had pursued the Gargoyle returned empty handed. Bodies pressed close, and a Dwarf stepped on my bandaged foot. I grimaced and moved away, but the stocky soldier didn't notice.

What Aviel had said unsettled me. As long as the enemy had one of the keys, were any of us safe? Could we really return to our homes, either topside or underside and function in a normal way? I doubted it. If the sword wasn't safe this *thing* wasn't over. I felt it in my bones.

"King Aviel," Queen Judith nodded toward her royal counterpart. "Yer son, Prince Xander, intercepted my entourage moments ago and explained this miraculous turn of events. Without the immense physical presence offered by yer warriors, we would not have avoided an unholy amount of bloodshed. Truly the Vituvian and Berganstroud armies are indebted to your swift, all-encompassin' aid."

Aunt Judith clapped her hands over her head. "Let's show the Calamus army and king our appreciation, shall we?"

Cheers ramped up again. The queen beamed and

applauded enthusiastically with the onlookers. Brock stood with his hands over his ears but otherwise looked okay.

The underdog had declared checkmate, and the world's most grueling game of chess was finished! For now, anyway.

Raising her arms, Aunt Judith hushed the crowd. "There's one thing I'd like to share, while I have everyone miraculously assembled here."

The murmuring sputtered to silence.

"I have some good news and some not so good news." Queen Judith's face grew somber. "I've recently learned that I have somethin' growin' in me brain. It'll likely be the end of me, though no one knows when. The estimate is that I've got about a year of livin' left, give or take."

I clasped my hand over my mouth, remembering Brock's secret.

Sophie flew into Mom's arms. Gasps of surprise and murmurs of sadness rippled through the crowd.

"All right, if ya want me to feel better, that's enough with the long faces, ya hear?" She wagged a scolding finger and smiled. "Now, the good news."

She motioned my brother onto the rocks.

Brock climbed up beside her. The more I saw him interact, the more kingly he became. Brock's newfound confidence—his purpose—made everything I'd endured worth it.

"This young man, me great-nephew Brock, has been apprenticin' with me this summer, as most of ya know." She smiled up at him admiringly.

The soldiers whistled and cheered.

Brock's fingers twitched. I knew how badly he wanted to cover his ears. Aunt Judith stood on her tiptoes and said something to him. My brother pressed his lips together and endured the rousing noise.

"Though the original plan was to have Brock spend the next few summers in trainin', my illness changes the scope of things."

"Oh, no it doesn't." Mom crossed her arms. Dad caressed the nape of her neck.

"I think everyone would agree that this summer has been a *thorough* initiation for kingship. Brock has been privy to more secrets and meetings and warfare than most monarchs see in a lifetime—in these parts anyway."

A smattering of laughter trickled through the soldiers.

"Therefore, 'tis me proud duty to recommend Brock's coronation be set for some time next spring." She raised a hand to hush the crowd before they could rev up. "That gives time enough to prepare, and—Lord willin'—time enough fer me to walk him through his first few months—and hopefully more—as king."

The crowd broke into a clapping cheer of: "King Brock! King Brock! King Brock!"

Mom turned smoldering, indignant eyes to my father. "Are we going to allow them to take our boy away this soon?"

Dad brushed Mom's hair off her cheek and smiled. "Look at him." He nodded toward Brock. "He's come into his own special place in the world. A world that loves him and respects him. Our boy has become a young man."

CHAPTER FIFTY-TWO

I STOOD BEHIND SOPHIE, MY HANDS on her shoulders. She stood next to Aunt Jules's bedside, fingers entwined. Uncle Daniel's bed was pushed against the opposite side of hers, or I would have been over there grasping her other hand in mine. But I was happy to let Uncle Daniel have handholding duty, as he had a great many years to make up for.

Someone had fitted my uncle with a double eyepatch. His color was good, and he looked healthier than ever.

It was a bittersweet gathering...and gathered we were. All of us Larcens, along with Aunt Judith, crowded into Aunt Jules's and Uncle Daniel's hospital room. We surrounded the two of them like a protective grove of trees.

My family was here to say their goodbyes—temporarily. Doc Keswick wanted Daniel to stay until his mental health was stabilized and Aunt Jules was back to her sprightly self.

"Oh, yer makin' such a fuss." Auntie blushed. "Truly, I'm feelin' right as rain. But Doc Keswick isn't ready to release Daniel yet. And if Daniel is stayin' here, goodness knows that I'm stayin' too. There's no separatin' us now. Not ever again."

"You'd have to fight me to take Jules with you anyway." Uncle Daniel patted her hand. "You all would have to be blind to think you could take me on."

We shared a good laugh at that.

Mom patted Auntie's leg from where she stood at the foot of the bed. "You know we love you and will miss you terribly. But I'm also missing Nate and Nicole something fierce."

"Oh, me! Yes, indeed, ya must get back to those wee ones." Aunt Jules's face morphed from a crinkly smile to a look of alarm. "But watch out fer that wily neighbor. I know ya can't get the authorities involved—but so does he. Let's hope he's learned not to mess with the Larcen clan."

Dad's eyes narrowed. "Oh, we're going to have a nice little face-to-face chat when I get back. The man better be putting a 'for sale' sign in his yard if he knows what's good for him."

"Let's hope so, Liam." Auntie raised her fist. "Or he'll be chattin' with me and my fist next."

More laughter bubbled over.

Sophie gave Aunt Jules a hug. "You're so funny. I'm going to miss you."

"Me too, doodlebug. I hate goodbyes." Auntie looked thoughtful and sad. "They're so unpredictable. Who would've dreamed when we said goodbye to Nate and Nicole that we'd be kept apart fer so long? Of course," she looked at her husband. "I never would have let this man go had I known how long our goodbye would last."

Uncle Daniel lifted her hands to his lips and kissed her fingers. "So much sweeter the reunion, my love."

Sophie grasped my hands that rested on her shoulders, as if moved by his tenderness. Her fingers found my new ring. She yanked my hand in front of her face. I heard her gasp, and she swiveled around, mouth open.

I placed a finger to my lips and pretended not to see her curious stares. My mouth went dry thinking about how I would explain the ring. If my family knew that this ring was really *the key*, they would have to protect my secret as well. I couldn't place them in such danger. But I also didn't want to lie.

I sighed at how utterly complicated the simplest things were any more. But I had to admit...I kind of liked it.

Dad cleared his throat, which, in Larcen language meant it's time to get a move-on. "So, Aunt Jules, won't you *please* stay put and stay healthy. That goes for both of you. We want you guys back where you belong as soon as possible."

"Where I *belong*, Liam?" Aunt Jules raised an eyebrow. "I would think that after all we've been through, ya might choose yer words with more care. Because this"—she gestured around the room and gave Dad a knowing smile—"is where all of us belong."

Now, a Sneak Peek at Book Three

The Genesis Tree

CHAPTER ONE

"KATU Channel Two News. We'd like to ask you a few questions." A female voice called through the front door.

My eleven-year-old sister, Sophie, catapulted from the couch. "I'll get it!"

"Hang on." I heaved myself out of the beanbag chair—my favorite place to curl up with a good book—and hobbled to the door. With my foot in a walking cast, everything I did took twice as long. "Let me see if it's for real."

Sophie stepped aside, hand on the knob. "What do they want with us?"

I squinted through the bubble of glass without answering my inquisitive little sister. A distorted camera lens stared back at me from the shoulder of a guy with a goatee. He stood behind a lady whose face looked misshapen through the peephole. "Looks legit."

Sophie twisted the knob on one of the deadbolts. Though we had three installed for our sleepwalking brother, Brock, we only used one when he was gone. My sister pulled the door open dramatically, which is pretty much how she does anything.

A redheaded woman wearing a pale blue dress and too much make-up blinked at Sophie, then me. I recognized her from television.

"Hello!" She gave us a syrupy smile from behind her microphone. "I'm Michelle Gaelyn with KATU Channel Two News. Is this the residence of Sasquatch specialist Amy Larcen?"

The hipster cameraman pointed his lens at us. A red light blinked, indicating he was recording.

Sophie glanced at me. Our mother—and said Sasquatch specialist—wasn't home. I guessed my sister was uncertain about how to answer.

"She's unavailable at the moment." I stepped closer to Sophie.

Michelle, blinked again. "We wanted her to weigh in on your neighbor's claim to be in possession of the body of a dead Bigfoot." She jerked a thumb behind her, indicating the house across the street. "What a crazy coincidence that the man who swears he has a Yeti lives across the street from a Yeti expert."

I faked a laugh to cover a gasp of indignation. Our diabolical neighbor had called a press conference to show off the body of a Bigfoot? Though I was well aware of the corpse, I had no idea the creep planned to play show-and-tell with it. Such publicity would be dangerous.

The reporter stuck her microphone in my face.

"Yes. Crazy." My heart hammered a distress call. "Um, I'll let my mother know you came by."

"Has she inspected the body?" The redhead shifted into the doorway. "Surely your neighbor, Joseph Marshall, has asked your mother to lend credence to his claims. Normally we would dismiss such hype as yet another hoax, but Mr. Marshall emailed some very convincing photos."

I stiffened. Though this woman could have no idea of the bad blood between us and our neighbor, she was quickly gravitating toward my disagreeable side by mentioning him by name. His *fake* name.

"This is the first I've heard. I'm certain she'd have said something if she knew." I shrugged. "Also, you might want to do a little fact checking about the man himself. Joseph Marshall isn't his real name, so who knows what he plans to display to the media today. I'd be careful if I were you."

The reporter took a step back, bumping into the cameraman. "Really?" She pressed her lips together and smoothed her skirt with her free hand. "Well. I thank you for your time. And the tip."

"You're welcome." I smirked at her reaction.

Sophie waved. "We'll tell Mom you came by when she gets home."

"*Sophie.*" I yanked her behind me.

"Oops."

"Here's my card." The woman shoved her business card at me. "Please have your mother call if she has anything to add after the broadcast. She has an excellent reputation. I'm flabbergasted that your neighbor has kept this to himself."

I closed the door and leaned against it, eyeing my sister. "Breaking news. Joseph *Delaney* isn't going to mind his own business and stay out of our lives."

"Mom's gonna flip out when she hears this." Sophie shook her head and ambled back into the living room.

A door creaked upstairs. My brother Brady towered from the top step, his blond hair wet, a piece of toilet paper stuck to his jaw where he'd evidently cut himself shaving. "Mom's going to flip out about what?"

Before I could answer, Sophie squealed. "Oh, my goodness! A van from Animal Planet just pulled up to the curb."

I lurched over to the couch, followed by my brother. The three of us perched on our knees, peeking through the blinds at the boxy vehicle enveloped in the bright, catchy logo of the Animal Planet channel. They'd parked on our side of the street.

"What's going on?" Brady nudged me.

"Apparently, Mr. Delaney—aka Mr. Marshall—plans to capitalize on that Yeti his wife Abigail killed helping dad escape from their basement. He's holding a press conference or something."

"Seriously?"

Sophie bounced on the cushion beside me. "Yep! Channel Two News just knocked on the door 'cause they wanted to ask Mom a few questions."

Brady groaned. "Mom *is* gonna flip. This is not the kind of exposure she needs."

The driver of the van got out and walked across our grass to the back of his vehicle. He opened the rear doors, which blocked our view of his movements. Another man slid out of the passenger seat then disappeared on the other side.

A pickup truck from KOIN TV Channel Six pulled up behind the Animal Planet guys.

I raised an eyebrow at Brady. "He's got quite the audience. Since when do major news stations take Bigfoot findings seriously? They've stonewalled Mom for years."

"That reporter said Mr. Marsh—*Delaney*—sent very convincing pictures." Sophie hopped off the couch. "I'm gonna go outside and watch."

"I don't know…" Before I could finish my thought, she was out the door.

"Good luck keeping Sophie in the house when there's a circus out front." Brady chuckled and offered me a hand. "Besides, aren't you the least bit curious? We should probably keep an eye on things."

I grasped his forearm and pulled up with most of the weight on my good leg. Brady helped me hobble to the door. It occurred to me, with a stab of surprise, that his shoulder was now level with my chin. Though younger by seventeen months, and about my height at the beginning of summer, he had shot passed me by several inches. It startled me to imagine Brock being this tall. Brock was Brady's identical twin that I had barely seen throughout our family's very peculiar summer.

Sophie stood in the middle of our driveway, gaping at the reporters and camera crews milling across the street. Brady and I stood behind her.

"I'm gonna text Mom." What would she say to this craziness? I pulled my phone from my back pocket and noted the time. Nearly four in the afternoon. Though she'd probably be home any minute, I went ahead and divulged the news. When the wrath of Mom arrives, this circus will come to a screeching halt.

Other people gathered on their front porches or in their yards, peering at the commotion. Our next-door neighbor's kids, RJ and Bethany, dashed across the lawn and set about mauling the Animal Planet van.

The irony of the situation made me shake my head. Mr. Marshall, who we now knew to be Mr. Delaney, has been the world's nosiest neighbor for the five or six years that he's lived across the street. He has spent his retirement, it seems, staring at us from his front porch, or from the front window of his home, blurred by a haze of cigar smoke. We used to joke that he'd moved here just to gawk at our homeschooled family, like we were some sort of novelty or lab specimen.

The unfortunate truth of it, we recently discovered, was worse than our silliest speculations. He knew secrets about my family, secrets I had only learned at the beginning of summer. The man *had* been watching us. Watching and waiting.

Now all eyes, and cameras, were on him. What did he hope to accomplish?

I had a sinking feeling he was trying to revive something that recently died—and it wasn't Bigfoot. It was his sick agenda that my family had managed to sabotage a month or so back. It looked as if Mr. Delaney wanted to resurrect his foul and nefarious plans right in our faces.

My hand instinctively sought the little book charm hanging around my neck, a gift from my dad. Though I often messed with it absentmindedly, stress drove me to zip it back and forth along the silver chain like it might start a fire. At this moment, I was smoking mad at what I was witnessing across the street.

The front door of our neighbor's house opened. Reporters and onlookers turned to watch. A cloud of smoke preceded Mr. Delaney's stout body like unintended special effects. He tipped his newsboy hat and stuck his thick thumbs in his suspenders, waddling toward the garage door. The crowd shifted to his driveway and would have blocked our view if not for his property's steep incline.

The man grinned, cigar clenched in his teeth on the side of his mouth. "Glad you all could make it today. I promise it'll be worth your time. You'll have an opportunity to take a brief look and snap some photos. Then I'll answer a few questions."

Through the veil of smoke, I saw his beady eyes peer at me and my siblings, as if daring us to speak up, and threatening us if we dared.

He removed something from his pocket—a garage door opener—and pressed a button. The mechanical humming commenced, and the door lifted like a slow motion curtain revealing a stage.

Bright lights set up inside the garage beamed onto the large silhouette of something lying on a table beneath a blue, plastic tarp. Mr. Delaney walked to one end, grasped the cover, and pulled it away with a *swoosh.*

Releasing Late Summer of 2017

About the Author

Heather FitzGerald grew up in Orchards, Washington (considered part of Vancouver). She loved creative writing and loathed math. In third grade she began her first book, *Rubber Bands and Mashed Bananas,* pounding it out on an old-fashioned typewriter. With no typing skill or knowledge of White-Out, Heather eventually gave up.

Though she married and settled down in Texas, "write a book" remained on her Bucket List. Family life included homeschooling four children, one with autism. A favorite past time was reading adventures with the kids. After they read through The Chronicles of Narnia, Heather's desire to write became too powerful to ignore.

She began to blog and work on story ideas. When author Susan K. Marlow read Heather's book review of *Trouble with Treasure*, she contacted Heather and asked, Are you a writer?" By God's grace, Susan saw something in Heather's writing and began to mentor her.

Heather joined North Texas Christian Writers and attended writing workshops. A prompt from Susan Marlow sparked Heather's original ideas for *The Tethered World*, book one of The Tethered World Chronicles. Though the novel is YA Fantasy, Heather prefers to call it Family Fantasy. She hopes families will read it aloud and enjoy the adventure together.

Acknowledgements

My heart is full, thinking of the many faithful family members and friends who have journeyed with me through books one and two. I believe I was even more amazed when I finished *The Flaming Sword* because I actually did it *again!* Turns out this writing thing wasn't a fluke, y'know? Though it was a surreal accomplishment to me, there are others who never doubted me for a minute.

My family, first and foremost, inspires me every day. What would I do without my devoted, supportive husband, who makes me feel like the cleverest woman in the universe? His faithfulness and hard work motivate me to excellence. By the time this book sees any sales, we will have celebrated twenty-seven years together! ***throws confetti and frolics around the house***

To my beautiful kids who have grown up while my nose has been glued to a computer. Thanks for patiently pulling for my dreams. McKenzie (and son-in-law Gary), Garrett, Delaney, and Olivia, you guys have always been my greatest adventure! Between working on *The Tethered World* and *The Flaming Sword,* I've had the distinct joy of becoming a "Mimi" with the birth of my granddaughter, Whittley (aka Lake Whitt). I can't wait to share these stories with her one day.

A massive thank-you to the professionals at Mountain Brook Ink. You guys are a small but formidable crew of awesomeness, dedicated to making us authors look good! Miralee, I've learned so much from you and am inspired by your work ethic. It's been such a pleasure to be part of your team and to get my creative bearings with your guidance. Nikki, thanks for patiently helping me with my website, my blog hop, and any and all technological crises. I'm sure there will be more, and you'll continue to rescue me from my ignorance.

Lissa Halls Johnson, you're the most perceptive editor yet! I'm grateful to have benefitted from your wisdom, your (near) omniscience with scenes, and your precision with the English language. You truly gave *The Flaming Sword* the polish to make it shine!

To my closest writing circle in the Manet Writer's group—Stephanie, Patricia, Rachel, Naomi, Ariana, Deanna and Abby (in spirit!)—it's a joy to be with you each month. To my mentor Susan Marlow, so much of what I know is because you patiently taught me...especially the use of a good cliff-hanger.

And to my other family members and friends who have encouraged me along the way: I hope the inclusion of many of your names, in one form or another (some more recognizable than others), lets you know how much I value our relationship.

Most importantly, all glory and honor and thanks be to my Lord Jesus. I'm blown away by the privilege of the gifts He has bestowed and allowed me to use. During the writing process, I feel His hand and Spirit whispering ideas and guiding me. Many chapters of *The Flaming Sword* felt like a desperate prayer tossed onto the computer screen. I'd make it to the end of many scenes and gasp at the wild ride God brought my imagination through. This happened repeatedly, with awe and thanks from my disorganized writing persona. I'm a "panster" (aka I write by the seat of my pants and have no idea what to do with an outline). This weakness of mine leads to a book that is truly written by faith and not sight—let alone intentional planning on my part.

That means if anything good comes from this book, if anything wonderful is communicated in its pages to my valuable readers...it's all God's doing! Yay! **throws more confetti and cartwheels across the living room**

This suits me just fine.

"Every good and perfect gift is from above, coming down from the Father of the heavenly lights..." James 1:17

Book Club Questions

1. Brady was bummed about cutting his hair for his driver's permit, but it became an unexpected blessing later in the story. Have you ever been opposed to something, only to find out it was exactly what you needed? Even everyday things we don't pay attention to can be a blessing in disguise. What sort of unexpected benefits have you experienced from the seemingly mundane?

2. Aunt Jules and Uncle Daniel share a very special love story. Is there a married couple in your life that has inspired you and reflected God's unconditional love? In what way? What about Aunt Jules' secret? Would you be able to hide something in plain sight for such a long time, without telling anyone? Can *you* keep a secret?

3. We meet a new creature in this sequel who is a master of disguise. What are ways that Satan tries to deceive? Is it easy to recognize his disguises? How can we test whether a statement or opportunity is from the Lord?

4. There is a shocking traitor that comes to light in this story. Have you ever been betrayed by someone you believed was trustworthy? How did you handle it? Were you able to forgive that person? Similarly, have you or others you've known been able to rise above bad choices made by parents or another family member or close friend?

5. Although Sadie was often afraid, her fear took a backseat to doing what was right. Have you ever faced your fear by speaking up for what's right, refusing to do something you believed to be wrong, or by helping someone in need? Do you believe that good will always

prevail over evil? Why or why not?

6. Just for fun: Although the Tethered World is not real,
    would you want to visit such a place if you learned of its
    existence? What about another planet? What would be
    the pros and cons of visiting such a different place from
    our home on earth?

More Ways to Connect with Heather and The Tethered World

Learn more about the characters
and creatures of The Tethered World:
www.heatherllfitzgerald.com

When you visit, sign up for Heather's newsletter
and be the first to learn about the release of Book Three,
The Genesis Tree, plus get a free novella.

Heather's Author Page on Facebook:
www.facebook.com/groups/1731996177017368

Follow The Tethered World on
Instagram: Tetheredworld

Tag your quirky and mysterious photos with
#tetheredworld!

Twitter: WriteFitz

Follow Sadie Larcen on Pinterest:
www.pinterest.com/sadielarcen

Follow Amy Larcen's Bigfoot Blog:
www.landoflegend.net

I would love to hear from you,
however you'd like to stay connected!

Cast of Characters

FAMILY, etc

Sadie Larcen: bookish, sixteen-year old. Prefers reading about adventures over experiencing any; fears roller coasters and failure; resides with her family in Orchards, Washington.

Amy Larcen: Sadie's mother; leading expert on Bigfoot; blogs about all things myth and legend, particularly Bigfoot. Kidnapped by Trolls, tortured by Ogres in *The Tethered World*. Visit her blog at www.landoflegend.net

Liam Larcen: Sadie's father; cosmetologist; previously kidnapped with his wife, Amy.

Brady Larcen: age fifteen; protective twin to Brock; easy-going and bighearted; Sadie's right-hand man in the Tethered World.

Brock Larcen: autistic twin to Brady; High King of Vituvia in training; excellent memory and fighting skills.

Sophie Larcen: clever and adventurous eleven-year-old sister; pretends to live in medieval times; desirous of moving to the Tethered World; brave beyond her years.

Nicole Larcen: sweet, seven-year-old sister; a big help with her baby brother, Nate; loves the color pink; oblivious to her family's connection to life below ground.

Nate Larcen (aka Nate the Great): adorable baby brother adopted from Ethiopia; two-year-old toddler.

Great-aunt Julie McGriffin (aka Aunt Jules): Fun-loving Irish aunt and twin sister to Judith, Queen of Vituvia; Sculpts garden gnomes; key keeper and family historian; has never given up hope that her husband, Daniel, may be alive; resides in Cannon Beach, Oregon.

Daniel McGriffin: went MIA in Vietnam shortly after his marriage to Julie.

Queen Judith of Vituvia: twin sister to Jules McGriffin; training Brock Larcen as her predecessor so she can retire; savant.

Joseph Marshall: nosy neighbor who lives across the street from the Larcens; smokes like a locomotive.

Brent McGriffin: Amy Larcen's brother: black sheep of the family; walked away from involvement with the Tethered World.

CREATURES

Gnomes: Approximately eighteen inches tall; stout bodies; pointy hat adds another eight inches; small but deadly; will protect the Flaming Sword of Cherubythe at all cost; reside in Vituvia.
- Reiko: head of Special Forces, officially known as Stealth Gnomish Warfare and Clandestine Operations (SGWCO); visits the Larcens to urge them to return to the Tethered World
- Sir Noblin: Premier Advisor to Queen Judith
- Revonika: Noblin's assistant; in charge of public relations
- General Muggleridge: military advisor and commanding officer
- Colonel Smarlow: Chief of Covert Reconnaissance; answers to General Muggleridge
- Mighty, Muscle: sibling soldiers in the SGWCO; answer to Reiko

Meadow Faeries: resemble butterflies with tiny arms and legs, carried by gossamer wings; transports the Larcens to Vituvia in their faery cyclone; reside on plant stems in the meadow between the Woods of Willowmist and Vituvia.

Leprechauns: stand approximately two feet tall; well-proportioned bodies; male leprechauns born with a beard; affinity for moss, mushrooms, and gold; reside in the Hallows of Nimmickdell.

- Skoon: snitch and traitor
- Thistle: Skoon's cohort

Dwarves: half as tall and twice as wide as the average topsider; fond of facial hair and pipes; Reside in the Berganstroud Mountains.

- Chief Wogsnop: leader of the Dwarves of Berganstroud; head of the Berganstroud army
- Glavashian (aka Lava): soldier in the Berganstroud army; has a special connection to Sadie
- Joanie: motherly nurse/housekeeper
- Doc Keswick: Berganstroud's one and only physician; terrible bedside manner
- Trinny: Lava's daughter; assistant to Joanie and Doc Keswick
- Bennett: soldier in the Berganstroud army
- Grimpenhauser: garbage collector: traitor: fancies himself a revolutionary

Dark Dwarves (aka Stygians): same stature as Dwarves; pale, grayish skin; patchy hair and beard; allied with the Trolls and Gargoyles; reside in the dens beyond Berganstroud.

Trolls (aka Bigfoot, Yeti, Sasquatch): hairy, broad-shouldered creatures; ape-like faces; XXL feet.; reside in Craventhrall or in the Eldritch on Mount Thrall.

- Chebar: sixth son of Chief Nekronok; loyal to Queen Judith; a mole living in the Eldritch, working against his father
- Nekronok: chief Troll; prefers to be addressed as "Worshipful Master"; wants control of the Flaming Sword of Cherubythe
- Rooke: first-born son of Nekronok; next in line for the throne
- Keturah: kind Troll that befriends Sadie

- Gwendolyn: Chief Nekronok's wife

Gargoyles: the physical counterparts to the stone gargoyles perched on medieval castles and cathedrals; shape-shifters; working with the Trolls.
  - Prince Malagruel: leader of the Gargoyles; rival to Nekronok; winged with the tail of a serpent
  - Ophidian: Malagruel's "worm" who serves without question; flightless

Nephilim: half angelic, half human; average height eight feet; well proportioned; wings a recessive trait, mostly seen in the royal family; reside in Calamus; refer to Genesis 6:4
  - Prince Alexander (aka Xander): first-born son of the royal family; commands the Nephilim army; infatuated with Sadie
  - King Aviel and Queen Estancia: monarchs of Calamus
  - Gage: seasoned soldier and Xander's right-hand man
  - Vincent: guard and soldier loyal to Queen Estancia
  - Typhel and Holt: warriors that train as Guardians of the Sword in Vituvia

Clovenboars (aka Toboggans): curvy horns, fangs, and dreadlocks; size of a panther; the Gnomes' transportation; able to see invisible Leprechauns; native to the wilds of the Tethered World and also kept in the paddocks of Berganstroud and Vituvia.
  - Thrym: Reiko's mount

Hippogriff: winged creatures with the head, breast, and talons of an eagle and the back legs and rump of a horse; offspring of a mare and a Griffin; easier to tame than their legendary counterpart; utilized for travel and war by the Trolls; reside in the wild and in Craventhrall.

Griffin: winged creature with the fore-body of an eagle and the back legs and rump of a lion; less popular than Hippogriffs, but still utilized by the Trolls

Ogres: large and thick-bodied; average seven to eight feet tall; tortured the Larcen parents; reside on the Isle of Skellerwad in the Sulfur Sea

Elves of Willowmist: slender, petite creatures with pointy noses and ears; shy but playful; can turn invisible; reside in the Woods of Willowmist

*See the map at the beginning of book for an overview of the Tethered World.